Advance praise for

A WOLF BY THE EARS

"*A Wolf by the Ears* chronicles the ordeals of two slaves among thousands in Maryland and Virginia who joined the British side in the forgotten War of 1812 against the American 'republic' and its hypocrisies, all for the cause of freedom promised by their monarchist allies and denied by a democracy built on slavery. Karlin makes this profoundly ironic and contradictory history so human and intimate, so tragic and yet redemptive, testimony to his great skill as a storyteller and his experience with the realities of war."

—Martín Espada, author of
Vivas to Those Who Have Failed: Poems

"Here is a complexly imagined record of the catastrophes and dreaming out of which the nation emerges. A dissection of the country within 'The Country,' the then within the now. But what makes this work pulse with vitality is Karlin's attention to that which is fleeting—the smallest instant, the slightest flesh. Lush, elemental, seeping with place, this novel is a reckoning, a confrontation, an excavation of a history made of breath and touch."

—Aracelis Girmay, author of
The Black Maria

A
WOLF
BY THE
EARS

ALSO BY WAYNE KARLIN

NOVELS

Crossover
Lost Armies
The Extras
Us
Prisoners
The Wished-for Country
Marble Mountain

NONFICTION

Rumors and Stones: A Journey
War Movies: Scenes and Outtakes
Wandering Souls: Journeys with the Dead and Living in Viet Nam

AS CO-EDITOR, CONTRIBUTOR

Free Fire Zone: Short Stories by Vietnam Veterans
with Basil T. Paquet and Larry Rottmann

The Other Side of Heaven: Postwar Fiction by Vietnamese and American Writers
with Le Minh Khue and Truong Vu

Truyen Ngan My Duong Dai (Contemporary American Short Stories)
with Ho Anh Thai

Love After War: Contemporary Fiction from Viet Nam
with Ho Anh Thai

In Whose Eyes: The Memoir of a Vietnamese Filmmaker in War and Peace
with Tran Van Thuy, Le Thanh Dung, Nguyen Quang Dy, and Eric Henry

A WOLF BY THE EARS

WAYNE KARLIN

UNIVERSITY OF MASSACHUSETTS PRESS

Amherst & Boston

ISBN 978-1-62534-503-5 (paper)

Designed by Sally Nichols
Set in Adobe Garamond

Cover design by Rebecca Neimark, Twenty-Six Letters
Cover art by West Smithfield. Detail from the wood engraving
The taking of the city of Washington in America, August 24, 1814.
Print shows a view from the Potomac River, under attack
by British forces under Major General Ross.
Courtesy of Library of Congress Prints and Photographs
Division, Washington, D.C., LC-DIG-ppmsca-31113.

Library of Congress Cataloging-in-Publication Data

Names: Karlin, Wayne, author.
Title: A wolf by the ears / Wayne Karlin.
Description: Amherst : University of Massachusetts Press, [2020] | Series:
Juniper prize for fiction
Identifiers: LCCN 2019044407 | ISBN 9781625345035 (paperback) | ISBN
9781613767504 (ebook) | ISBN 9781613767511 (ebook)
Subjects: LCSH: United States—History—War of 1812—Fiction. | GSAFD:
Historical fiction.
Classification: LCC PS3561.A625 W65 2020 | DDC 813/.54—dc23
LC record available at https://lccn.loc.gov/2019044407

British Library Cataloguing-in-Publication Data
A catalog record for this book is available from the British Library

The chapter "Passing the Fire" was previously published in
Mānoa: A Pacific Journal of International Writing.

for Lucille Clifton: in memoriam

But as it is, we have the wolf by the ears, and we can neither hold him, nor safely let him go. Justice is in one scale, and self-preservation in the other.

—Thomas Jefferson, letter to John Holmes, April 22, 1820

loaded like spoons
into the belly of Jesus
where we lay for weeks for months
in the sweat and stink
of our own breathing
Jesus
why do you not protect us
chained to the heart of the Angel
where the prayers we never tell
are hot and red
as our bloody ankles
Jesus
Angel
can these be men
who vomit us out from ships
called Jesus   Angel   Grace Of God
onto a heathen country
Jesus
Angel
ever again
can this tongue speak
can these bones walk
Grace Of God
can this sin live

—Lucille Clifton, "slaveships"

A
WOLF
BY THE
EARS

PART ONE

TOWERHILL SEPARATION

MARCH
— 1814 —

ONE

TOWERHILL

THRICE-BORN

His paddle breaks glowing threads of phosphorescence that trail the blade in the black water. Clouds of fireflies dance like drunkards over their own mirrored images on that opaque surface and are mirrored themselves in the white swirls of stars overhead. Observing this trinity of light, Towerhill feels he is standing just outside some secret door of understanding.

At the same time, in this world, he wishes it were darker. All of this agitated illumination increases the danger that patrollers will spot him, a black silhouette hunched against the heavens.

He pushes his mind, his arms, back to the simple rhythm of paddling. Tells himself there is nothing to fear. The word *mirrored* comes back into his mind, as if someone whispers it into his ear. The night is the reverse world, the world in the mirror, the black world. His world. He knows the lay of the land in the darkness; he knows the way all the familiar landmarks of the day shift subtly; he knows, day or night, the secret trails, the hidden hollows, the skein of creeks through marsh grass, the shifting currents of the river, the hidden Wesort paths through the forests. They are the coinage through which he will buy freedom. They are what he has to sell, as he had once been sold.

As those words come into his mind, his thoughts flow into a different channel of memory. The touch of a breeze on his skin dries the sweat on his forehead, awakens the way he had felt when he was five years old and naked on the selling block, torn from the arms of his dead mother. Or must have felt. His vague recall of terrifying shouts and barking laughter, of looming forms and distorted red faces and painfully poking fingers are all couched and framed by the sight of the children he has since seen sold or by the stories he had been told by older slaves. And by the man who had bought him on that day. Brought out from the belly of a ship called *Jesus Christos* as if to a new birth, the baby Sarai clutched in his arms, both of them waiting for their names. His mother, *Jesus,* the selling block. Thrice-born.

And now moving through this water to a fourth birth. This time he will sell himself. Sell or be sold. He paddles harder, singing the phrase under his breath, the way the field slaves sang a rhythm into their labor. Sell or be sold. Though he knows that Jacob would never sell him, never sell Towerhill the slave to save Towerhill the plantation. Master Jacob Hallam would never sell him, not to pay his debts to the merchants in Boston and New York and Baltimore for failed crops, for lace curtains, for heavy oaken furniture, for Madeira wine, for damask carpets, all mildewed, rotting, crumbling, for all he has heard Jacob call the *veneer* of civilization. Pronouncing the word with an ironic twist of a smile as if to distant himself from such pretentiousness. The Good Master, the defender of liberty and the Rights of Man, will not sell him, Towerhill, the fashioner and maintainer of that veneer. Will not sell him, the slave Jacob and his father had erected like a statue to their virtue. And he will not sell Sarai for the same reasons. As well as for reasons Towerhill does not want to think about. He will sell those rhythmic field hands, or their children, or the old woman Meg. He will sell them with a tear in his eyes, a tremble in his lip, his face twisted in a delicious moral struggle he will write about in his journal. Towerhill sees that image as clearly as if it were one of the portraits of Jacob's ancestors hung on the wall. The old man, Cedric Hallam, who had bought Towerhill and Sarai off that block, staring reproachfully from his gilded frame at his wastrel son.

He shakes these thoughts out of his head. His mind is drifting off down too many twisty creeks and channels, threatening to get lost. He dips the paddle deeply, pulls it back against the tug of the water, loops it around and dips it in again. Sell or be sold. Dip, tug back, loop. Sell or be sold. He paddles into the black mirror of the black night, a black man looking for a white man in a red coat.

A black man who will be late. He had arranged with Scott to meet around two hours past sunset. He glances up at the moon. It must have been more than three hours since he had slipped down into the gulley behind the Quarters, an easy passage from the plantation into the night country. Sarai had been in the manor house letting Jacob moon over her, and Hiram Bertram, the chief overseer, was occupying himself that night with other amusements. He tries to banish the memory of those amusements from his mind, force them into a lidded corner of his mind, as he has trained himself to do. Forces himself to again concentrate on the rhythm of the paddling. Towerhill the slave leaving Towerhill the plantation. Towerhill the man leaving Towerhill Separation. Separating. Had his name been bestowed out of laziness, or as another way to chain him to the place? Chain him, name him, claim him. Why not name all slaves Towerhill then? Why give them the hollow gift of names chosen by whim? Rebekkah, who still dimly remembers stories from a dusty village of wattle and mud in Africa, has told him how names, the very sound of them, are what call humans to life and reveal their way in the world. "Take our name, stronger than chain," she says. He tries to occupy his mind with these ancient, idle questions. Tries to keep from thinking about Sarai and Jacob. Tries to keep from thinking about Bertram and his night games. Sell or be sold. He will sell himself and the others into transitory servitude in order to be liberated from eternal bondage. That simple.

A few moments later, just where it is supposed to be, he spots the pink cloth that would seem to white eyes to have blown here accidentally, wrapped itself around the sharp nub of a broken branch sticking up from a dead, half-submerged tree, its trunk shining wetly in the moonlight. As he passes the branch, he swings the canoe to the right, through a curtain of marsh grass that parts easily, the stalks brushing the sides of the boat, whispering to him. He is paddling now down a thin vein of water that winds through the cord grass. A large blue heron, startled, its eyes reproachful, rises screeching from a clump of reeds, unfolding into the grace of its flight. If he could fly with it, he would see the pattern he can sense under his skin now, the skein of narrow creeks snaking through the pale, undulating body of the marsh, glinting here and there in the moonlight. The marsh grass pushes in around him, the miniscule but combined weight of clinging snails bending blades to the water, the sudden dazzle in the moonlight of a spider web spread like a shroud over an acre of marsh. In the middle of it all, he, Towerhill. A black dot in a dugout canoe.

Ahead, a small hummock rises out of the swamp. He hears the sharp blow of a rock striking flint, see sparks gyre up between the black trunks. Lieutenant Scott, his red coat mud-stained, is hunched over a small fire, Sergeant MacDougal squatting next to him, saying something to him. The heron should have been a herald announcing his arrival to them, but neither of these men had paid attention to it. His new allies. He paddles harder, wanting to see when they will notice him. He is close when MacDougal finally rises and raises his Baker rifle, pointing in the general direction of the canoe. Towerhill takes two more strong strokes and then turns the paddle sideways, bringing the canoe parallel and flush against the hummock, its bank too high for him to run aground. He grabs onto an overhanging branch for balance and carefully steps out into the water; it comes only over his ankles here. Scott gets up, brushing off his trousers, and he and MacDougal walk over to help lift the bow of the canoe. The three men grunt with the shock of the weight—the craft is fashioned from a log scraped hollow by oyster shells and fire, a construct from the Wesorts for which he had traded stolen tobacco and whiskey. The two British soldiers drag it onto the higher ground as Towerhill lifts and pushes the stern.

He half-expects Scott to chide him for his lateness, is ready to resent him for not understanding the difficulties endured by a slave sneaking away from his plantation. But the Englishman simply holds out a hand. Towerhill stares at it for a second, the hand of a white man extended towards him calling memories that pushed down the rise of his own hand as if a manifested physical weight were pressing it. He fights it, grips Scott's hand, shakes it.

MacDougal, on the other hand, does not disappoint his expectations. Or not on the other hand, for he keeps both of his tightly tucked under his armpits. "What kept you, Blacky?"

"Was your journey difficult," the lieutenant asks, gently, as if to defuse his sergeant's words. He smiles, the firelight exaggerating the somewhat rabbity protrusion of his teeth.

Towerhill doesn't answer. He releases Scott's hand, walks over and kicks dirt into the small fire, extinguishing it. MacDougal snarls and starts towards him. Scott stops him with a look.

"I say, man . . . ," the lieutenant starts to say.

"Do you know how far that can be seen?"

Scott stands still for a moment, staring, as if gauging his response, or, perhaps, as if seriously engaging the question. Finally, he nods. "How idiotic of me," he says.

MacDougal snorts in disgust, but says nothing. He squats down, Indian-style, Towerhill remembering that the man had once lived with the Iroquois. They had left him with two oyster-shell-shortened fingers on his right hand. And the nubs that had once been ears on the sides of his face.

But it is the second time in the last few moments that Scott has surprised him. He wonders if the gestures: Scott's handshake, his acceptance of chiding from a slave, his ignoring—if he had noticed it at all—of the deformity on Towerhill's right hand, all are part of a tactic to disarm, Scott thinking he can read and turn his expectations. He likes the idea. It reveals that the man needs him, needs what he has to sell. He regards Scott. The bright moonlight gleams off the brass buttons of the uniform, the wide white leather belt, the pommel of his sword. The white goat's hair wig he wears is askew on his head.

"You're a fire yourself, lieutenant."

Scott looks at him, puzzled, and then raises his left arm, brushes the brass buttons on his sleeve with his other hand as if to erase them. He nods again. "Quite. Thank you, Towerhill. I must learn to dress for the occasion, I suppose."

"You know what I risk."

MacDougal spits into the ashes of the fire.

"Of course. And I would prefer as well not to have my own neck stretched by Yankee hemp."

For the first time, Towerhill smiles. At the image those words bring into his mind.

"You had no difficulties getting here," Scott asks again.

The image vanishes. It is replaced by the memory he had tried to repress. He feels it now; the muscles in his arms and back knotting, twisted and frozen by a rage he had to turn inwards to himself to keep from screaming.

The difficulties it had taken to get here.

He had only been paddling for perhaps fifteen minutes when he heard the screams. There had been enough time to glide under a bower of branches, and then stay completely still, watching Bertram and his patrollers at their night games.

He didn't know whether the couple had been stripped by the patrollers or discovered that way. Their hands were tied to the same overhead branch, bodies half lit in the fire light. One of the patrollers had dropped his trousers, his hairy arse clenching and unclenching as he thrust into the girl, her legs draped over the bend of his arms, his hands clasped behind her head. At first Towerhill could not make out her face. Then his eyes had adjusted and he recognized her. Sally. Sally and Lucius. He'd known the threat of being sold away from each other would compel them to run but had not thought it would be on this night. The red bristled jowl and shaven head of Hiram Bertram came into focus. The overseer had gripped the boy's narrow face between his thick, splayed fingers and was making him watch what the patroller was doing to the girl. Lucius was bleeding from the corner of his mouth. He tried to lower his head, close his eyes. Bertram yanked his face up, his finger pressing hard into the boy's cheeks. Towerhill became aware that his hand was gripping the paddle in the same way Bertram was clutching Lucius's face, involuntarily squeezing the wood, mimicking what the overseer was doing, as if his hand did not belong to himself anymore. "You look, nigger," Bertram had hissed, "use them eyes or I'll gouge them out. You look and learn." He laughed suddenly, a sound that stabbed an icicle into Towerhill's heart, then said, "The hell, you don't need both, do you?" He clutched the back of the boy's head with one of his large, splayed hands and pushed the thumb of his free hand into Lucius's left eye, the boy screaming, Towerhill looking away as if to save his own sight, but then forcing himself to look back, burn it into his memory: the press of the overseer's thumb inevitable, the thumb hooking in, scooping out, Bertram shaking the eyeball off his finger with a flick of the wrist. The soft plop of it into the water. He had felt Bertram's rough grip as if it were on his own face, as if the overseer was forcing him to watch along with Lucius. He had watched until he knew they were too busy to spot him, and then dipped his paddle softly into the water, turned the canoe, let it drift off silently with the current.

"None," he says now to Scott.

"Good." The Englishman extends a silver flask. Towerhill drinks deeply. It has become a custom, this sharing of rum. Last Sunday after church, Jacob had also opened a flask of rum, poured a pewter pot which was passed among the male slaves, giving them something, Towerhill supposed, to wash down the bitter taste of Bertram's hire. He had watched Jacob smiling uncertainly as the overseer stared hard at each slave, making sure only one swallow of rum was taken by each. Bertram and his underlings—he hired his own crew—had arrived the week before, brought over from Towerhill Proper, the portion of the plantation owned by Jacob's brother. To help stem, Thomas Hallam had said, the steady bleed of money from Towerhill Separation that had occurred due to Jacob's lax treatment of his slaves, their shortened hours, the indulgence of their weddings and other ceremonies, their increased rations. Bertram was a gift received unwillingly, Jacob had confided to Towerhill; his brother held lien and lease on the plantation and could repossess it directly into his own property. Towerhill didn't believe him. Bertram was the malevolent imp held in Jacob's own soul.

Scott's rum burns his tongue now, warms his throat and limbs, and he takes another swig, tries to wash Lucius and Sally out of his mind.

"How many men can you bring over?" Scott asks.

Men, the Englishman had said. Not slaves. And so passes another test. And so it would be. Every word that passed from the lieutenant's mouth and every word held back would always be part of a test he would apply to the man, to any white man. *Men,* Scott had said. Not slaves. Not niggers. But also not women and not children. The words held back. The British wanted only scouts and fighters for the Colonial Marines, the regiment of runaway slaves that had been raiding along the Tidewater for the past two years. Towerhill takes another drink, hands the flask back.

"Thirty from Towerhill," he lies. "That number and more from the other plantations."

"Towerhill," MacDougal, still squatting says. "You are named after the plantation?"

"It is sometimes the custom. Though the plantation on which I live is Towerhill Separation, since it was divided between the Hallam brothers."

"Have you that family name? The name of the man that owns you. I ken that is also the custom. What's your family name, Blacky?"

"Separation," he says.

Scott grins. "Let us work to that happy title."

MacDougal spits. "Where will you be getting the vessels?"

"If we need them, we'll steal them from the plantation." He waves at the dugout. "Or buy them from the Wesorts."

MacDougal laughs, presumably at the name. "Half-breeds," he says.

"You're in their territory here. As most of the swamp lands are. They've been watching you since you came." *Watching me,* he thinks.

"Will they help us also?" Scott asks.

Meaning, would they fight for the British?

"They take no side but their own." The Wesorts carried the blood of runaway slaves, runaway white indentured servants, and renegade Piscataways in their veins, their name encompassing all who did not fit within the firm boundaries of the white or black or red worlds. We sort of people.

"In the Piedmont," Scott says, gesturing at MacDougal, "the Iroquois are our allies. The good sergeant here has fought with them."

"The Wesorts will not fight for you or for . . . the Americans."

Or for . . . the Americans. He had hesitated before using that word, as if his tongue were reluctant to exclude himself from that name and what he once foolishly believed it would encompass.

"Wesorts," Scott says. "A charming name. One day you and I, Towerhill, will stand on the deck of a fine English frigate, drink more of this Barbadian rum, and you will tell me stories of those Wesorts and other wonders."

Towerhill nods. As he would nod and say nothing to all promises of the future Scott or any white man made. Deliberately, he walks over to MacDougal, extends the flask to him. MacDougal's eyes fasten on his hand, and he spits again.

"What the hell kind of sport of nature are ye, ye wooly-pated freak?" He takes the flask, drinks deeply.

Towerhill holds up his right hand, spreads his fingers to draw attention to the sixth digit. "'A family trait."

"I saw a cow born once, two heads. We killed it outright."

Towerhill points to the nubs on either side of MacDougal's face. "Are those a family trait also?"

To his surprise, the Scot grins crookedly at him. "Nay. A gift. Though they gathered me to a new family, Blacky."

Towerhill catches Scott staring at his hand also. He looks quickly away. Towerhill holds his right hand up. "A help with my carpentry. And other skills."

Such as stirring shapes and voices from the murk of time, he might have added, words he had said once to Sarai, trying to describe to her that for which he had no words.

"Of course," Scott says. "It would be, wouldn't it?"

MacDougal looks disgusted. "Scratching your bunghole too, in't?"

"That will be quite enough, sergeant major," Scott snaps.

"Yes, sir. Just trying, as it were, to *grip* the situation as it obtains, sir."

Scott ignores him. "Towerhill, we will be coming back up the Patuxent next week, moving north from Point Lookout. Can you get your people to us? Admiral Cockburn will continue to punish the plantations in this region. At the moment, our preference is to accomplish that with our cannon, rather than with shore parties. Once more of your young men join us, we will be coming ashore, as it were, more often. For now, well, if it is feasible, we will raid Towerhill Separation. But we prefer that your group simply slips away."

So that they would not be burdened with the women and children and the old. The words Scott is not saying. He stares at the lieutenant, his sixth finger invisibly stirring time and vision, forcing him to see the patrollers, see Lucius and Sally once again, and then a sight that grows not from memory but from premonition: Sarai hanging naked, wrists bound to a tree limb, as he had seen Sally so hung this night. His stomach hollows with fear and sickness. And rage. What had been conjured in the thick, damp air above this hummock was a vision given to him so that he could erase it. So he tells himself. A wave of hatred for Bertram, for these two white men in front of him, for his own helplessness, shudders through him. He tamps it down.

"It would be less risk if you did come ashore. If you burned the place."

"Old boy, I understand that. But at this time the admiral's policy is to attack and destroy only those plantations or towns that offer resistance. As I said, we prefer you come to us."

"Do you think you can manage that, Digit?" MacDougal asks. Christening him with a new name.

TWO

JACOB

~~~

A LISTING

The wooden duck Towerhill carved and painted for him sits on its shelf in the recessed niche across from his desk. The duck, the niche, the desk, all the work of those hands also. Of that six-fingered hand. Something Jacob has not thought about for years, so common has it become to his sight. He grew up with it, and when he was very young he assumed all blacks were so assembled. When he was somewhat older and had learned—one day in the Zekiah Swamp—the differences in station between himself and Towerhill and Sarai, he had seized on that extra finger, even more than on the color of his friend's skin and his wooly hair, to reassure himself of the dissimilarities between himself and Towerhill and, more importantly, between Towerhill and Sarai.

Lit by the candles on his desk and in the sconces on the wall, the shadowed form of the carved mallard shifts in his vision, and he lets his mind play with the forms it suggests, drift into the memories of what had existed between the three of them when they were younger, a time he wishes he could retreat into and wrap around himself now, the way he would pull a blanket over his head when he was a child to shut out the growing complexities of the world.

He hears the rustle of Sarai's dress in the other room. The sound dances on his nerves.

He forces himself to look back at the columns of figures. Of names. They flicker in the candlelight as if he could affect them according to the angle of his vision. As if he could see them only as the numbers they need to be. His quill swings back and forth over the parchment like a hesitant osprey dangling over the river. He thinks of calling Sarai in; her presence is usually a comfort. But he can picture the forced smile on her lips, her eyes darting as if looking for egress. He wonders if he is picturing some manifestation of his own shame. No, he is certain of it. He dips the quill into the inkwell and then lets it sit there, the feather trembling as if quickened to some life. As if the ink were blood.

"Why are you hesitating, brother?" Thomas had asked him the week before. Doubting Thomas. Sneering Thomas. Practical Thomas. "It is why people look at you as a weakling," his brother had said. "Do what must be done. I will not sell any more of my own niggers to meet your debts."

"Our father never sold any of our people."

"Our people?" His brother had shaken his head. "Yes, I know. It's true. We are both the children of a childish father. Our father-who-art-in-nigger-heaven. Our dreamer of a father. But now I am a man. I have had to put aside childish things. When will you attain that necessary state?"

Their conversation echoing all their other conversations, their eternal argument.

Echoing the conversation they had had eight years before. Thomas had sat in the same horsehair chair that stood, empty now, across from Jacob, on the day he had leased half of his inheritance, half the plantation, over to Jacob. "As if it were the infant judged by Solomon," Thomas said. As his brother held out the property deed to Towerhill Separation, the name Jacob's portion of the land would now bear, Jacob had passed him the manifesto he planned to present to the Maryland legislature: his plan for the gradual abolition of chattel slavery. Thomas read it, nodding, and then had put the parchment down on the small settee between them, next to the deed. He stared at Jacob for a long time, the way Jacob had seen him

staring at a field lying fallow and profitless, as if puzzling out its unwillingness to sow itself. And then began speaking very slowly. As if to a child. His
left hand petting Claret, Jacob's favorite hound, grown old and feeble even
then, long dead now. The forefinger of his right hand running over Jacob's
words on the paper. Claret had laid his head on Thomas's knee, gazing
up at him, eyes heavy with great wisdom, slobber dripping on Thomas's
trousers.

"This manifesto expresses our father's dream," Jacob had finally said.

"Yes. Occasionally shared, when necessary for domestic tranquility, by
our mother," Thomas said dryly.

He filled two goblets with Madeira from the decanter on the settee,
and handed one to Jacob, who gripped the cold pewter tightly, his fingers
trembling. Thomas drank, put his goblet down, reached across and lightly
touched the deed, almost a caress.

"Did you hear what Plater said when our former and unmourned—
and unmoored—preacher, Andrew Carter, assured him that the holding
of niggers in bondage would surely place his soul in hell? 'I'll take that
chance,' Plater said. 'I'll take that chance rather than take the food out of
my children's mouths, sir.'"

"I experience no surprise at those sentiments from George Plater."

"I want you to consider this, Jacob. You assume you share our dear
father's belief. Your nigger manifesto is a continuance of his legacy. But
there was no reason, no law of primogeniture, which forced him to will
the entire plantation solely to me, to the eldest son. Yet he did so. Our
enlightened father who would agree with every word you have written
here. Who regarded me as a beast or at best an ignoramus who could never
understand how the institution that nourishes us exposed the hypocrisy
of our democracy. Have you asked yourself why he did that? Why did he
leave the plantation to the prodigal son, the son who abandoned his belief
in the uplifting of the niggers?"

"You need not do this, Thomas."

"He knew I would do what is needed to keep Towerhill extant," Thomas
continued.

"It is all, as you say, your inheritance. I appreciate your generosity, but . . ."

"It's not generosity; you will pay the lease on Separation. You are my brother. You have nothing. I either give the land to you or I sell it; I can't afford what I would need to keep it. Pick up the deed," Thomas said. "Hold it. Now pick up your nigger manifesto, in your other hand."

"Don't be ridiculous."

"Do it," Thomas growled. "Do it, or on our parents' graves I truly will snatch this deed back."

For a second, Jacob felt a wave of relief, a weight being lifted from him.

But he picked up the deed. Held his manifesto in his left hand, lowering it as he raised the deed as if it were heavier, attempting to affect a theatrical mockery, a strained smile trembling on his lips.

"Is this how you would have it, Thomas?"

Thomas slapped at the manifesto, Jacob feeling it like a slap to his face. Then his brother tapped the deed with his forefinger, lightly and quickly, as if it were on fire.

"You cannot have both. You now own Towerhill Separation," Thomas said. "Let us see by tomorrow, or next week, or next year, if you still stand by your manifesto—let us see which parchment weighs more heavily in which hand."

He plucked the manifesto from Jacob, looking at it again, nodding occasionally. "Have you even considered the cruelty of sending our niggers back to the savage country of their ancestry?" He ruffled Claret's ears. "It would be like sending old Claret here to live in the forest with wolves." He seized one of the hound's ears and twisted it. Claret yelped, looked at Jacob reproachfully, and shuffled out on his arthritic legs. Outraged, Jacob started to rise.

"Sit, brother," Thomas said. "I only wish to make my meaning clear."

"Cruelty to an innocent animal, one who loves you, is odious."

"Ah," his brother said.

Between that "ah" and today lay the parallel columns of words and figures on the two sheets of paper in front of him. Like the bars on a debtor's prison cell, he thinks, then rejects the simile as morbid and self-pitying. Again two pieces of parchment, two choices in binary opposition. One sheet a list of the debts he owes Wm. Cleary and Co., Boston, for the shabby comforts of this room, the molding curtains, the sagging floor, the shelves filled with books, the chattel near starvation under the sagging roof of the corncrib, those arrears not including the lease obligation Thomas holds over his head. The other sheet listing the property, what he would sell to meet this year's interest on his debt, the sad inventory of what had once been a prosperous and, he liked to think, happy corner of the world. Had it been Thomas's intent all along to put him into this position, another lesson in the realities of the world cast against their father's beliefs? Jacob had found out, years later, that Thomas's deeding of the Separation to him had not been solely an act of brotherly generosity, done to reinforce Jacob's understanding of the economic necessity of chattel slavery. Their old solicitor, Hiram Redmond of Leonardtown, had confided in him that he had seen a codicil to Cedric's will indicating his desire to eventually have the land divided between his sons, "upon Jacob Hallam's maturity."

Jacob looks down at the list:

March 5, 1814

A Partial Inventory, with the Exclusion of Acreage and Crop, of the Goods, Chattel and Personal Estate of Jacob Hallam, planter, Towerhill Separation, appraised in dollars and cents, upon the request of the Estate Owner, by Thomas Atkinson, Esq.

Negro Towerhill	carpenter	age 30	600.00
Negro Hillary (male)		age 32	600.00
Negro Nebuchadnezzar		age 27	350.00
Negro Ulysses		age 23	450.00
Negro Agamemnon		age 18	450.00
Negro Mingo		age 30	300.00
Negro Nero		age 28	300.00
Negro Ben		age 28	300.00
Negro Samuel		age 32	275.00
Negro Henry		age 25	300.00
Negro Telemachus		age 22	450.00
Negro Achilles		age 21	450.00
Negro George		age 20	450.00
Negro Craney		age 20	450.00

Negro Lucius		age 17	500.00
Negro Nestor	boy	age 15	325.00
Negro Leander	boy	age 10	250.00
Negro Homer	boy	age 14	275.00
Negro Chapman	boy	age 10	200.00
Negro Hattie	woman	age 30	300.00
Negro Milly	woman	age 45	125.00
Negro Cecilia	woman	age 26	275.00
Negro Phibs	woman	age 18	300.00
Negro Sally	woman	age 16	300.00
Negro Mariah	woman	age 15	300.00
Negro Lucille	woman	age 15	300.00
Negro Rachel	woman	age 17	300.00
Negro Rebekkah	woman	age 43	250.00
Negro Agnes	woman	age 30	275.00
Negro Yael	woman	age 24	275.00
Negro Biresis	woman	age 22	275.00
Negro Meg	woman	age 60	10.00
Negro Caleb	boy child	age 3	75.00
Negro Martha Ann	girl child	age 3	50.00
Negro Emmeline	girl child	age 2	50.00
Negro Julian	boy child	age 8	150.00
1 bull			20.00
1 white cow			7.00
1 white cow broken horn			7.00
1 black buffalo			7.00
1 red heifer with white belly			7.00
4 yearlings first choice			8.50
10 sheep first choice			20.00
10 hogs in pen first choice			60.00
10 shoats first choice			15.00

He holds the quill over Towerhill's name. Of course he will not sell him. He had placed him on top of the list as a kind of, what? Dare to himself? He had placed his name there because he could. He is not proud of the act. He is not certain it is an act, in another sense of the word.

A shadow falls across the list. Jacob tries to cover Towerhill's name with his hand, forgetting the quill he clutches. A black blotch spreads over the name. He closes his eyes, knowing not only who has walked in behind him, whose breath he imagines he can feel on his neck, the hairs rising there, but also what the reproachful expression on Sarai's face would look like.

"Please do not come up on me so stealthily, Sarai."

"Do you fear I would do you harm?"

"Look what you made me do." He smears the ink stain over the first name on the list. Had she seen it? He turns to look at her. At the name not on that paper. Negro, Sarai, woman, age 25. And what value would he place upon her?

Instead of the expression he had imagined, her face is blank except for that flare of her nostrils which always causes his blood to quicken; that blankness a mask which more and more these days he has seen settling over her face, standing between them, a distancing greater than the differences of skin he no longer, not since they were children, sees as separation but as a natural completion. So he tells himself, but in the telling now, in the blossom of dread and anticipatory loss opening in his stomach, he allows himself to imagine her hair less kinked, her skin less black, a difference of shade, a shade of difference, that would allow the dream of taking her from this place, disappearing into the Western territories where no one knows who they are. He had, idly, shared that vision—the disappearance, not the lightening of her skin—with Sarai once; she had only snorted and said if that was the shape of their lives he desired, they hardly had to go so far when the mixed-blood Wesorts lived a scant twenty miles from where they stood.

"Do you remember our fortress, Sarai?" It had been—is, for it still tentatively stands—the ruin of the watch tower that had given the plantation its name, its termite-latticed logs collapsing inwards, the clay between them long rotted away, too far gone and far away even for slave quarters, too many stories haunting it, so that all the other slaves stayed away. The three of them, he, Sarai, and Towerhill, had made it their own, its age and distance allowing it to exist outside the border of the world that they knew, even then, would encroach upon their friendship. "Do you remember the copperhead sitting at the bottom of the old root cellar? How Towerhill grabbed it by the tail and snapped it, broke it, how you clung to me, weeping, saying it was its place, the snake's place; he was the king and we had been the guests of the king."

She touches the list. "Who will it be?"

"Not you. You know that."

She says nothing.

"There is really no choice." He reaches up, runs his finger over her face, forehead to chin. "I owe too much. I could lose everything, end up in debtors' prison. If I do, everyone will be sold."

She says nothing.

"Sarai, have I not treated you all well?"

"Yes," she says. "And the shoats, and the white cow with the broken horn, all well. Only your father did not have the latter taught to read and write."

"Was he wrong?"

"No. Only cruel."

"You sound like my brother."

"But I am clearly not your brother. Nor your sister. That tower has fallen. Who is on the list?"

"I have tried to be as fair as I can."

They stare at each other. He closes his eyes. Shuts away from his vision the blank expression on her face and replaces it with the face of the girl who had smiled at him, eyes bright, from the dangerous wall of that fortress.

THREE

SARAI

A WALL OF BOOKS

The hand of God hovering over the list on the desk. She wishes she could cause him to spill more ink, blot out all the names.

She bends to kiss him. To kiss him. To kill him. She knows he would not sell her nor exile her to the fields if she refused him her body. Nor would what she is doing prevent him from selling any of her brethren; she cannot play the wanton seductress with him, as Towerhill wanted to think. She is certain that convenient lie is not even one Towerhill believes any more. If she is to sin, at least let it be without the hypocrisy exhibited by this man, rising to kiss her back now, the familiar hardness of him pressed against her, her body reacting as if trained by habit. "He doesn't only own you," Towerhill had said bitterly. "He created you. Just as his father created us. Educated monkeys. Malleable brown clay." She seals her mouth to Jacob's.

She is a story in one of the books on these shelves that only came to life when it was read.

A faery story. The ruined tower on the hill the embodied fortress of their childhood, a connection that Jacob had referred to now, as if he needed to remind her. Jacob and Towerhill were both, as far as she knew—she had been an infant, born between continents—five years older than she. But outside of age and sex and law, the three of them were equal, in their own minds, until one summer when she was seven, the boys twelve, and the three had gone into the Zekiah Swamp and two had come back as slaves. She knew Towerhill was right, had known even before he put it into words. Jacob's first intimacy, even before the night he had made love to her in this room, had been to reveal to her the agonies of his soul about their disparate and unequal conditions. Agonies she is now convinced that he clung to in order to feel he had a soul. "How can I exist with these contradictions, Sarai?" he would ask her, as if she were the representative of the bonded. "But to take our slaves is to enslave us, Sarai. It is to lose the ground we stand upon. The existence of this plantation, this *separation,* this *fortress,* is the only way I can continue to protect you."

"Don't worry," Towerhill had assured her, just the week before. "He will never sell us, not you and me. We're the monument to his virtue."

How attractive Jacob's struggle to exist as a moral man had once seemed to her. It had entered the awakening sap of her body as it entered the awakening awareness of her mind to the injustice of the world. This man, her lover, was sincere in his hypocrisy. At times, she hated him for that. At other times, she regarded it in the same way one would see a scar or deformity on the body of a lover. Of a still loved one.

The irony does not escape her that one of the many gifts he had given her was the capacity to see his self-deception.

How can I exist with these contradictions, Jacob?

How she exists, she supposes, is in boxes. In this book-lined room and the windowless room Jacob had built for her after his wife Abigail's death, a small, separate cabin set between the manor house and the Quarters. A single bed, white-washed pine-board walls, a shelf of books leaked from this room, a candle, a door that faces the rear of the house. Easy access for nocturnal visits. A perfect geographical referent for her life. Though these days she has been spending more time in his bedroom, next to the larger room where his late wife had spent her brief, bitter, barren reign, creating new ways to torment her and the other house slaves.

I'm sorry, Sarai. She controls me.

But what his wife controlled, Sarai knew even then, was the money his marriage to her, a sickly woman past the age of eligibility, brought to Towerhill Separation. Before the relief of that woman's death, Sarai had slept curled on the floor in front of the paneled oaken door of the master bedroom, available to be called at her mistress's whim, exhausted from a day of scrubbing clothing and dishes, of cooking and serving and polishing.

She was fifteen the first time Jacob had come to her, a few days before Christmas that year. His wife's door was tight shut to hold in the heat from the small fireplace, the parquet hallway floor at the threshold where Sarai slept cold as ice. "Slept twitchy," as Rebekkah described a house slave's night, her brain always ready to be jerked out of dreams. So that when she first became aware of Jacob in his long nightdress, he was moving towards her in the space of the hallway, lambent, trailing in and out of a dream, the candle in his hand throwing a flickering light that made his smile do odd tricks, as if the features of his face were malleable. He had extended his other hand to her, and she took it, let him pull her to her feet, pull her to this room. She was fifteen but she had read the new Romantic poets now being published in England, their books shipped through the same port that landed slaves, and she read Malory and Shakespeare and they had prepared her for lovemaking with a king, or a god, or an ardent fool. Though not for the details of the act. But she had grown up on a working plantation—had Romeo appeared to Juliet as that unsheathed bull in the North Pasture?—and, besides that, Rebekkah the midwife had described in detail what awaited her.

He had stood, staring at her, as if expecting a slap or a blessing, the tug between power and conscience that would always be there confused in his eyes. The same tug she supposed she had felt. But for each a different meaning. The power to do what he wished without consequence. The power to use his guilt about that to control him. At fifteen she had known that already. And under all of it, stronger than any of it, was curiosity and desire. He had stood, paralyzed, but she had raised her shift, pulling it up to her chest, parted her legs slightly. He groaned, raised his own nightgown in a parallel action to her own, presenting a sight that forced a laugh from her, at the practicality of bodies. When she cried out in pain a few seconds

later, he had covered her mouth with his hand. An act of ownership, more
so than the lovemaking itself. Had his wife lay abed awake and heard that
cry? If not that night, then surely on others when its nature changed.

But on that night she lay under his weight, and her eyes went to the
books in the shelves above them, their smell of leather and glue and paper
becoming for her part of the smell of sex. The books seemed to be witnessing this human act, and as he thrust into her she fought her own desire,
put herself inside their covers as she still did from that day, seeing herself
and what was happening to her as if she was in the safety of a story. Or in
a Shakespeare sonnet. *I lie with her and she with me, / And in our faults by
lies we flattered be.*

Now she unbuttons his shirt and places her lips on his nipples and he
groans, his hand waves, and, as if directed by her fierce wishes, knocks over
the inkwell. He tries to snatch the paper out of the way before the other
names on it are covered, as she had seen Towerhill's had been. Too late. It is
ruined. But the names are still there, under the ink, an inventory of those
she loves, of those who would be separated from the body of each other.
For that was what they were; they were a body, one this man could punish
with cruelty or kindness, but which he could never enter.

She touches him, lingers, feels how much he wants her, and, yes, of habit
her body, her betraying body, responds. Her mind, though, is detached,
hovering, though not this time mooring into the haven of a book. Her
mind is floating down Hallam's Run with Towerhill, trying to envision the
place where the man in the red coat awaits him.

FOUR

TOWERHILL

THE GEOGRAPHY OF NIGHT

MacDougal spits into the cold ashes left from the fire.

"You have a comment to make, sergeant," Scott says.

MacDougal shrugs. "More a question, sir."

"Then say it, man."

"Why do we need these savages, sir?"

His look and his question are directed straight to Towerhill, who suddenly understands the play these two have been performing. The benevolent Scott; the surly, hostile MacDougal. He had seen that drama before; he knew it in his bones. His so-kind, so-paternal master, Jacob, pouring from his flask of rum as his factotum Bertram hovered behind him, sneering. What is happening here is more deliberate, conscious, a tactic decided beforehand. A test. Towerhill sees MacDougal's eyes widen, and then a small grin flits quickly over his lips, as if the sergeant has understood his comprehension.

"Chasen's Run," Towerhill says.

He is gratified to see MacDougal flush. The Run, in the Northern Neck of Virginia, had been the site of an ambush in which a British column, lost and tangled in thick forest, had been cut to pieces by American militia.

"I was not at Chasen," MacDougal says. "More the pity; I would have been useful. I learned to fight American scum in the Piedmont, from the Iroquois."

"We are the Iroquois here."

"Explain how that is true, please, Towerhill," Scott says. "Sergeant Mac-Dougal's rudeness has the advantage of revealing questions my superiors will ask as well."

Towerhill grins at MacDougal. Sees he has the intelligence to grin back, understands the farce is over.

"There is a woman who has slaved on Towerhill for all her thirty years, Agnes Hallam; she's a skilled cook and seamstress."

"May her cunt curl with the pox. Answer the lieutenant's question."

"Agnes had a husband, Samuel, and three children, all girls," Towerhill goes on, as if MacDougal has not spoken. "Samuel died of the bloody flux, and last year the girls were sold. One down South, which is the same as dying. Another to Sotterly, and the last to Mulberry Hill, our neighboring plantations."

MacDougal spits. "Did they fetch a good price?"

"Two obstacles, two walls stood between Agnes and her children. One was slavery. The other was geography."

He picks up a stick and stirs the dead ashes of the fire.

"Make your point," MacDougal says.

"Agnes overcame both those walls. She would see her children. To do so, she needed to move at night, when her time, however briefly, became her own, and she needed to know the secret trails and ways to go invisibly between those plantations. She needed the help of other slaves and the knowledge of how to secretly ask for and receive their help, and the knowledge of the land that so many of us have. She has not been the only slave who has needed the geography of night. The black geography. The landscape we know and in which we move."

—

The geography through which he is moving now. Sell or be sold. Sell or be sold. Nothing but that blackness around him, the air thick and cold on the river. The moon gone behind clouds, and now a light rain starting, cold on his head, rivulets moving down his spine. Can they trust the British? Of course not. No more than the British can trust him. It doesn't matter. Need is a stronger bind than trust. He smiles at the phrase, thinking how he will speak it to the others. And distracted by thoughts of his own cleverness, his attention strays. If not for the crack of a branch from the wooded shore, that cleverness would have hung him.

He freezes, his paddle still in the water, trying to make out the direction of the noise. Listening so hard all that of his muscles tighten and his senses open to the world, the way an iris widens to capture light as it dims. Another crack. The sound of metal clanking against metal. And then a curse, muffled but loud enough for him to identify as belonging to a white man. The voice and that carelessness in the way white men move through the world, as if they believe they own it. A belief that both the world and his own circumstances tend not to contradict. As if to confirm his thoughts, more voices rise now: another curse, a laugh. Towerhill is drifting towards a bend in the creek; if he continues at this speed, in this direction, it will be his meeting place with what has to be a party of patrollers. Perhaps even Bertram. On his left he knows there are rocks that will, at the least, scrape the boat; the passage between those rocks and the shore too narrow; he will be spotted.

The rain stops. It would have provided some cover, a blanket of sound at least. He turns the paddle sideways, swinging the bow towards the shore. The drift catches him, and as he draws close, he grips the paddle in one hand, grabs a low-hanging branch, and pulls the canoe in between the bough and the thick brush on the shoreline. As he does, a lower appendage of the same branch scrapes the craft, not a loud sound, but strange enough in these woods to draw attention, if someone knows how to listen. Someone does. The voices stop. Someone starts to ask a question; he cannot make out the words, but hears the man's voice rising. A sharp command. "Shut yer mouth." Bertram's voice, he's sure of it. Silence again; they are listening. He holds his breath. And hears them advance, closing on him.

He throws his head back and howls.

A wolf's howl, long and drawn longer, rising and falling. Joseph had taught it to him, drilled it into him.

The patrollers fall silent, stop. The sound pins his location for them. It will either scare them or draw them to him. That's the gamble. He touches the knife in his belt.

"God's teeth, move yer arses," he hears Bertram shout. "We got the bastard. That were no wolf."

"For fuck's sake, yer too damn right, Bertram," another voice says.

He smiles. They are armed and they know that any wolf will flee from them. But they have all heard the stories, the Wesort lycan legends—cultivated, he is sure, by Joseph—that keep people out of the Zekiah. They are not in that swamp, but this place is swamp enough and they know enough to be scared that it may not be a wolf.

"You will damn well move or I'll gut you like a fish, Wallace," he hears Bertram say. The sound of brush moving. The sound of a slap, a grunt.

He draws out the knife.

The clouds draw back and suddenly the moonlight pours down upon him. Through the weave of branches on the shore he sees a white face appear, just a blur. He is certain it's Bertram, a glimpse of the man's red beard stubble, the shaven head reflecting the moon, but he is not certain that he has been seen. The moon darkens and the rain begins again.

Another howl splits the night.

It comes from the other side of the patrollers' position. No, it comes from everywhere. From the forest and the creek. From outside him and from inside him. Everything that he tamps down in his guts has suddenly been loosened into the world, and he joins it, the noise bursting from his throat, rising, though he hears now how the sound that emerges from him is only a shadow of the pure rage of that howl that seems to sink teeth into the flesh of the night and shake it. And then it stops.

He hears panicked shouts, the noise of branches breaking, Bertram cursing his men.

Sell or be sold. Sell or be sold.

FIVE

SARAI

——

ORIGINS

Royal Africa Company
Cape Coast Castle, Africa

May 2, 1789
Capt. Alvarez joyned with Mr. Wm. Bowles on a trading Voyage
to Windward. Will consign the Negroes to Mr. Cedric Hallam at
Patuxent River in Maryland.

August 9, 1789
Shipd on board the vessal Jesus Christos 260 slaves vixt. 124 Men
112 Women and 16 boys and 8 girls.

"You an Towerhill was born a Jesus," Rebekkah had told her, singing it like a hymn, and Sarai had not understood until she found the document in an old ledger in one of the bookcases that lined the study. A ship called *Jesus.* "Two mother, two dead," Rebekkah had sung. Her mother dying as she was born at the same moment Towerhill's mother gave birth to a stillborn infant, his brother or sister. She taking that child's place, sharing his mother's breasts with Towerhill, until his mother also succumbed. A boy too old to be so fed, but that milk saving both of them.

Saving two Negroes not consigned but purchased anyway by Mr. Cedric Hallam at Patuxent River in Maryland. To lives their mothers could have never imagined.

SIX

JACOB

THE FEARED FUTURE

Thirty-six. That is the final tally of those he will sell. There seemed something portentous about the number, some meaning to be found in it, as the Cabbalists find prophecies wrapped in certain numerical combinations. Thirty-six slaves. Chattel. He will force himself to think of them that way, not with their given names, though he knows such verbal and numerical evasions will do him no good. Finally no good. In the end no comfort. He is not capable of the self-deceptions that are the unspoken currency of the trade in flesh. He will press their names to his forehead like a crown of thorns. Thomas comes to his mind; his brother, he knows, also refuses hypocrisy, but does so with a relish that both disgusts and pulls Jacob. "We must accept Necessity and not fall into Hypocrisy," Thomas has said. "The most fundamental liberty the British would take from us is the freedom to deny our slaves their liberty. Say that. If not aloud, then say it to yourself, because you know it is true."

—

Two years before, Jacob had been ready to go to war against the British, as his father had done in the Revolution. His status as a plantation owner would have granted him an immediate commission in the Maryland militia, attached to the 36th American, a regiment of the regular army. Thomas had talked him out of that also. "What will happen to your beloved darkies if you go?" Finally, reluctantly, he had accepted another privilege of his status: a planter's exemption from military service.

The day before he made that decision, Towerhill had come to his study. Jacob was somewhat shocked to see him striding down the hallway in his sweat-stained clothing; since Cedric's death, he had not come into the house except to do repairs. He stopped at the doorway to the study, looking silently at the shelved books, many of which had been the core of the curriculum designed by Cedric to awaken the minds of Towerhill and Sarai, to demonstrate to the world—to his Tidewater world, in particular—that such minds in fact existed. Towerhill was holding the carved mallard that Jacob, sitting at the same desk, surrounded by the same books, touches again now, its smooth contours filling his hand as he remembers their conversation.

"How your skill has grown," he had said, taking the carving, feeling a warmth spreading through him at what he took for Towerhill's gratitude. "Thank you, Towerhill."

"It is a farewell gift."

Jacob laughed. "Are you planning to run off to the British?"

Towerhill didn't laugh.

Jacob's heart lurched. "This is not the time. Everything will change, Towerhill," he said, hearing the double meaning of the word that came out of his mouth and into the ears of this man named for the land. "I promise you that. The legislature . . ."

"You mistake my meaning. This is a farewell gift. Not a farewell."

"I don't understand."

"I wish to accompany you."

Jacob laughed in relief. It was the moment to tell Towerhill of his decision not to go into the militia. But he was still reluctant to actually put that statement out into the world, especially, for a reason he couldn't understand, to Towerhill.

"I cannot bring a servant," he said.

"I don't mean to come as your servant."

They stared into each other's eyes. Jacob had already bought his uniform; it hung empty in a corner of the study, representative of a choice he would not take. An image of Towerhill, standing in the shadows in military kit, a musket and bayonet in his large hands, formed in his mind.

"Towerhill, it will come."

"I would take it with my own hand," Towerhill said.

He held up his right hand, five fingers and the misshapen sixth outspread, and then slowly clenched them into a fist.

Jacob said nothing.

"There were free Negroes, and slaves, who fought in the Revolution. I remember your father telling us of that, of how most of the Rhode Island volunteers were black. And of others. So do you."

"What did you call him?" Jacob asked sharply.

Towerhill looked puzzled. "Cedric? Your father."

It must have been so. But what Jacob had heard from that black mouth was "our father."

"Do you remember what he told us about Camden?" Towerhill asked.

It had been the only time Cedric had ever spoken in detail to them about his time in the Revolution. He had told them the story after they had attended the funeral of a freedman, Peter Forrest, who had once been a slave at Towerhill and who had been in that battle. He was buried on the land his family had been given, near Dameron, and afterwards Jacob, Cedric, and Towerhill had sat on a dock on Flat Iron Creek. Sarai had come with them to the funeral, but had been sent back home afterwards. Cedric, legs dangling just above the water, had begun speaking as if one of them had asked him a question about the battle. It had not seemed he was speaking to them. His face was turned towards the center of the creek, sun-maddened clouds of gnats and darters circling frantically as he spoke, his voice so low it mixed with the soft gargle of the creek so at times it seemed to emanate not from his father's mouth, but from the water.

Until then, Jacob had read of war only as accounts of the mass movements of armies, the strategies of generals, heroic stands and charges. But in Cedric's telling he sensed some adult truth about the matter that, like the details of human coupling, had been held back from him. The British then—as they were doing now—had promised freedom to any slaves who would run away and join them. Those who had taken up the offer had been formed into what was called the Ethiopian Regiment. Cedric's battalion had fought them at Camden, in the Carolinas. It had been a disaster. The American irregulars, the militias, had fled that battlefield, leaving the Continentals—Cedric's regiment among them—on their own. Their commander, General Gates, had fled with the militias, into his own disgrace.

His father told how his company had been sweeping in a flanking movement through some stinking Carolina swamp, its black water picketed with cypress trees and stumps all blasted and shredded by the earlier fighting. Corpses, or parts of them, were strewn through the fetid water. The Americans had struggled in a ragged column through those evidences of an earlier skirmish or ambush, the mud sucking the boots and shoes off any of the men who still had such luxuries. Each step was an epic. That mud seemed animate and malevolent, as if it were reaching up to grip the soldiers, strip their flesh, snatch them down into it. Scattered fragments of bone and shards of metal from the morning's fight shredded their feet and ankles, their blood joining what had already been gathered into that hellish soup. Mosquitoes, driven insane by the rich bounty of meat come into their country, covered every inch of exposed skin, and worked themselves down under clothing also. The high-pitched whine of the insects in the soldiers' ear canals drove the men almost mad, distracting them so much that at first they did not even hear the volley of musket fire the black soldiers of the Ethiopian Regiment blasted into the American ranks. Men who one instant were swearing and swatting their faces were flung backwards into the mire as if they were puppets strung along a cord that had suddenly been yanked. The blacks came at them out of a copse of palmetto trees, their eyes wide and white against skin caked with mud, their bayonets pointed at the Continentals' hearts. They charged out of the trees like a wave from the feared future.

The feared future. His father's words.

The mire forced the enemy to come at them with what seemed to be a preternatural sluggishness, as in a nightmare in which one's movements become leaden. Sloughing off the heavy fatigue that weighed down their bodies and minds, the men raised their muskets, managing a ragged volley as the blacks thrashed about, trying to pull their feet out of the muck, their arms waving as they struggled to keep their balance while pointing their bayonets towards the Americans and firing their own volley. The soldier next to Jacob's father, a Sergeant Hammett from Charlotte Hall, was hit in the gut—out of the corner of his eye, Cedric saw him clutch at his belly—but was still alive, on his back, his intestines trailing and writhing snake-like in the muck, his eyes desperate as the mud closed over his face. Cedric saw this only in a glance, for in spite of their impeded movement, the blacks were almost on them: a huge buck grinning malevolently as he thrust his bayonet forward. He was so close Cedric could see the mosquitoes, undeterred by the slaughter, covering his face, moving in the caked mud like visible nerves. Cedric swung his saber around to catch the Negro's thrust, awkward because his feet were frozen in the mud, but before he connected, he saw him gasp, drop the weapon, and move his hands down to his privates, through which Sergeant Hammett had thrust his own bayonet, the movement that saved Cedric's life pushing Hammett completely under the mud which became that brave man's tomb.

To his left, Cedric heard another volley of musketry and saw the line of blacks crumple. A skirmish line of Continental soldiers had crossed the T of the enemy formation and were pouring volleys of fire into the Ethiopians. He could hear the thud of leaden balls striking into flesh; he could see the mouths of men—from both sides—open in screams, though he could hear nothing. And then he saw something that made him doubt his own vision, as if the battle had shaken his brain in its pan and some strange pocket of his mind were drawing apparitions in the air. For the Continental soldiers who were saving them from the blacks were black themselves: across the swamp, not fifty yards from where Cedric stood between the corpse of Sergeant Hammett and the man who had tried to stick a bayonet into his guts, was Peter Forrest, a runaway from Towerhill Plantation, wearing the uniform—if his bloody, tattered rags could be called a uniform—of the Continental Army.

Until that transformative moment, Cedric had not put his mind to the contradiction between the cause for which he was fighting and the institution which gave him and his family their sustenance. The fight for freedom from the British was an obvious and clear choice for him, but what would be its attraction to a man such as Forrest, for whom an American victory could only hold the promise of bondage? He put the question to Forrest that night as they shivered around a campfire. "Well, cap'n," Forrest had said, poking the fire, "sometimes you see the embers under the smoke." It was all he could get the Negro to say, but that enigmatic sentence had stayed in his mind, and he had mulled over it again and again. It had led eventually to his purchase of Towerhill and Sarai, and his plans for them. That and the memory scored into the tissue of his brain of the black faces of the Ethiopians charging at them out of a copse of palmetto trees, their eyes wide and white against skin caked with mud, their bayonets pointed at the Continentals' hearts.

The feared future.

"I remember the story," Jacob had said to Towerhill as they stood in the book-lined study that had been the womb of their brotherhood.

"Why did your father give me my name?" Towerhill asked suddenly.

"I don't know. You never asked before."

"It doubles everything."

"I don't understand."

"Is the name of this plantation on me, or is my name on it?"

"You know who you are."

"I does. I's one huge buck, massa."

"Stop it."

"You don't think I can speak nigger?"

Towerhill had unclenched his fist, stared at his palm, at his sixth finger, as if searching for a future writ there.

"Are you your father's child?" he asked Jacob softly.

—

Is he? He had thought so in those days, before he came to resent the moral stance that, until the death of his parents, had made their family social pariahs among the other plantation families. He runs his finger over the smooth wood of the carving. In many ways, Towerhill and Sarai were Cedric and Emmeline Hallam's children—his mother a silent, frightened partner, but always loyal to her husband. In some ways they were more his parents' children than he and his brother: their bond to their parents was merely through blood, while Towerhill and Sarai were bound through his father's words. The two had been bought by Cedric—Sarai an infant clinging to Towerhill—not to be groomed as house slaves, but as an experiment, a demonstration in flesh that those held in bondage possessed the capacity, in intellect and in morality, for freedom. They were the premises of an argument. At William and Mary, Towerhill had accompanied Jacob, officially, as his manservant, but the two of them had learned together, read the same books, parsed and argued through long, sleepless nights. He thinks now of the hours, days, months, years Towerhill and Sarai had spent in Cedric's study, here, being taught by the various discreet tutors, northerners hired by his father. His father's delighted laughter at something clever they had said drifting out through the door, stabbing Jacob like a knife. His brother, listening also, would sneer, mock. "How clever you are, Master and Mistress Monkey," he would whisper, and then snort and cavort like an ape. Jacob would chide him, and sometimes he would fight him. He loved Sarai and Towerhill and his strange parents. But at times he would join his brother's mocking laughter. If one can say that a child is clay formed by his parents' hands, then, yes, surely those two were more his parents' children than he was, and infinitely more so than his brother. His mother and father had chosen to nurture their black shadows over the children of their own blood. He hoped, in the feared future, whenever it would come, that he would be beyond such jealousy. That he would be able to see the embers under the smoke.

SEVEN

SARAI

⎯

A RENDERING

She goes to the creek afterwards, squats and tries to wash him out of herself. But there is no trace of him left. She wishes there had been, so she could see him leave her. She has no illusion it would keep his seed from taking; like him, it would do as it pleased. The women and girls on the plantation had many ways to keep their wombs from quickening, or the opposite—some wished for a half-white child, deceiving themselves that it would gain them privilege. To kill the seed, hold a divining rod over your parts afterwards; this will distract the flow. Eat a paste of ginger root and ground oyster shell. Drink the urine of a pregnant goat. To Sarai's relief, Rebekkah, who serves as the plantation's midwife, has told her that these and other methods just as unpleasant are all nonsense, and the number of light-skinned children on the half of Towerhill belonging to Thomas Hallam have proven her correct. Though in truth Sarai would drink a bucket of goat piss if it would keep her from becoming pregnant by Jacob.

Or would she?

Later she works with Rebekkah making lye for soap. They work outside the laundry room, but still the stink enters and fills her nostrils solidly, like plugs of rotten lard. As she renders the animal fat, the drippings saved

37

from all the cook fires of the plantation as well as the fat from the butcher-
ing done last week, the fumes burn her eyes and skin and private parts. She
welcomes it. The cold, clean water of the creek had not been enough. She
wants to burn herself clean.

Hours go by. Neither she nor Rebekkah speak. This is not like the midwife. Her eyes are red and inflamed, the skin around them swollen, her
mouth downturned, her face soaked with sweat. Sarai looks at her hands
as she places a potato into the boiling kettle of lye; they are scarred and
patched with burn marks, rough hands that have pulled so many children
into the world. The potato sinks, bobs up, a coin-sized portion of its skin
floating above the surface. If any more or less showed they would have to
boil lye down more to make it stronger, or add water to weaken it. But it
was perfect, the lye ready to be made into soap. Rebekkah would look at a
girl's or woman's belly with equal skill, knowing exactly when the child was
ready to be rendered. It is the exact word, Sarai thinks. Rendered. Made
into caustic material that could be used, and be worn down in its use,
returning finally to a melted mess of stinking animal fat.

"You don't need be at this, you," Rebekkah says. She does not say it kindly.

"You think I'm the lady of the house?" Sarai starts ladling the lye out of
the kettle into a pot.

"Talk like it. Talk white. Fuck white too."

She glares at Sarai, puts her hands on her broad hips, log-like legs
planted apart, her boat prow of an ass jutting out.

"Why are you angry with me, Rebekkah?"

"Why are you angry with me, Rebekkah?" the laundress mocks. "You
and t'other white nigger, Towerhill. Get all us dead. Or wishing we dead."

Sarai is surprised. Before, when they had spoken of plans to run away to
the British, Rebekkah had been enthusiastic.

"What we know these strange white men? You saying they don't keep
slaves?"

"They've promised us freedom," Sarai says.

"Promise, you say? How we know what be out there?"

"We know what's here. Hallam will begin selling folk."

Rebekkah snorts, looks at the kettle. "Stir this, use a sassafras stick, or it don't take. You know that? You see what I be doing here, these two days? Put ashes in the barrel, boil down the grease, just so. Know when it be ready." She points at the pot. "Cool it down, shape the soap cakes, who else know to do that? Massa Jacob? You? Some other nigger? Who know how to pull a baby, he get all twisty up? Just me, Auntie Rebekkah. Auntie Rebekkah ain't going nowhere. I here, and I know here." She spits into the pot.

Sarai knows this is true. Immersed in her own tasks, she's still been watching Rebekkah over these past few days. No, she can't use the word *immersed* for what she does; that word is owned by Rebekkah. The way she works. What they are doing now is rooted in the disease that has ravaged the plantation's already small herd of cattle, forcing Jacob to butcher many of them. Along with the grease the slaves collect all year from their cooking fires, and the animals' tallow, all must be transformed into soap. Another wrong word. *Transformed* is how Jacob and the other whites must see it—the square, crumbling chunks of soap appearing, as if by magic, in their hands. How does it form their vision of the world, to be so separate from the process of transformation, ash to lye, lye to soap, tree to dwelling, seed to plant? That magic belongs to the slaves; the whites are helpless without them. Rebekkah knows this, though she has neither the words nor—until now—the need to say so. Sarai knows men and women who perform their assigned tasks slowly, slovenly, oft-times damaging what they service, while at the same time working skillfully at what benefits themselves and not the master: tending their small garden patches, trapping squirrels and raccoons or crabs after working all day in the fields, building and caring for their quarters. Sarai understands them, and why not? She has spit into the cook pot herself. But Rebekkah does her tasks—boiling lye or laundry, or bringing a new soul into the world—with skill and love. It is a kind of freedom for her, a mastery she can own; that she can do what no white woman—or man—can do is her pride. She knows that what is made belongs to the one who makes it. Less metaphysically, she knows her skills are what keep her from being sold. Sarai watches her now, as she has watched her over the past few days, learning a world she hopes to soon

leave: Rebekkah placing wood ashes in the bottomless barrel that sits on
a grooved stone slab, layering straw and twigs as a filter to keep the ashes
from mixing into the lye. The principal of separation at the heart of all
they do and all they are. She pours the water slowly over the ashes, judging
ebb and flow until brown liquid oozes out of the base of the barrel, flows
into the grooves, drips from the slab's lip into a clay jar. Her work is a ceremony of exactitude. And Towerhill is the same. Cedric Hallam was wise
when he insisted on apprenticing him to a master carpenter so he might
gain the skill that would keep him valuable, even as his intelligence, his
store of words, would infuriate whites. Cedric insisted on no such skill of
the hands for her, thinking, Sarai supposes, that her face and body would
ensure her value. To her he had given only the curse of understanding. He
allowed her to open books, doors that let her see into the world around
and beyond herself. But Rebekkah knows only the place she lives in, and
her son, and the work that may keep both of them together in it. Who can
tell her that elsewhere will be better?

"And Lucius?" Sarai says. "Are you sure he will not be sold?"

At these words, Rebekkah's face softens and seems to collapse in on
itself, melting like lye. Tears begin trickling, then streaming down her
scarred cheeks. Sarai knows that the dread her son will be sold is not new
to Rebekkah, but her reaction now seems charged with a new fear, one that
has built a wall of anger around her all day. The mere sound of his name
has collapsed it.

"Auntie, it will be good. We'll go together."

"Ah, missy, I sorry, I sorry, but what to do? That boy, off tomcatting with
his Sally slut. Left last night. Maybe running."

Sarai feels a stab of fear. Will this jeopardize their plans?

"They be all right, auntie."

"Naw. They love," Rebekkah says. As if the last word is an accusation.

EIGHT

A NOTICE

Towerhill Separation, March 24th, 1814

On the first day of April next, will be offered for sale at the Scribers Float on the Patuxent SEVERAL Negroes, to include as many as 36 able-bodied men, women, boys, and girls. Credit will be given on bond and good security. These Negroes are sold for no fault, but for the need of the proprietor.

NINE

TOWERHILL

—

WE'LL PRAISE HIM AGAIN
WHEN WE PASS OVER JORDAN

He is back by dawn. It is Sunday, and there is no work, though, as is the custom, Jacob will have them walk to church. Towerhill would prefer a day of carpentry, bent in his own manner of prayer over a beam of wood. He is exhausted, his mind still spinning with the events of last night, and the thought of their forced pilgrimage, a meander which normally only bemuses him, makes him feel light-headed with rage. Jacob regards the church visit as an act of compassion, as well as a display to his fellow planters. A feeding of the spiritual hunger that his fellows refuse to acknowledge even exists in the bosoms of their slaves. He has heard Jacob describe the Sunday custom in those words to Sarai. But the closer they come to the planned escape, the more unbearable become Jacob's blindly cruel gestures, perceived by him as kindness. The cruelty that grows from Jacob's need to see himself as benevolent. He gives his work-exhausted slaves the gift of God by marching them ten miles to St. Cecilia's Church (leading the way in his carriage), where they can sit on hard benches in the nigger balcony and listen to Father Clements assure them that their condition in the world fulfills the intent of the Lord. And then walk ten miles, through the Maryland heat, back to Towerhill Separation, where they must scramble to find and prepare their suppers and sleep for the few hours left before the next day's work begins.

He detests Jacob's hypocrisy: the Jacob who embraced his father's grand experiment in educating slaves is the same man who accepted Bertram from his brother when the British raids began stirring unrest throughout the Quarters. In the past he could see Jacob as a lost brother, to be mourned rather than despised. Jacob's peers, his brother and cousins and the sons of other plantation owners, find something alien in him; they squint uncertainly at him as if he were a looking glass that reflects back a face they recognize but would rather not own, and this, for a time, had allowed Towerhill to keep loving him. He had understood that the unease and repulsion other whites feel towards Jacob comes from his inability to see him and Sarai—and so by necessity his other slaves—as less than human. But it is that incapacity that has finally twisted his love for Jacob into hatred. Jacob knows the monstrosity of their lives and is torn by it and chooses to continue it while he pretends munificence. As his parents had done. Until now, love—the affirmation which means the most to Jacob—has been the only profit from their relationship that Towerhill can deny him.

He prefers Bertram's malevolence. There is at least no hypocrisy to it. At least with Bertram he does not have to construct the chambers of his heart into a replica of the cherrywood desk, filled with secret compartments, which he had once built for Jacob's study. Pull out one drawer and there they are, he, Sarai, and Jacob, huddled over a candle in Jacob's childhood room, reading the books Jacob has sneaked there from the study, the flame flickering against their faces and reflected in their eyes like the fire slowly being lit within them. Pull out another and there is Jacob's wife (he refuses to even think the dead bitch's name) and Jacob letting her use Sarai as a door rug. Another, and there is an island on the flank of the Zekiah Swamp where three children, two black and one white, and a companion wolf romp and laugh in utter freedom, their surroundings like a deep moat between them and the world into which they will grow up. Another, and curled within, is the whip that lays open his back when that reverie ends.

And a large drawer that he tries to stuff with images of what Sarai does for Jacob—stuff full, and close, and lock, and throw away the key.

Just after he returned to the cabin near dawn, immersing himself in the familiar miasmic odor of sweat, the weave of smells, sighs, coughs, and snores from the fifteen adults sleeping on the dirt floor (the loft above, wedged between the ceiling and the eaves, populated by a mouse tribe of children), Sarai had come to the front door. What they called the front because it faced away from the plantation house; for the whites it was the rear door. He lives in the reverse world, the night world, where every word means its opposite. She kissed his cheek and handed him the advertisement placed by Jacob in the *Courier.* He read the words that Jacob had wanted to be kept from them until Bertram gathered the slaves for the actual sale.

"We only have a week," she said.

"The arrangements with the British are made."

Instead of asking about the details of those arrangements as he'd expected, she said, "I think Rebekkah's Lucius ran away with Sally. Did you see any sign of them last night?"

Towerhill had said nothing. He couldn't speak. She looked into his face and then bit down on her lower lip, clutching his arm, her fingernails digging into his skin. Before he could gather the words, Caleb Hewitt, one of the lesser overseers, burst into the cabin and screamed to them to get ready. Towerhill felt relief at his interruption. And shame for that feeling. He accepted that if he had tried to intervene, he would not only have died, but would have destroyed the plans for escape. But the vision of Sally hung like meat from a tree branch as the patroller pushed into her, of Lucius's face pressed between Bertram's hands, the thumb with its filthy nail digging into the boy's eye, flickers continually on the periphery of his mind and vision; he sees them whenever he drifts from the urgency of purpose.

Now some of his brethren sing as they trudge along the dirt road, an old Indian trail that leads to the church. Bertram is not here. Towerhill sees Sarai riding ahead with Jacob, the wheels of the carriage churning up a red dust that settles on the marchers. The air is hot and heavy-wet, like a clinging, itching garment. There is no relief in the shade: the thick canopy of trees just seems to compact and press the heat down upon them. It is no more heat than they endure working in the fields. But there is an undercurrent of fear in the singing. Word of the sale has spread. Usually most of the other slaves are happy to go to church, despite the long walk and even though it is Church of England and some are Catholic or Baptist. Many these days, particularly among the house slaves, have become followers of the Reverend Richard Allen, a freed slave who, it was whispered, had started a Negro Episcopal church. Whispers, Towerhill knows, which had been started by Jacob himself in one of his strange and strained efforts to soothe his own conscience since hiring Bertram and planning the sale. Sarai, with Jacob's knowledge and blessing, had been secretly teaching verses from Allen's hymnal. Towerhill does not include himself among the believers of any creed. He came away from his "studies" at William and Mary as a Deist, as did Jacob. But he does not begrudge or attempt to dissuade the others from their faith. They had built a God to the measurements of their own need.

When they finally arrive at the church, though, he regards it, as always, with some measure of affection. It was his first large brick construction, and William Boulton, the white master carpenter to whom he had been apprenticed, had prepared him well. He still knows the measurement of each brick and board, can still feel the moment when he and his crew cut and planed and hammered and laid each brick into place. He runs it all through his mind like a silent chant. His prayer. And the Lord commanded Towerhill to make two steeples flanking the door, the inset portico and Palladian window on its exterior. And the Lord said the exterior shall be fifty-five feet in length and forty in width and the foundation three and a half bricks thick and the pews wainscoted, the pillars fluted and capped, the aisles laid with flagstones, the roof planked with sweet cypress shingles.

Now he can see the nebulous cloud of white men and women claiming its entrance. They mean nothing to him. They mean nothing to this edifice, built by black hands. By his hands and mind. He would burn it to the ground. It doesn't matter. He possesses it already. Jacob helps Sarai from the buggy, and some of the white women among the congregants waiting outside mutter. The words "nigger whore" float in the air. The white congregants' usual vehemence is underscored by their fear, a mirror reverse of the fear weighing on the slaves; accounts of the British-aided slave risings and escapes are being whispered everywhere. Jacob does not take Sarai inside with him. Towerhill knows that he would, if he could get away with it; riding with her as he does defies and defines what most of the planters do discreetly, their silence about their black mistresses fulfilling a contract with their wives, whose acceptance of that custom is the payment they render for the lives they lead.

Towerhill leads his people up the narrow staircase into the balcony rows set aside for them. Nigger heaven.

What is his own contract of silence? For him, the fact that Sarai fucks Jacob (he refuses to prettify the act with soft words) is something he is able to accept because she has no choice, because she feels no love, because her being with him enables her to know his plans. These are the three beams that support his acquiescence. Yet the base of the second pillar at times feels termite-tunneled and eroded.

He hears the preacher, dour Father Clements, preach to the slaves to obey their master as if he were God. To not hold back in work, to not sass, to not be eye servants. Towerhill sees Lucius's eye flicked into dark water. Some of his own people, and then more, turn to look at him. The last is Sarai. Then big Mingo nods to him, takes a deep breath, and, to Towerhill's horror, begins to sing. No, he thinks. Not now, Mingo. "The voice of free Grace cries escape to the mountain," sings Mingo, a grin on his face, his deep voice booming, drowning out the priest's drone. Towerhill recognizes the words; they come from one of the songs in the Reverend Allen's forbidden hymnal. "Hallelujah to the Lamb, He hath brought us our pardon," one of the women cries out, and Mingo takes it up: "His blood flows most freely in streams of salvation / We'll praise Him again when we pass over Jordan!" Hewitt and two other overseers, sitting at the end of the row, leap to their feet. "Shut your mouth, nigger!" Hewitt screams. Towerhill looks down at Jacob, who is in the first row below. He sits, head hanging down, hands clasped as if in prayer, ignoring the songs he has given to those he calls his people as if he has never heard them. The three white men are running among the slaves, yelling, punching, the murmur of the congregation below rising to them, and then a white woman screams, and then another. A woman faints. Mingo and Agamemnon, and now Abigail and Neb—Nebuchadnezzar—all look at Towerhill as their voices start to harmonize sweetly into more of the verses. Freedom songs. Fleeing songs.

> *With joy shall we stand, when escaped to that shore;*
> *With harps in our hands, we'll praise Him the more;*
> *We'll range the sweet plains on the bank of the river,*
> *And sing of salvation for ever and ever.*

Most of the white congregation are on their feet, staring upwards at nigger heaven with hatred, or at Jacob with reproach. He still has not moved. Another woman faints. Others fan themselves frantically. The black singers all turn again to look at Towerhill, except for Mingo, who looks down at the white congregation and sings in a low voice only those around him can hear now:

> *Brethren, farewell, I do you tell*
> *That you and I must part.*
> *I go away, but here you stay*
> *But still you join in heart.*

As Hewitt reaches them, they fall silent, but Mingo has time to say, "I's sorry, Massa Hewitt, we just taken by the Holy Spirit," before Hewitt strikes him full in the mouth, his knuckles drawing blood. Mingo still stands, swaying only a bit and then coming back to true. Towerhill feels a swell of pride and envy, along with a great need to strike Hewitt down into the earth. *His blood flows most freely in streams of salvation.* But sufficient unto the day is the act of defiance thereof.

They are marched back under blows and curses, and without the company of Jacob, who pushes ahead in his carriage, Sarai still next to him. Towerhill is not surprised when Hewitt and the other overseers drive them, cursing, not to the Quarters, but to White Meadow. It is filled with a glory of Queen Anne's lace, the acres of delicate white flowers that give the place its name bobbing and dancing in a breeze that roils them in waves.

Mingo smiles at Towerhill, shrugs, as if to say he can take the whipping. The meadow cannot be seen from the plantation house. Bertram waits for them there, next to the three whipping posts, his own altars, scrawled with the sacrament of blood, the foundation of his faith. And then Towerhill understands they have not been brought here just to receive and witness punishment. He hears Auntie Rebekkah's hopeless scream, sees Sarai and the other women surrounding her, patting her. He thinks, absurdly, how good it is that Sally was sold away from her mother very young. She and Lucius hang naked, lashed by their wrists to the posts, their arms above their heads, their mouths open, each gasping for breath in a strange unison. Both their bodies are already crisscrossed with bleeding welts, their flesh hanging down in strips. Lucius's face is uptilted. At first Towerhill thinks the boy has raised his own face, to bathe it in the sunlight. But then he sees the rawhide around his forehead, keeping his face in that position so that all of them can see the empty socket, a tear track of blood bisecting his cheek.

TEN

JACOB

EYE SERVICE

Bertram stands before him, unrepentant. "If I am to do my work, I must do it as I see fit. On your brother's plantation, I . . ."

"Where are you standing, Bertram?"

"They were running away, Master Hallam. And you were at the church today. If an example . . ."

"I asked if you know where you are."

"Yes, sir. I grasp your meaning, sir. I work for you, not your brother. But he sent me here to . . ."

"There is only one part of what you are spewing from your mouth that concerns me, and that should concern you. You work for me and not for my brother. Is that something you truly *grasp*, Bertram?"

Even as he says it, he knows it isn't true. When his brother had insisted he take on Bertram, he had refused at first, but finally had given in. Had even felt, to his shame, a certain vengeful thrill. Didn't his people understand how painful it was to be forced to sell some of them? To sacrifice some so that the rest, so that the world he and his father had created, would continue to exist, a construct that modeled the possibility of fairness and, yes, kindness, that shielded Towerhill Separation, that *separated* it from the world where creatures such as Bertram reigned.

But there is no doubt for whom the overseer truly works.

Bertram shuffles, like a schoolboy caught in some mischief, but his eyes are still locked to Jacob's, his mouth twisted as if he has eaten something foul. A bull of a man, as are most overseers Jacob has known. Bertram's massive head is shaven, a soot of coarse red hair bristling on top, and on his cheeks, and on the roll of fat crushing his collar. His scraggly eyebrows over-arch a small snout, black-pocked flesh scrunched over two gaping, cavernous nostrils. Heavy jowls wing both sides of that stub, pulling the skin between them taut and strangely smooth. Did the face make the man's life, or had his life created this face? The comic exaggerations of Bertram's visage do not encourage laughter but fear. His head is set, seemingly without a neck, on shoulders layered with muscle; his thick torso, his corded arms, his cruel hands limn a latent, menacing strength, an effect broken only by a pair of skinny, bandy legs he keeps covered, most days, in over-sized homespun trousers that flap like sails as he walks.

For now, though, he stands on those legs. Insolently meeting Jacob's gaze.

"Sir, Mr. Hewitt told me what happened. You need to let the niggers know you know. Those were runaway songs, Master Hallam. Songs you let 'em sing elsewhere. No whipping. No stocks. You take from my wages if you see me cursing some lazy buck. How you think they take that? Six days' labor and even that not first light to no light. Singing, dancing. Reading scripture to them. Nigger paradise here. But how's that helping you, sir? Niggers are my work, sir. And I know my work."

Jacob had seen his work not an hour since. In a meadow configured by this man into a form and purpose Jacob had forbidden to exist on Towerhill Separation. The peace he looked forward to on Sundays, looked forward to sharing with his servants, shattered by their ungrateful insolence and now the actions of this beast Bertram. Towerhill, his face blank, had merely looked at him and asked if he could take the pair down. "Of course, and quickly," Jacob had snapped, unnerved by Auntie Rebekkah's piercing cries. "Get them down immediately." Towerhill had taken the two to the parlor, where Sarai and some of the other women were now attending them. Rebekkah had joined them after a few moments. She was no longer crying. She was stone silent. Her face, as Towerhill's had been, as had all the other slaves', was set and hard.

"Get out of my sight," Jacob says to Bertram.

"Sir, you said I work for you and not your brother."

He is at the end of his patience. "What is your question?"

"Why, whether 'tis still the case."

For a few second Bertram stands uncertainly; he wants the matter resolved, undoubtedly wants Jacob to throw him off Towerhill Separation, whereupon he will go back to Thomas. Who may or may not take him in again. No, there is no question. Thomas *will* take him, another lesson for his soft younger brother, more evidence of Jacob's failure to know how to move through the world of men. He thinks of the day he had grasped for the deed to this place, wishes he could reach back, seize and still his hand. The life of a second son, landless but able to live comfortably within the security of the law or the university or the church, or even rebelliously at sea, a life liberated from the ownership of slaves, appeals to him more and more.

Bertram clears his throat, looks down, shuffles, clears his throat again. To hell with him. Let him hang suspended between heaven and earth, between Towerhill Separation or Towerhill, until Jacob makes his choice, until he decides whether the plantation can function without the overseer, until he decides which action will fulfill more completely his brother's need to be disappointed in his behavior.

"Damn your eyes. Leave me. Wait in your quarters."

Bertram looks up, into Jacob's eyes, naked contempt written on his face. He turns sharply, like a soldier, and leaves the room.

Like a soldier. Is it possible to run the plantation without Bertram? Jacob knows the danger he now faces; a British raid has already freed George Plater of Cremona from the slaves he always complained enslaved him in turn, with their whining and laziness and need for discipline. The

British admiral, Cockburn, has freed Plater into desperate poverty. It is another reason to sell as many slaves now as he can. More than—or along with—the British, Jacob fears the threat that may rise from within Towerhill Separation, and from within the man named for it, who—as Thomas has warned him—hears the second part of that name as a call to action. A feared future. Last week, Thomas sent him copies of eight-year-old dispatches from Saint-Domingue: accounts of how the colony's slaves had massacred French planters in their beds, their brutal torture and rape of white women and children. Thomas included no explanatory letter with the yellowed copies. Nor did he need to.

In truth, Jacob does not know what Towerhill and the others will do if given such a choice by the British. Surely the kindness and fairness with which he has endeavored to treat his servants, the beauty and certainty of life here, will weigh in favor of their loyalty. They will understand that Bertram has been forced upon him, how necessary but painful it is to sell some of them to preserve the rest. He will do all he can, when he can, to not separate families, to keep people here in the Tidewater and not send them South to the living hell of the cotton plantations. Surely Jacob's disgust at Bertram's brutality will be noted by them. He feels another wave of fury at Bertram: did the man not understand what the cost of his cruelty could be? But he is certain, he tells himself, that Towerhill and the others will not let one incident, no matter how cruel, push them to the British.

The howls all around him grow louder and then louder. It is a moment before he lets himself understand they are coming from Rebekkah still in the parlor.

Yet when he goes there to comfort her, she falls silent, her face contorted into frozen grief, as if the scream is trapped forever under her skin.

—

He sends a buggy for Dr. Biscoe, who cleans and bandages Lucius's eye socket. Jacob lets him use the study to do his work. Biscoe, a plump, balding man with a bulbous, mottled, drinker's nose, does not look at him, even when he is not concentrating on the wound. There is little he can do for Sally, who shrinks into herself when he moves to touch her, resting her face on her knees and hugging them, as if to make herself as small as possible. Biscoe snorts, yanks her up brutally, pushes up her shift and, with a hand on each of her knees, spreads her legs and examines her privates. Jacob turns his head, but not before he sees the angry scarlet scrapes on her inner thighs. All the while Rebekkah stands, staring. Her silence after her first cries worries him. She is pushing everything inside herself where it will fester and grow poisonous, a diagnosis he does not share with Dr. Biscoe.

He hears the clop and snort of another buggy horse pulling up under the porte-cochère. A moment later Thomas walks into the room, tall and saturnine and smiling smugly, as if a prophecy has been fulfilled.

"This will not stand, Jacob," he admonishes. Then, as if remembering something, he turns to Rebekkah. "I am sorry for what happened, auntie."

"I will deal with Bertram," Jacob says.

His brother waves languidly at the five blacks in the room.

"And how will you deal with them?"

"I don't take your meaning."

"I heard what occurred at the church. Bertram must be disciplined, perhaps even arrested and charged. We are not barbarians. But surely you understand that applying your slipshod theories to your slaves causes such incidents. Those slaves involved must be punished also."

Dr. Biscoe nods vigorously, and for the first time looks at Jacob. "Listen to your older brother. I hear the muttering among my own servants. They speak of Towerhill Separation as if it is the Garden of Eden. You are causing unrest throughout the peninsula."

"In these times," Thomas says, "we need to be particularly vigilant."

"Exactly," Biscoe says. If he nods any faster his neck may break. Jacob enjoys the thought, but only for a second. Biscoe cuts a comical figure, which makes it easy to dismiss him as a joke, but he also represents, Jacob knows, vox populi, the voice of his neighbors. Still nodding, Biscoe folds the white cloth left over from the bandages he cut, stuffs it and his instruments into his bag, and makes his exit.

"Perhaps if we gouged out all their eyes," Jacob says, "they would be easier to control."

"You joke. But your laxness encourages a relaxing of necessary boundaries." Thomas purses his lips and smiles slightly, as if pleased with his word play. "Spare your slaves the illusion that they are not inferiors. In the end it will be more merciful than this." He pokes his forefinger into the bandage over Lucius's empty socket. The boy cries out.

Jacob glances at Auntie Rebekkah, but she does not move.

"What do you think you are doing?" Thomas asks. "Who do you think you are?"

"I am a Christian and an American."

"We are all Christians in this place," Thomas says. "And we are all Americans."

"Even them?" He points at the five blacks, who remain motionless, as if they are trying to become as invisible in reality as they seem to be in his brother's regard.

"They are what allow us to be Americans," Thomas says.

"And that does not torment you?"

"Don't be a fool. The British would strip us of our property and make us into slaves ourselves. It is for that we fought against them and will do so again."

"Yet Towerhill once expressed his desire to serve with me in the militia, as blacks did with our father, in the Revolution."

Thomas's eyes flash. "Armed and killing white men. As if it weren't enough to arm him with books. I understand you even had Sarai trying to teach the pickaninnies to read and write. Our father's notions were mistakes for which you are still paying. For which we are all paying."

He moves swiftly over to Sarai, who is standing with her back against the wall. They all are, except Lucius, who sits like a statue of justice, with the bandage draped over his eye and half his head, and Sally, who is still configured into a comma. Thomas strokes Sarai's cheek. She stares into his eyes and does not flinch. "You are looking particularly beautiful today, Sarai," he says.

"Stop acting like a stage villain," Jacob says.

Thomas laughs, lets his hand drop lower, to her neck.

"Did you come here to provoke me?"

His brother takes his hand away, turns swiftly towards Jacob.

"I came, little brother, at the request of our peers. Your methods, your strange illusion of the intelligence of these beasts of burden, these hewers of wood and bearers of water, are causing unrest at a time when we can little afford such, not with the British encouraging revolt."

"Illusion? Towerhill . . ." he starts to say.

Thomas shakes his head, smiles his little smile. "Spare me the demonstrations. Once I saw a marvelous sight. It was in Philadelphia, in the theatre. A man had trained a monkey to do most clever acts. The beast was dressed in human clothes and seemingly could count and add and eat with utensils. Oh, it was so amusing! Near the end, a girl monkey was brought in and the two beasts held hands, kissed and cooed at each other. It was so touching and amazing to see what they could be trained to do."

He walks over to the cabinet, pours himself a glass of Madeira. Does not wait for Jacob's offer, does not offer to share a drink with him. He raises the glass in a mock toast and then flings it at Towerhill, who leans casually to one side. The glass shatters against the wall near his head, wine and shards of glass showering the duck he had carved for Jacob. Thomas walks up to Towerhill, brings his face close. "Clean that up, nigger."

And he turns and goes, leaving Jacob alone with the five of them. Having insulted him in all ways except by calling him a hypocrite. The one insult which would have been true.

ELEVEN

SARAI

QUARTERED

Sally sits curled and broken on the chair. Lucius sits silent and broken near her. Rebekkah stands silent and broken.

And Jacob stands silent and broken also. And if he is broken now he will be broken more when they leave. So be it. Sarai knows that his fragility, like his kindness, can only seduce her away from freedom. She knows he sells his soul. She knows that he understands this, and the agony of his understanding and even his indulgence of it pulls her to him even as it pushes her away. He has never forced her into his bed. Towerhill, to live with himself, insists that he has, that she has no more choice than a field slave. Towerhill, to live with himself, insists on believing that she is forced to sacrifice her body as a strategic distraction. And, to live with herself, at times she has tried to believe the same. But their lives are twined around each other, hers and Jacob's. What is broken in him is broken in her. What he has sold himself to, she has sold herself to as well. For the comfort of her position, for the luxury of the time stolen from her brethren, who, since the arrival of Bertram, labor first light to last light and then labor more for the privilege of foraging for food to eat, lugging water to cleanse them of the filth and sweat of their days, building and repairing the walls that for a few fleeting hours embrace them with the illusion they will always be together. The theft of time, of time even to think of how their time has been stolen, enslaves them more than the whip of the overseer. That time is the gift that Jacob has given her; it is the chain she cannot refuse to wear.

He continues to stand, motionless, silent, even as she helps Rebekkah and the two young people from the room. Rebekkah is quartered in the small room above the kitchen. *Quartered.* Jacob lives here. But they are quartered. Quartered in the Quarters. Though not her. She is quartered— when not called to him—in the small, windowless structure he has built for her near the main house. A quarter of herself. She has never questioned how they use that word, how well it reflects the fragmentation of them- selves. Of herself. So when Towerhill appeared not at, but inside of her door one night, urgent with need, she had not refused him. It had hap- pened only once. Afterwards neither could look at the other, knowing it had not been about them, their fused years together; it had been about Jacob. It was a matter of justice. Of balance. Of defiance. Of revenge. Whereas with Jacob it was a surrender. Not only to him, but to herself.

As she pulls down the ladder stair that is the only access to the room above the kitchen, Auntie Rebekkah suddenly grips her right wrist and stares at her fiercely. When she releases it, Sarai sees that the woman's nails have punctured her skin, droplets of blood forming on the wound. Rebekkah points, her finger shaking, at her son and his lover. Lucius has his arm around Sally's shoulder now, and she is leaning against him. The white cloth draped around his head and over his eyes is spotted with blood, echoes of the droplets Rebekkah has raised from Sarai's skin. His tattered shirt is striped with blood as well. Rebekkah will not speak. It is as if she is afraid that if she opens her mouth, any sound that comes out will peak into a scream. Yet Sarai understands what she wants. Lucius and Sally are not allowed to sleep in the main house. They should be taken back to the Quarters now, and some of the other slave women are waiting outside for them, under the little overhang beside the kitchen, where the field slaves line up on Saturday to receive their cornmeal and fatty pork rations. But Rebekkah, wordlessly, has told Sarai that she needs them to stay with her.

Sarai tries to help them up the ladder, but when she places her hands on Sally's waist, the girl cries out, and Lucius gently pushes Sarai aside.

As he reaches for Sally, she seizes his hand and kisses his fingers.

Afterwards, Sarai walks through the house in the dark, like a ghost. *Quartered.* Is that fraction of her fractured self rooted within these walls, or is it outside, down the hill, where even now Towerhill is making his plans? Is that quarter of herself down there with him, in the warm, squalid nest of a cabin he built with his hands, just as he had fashioned so much of the place she haunts now. She passes the empty room where Jacob's wife had nested in her solitude, but even though it is kept as it was when she lived, the four-poster bed made, still waiting for the conception of an heir who will never arrive, there is no trace of that cold breeze of a woman, barely here even when she was alive. Sarai drifts down the Chinese Chippendale staircase, its banister a pattern of vertical and horizontal rectangles. Seeing it every day, she has become blind to the cleverness and intricacy that must have gone into its making. As she has to the shell alcove over the mantle, made, Towerhill had once explained to her, with strips of wood that had to be curved and softened and made to look as if they were one piece. She searches the rooms for the touch of Towerhill's clever hands on the furniture and alcoves and mantles, but the craftsman, as he once told her should happen, has disappeared from his craft. Her skin, the skin of a ghost, disappears as well; she wants to be absorbed into the red ochre of the wall. The house is in her as she is in the house, and the house, no matter how much of it is the work of Towerhill's hands, is Jacob. Jacob as she saw him today. Jacob broken. Halved.

She goes to him. He did not ask her to; she does not even think he wants her, not after today. But it is not his need that draws her into his bedchamber.

Afterwards, she sees a blood stain on the sheets, as if it were the first time for them. When she tentatively runs a finger over it, testing whether it is truly there, Jacob, as if answering that unspoken question, traces the forgotten punctures on her arm Rebekkah's nails had gouged into her skin as she gripped Sarai to keep her own soul from floating away. The wound must have opened during their lovemaking. He kisses it, brings the blood written on their skin and their sheets down her body to the center of her, where she lies open to him. She feels, tries to feel, wants to feel, something in both of them struggling to be restored.

TWELVE

TOWERHILL

HATING THE MOON

Consider the small ditch dug around the cabin.

The dwelling lies on the slope of the large hill which runs down to the river, next to the Rolling Road, the packed dirt path where hogsheads of tobacco are rolled to the dock—though *roll,* Towerhill thinks, is a misleading word, easy-sounding, *rollll.* In truth the field hands must control the downward rush of thousand-pound barrels, and he has seen more than one crushed under them.

Without a ditch, the cabin's hard-packed dirt floor, always swept clean, would flood each time it rained. That drainage, like every other improvement in the dwelling, was the idea and the work of its inhabitants, for the cabin was sited where it would be convenient for the labor of the plantation, not for the comfort of those who dwelt within. Towerhill has always known this but has not thought of it for a long time. Has not considered this ditch. He lights his clay pipe, looking at this place, which one way or another he will soon leave. Now that he knows he will go from it, on his feet or on his back, he finds he is fastening it, as with certain meadows, copses of wood, stretches of wind-riffled water, part by part, into his mind. What he will carry away. The moonlight bleaches the cabin into a ghost of itself, as if it is already a picture held by memory. He touches the lintel, runs his finger along the smooth pine, his hand recalling the glide of the adz. He listens to the breathing and rustles and soft moans of the sleepers inside, fifteen lives notched together, nested inside the fourteen-by-sixteen rectangle of the walls. It is the best-built of the slave cabins: the Thompson family, with whom he resides, are all valuable house slaves or craftsmen: laundresses, coopers, wheelwrights, and joiners. He had worked with them to fashion it of pine logs, hewn and square-notched, with four cedar posts dug deep into the earth to hold it firm. He had helped to build its brick chimney (Jacob letting him use the extra bricks from a cargo brought from England to build and repair the manor house) and the loft where the children now sleep under the pitch of the roof, freeing more sleeping space for the adults on the dirt floor, though keeping the ceiling low, so that a man of Towerhill's height is always bumping his head against the joists. Some of the clay and hog's hair and oyster-shell mix used for chinking between the logs has been removed now, to let the spring breezes in. The inhabitants will put it back in the fall, but this is a task he no longer needs to schedule. He has no love for this place, he tells himself; like everything else here, it is his but not his.

No, he thinks. That is wrong. It is not his but it *is* his. As is everything else that he will leave behind to weigh on this land, none of which would exist without his six-fingered hand—not the plaster scrolling and wainscoting and carving in the manor and in the church; not the bone and oyster shell and lime whitewash he invented from need and spread on the walls of this cabin to keep the termites and plaguing insects away, to bring light to the windowless space. It is not his but it is his. Through the door, he sees Hattie Thompson sit up, wave to him, and then rise and walk towards the iron pot hanging in the fireplace. Her wave awakens, or makes him aware of his hunger. There is still a small fire under the pot. He picks his way as quietly as he can over the sleepers, takes up the wooden bowl near his bedding, returns to the fire, and ladles the stew. Rabbit and squirrel and a ration of fatty pork. What is there has been saved for him by these people who are always on the edge of hunger, and he feels a swell of love for the sleepers around him, lying on grain sacks stuffed with corn husks or pine needles, the breathing, moaning, farting human mass of them, glued by their sweat and toil and servitude, their breaths knitting together, the planet of them here, creating their own air. These people who are not his blood but surely are his family, as are all the exhausted dwellers, perhaps some lying sleepless now, dreaming while awake in this string of cabins between the sharp downwards slope of the Rolling Road and the creek and wooded gulley that meanders down to the Patuxent, the watery road that brought many of them here and that he hopes will take him, and as many of them as he can, away from the beloved prison of these walls.

He goes outside again to wait, moving into the shadow of the trees.

Considers his dilemma.

The two thousand acres of Towerhill's Separation slope down to the Patuxent River. The Rolling Road follows the same creek, which descends, in a meandering fashion, in the gulley next to the Quarters, these slave cabins strung along the path and the creek. It is the easiest access to the river and thus the most watched, the most guarded. The defiant singing at the church, the unrest after the abuse of Lucius and Sally, have alerted Bertram, and he and the other overseers will be particularly vigilant. Towerhill needs to get everyone out through the same indirect route he took to meet James Scott; they need to disappear through that same skein of waterways.

He moves deeper into the woods. The moonlight is bright, too bright, and he thinks, *I hate the moon,* and then he thinks that what he hates is that perversion of his perception, the circumstances of his life that must twist beauty into threat.

He does not have to wait long.

Earlier, Hattie had hung a quilt with the drinking-gourd star pattern over the worm fence along the creek. As soon as he hears the rustle of bushes to his right, he snuffs out his pipe. He has been alert for the noise, knows the brief whisper of leaves was not accidental. He has seen Joseph move without a sound through the thickest underbrush, even on carpets of dead leaves.

They embrace. Joseph has that particular, not unpleasant smell that always conveys "Wesort" to Towerhill: pine resin and sawgrass and the fragrance of wildflowers but also of something feral, sharp, and acrid that does not repel him, but rather stirs his blood.

They move away from the cabin, towards the gulley.

"Thank you."

Joseph shrugs. The quilt was hung, he would come. He says nothing. In Joseph's telling of it, mouths are only given a certain number of words; once they reach that number, humans have nothing left to say and can die.

"Not only for coming now. Thank you for coming to my aid last night."

"Towerhill," Joseph says, using up one of his words. He grins.

"What is it that you always find comical in my name?"

Towerhill hears whistling from further up the Rolling Road. Hillary Thompson is standing watch there. The tune is "Fiddler's Lament," a serious warning. They can go deeper into the gulley, but that could also be a trap. Bertram is no fool; he often has his overseers walk towards each other in a scissoring movement, catching his victims between the blades. As if to confirm his fear, Towerhill hears a branch break in the other direction, along the creek. He takes Joseph's arm and draws him inside the cabin. Several people look up as they enter; they have to move over the bodies of the sleepers, but they know to remain silent, and silently also they clear a space over the root cellar before the small fireplace, most of it filled with the common cooking pot. Towerhill opens the trap and Joseph lowers himself down into the narrow, conical shaft that opens out at the bottom into a small hollow where vegetables are stored in the cool of the earth, along with nails, twine, and some flints stolen from the house, and a rusted cutlass found buried near the river. The top of the door is covered with a layer of dirt stuck with resin over a reed-woven mat. But the overseers know there is a root cellar; each cabin has one; and Towerhill does not like this way of hiding Joseph, would not do it if there were a choice. As soon as the trap door is closed, he lies over it on his stomach, and the others inch and roll close in around him, a human mat. He hears their breathing, along with the usual insect noise outside, the chorus of crickets and cicadas which is his other warning picket. And just as he listens, their noise stops. Footsteps. He keeps his eyes closed, but he can feel the pulse of the room running through all of them, quickening, the heat rising as a new presence enters the cabin. He opens his eyes slightly, as the Thompsons stir around him. The overseer, Hewitt, holds a lantern, its light splashing around the room, making the shadows of tools and traps hung from the joists jump and jar. Hewitt counts the inhabitants, aloud. Then he asks, "D'ye all sleep well, niggers? Having good dreams?"

He starts towards the fireplace, stepping on Hattie Thompson's leg, kicking at Samuel, the light from his lantern bobbing crazily. Towerhill opens his eyes all the way and sees the overseer's feet, planted apart in front of his face. He rolls over; to keep lying motionless would only bring suspicion.

"Ah, Tow-ah-hill," Hewitt drawls out. He steps over to the fireplace, kicks the pot aside. The embers that had kept the stew warm had gone out. "No fire tonight, Tow-ah-hill?"

"It's warm, sir."

"'It's warm, sir,'" he mocks. "You a bright nigger, all book-learned, in't it? Tell me ain't no fire, sir, 'cause it's warm. That why you sweating so much, lying here? Nervous about something?"

He knows Joseph can hear these words. He imagines him drawing the knife from his belt, waiting. A part of him wants to see that: Hewitt opening the trap door, Joseph springing, sinking the knife into his chest. But it's too soon, the moon too bright, the way too guarded, and no boat yet awaits them.

The room is dead silent.

"Naw, Mr. Hewitt, he good," Mariah Thompson says suddenly, rising to her feet: a slender fifteen-year-old, Agnes's daughter. A girl Hewitt has taken from this house on other evenings.

"You lie down, girl," Agnes says helplessly.

"Place makes us all sweat, Mr. Hewitt." Mariah runs a finger down from her neck to her breasts and then over the front of her garment; she is wearing only a coarse flax shift. "But we all good."

Hewitt holds the lantern up and then brings it around in a circle, throwing light on the people on the floor, stirring, staring at him stone-faced.

"We all good, Mr. Hewitt."

Hewitt laughs. "I don't know about that, Mariah. This don't look like no happy bunch of niggers. Master Hallam, you know, he wants happy niggers. Singing niggers, that right, Towerhill?"

"I'm a happy nigger, Mr. Hewitt," she says.

He laughs again. "Y'all trying to *dis-tract* me, somefing, Mariah?"

She pulls the flax cloth away from her skin, peers at herself. "Think I could do that, man like you?" She blows down onto her breasts, a grotesque parody of seduction. Towerhill is filled with pride at her courage, with rage at the way she must use it. He wants to kill this man. He lets—tells himself to let—the first emotion override the second. He hopes everyone in the room is doing the same. "This nigger cloth so damnable itchy," she says.

This is enough for Hewitt. He growls, deep in his throat, grabs her arm. "Come on, girl," he says, his voice strained. "Les go scratch that itch."

He pulls her from the room.

Everyone is dead still. At first Towerhill doesn't move either. Then he leans in to the trap door and whispers Joseph's name.

"Still here, Towerhill," Joseph says from the earth.

Towerhill remembers reading about how supplicants would speak to the oracle at Delphi; Joseph's voice rising from the hole like a soul whispering from Hades. He feels everyone's eyes on him. In the wake of the silent helpless rage Hewitt left behind, people are sitting up in the darkness. He can hear Agnes crying softly, holding in her grief and anger. He is sure Hewitt knows, or at least thinks, they are planning something. Only one more day, he tells himself. He needs to keep them calm.

"Towerhill, let me out this place," the voice from the earth says.

"You hear something?" he asks the room. "Think we got us some mice, down the root cellar."

Joseph pushes against the door, raising it slightly. Towerhill rolls over on it. People are lifting their heads. Grins. A soft, deep chuckle. The door pushes up against him.

"My, that's a big mouse," he says. "Hope it don't like potatoes."

"Hope so too," says Ben Thompson, a thirty-year-old cooper. "Stole those myself. Took some time, some thinking to free them from their bondage to Massa Hallam."

"Towerhill," the voice from the earth says.

"That's a smart one," Ben says.

Laughter ripples through the cabin.

Towerhill is filled with gratitude towards Ben, towards all of them, towards Mariah. His people.

"Towerhill," the muffled voice calls.

"Not much of a talker, though," Hattie says.

"Still pretty smart for his kind, talking at all," Ben says.

Towerhill lets the trap door up and Joseph emerges, dirt on his hair and face. He looks around in mock indignation, and Towerhill sees he understands.

The laughter, for a moment, drives out some of the tension of Hewitt's visit, Mariah's absence, the horrors of the day. As they all knew it would. He is sick to his heart with his hatred of this home they have made for themselves, this place where every wrenched moment of joy is fastened to a conspiracy of survival.

He and Joseph go outside, to the gulley. He sees Hillary near a huge tulip poplar; the man nods to Towerhill—everything is secure—and moves back into the shadows. Hewitt must have taken Mariah off some distance, into the woods. For a moment, he stares into the darkness, and then takes a step towards where he knows Hewitt will take her. Joseph grabs him by the shoulder, spins him around. He keeps his hand firmly pressed down.

"Don't ruin her sacrifice."

Towerhill feels his muscles twitch against Joseph's grip. He closes his eyes, stands still until the urge to kill Hewitt passes. No, not passes.

"Joseph," he says.

Joseph nods, releases his grip.

"How many do you have?"

"All that will go. At least thirty-six. More from Sotterly and Mulberry Hill."

Joseph raises his eyebrows. "That's more than we spoke about."

"We need to get out along the northern creeks," Towerhill says. "You heard Hewitt. They know we're planning something. They'll be watching the shoreline here."

"Then wait for a better time."

"The sale and the British have determined the time."

"The creeks, then. Though not all of you will succeed. You'll be split up, and you all must get to the river at the same time. I can have the barge where you wish. But even if you get to the river, it will be difficult. Open."

"You're talky tonight."

"But you do not listen."

"Joseph, what if I can get them first up to Zekiah Fort, to hide with your people? If we can shelter there for a few days, until I make other arrangements with the British?"

Joseph remains silent for a moment, peering out into the darkness.

"You know what I will say."

"But I need to ask."

"Yes. You need to ask."

"Your ancestors were runaways. Blacks, Piscataways, white servants."

"And now we need to survive to become ancestors. The only reason the Americans leave us alone is because we give them back any slaves that come to us. We're taking a great risk, helping you now."

"You do more than give them back. You capture them."

"We've had this conversation before," Joseph says.

THIRTEEN

TOWERHILL

~

THE BRAIDED STREAM

He had met Joseph when they were both twelve. Cedric Hallam had taken him, Jacob, and Sarai to Allen's Fresh and left them to go fishing and swimming while he did business with a tobacco factor who had driven his horse and buggy down from La Plata. Anyone—black or white—looking at the trio would have assumed that he and Sarai were Jacob's slaves. Which they were. Though it was not how they regarded themselves at the time. The end of that outing had marked the end of that fragile illusion.

Paddling a long, narrow, Piscataway dugout, the three of them had fished and crabbed in stretches of sun-splashed wavering cordgrass, at times slipping off their clothes in the heat and jumping into the silty water, their feet sinking into the viscous mud on the bottom, the fetid, loamy smell of the marsh clinging to them like a second skin, giving them a little protection from the clouds of mosquitoes. They set up a trot line between two poles cut from pine branches, tying eel chunks along its length, and gave seven-year-old Sarai the job of holding up another forked branch at the side of the skiff, the line traveling through the fork as Towerhill paddled and Jacob stood in the bow and netted the crabs that clutched at the bait, their hunger and greed landing them in the reed basket kept in the bow.

It was easy, too easy, and after they filled the basket, they got bored and decided to explore a little ways—only a little, they told themselves—up the Wicomico River and into the Zekiah Swamp, which begins at the Fresh. Cedric had forbidden them to enter the swamp, an admonition they read as invitation or dare.

"The Zekiah is a braided stream," Cedric had lectured. "A *braided* stream." He had repeated the words, but the phrase had not evoked for them the hopelessly tangled weave he had wanted to press into their young brains. Not until they had drifted past the sawgrass marsh along the Wicomico into the bewildering web of black shadowed creeks that meandered through thick, boggy, hardwood forest. Towerhill paddled from the stern and Jacob the bow, Sarai sitting between them like a little queen, humming some tune she had made up, until both he and Jacob, in tandem, told her to shut up. Ospreys circled overhead, emitting sharp warning cries when the boat came near their nestlings, and a giant blue crane rose in the disjointed way blue cranes do as they launch into the grace of their flight. Jacob told them of a waterman speared through the heart by the beak of such a bird when he surprised it at its fishing. Their eyes on the crane's flight, they tried to follow it, hoping it might find another such waterman and dispatch him for their amusement. They were gradually being funneled into narrow and then narrower passages, the forest closing around them, woven tree branches overhead making the channel into a dark tunnel, until finally Towerhill twisted his paddle around, dragged them to a halt, stood up, and they realized they were lost.

The silence was like a presence around them. After a moment, they started to hear small noises subverting it—the faint splash of a fish break- ing the water, the creak of branches in a slight breeze, the buzz of insects, their own heavy breathing. Jacob, and then Sarai, slowly stood also, careful with their balance, and they looked around and then at each other.

"Shit," Jacob said.

"Shit," Sarai said.

"Let's paddle on a little," Towerhill said.

They continued up the creek, until the trees began to thin again and sud- denly it opened into another sawgrass marsh, the creek fingering through hummocks glittering with spider webs. Towerhill spotted what seemed to be a thick line of trees fringing a hump of earth drawn straight along the horizon to their left, and called the others' attention to it.

"Maybe it's an island," he said.

"So what?" Jacob asked.

"So what?" Sarai echoed.

"Stop doing that, little crab," Towerhill said.

"Please," Jacob said.

She started to speak, but they both glared at her. She closed her mouth into a tight line.

"I don't know what it is," Towerhill admitted.

"Oh. Well, then certainly we shall go there."

"Certainly," Sarai said.

Suddenly they heard a loud splashing, moving parallel to them on the other side of a small hummock, as if something heavy were running through the knee-deep water. Sarai let out a small scream. Towerhill was glad she did; otherwise, it would have come from him. Without a word they began paddling hard.

They could not travel directly to whatever that tree line marked. As they started towards it, they were funneled into a different direction, and then turned onto another channel, working their way towards a destination which sometimes seemed to recede further from them, sometimes seemed fingertip close, sometimes seemed to waver as if it had turned into mist. The channels became shallower and narrower, bottom grass clinging to the boat so they had to dig in heavily with their paddles, panting, mosquitoes sticking in the sweat on their faces, buzzing in their ears maddeningly, clogging their nostrils. Insect bites swelled the skin around their eyes. Three or four times, when they stopped to rest, they heard the same splashing sound, *patter-patter-patter-patter*, parallel to them, until Sarai, angry tears in her eyes, slapped her hand against the water in the same rhythm, as if mocking it. "Ba-dup, ba-dup, ba-dup," she said. "Shit," she said. He and Jacob grinned at each other.

It took them two hours to reach what they had come to call the island, a destination towards which they had worked for no other reason, Towerhill came to realize, than to *have* some destination in that trackless place. Tall loblolly pines, oak and hickory trees crowded a long, thick finger of land hunched up out of the bog, fringed by a muddy strip towards which they aimed the canoe, calling on the last of their strength, stroking hard, driving the bow up between clusters of black, wet, snail-crusted roots. Towerhill jumped out first and pulled the boat up onto land, and then they went under the shade and lay face down on the grass. A cool breeze riffled the leaf canopies and came through the trees, kissing their skins.

Jacob passed their flask of water to Sarai, and then to Towerhill, before taking a sip himself. They were hot and exhausted and welted with insect bites, but they felt light; something about the place, its trees and foliage, un-swamplike and familiar, that made them feel they had arrived at a place of refuge.

But they were nearly out of drinking water. Towerhill peered through the trees.

"There is probably a spring here," he said.

"Maybe," Jacob said.

"Maybe," Sarai started, but then closed her mouth at their glare.

They walked deeper into the island, Towerhill leading, Sarai in between.

The foliage around them evoked Towerhill Separation in their minds. But that impression did not last. What it brought instead to Towerhill was one of the paintings he had seen in the salon of the manor house. A scene in an English park: a group of young women wearing hooped, frilly dresses and armed with umbrellas having a picnic in the shade under the trees, near a rock-studded brook. The painter had rendered those rocks marvelously well, capturing their sheen of water. But what had always struck Towerhill about those woods, in contrast to their own, was the lack of tangled, thorny underbrush and weeds; he put the difference down to the imagination of the artist. This island reminded him of that park, the earth under the canopied shade of the trees free of the annoying tangle and grab of brambles, carpeted by moss or soft pine needles that were a blessing to their bare feet. It wasn't until some days later that he learned that the Wesorts, who used this place as one of their hunting camps, followed the old Piscataway custom of periodically burning out the underbrush.

As they walked, they heard only the faint sound of their footsteps. Suddenly Sarai stopped, stared at a cluster of plants, squealed in delight. "What is it, little crab?" Jacob asked, annoyed, but then craned his neck forward, staring, and Towerhill followed his gaze. There was a crown of green leaves on the plant, some of the leaves shaped and opening like butterfly wings, their edges fringed with tiny spikes, their insides a meaty red. A large horsefly had lighted on one, and as they watched the two wings closed over the insect like a trap. No, not like a trap, Towerhill thought. It *was* a trap. A chill went through him. What kind of place was this? He turned to walk again, then stopped, and in that second thought he heard an echoing pad of his steps, continuing, and then abruptly stopping. The others heard it also. They looked at each other, Towerhill thinking of the plant, the two crushing, trapping lids closing in.

"Come on out, you son of a bitch," Sarai yelled suddenly. "You're not scaring us."

They waited. The breeze that had been creaking the trees stopped.

After a long moment, they saw a figure coming to them out of the shadow of the trees. Sarai let out a sharp squeal, and then caught her breath as the shape solidified and clarified: a boy, perhaps of Towerhill's or Jacob's age, and sharing their height and build as well. Towerhill suppressed his own desire to squeal. The boy coming towards them in a silent glide was bare-chested and brown-skinned and wore homespun trousers, wet to the knees, with a sheathed knife held by a hemp rope around his waist. His long black hair, tangled with twigs and leaves, hung to his shoulders, framed gray unblinking eyes, a high-bridged nose, a sensual mouth, lips sealed tightly as he stared at them with what seemed accusation. Three ochre red lines had been painted on his forehead and in parentheses around his mouth, and he bore red and black circles on his chest. His hair and body were wet as well, and Towerhill thought it was strange that the painted symbols had not blurred or run, and then wondered if they were tattooed onto his skin. Later he found out they were not. But what he saw then was an apparition that made him catch his breath.

"You should not be here," the boy said.

Towerhill could not agree more.

"Who are you?" Sarai demanded.

"I'm the son of a bitch, little one."

"Were you following us?" she asked. "How did you go through that water, you?"

"Shut up," Jacob said. He stepped forward, gravely holding out a hand. "My name is Jacob Hallam, of Towerhill Plantation, and these are my hand servants."

Sarai and Towerhill glanced at each other; they had never heard Jacob use that word. But said nothing, understood instinctively, some knowledge bred in the bone, that it was the wisest way to describe their triad to an outsider.

"I assure you my father will award you handsomely for our return."

"I assure . . . ," Sarai started, but Towerhill slapped the back of her head lightly.

The boy ignored both the statement and the outstretched hand.

"You all better come with me now," he said.

In later years, Towerhill would try to remember the labyrinthine route Joseph had used to take them to the Wesort settlement at Zekiah Fort, but its purpose had been to subvert memory, and all that remained to him was the possibility of informed passage. What had seemed at first to be an impenetrable, tangled mass of vegetation was webbed with trails and ingresses and waterways, a scrawled history of habitation that began with gameways pushed through forest and marsh by the buffalo and cougars that were hunted by shadowy, legendary ancestors the Piscataway had honored but could no longer name. Those ancient beasts and most of the Piscataway themselves had long been killed off or driven north, their tunneled trails inherited by deer and brown bear and wolf and Wesorts. The paths formed a skein of stories threaded now into the story of the Wesorts, progeny of escaped black slaves and white indentured servants and renegade Indians whose sole commonality was un-commonality. That and a need to flee.

(These thoughts coming now to Towerhill, as he stands with Joseph and the people who have become his tribe now, the brave Mariah and singing Mingo and all the others whom Jacob would delete from his life tomorrow.)

Zekiah Fort had been a last refuge of the Piscataway before most of the Piscataway left the state to become Piscataway Conoy, Piscataway Gone. It sat on a hilltop with a freshwater spring on the edge of the swamp, the posts in the stockade that surrounded it tilted and rotting, with some logs missing, leaving gaps large enough for a cart to pass through here and there. The Wesorts had kept or rebuilt some of the original longhouses, but most of the dwellings were log cabins. Joseph took them into one of the longhouses. It was much closer than it seemed from the outside, the sharp permeating odor of smoke and sweat and drying fish sweetened by the smell of cedar and leaves. Baskets, nets, fishing spears, muskets, and powder horns and an ancient-looking quiver of arrows hung from the poles; the only light came through a smoke hole in the roof.

Sitting cross-legged on the ground inside was a thick plug of a man, his features more Indian than black or white, dressed in a red shirt and deerskin trousers. He looked askance at Joseph, ignoring the other children, and said something swiftly in a language that hinted at English, but a kind of English heard through a muffling blanket. Towerhill couldn't understand most of the words, but the tone was plain enough. The man squinted at them.

"You should not be here," he said.

"We should keep them," Joseph said. He patted Sarai. "Specially the little one, someone need a good cusser."

Sarai stiffened in fright, and Jacob and Towerhill moved in close around her, but Joseph winked at him.

"This is Lombroso," Joseph said.

"Is he a chief?" Sarai asked, impressed.

"He'd like to be, little cusser."

(A dialogue that had also stayed in Towerhill's mind. Later, he would hear whites, plantation owners and overseers, speak of the rivalry between Joseph and Lombroso as if some tribal conflict, Israel against Judah. He knew both would have it that way, each trying to shape the Wesorts into his concept of a tribe, harking back to their Piscataway blood and what they remembered or created as Indian folklore and custom. What they were, though, were families; some of the younger people drawn to Joseph's vision; some of the older Wesort clans allying with Lombroso, some refusing all such definition and going their own way, trying to blend into the free black or white population. Towerhill didn't begrudge either man his ambition; the world, he'd heard tell, could be shaped to a dream.)

The man said something angrily, in the midst of which Towerhill heard his own name. It startled him, as if Lombroso had known about him before this meeting. The man, Lombroso, said a few other words, his tone angry, and then waved Joseph and the others outside.

"My father will certainly pay . . . ," Jacob started to say as soon as the mat closed behind them.

"Lombroso, he send a message, no worry. Your daddy knows you are here."

They spent the next three days back at the island where Joseph had first met them. Towerhill wondered briefly why the Wesorts hadn't kept them at Zekiah Fort while waiting for Cedric to fetch them. But they were content to be by themselves. That wooded rise of ground remained the refuge it had first seemed to them. Towerhill had been right about the availability of drinking water: a small spring bubbled through a U-shaped formation of rocks and a stretch of the hummock bordered a large freshwater pond, fringed with forest. They swam and fished with Joseph and feasted on rockfish, crabs, and oysters in the evening, meals spiced with the salty tang of tiny snails plucked off the cordgrass swaying on the shoreline. The air on the swamp side was sometimes fetid and skunky, but at dawn and in the late afternoon the light was golden, and the land they could see from the other side of the island opened in a way that promised choices and freedom. They did not want to leave. It was as if part of them knew that this time was steeped with the last sunset glow of their life as equals. Of their childhood. That, from this point on, the braided creek that was their entwined selves would unbraid, wind separately and unequally into the world that waited like a wolf past the border of the Zekiah.

The idyll ended on the morning of the fourth day. Towerhill woke up to find Lombroso suddenly there, arguing with Joseph, Joseph glaring at him, tight as a drawn bowstring, and then spinning around and leaving, brushing past the three of them.

Lombroso pointed at the children and said the only English word Towerhill had ever heard emerge clearly from his lips: "Stay." Sure. Where would they go? About an hour later, two Wesorts they hadn't seen before, one tall and very black, the other a mulatto, squat and square, like many of the tribe, came into the shelter and without speaking grabbed Jacob and Towerhill by the arms and started to drag them outside. They didn't touch Sarai until she kicked one between the legs. Doubling over but controlling himself, he took her by the hair and yanked, dangling her as she screamed, Towerhill and Jacob struggling to go to her.

The men brought the children down to the shoreline, and then bound Towerhill's and Sarai's hands with rawhide. When Jacob began to object, the Wesort who had been kicked slapped him with casual contempt. Tears welled in his eyes, but he started forward anyway, his hands clenched into fists. By that time, the other man had tossed Sarai and Towerhill into the canoe they had dragged onto the sand.

"You leave them be, you," someone shouted, and Towerhill saw Joseph running across the sand to them. "We promised them," he yelled. The yellow man shook his head, stuck his hand into the canoe, brought up a paddle, and struck Joseph across the face, all in one smooth motion. He fell to the sand and remained motionless. Towerhill and Sarai did not; they were wiggling like fish, struggling to get onto their feet, until the black Wesort picked up a paddle and shook it at them. As Jacob stood helpless on shore, the other man pushed the canoe off and jumped effortlessly into the stern, paddling off and leaving him. Lombroso, they discovered later, had decided there was more profit in peddling them to slavers than in returning them; selling runaways caught in the swamps or turning them in for the reward had become a business for some of the Wesorts, and he had received an offer that trumped Cedric's.

Towerhill didn't know how long they paddled back into the net of creeks. If either of them moved too much, or tried to speak, the mulatto would smack them casually with his paddle. Sarai pulled her legs to her chest and remained silent, her mouth in a tight line. Towerhill wanted to cry, but looking at her anger shamed him out of it. After some time, they went through one of the thickly wooded areas where the trees stood in shallow black water just deep enough for their passage, the paddles at times sinking into and scooping up mud, clouds of insects rising from it, the men cursing. It was during this passage that Towerhill began to hear a faint intermittent splashing running parallel to them. Sarai caught his gaze, her eyes brightening. It was the same sound they had heard when they had found their island.

When the two Wesorts finally hove in to shore, he knew the canoe was out of the Zekiah. They were led down a dirt path to a small clearing, a crude shack in its center. Two white men waited there. The Wesorts pushed him and Sarai to the ground at their feet. One of the white men handed the Wesorts a small leather bag and they left without a word.

The man who had paid for them wore stiffened buckskin trousers and a stinking leather vest over his bare chest, his musculature defined and cruel, arms laced with thick veins, skin caked with patches of dirt, sweat runnelling through them. A bull-pizzle whip was curled at his belt. Towerhill couldn't remember what the other man was wearing; his odd appearance pushed the particulars of his dress out of his mind. The man had an egg-shaped head, the top elongated, but all his features crowded into the middle, his wide, white cheeks and chin winged out around that little cluster of eyes, nose, mouth, and tapering up to a bald white scalp netted with blue veins. He pulled back his thin lips into a grin, his grayish teeth splayed in all directions like old, neglected tombstones in a cemetery. A musket was slung over his shoulder, and a cutlass stuck through the rope he used as a belt. Sarai looked up at the two of them and screamed. The man in the buckskin vest kicked her, and Towerhill struggled to his feet and ran at him, head down, hands tied behind his back. The egg man stuck out a foot and he went sprawling into the mud, gasping and sucking some of it into his nostrils and mouth. Buckskin unfastened his whip, snapped it next to Towerhill's ear, and then flicked it at his arms and chest, each snap a fire on his skin. He almost cried. From the insult of it. This was not something that happened to him or to Sarai. "We're from Towerhill," he started to say, as if knitting his name to that place would protect him, let them know who he was.

"I'm Towerhill," he shouted.

"Shut your mouth, nigger," the man with the whip said, giving Towerhill the name that had been waiting to claim him since his second birth. The man cracked the whip across Towerhill's chest and, as he raised his arms to protect his eyes, opened a gash on his cheek. He could have claimed that the humiliation was worse than the pain. But it wasn't. He screamed, tried to run, but the slave trader tripped him, whipping his back and buttocks as he squirmed on the ground. Sarai was trying to get to him, but the other slaver grabbed her by the hair and again yanked her off the ground by it when she tried to kick him. The man with the whip hesitated for a second, distracted by the sight, then raised the whip again.

"Don't mark him much," the other said.

Those words were interrupted by a gut-churning howl from the woods behind the shack. "They fuck," the egg man said. He pulled out his cutlass and went behind the shed and into the trees. The howl split the air again, and then a new voice: a scream of pure terror. The man with the whip raised it, lowered it, raised it again, frozen into a pattern of motion. Finally he looked up—Towerhill presumed he meant to call his companion's name. He opened his mouth. An arrow pierced his throat.

A moment later Joseph, his painted face calm, walked out of the woods.

The next day, he had them back at Towerhill. Already, two of Joseph's friends, twins, a boy and a girl with African hair and blue eyes, had retrieved Jacob and returned him. The reunion of the three friends was awkward. Jacob would not meet their eyes.

Towerhill understood Jacob's shame. He understood it would always stand between them. But he refused to see it as the moral equivalent of having his back shredded with a bull-pizzle whip.

—

"We have had this conversation before," Joseph says to Towerhill. The boy growing into the man. But the savior apparently gone.

"Never so urgently."

"I can do nothing else. The canoes are at each of the usual places on the creeks, as before; we have not removed them. But we can't help or shelter your people."

"Joseph, you are going to lead the Wesorts." Towerhill doesn't say this as a question.

Joseph laughs.

"There is no ruler. Lombroso does not rule us, not as you think. We're free people, us."

"Yes," Towerhill says. "I've heard of the concept."

"Towerhill," Joseph says, and there is no note of amusement in his voice now. "Towerhill, you must listen to me. We must be with the Americans."

"With the whites."

"This is our place. Do you understand? It is not Lombroso. He is nothing, an old man. You are right; it is me. It is what I want. We will help you get out onto the creeks as we agreed. But afterwards we cannot help you anymore. I came here for our friendship, but I came here to tell you that as well. I cannot help you anymore. If you join the British, you must learn to see me as your enemy."

FOURTEEN

TOWERHILL

IS YOU US?

At first light, he looks down the slope over the two miles of field and meadow to the Patuxent. A breath of mist hovers over the river and then parts, as if blown upon from above, to reveal the sailing scow that will take those to be sold out to Scriber's Float, anchored at the plantation dock. It lies alongside a sloop from Baltimore that had come down for a load of tobacco, though there's been little to harvest from the poor, worm-plagued crop this year. The Float waits in the river like a promise. Floats. He hears the familiar screech and grind of the screw press, run by Henry Thompson, compacting sotweed into a hogshead barrel. Field slaves are coaxing a full barrel down the Rolling Road, controlling its descent with poles in front, ropes behind. An overseer, the porcine Charlie Dodson, is standing on the road, holding a musket which he casually points uphill at the men slowing the barrel. Towerhill feels a shiver run through the net of his nerves; he has never before seen the overseers armed with more than a whip while supervising the daily tasks of the plantation. He forces himself to walk over to the barn, trying not to think too much. There is nothing to do now but wait for dark. Get through the day. Everyone who will go knows where to go, what to do. Word has been sent to those family members on Towerhill proper and even to those on Sotterly and Mulberry Hill plantations who will join them, and he's dispatched Chapman, a ten-year-old who works on the dock, to sneak downriver in a canoe to alert the British that they will be coming. The timing will be difficult. Each group has a captain, but they all have to get to the river as close to the same time as possible.

At the barn, he watches Mingo heat a five-foot-long piece of bar iron and lay it on the anvil. Mingo glances at Towerhill as if asking a question and, when he nods, hands him the hammer. Towerhill strikes the bar with the flat of the tool, tapering the iron to about an inch thick at its end, a skill Mingo has been teaching him, on Bertram's orders. They both know what this means—Mingo is on the list to be sold, as is his wife, Phibs, with no promise they will be sold together. The tension he sees bunched in Mingo's huge shoulders, the muscles on his forearms corded and tight as drawn bowstrings, reflects his own exhausting tautness, waiting for tonight. George Adams, a tall, thin overseer with an acne-scarred face, walks into the barn, eyeing the two blacks nervously. He is only nineteen years old, the son of Dick Adams and inheritor of his father's job after Dick was paralyzed by a falling log while clearing forest with a party of slaves. He scowls at Towerhill, imitating his father, but he has already been warned by Jacob not to interfere with the work. With the peen, Towerhill notches the tapered end of the heated bar, thrusts it into the hole drilled into the anvil to fit its size, snaps off the nail, flattens its top with a few blows of the hammer, pops it out of the hole with a smart upwards strike. He begins to name each nail as he tosses it into the bucket at his feet, trying to envision the list Sarai described to him, the names evoking faces. She had not said his own name was on the list, but he had seen that in her eyes as well.

Mingo
Nebuchadnezzar
Ulysses
Agamemnon
Hattie
Samuel
Telemachus
Lucius

Sally
Nestor
Leander
Homer
George
Mariah
Agnes
Nero
Milly
Cecilia
Rebekkah
Yael
Lucille
Rachel
Sukey
Phibs
Craney
Biresis
Emmeline
Julian

At Julian everything goes to hell.

He hears a man scream—he thinks a man, even though it is high-pitched and finally spirals into something more like an animal would make than a human being. And then a gunshot. He and Mingo look at each other. They both know. They do not know who or why, but they know that scream. Their ears have waited for years to hear it and it has hovered at the edge of this day's long waiting. Without a word, almost calmly, Mingo picks up the next iron bar meant to become the nails that will hold this place together and smashes it into the side of Adams's head. He falls deadweight to the ground and Mingo raises the bar overhead and brings it down again and again. Towerhill can hear the bones of the boy's skull cracking and breaking and when Mingo is finished there is nothing recognizable as a human face on the floor. Mingo smiles at him, almost shyly. A few moments before Towerhill had been regarding Adams with a kind of contemptuous amusement, as if he were a boy trying on his father's too large britches. He should be horrified. But he is not. Something has been released in him and he knows that, even if he never makes it to that British ship, from this moment on he is a free man.

They run out of the barn, Mingo still holding the bar and the hammer still in Towerhill's hands. The screaming is coming from the overseers' quarters, and as Towerhill tries to see what is happening there, Bertram comes stumbling out of his cabin, clutching his eyes. "Ye blinded me, you fooking bitch," he yells, and Auntie Rebekkah comes out after him, holding a bucket by its strap in one hand and a ladle in the other. Towerhill pictures her standing over his bed, pouring the lye into his sockets as if making her soap. She arcs the ladle and liquid falls on the back of Bertram's head, making a sizzling sound, like frying fat. He screams again, and as he turns to her, hands clutching at the air, she throws more lye at his face. Towerhill can see now what the lye has done to his eyes. He steps in front of Bertram and swings the hammer at his forehead. It connects solidly, the handle vibrating in his hand. Mingo grunts, comes up next to Bertram, and brings the iron bar down on top of his head. Rebekkah is standing still, her feet planted, looking at the man on the ground, a slight, mad grin playing on her lips. Towerhill hears the boom of a musket shot and feels the ball buzz past his head. It strikes Rebekkah squarely in the forehead. He spins around and sees Dodson reloading his musket, pouring powder down the barrel. So do the men coaxing the hogshead down the slope of the Rolling Road. It is as if he, Towerhill, and they are all having the same thoughts at the same time. They pull out the holding staves, release the ropes and stand aside. Dodson looks up from his musket, too late to even scream as the barrel runs over him.

Towerhill laughs.

He gestures for those men to come up to him. They run, laughing also, giddy with murder. Grab tools from the barn and the corncrib—axes, hoes, scythes, the staves they already have. And then stand and look at each other, uncertain about what to do next.

Towerhill taps Samuel's shoulder. "Run down to the Quarters, tell everyone to gather behind the Thompsons' house." He must speak and act as if he knows what he doing. But above all, he must act. He tells the other man, Ulysses, to get to the field hands, bring them also. He looks down towards the river. The sailors on the merchant sloop, a three-master with a two-pound cannon mounted on the stern, do not yet know what has happened. The gangplank is down. They need to seize either that ship or the ferry.

"The overseers?"

Towerhill looks at him. There is no need to answer his question; the answer is in its statement. Samuel draws back his lips in a fierce grin.

"What we do at the big house?" Nebuchadnezzar asks Towerhill. Neb's eyes, bloodshot, dart back and forth swiftly as if registering the turmoil in his own brain. Towerhill understands what he is feeling. His own thoughts cannot keep up with the lightning shifts of the world.

Neb jabs in the direction of the manor with the iron stave. He shifts the stave back and forth in his hands.

Towerhill looks at the house, Jacob's house, up on its hill. It still holds the peace of the morning, as if it exists in a time separated from the events of the past ten or fifteen minutes. He thinks of Sarai; is she there now?

"No. Not yet."

Neb sneers. "Why that?"

"More important now to spread the word, get everyone together."

"Mr. Hallam your own massa, Towerhill? You still taking care of him?"

Mingo scowls. "Shut your mouth. Towerhill is boss man this day. Get it?"

"Got no boss man this day, Mingo," Neb says.

Towerhill thinks about Jacob and then tries not to. He knows what he needs to burn. But he also needs to get Sarai out of there. "First the ship. We have to have a way we can get downriver, fast. Fire will bring the militia."

Neb nods. "That ship, she first."

"Tell whoever you can."

The men, except for Mingo, scatter.

When he gets to the Quarters, about twenty people are already waiting—he doesn't count heads yet—men, women, children. Most of the adults are armed, with tools and axes and kitchen implements. Two of the men have gotten hold of muskets and powder horns. Mingo's wife, Phibs, stands with her feet spread, a cleaver in her hands, blood on her dress. She lowers the weapon as Mingo joins her, and the two embrace, eyes closed, rocking together. The sight of them, the bond that holds them in defiance of the imposed transience of their lives, hits Towerhill fiercely. He will do anything for these people.

"Where are the others?" he asks Phibs.

"Some wait, see what happen," she says. "Others, they afraid, not going anywhere. Some down there. Some women." She points towards the gulley. He looks at her smile and a chill goes through him. He makes his way down to the women.

Mariah, Agnes, and three of the other Thompson women stand in the shadowed depression of the gulley. There is a waiting blankness in their eyes, as if their souls have fled for a moment but will return. They hold knives—Agnes an awl—and their hands and forearms are soaked and dripping with blood. Near them, but separated from the others, are Lucius and Sally. They are holding hands. Towerhill does not need to see the face of the corpse tied to a loblolly pine to know it is Caleb Hewitt. His face is mostly intact, the eyes wide. Not so his body. Mariah looks up, catches Towerhill's gaze, and light floods back into her eyes. She draws back her lips in a terrible smile, her teeth flecked with blood, and then throws the trophy she holds in her right hand away from her, into the creek. It barely makes a splash.

He doesn't look away. He wants his eyes to hold everything about this day.

"The other overseers?" he asks Ulysses.

"Overseeing hell."

They look at each other like mischievous children, smiles flitting across their lips. Rebekkah's face comes unbidden into his mind; he will mourn her, he promises, but not now.

"We've got to get that ship," he says. "We'll move down here along the gulley, board her before the sailors know what's happening."

There is a murmur of agreement.

They turn, as if they are one body, and begin to move down through the trees to the river.

They are nearly there when he hears the crackle of fire behind them. He stops, moves out of the woods, and look up towards the manor. Flames are licking up from the roof over the kitchen.

"Who set that?" he yells. He grabs Neb by the collar of his shirt. "You bastard, who set that?"

Neb shoots his hands up and flings them apart, breaking Towerhill's hold. "Us," he says. "That you too, boss man? Is you us?"

They stare at each other. The others have stopped, are watching them. As if waiting for Towerhill to answer.

FIFTEEN

SARAI

―――

THE GIFTS GIVEN HER

In her last morning in this place, she opens her eyes and sees Jacob standing naked at the window, staring out at the fields. The sight shifts something in her. It is not lust. It is, she supposes, pity for the vulnerability that is naturally called up by his nudity. It is her knowledge of what will happen tonight. It is his ignorance of it. He will be stripped. What should not be his will now be taken from him. He believes he is the master of everything he sees outside that window, the two thousand acres of tobacco field sloping to the river, the river itself and the creek that runs into it, and the forest around it. The souls on it. The bodies and the souls. Darkness will come and they will flow away into their claimed lives like the water in the creeks that will carry them off. He will be truly naked at this same window tomorrow morning. The image of him now, his edges blurred by the diffused morning light streaming through the window, a precursor vision of how he will stand tomorrow, shorn of the vestments of power: the boy she grew up with, the man struggling to find words to move the world towards justice, only to see those words shatter against the world. Will he be too weak to survive the unraveling that will happen tonight? The unraveling of what he thinks is his but knows is not. So that finally his life will be one with his faith. The unraveling of their two souls. So that they both finally can be free.

"Jacob," she calls, "come back to bed." Come back to the illusion of linen, to a life that likens to the condition of a child who pulls a linen sheet over his head believing it will keep away the monsters in the dark. An analogy she can make because of this man and his father, because she has lain in beds such as this one covered in linen sheets. An analogy her brethren, sleeping all their lives on coarse flax laid over corn cobs or pine needles or on the earth softened only by their sweat, tears, and blood, will never grasp. The gifts given to her, unasked for, but not refused. In this, they are the same, she and this man. In this they are as much brother and sister as lovers.

He remains motionless, a statue, though when she looks at him now, she does not see stone but flesh, a curl of black hair pasted onto his neck, a fine sheen of sweat on the muscles of his shoulders, one droplet running down into the cleavage of his buttocks, and what opens in her now is lust; she wants to feel the smoothness of that flesh under her hands as she pulls him into her.

But then his body jerks, and she hears a cry from his lips. He turns to her, shock on his face. Screams intrude into the room.

"What is it?" She throws off the sheet and joins him at the window. Several slaves surround a hogshead on the beginning slope of the Rolling Road. There is a strange jerkiness about their movements. What she sees now does not register in her eyes as an ordered sequence of events. The known world is shaking to pieces. Screams and cries reach her, but she cannot make out words. Bertram staggering as if drunk. Auntie Rebekkah swinging something in a wide arc. Towerhill swinging a hammer in the same motion, as if one action echoes the other. Mingo the smith striking downwards with an iron bar. Only now do her eyes let her see what he and Towerhill have struck. As if there has been a skip in time. As if the players were not all on stage. The crack of a musket. Smoke rising and dispersing from the musket's barrel. Auntie Rebekkah falling not straight down but as if someone is shoving her backwards, hard. Sarai feels Jacob's hand grip her arm painfully. As if they are on the rolling deck of a ship and he is trying to find purchase. The hogshead rolling down and over a screaming overseer. She thinks the word *overseer*. What does he see over now? She understands what has happened. Or rather she understands that whatever has happened has changed everything. There will be no quiet slipping away.

And slipping away is what she needs to do now. She needs to be with her people.

She hears noise from downstairs. A door flung open. Heavy footsteps. Milly, one of the house slaves, screaming something. Shouts.

Jacob looks at her, his lips trembling. But as he continues to stare, continues too long, they set in a firm line.

"The priest hole, quickly," he says, grabbing up the sheet. He is speaking of a space Towerhill built between the walls of this room, accessed through a sliding door that looks to be a wall. She understands he is thinking of her, that she needs protection. It is time for her to leave.

SIXTEEN

JACOB

―――

THE PRIEST HOLE

The walls and the darkness press in on them. The thick oak of the panel muffles and diffuses the noises coming through it. Something falling heavily. Something breaking. Laughter. Shouts. Curses. He feels a kind of relief. Waiting for this to happen has weighed so long in his guts and on his shoulders that he had stopped thinking of it. The weight of the wait. It is only now, by its lifting, that he realizes how heavy it was. He did not seek this justice but he will embrace it. He prefers, though, that it will not kill him.

And Sarai? She had resisted when he pushed her towards the priest hole, but only slightly. Surely she understands. He would have shut her outside to be safe with her people; his first impulse was to do so. But if they find her in his bedroom it will be no different from finding her in his bed. He has little doubt what would happen to her. Unless it is Towerhill who finds her. And what would Towerhill do, confirming what must have been his own fears and jealousies, the bedding he surely knew of but that neither he nor Jacob acknowledged to the other?

Unless it is Towerhill. Jacob moves his arm around Sarai's shoulder and presses his palm against the cool wood of the wall, picturing Towerhill pressing his own palm against the wall that separates them, in the same spot. It cannot be him, Jacob knows this. He who built this hole knows how to open it.

And Sarai. She stands silently in front of him. They sweat in the small enclosure. In the darkness. The darkness that is a curtain drawn between him and who he was, just moments before. A blackness which is as much liquid as it is color pours into his eyes, fills his brain. They are in their fortress, their secret place, their walls against the world that, deep inside each of them, they know waits outside like a wolf. He sees Towerhill and Sarai, hands gripping each other's forearms, spinning in a circle, laughing. He calls for them to stop; he wants to join them, but it is as if they cannot or will not hear him. They spin faster and faster, screams from somewhere past the trees passing into them so they shudder and spin even faster, and then he is there, he is gripping Sarai's wrists and she his; they are spinning, their bodies being pulled away from each other even as they tighten their grasp on each other, their wrists slippery with sweat, their hands losing their grip, slipping away, spinning faster and faster and they are in the water at Allan's Fresh, the three of them laughing and splashing, reeds scraping their bodies like prickly combs, Towerhill plucking small snails off the long stems, sucking out the meat of them, flipping the emptied shells at the others, one by one. They stop, the silty water warm on their skins, its funky, fetid smell thick in their nostrils. Take each others' hands. From somewhere he hears the crackling of a fire. The air is hot, pressing, moist. He puts his arms around Sarai and holds her body; they are glued skin to skin with sweat.

The reeds part. Reveal the face of the wolf.

SEVENTEEN

TOWERHILL

BOOK MAN

The sight of them sickens him.

He had rushed to the manor house, alone, save for Neb, who had refused to leave his side. Neb's distrust should have enraged him. But something in him needed and welcomed this watchdog vigil on his heart, heavy with dread at what he would see waiting for him in the house. As it was, though, the fire had only scorched the kitchen: an enthusiastic but ineffective attempt by Yael, a heavy-set, big-hipped woman, one of the house slaves. She stood in the doorway, panting and cursing as the flames destroyed a table and chair that she had smashed into kindling. The fire had flared up, licked the northern wall of the kitchen, erupted out of the window—the flames Towerhill had seen from the gulley—but then must have flickered out, or perhaps she had doused it—he saw a bucket nearby—out of some reasoning her mind, giddy with liberation, had fashioned.

"What you doing, woman?" Neb had asked.

"Cooking," she said.

She was standing in a pile of smashed crockery, pots and kettles scattered around the room. She looked drained, her hair a bramble of tufts as if she had been yanking at it.

"Y'all go on down the gulley," Neb had said. "We having some fun over there, us."

"Take her there, Neb," Towerhill had said.

Neb held his gaze, grinned. "Naw, boss. She know the way."

"Don't call me that."

"You right. You not boss man. You book man." He laughed, repeated the phrase.

Towerhill saw that the front door had been smashed open. As he stepped inside, Neb on his heels, he looked around quickly, but saw neither Jacob nor Sarai. Nor the former's corpse, as he'd half-expected, half-dreaded to find. He told himself that Sarai had probably already run out, as soon as she understood what was happening.

Some of the field slaves were rummaging through the drawing room and the dining room. They had pulled most of the portraits of the Hallam ancestors off the wall and shredded them; those few still on the wall had had the eyes and mouths cut out of their faces. Some of the men and women were cradling loot: silver candlesticks, china plates, punchbowls, bottles of rum. The thick damask drapes had been pulled down. Light filled the room. Pegg, another house slave, ran by, laughing, her mouth and chin golden with a powder of ground cinnamon, her hands and forearms covered in it. The shell alcove he had labored over for weeks was scored and gouged. A field slave, Pompeii, was smashing at the latticework on the Chinese Chippendale staircase with a heavy wooden mallet. Towerhill couldn't stand it, though whether he could not stand its destruction or needed to destroy it himself was unclear to him. He grasped Pompeii's wrist on the upswing and the man turned, his eyes glazed and uncomprehending, then slowly coming into focus as he recognized who it was.

"Towerhill," he said, his voice strangely gentle, filled with a kind of wonder. "Towerhill, we here." He lowered the mallet.

"Book man here," Neb said. "Book man protectin' what his."

Towerhill raised his voice. "Everyone, gather down the gulley. We're taking the ship at the dock."

People stopped what they were doing, looked at him.

"Where we running, Towerhill?" someone asked.

"To the British. To Cockburn."

The word passed from mouth to mouth like a prayer. Some of them, the ones to be sold tomorrow, already knew the plan. But putting the words into the air had made them real.

From upstairs he heard a thud and the sound of wood breaking. He took the mallet from Pompeii's loose grip.

"Get them to the others, Neb," he said. "See who else wants to go."

"Y'all listen to Towerhill," Pegg said. "Militia be coming soon."

He had rushed up the stairs. Up his stairs. In the bedroom, a man and a woman—Sukey and David—were bouncing up and down on Jacob's bed, laughing. The furniture had been smashed; a large highboy lay on its side, its door open. David wore one of Jacob's wigs askew on his head.

"Get out of here," Towerhill snarled.

"Naw," Neb said, suddenly behind him. "They funnin'."

Towerhill spun, the mallet in one hand, and slapped Neb across the face. Neb rocked back but then stood still, put his hand up to his cheek, caressed it tenderly.

"Boss man," he said. "Book man."

He smiled. The smile didn't reach his eyes.

Towerhill crossed the room, found the faux paneling over the entrance to the hidey-hole, hooked his fingers into the small slots, and slid open the door.

The sight of them sickens him.

"Well, looky this," Neb says.

Sarai's startling nakedness. A body Towerhill has known but is now strange to him, in this strange context. Jacob moves in front of her. Sukey laughs loudly, pointing. "Massa like her, he do."

Towerhill steps forward, gripping the mallet tightly.

"Here it comes," Neb says, laughing. "You wants to slap them too, book man?"

Sarai looks slowly around the room, first meeting his eyes, and then her stare moving from one face to the other. And then back to Towerhill. She steps next to Jacob, so they are flank to flank in the tight space, and puts her hand on his shoulder.

For a moment Towerhill stands frozen, stabbed to the quick by her action. Sukey's and David's and Neb's eyes on him. All their eyes on her. The sound of their breathing, all of them and his own, loud and in tandem, like the panting of something large and terrible. And then an even louder silence as their breaths catch. The silence of the world catching its breath. He slowly lowers the mallet. He wants to kill this man, his master, his brother. He wants to kill the serpent who had offered him the shining apple of hope, rotten and wormy at its core. The fruit of a rootless tree in the center of a false Eden. He wants to kill both of them.

He raises the mallet again, hearing Neb laughing behind him, as if from a great distance. Everything else but this woman standing before him, betraying him, has retreated into that same distance. He shifts out of himself, watches himself, all of them, as if he has floated out of his body and is seeing a diorama. He raises the mallet higher. Sarai stands motionless, their eyes locked.

EIGHTEEN

JACOB

NAKED IN GAZA

I want this man to strike me down. My brother. My slave. He has already torn me apart at the seams. The illusion of my goodness. The illusion of my virtue. The illusion of my hope. And so the temple will fall around me. On me. He has revealed the lie at the heart of the words that had sustained me. Has touched the flame of truth to that wishful lie. He has destroyed everything but the one article of faith that has proven not to be a mere vapor, diffused against the hard surface of the world. Sarai's love. I will die with that consummation. It is Towerhill who pushes down the pillars holding up the false temple of my life. But it is I who will die naked and triumphant in Gaza.

NINETEEN

SARAI

—

CURSE

I want him to strike Jacob down. Yes, I tell myself. It is the only way I will be free of him. I must move into the air of my new life, into the new country to which Towerhill invites me.

But when I look at his face, Towerhill is staring at me, his eyes bright with contempt and hatred, and when I look around at the others, I see that hatred fly like a spark to the eyes of every other black face in that room. Filaments of harsh light connect them. Their eyes are mirrors. They stare, silently. Their faces hard. Their contempt a wall. Their hatred a fortress. Their verdict clear. These people to whom I had once thought I could return.

As if I had lost all agency over it, my hand reaches up and touches the solidity of Jacob's shoulder. I step next to him. So be it. He is all I am allowed. His is the bed I made and lay in. We had floated holding each other in the darkness and listened as all that had snugged around us was broken, and then we stepped out to the light through the rupture and ruin of that thin membrane. My people will not have me. I belong nowhere. I have become Wesort. We are born now twined, stripped of all that separated us. So be it. I will never be free of him. I take this curse to be my man. I take this man to be my curse. Now and forever. Amen.

TOWERHILL

—

ALL THE WORK OF HIS HANDS

He pushes the two of them out through the front door, shoving the mallet handle into their backs when they slow, and even when they do not. The door hangs askew on broken hinges, and a part of his mind he no longer needs dwells for a second on the task of fixing it. He laughs. What is broken can no longer be fixed. He is no longer here to fix. He is here to break. Looking at the now bruised backs of the two people he had once loved, he is filled with anger and hate but also with a gyring freedom. He laughs again. These people, these dark people, his brothers and sisters, catch his laugh and join it, pointing at Jacob and Sarai. Yael shoulders her way through them and spits, first on one, then on the other. Sarai stands impassively, her face expressionless. Jacob looks stricken. *I have been nothing but kind to you,* he would say. Towerhill wishes that the words he knows are in Jacob's mind would drop from his mouth. Then he would spit on him also. But Jacob says nothing. It doesn't matter. They don't matter; they are people from a distant country where Towerhill once lived.

"Leave them," he says. "They mean nothing." He points towards the river, the two ships. As if his gesture calls it, the two-pounder at the stern of the sloop fires. He sees a white puff of smoke, the boom a half-second later.

He can't see where the ball lands; they must be shooting into the woods near the shoreline, the others moving ahead as he wastes time here bidding farewell to his old life. Hefting the mallet, he starts running downhill, not bothering to move into the trees. He hears the others following, Neb coming up alongside, fox grin on his face.

The cannon booms again and this time he can see the ball, its arc towards them; it thuds into the ground nearby and the people running with him do not slow, only laugh wildly, and he thinks, *That will change.*

As they draw closer to the river, he sees that the people he left in the gulley have gotten to the bank and are screaming at the sloop; its sails have been unfurled and the two sailors manning the cannon have raised the angle of the barrel and are tamping in powder, others cutting the lines moored to the dock pilings. Mingo steps forward, holding one of the muskets, bringing it smoothly to his shoulder, firing. One of the sailors screams, his face suddenly blossoming red, and falls into the river.

But the sloop is free, drifting out from the dock at an angle, and then the wind catching in its sails. Mingo is reloading, but it is too late. Towerhill shifts his attention to the flat-bottomed sailing scow. It is crewed only by the two sailors he had seen; one, his face twitching in panic, is struggling to free the stern mooring hawser—the bow is already undone—as the other, a red-haired man with a wild red beard, has raised the topsail and the mainsail, though the mizzen is still unfurled. Towerhill hurls the mallet with all his strength towards the first sailor; it clangs uselessly against the stern transom. But the others have gotten the idea and people begin throwing whatever is in their hands at the man, a shower of hoes, rakes, rocks, and boards hitting the deck around him. Mingo raises the musket and pulls the trigger, but there is no flash when the hammer falls. By now, several people have seized the slack of the stern hawser rope—its end still tight around the piling—and are pulling the scow back towards the dock, as the other sailor, a stubby man with a shaven head, frantically unwinds it from its cleat on board. His companion, not as foolish or as brave, dives from the bow and begins swimming upriver, along the shore. George, a field slave in charge of the tobacco prize, heaves an iron bar sideways at the boat; it slams into the remaining man's right knee. His mouth an O, he clutches at his leg, releasing his hold on the rope, but by now it does not matter; people are swarming over the side. The sailor is on his back, raising his hands in supplication. But people have picked up some of the objects they threw and they surround him, staves and hoes and now an axe rising and falling, men and women grunting as if they are working in field or barn, the sailor's screams earsplitting and then gone.

The scow is about forty feet long and eight at its beam, and there are, Towerhill estimates, about thirty of them, nearly the number of those marked for sale by Jacob. He knows Mingo and the aptly named Ulysses have experience sailing, sometimes taking this very scow, laden with tobacco, out to larger ships whose beams are too big to moor at the plantation dock, sometimes taking or bringing human cargo from Scriber's Float. He calls them over.

"We need to get downriver, to Point Lookout. The British have a warship there. But I don't know how long they will wait."

They nod grimly. The crack of a musket. A small hole punches through the lower edge of the mainsail. Another bang and wood splinters off the guardrail. Towerhill looks quickly towards shore. Several men on horseback and a line on foot are running towards them, the man in front dramatically waving a saber over his head. The St. Mary's militia. Wind has caught the topsail and the scow has swung out into the river, but the stern hawser is still looped around its cleat. One of the field slaves, Cecilia, is gripping an axe, her face slack with the expression Towerhill sees on many of the faces around him: dumbfounded with freedom. He yells at her to cut the rope. She shakes the lethargy out of her head and swings the axe down onto the section of the rope lying across the gunwale, once, twice, chips flying up from the wood, the tendrils of the rope stubbornly holding and then suddenly snapping, the two sections falling and they are free. Even as he thinks those words, he tries to shake them violently out of his head, imitating Cecilia. They are not free yet, not until they are on board the British vessel. The bonds mooring them to their pasts are still here, still taut. They are all exhausted by the speed of the change in their lives: the dreams they have been dreaming for years all crowding into the world within the last hour. It allows a deadly complacency he has to fight in himself.

The wind catches and fills the red brown flax of the sails and the scow moves ponderously slow away from the dock. Ulysses has the tiller. Towerhill laughs wildly. Ulysses has the tiller. He would have wax in his own ears, to block Sarai's cry of *no* as he raised the mallet to rid them both from the past that would pull them into the sharp, killing rocks. No, he would have needed to fill his entire skull with hot wax in order to block out that cry. Ulysses tacks into the wind and they are heading straight to mid-river. There are puffs of white smoke, a cacophony of bangs as the militia shoots at them from the shore. A ragged line of little geysers springs up from the surface of the river, but they are already out of range, Ulysses steering into the current. Some of the people on the scow are cheering, waving their tools, their weapons, at the white men on shore.

To Towerhill's surprise he sees the militiamen start to cheer also, pump their weapons up and down, as if applauding their escape, and for an instant he has the fantastical vision that his life had been a test, the whites judging that he has just now matriculated. A second later he sees, or rather hears, why they cheer. A loud boom, from the wrong direction, ahead of their bow. He rushes towards the sound, seized by dread. How could he forget? The cheering from the militia is loud enough to come over the water as the sloop hooves into view, moving out from behind a spit of land. In the bow, the red-haired scow sailor, dripping from his swim, is pointing at them, screaming something into the wind. Ulysses pushes the tiller hard to the right, but Towerhill can see that the sloop will cross their path. Its cannon roars again, and a spout rises near their bow. Mingo has come up next to him, with his musket. He steadies it against the gunwale, pulls the trigger, and this time the gunpowder ignites. But to no effect. Towerhill does not even see where the musket ball hits; it must have dropped into the water. The sloop's cannon booms again and this time the ball smashes into the wood of the bow just above the surface of the river. The gunner is aiming for the waterline. They cannot outrun the swifter boat in the heavy scow. The sloop will keep crossing their path, herding them without trying to board. All they need do is keep chopping away with the cannon until they sink the scow.

It is not all they can do. He hears the angry bee buzz of musket rounds going past his head. There is a scream behind him and he turns to see Aaron, one of the older field slaves, kneading his belly, blood gushing between his fingers, his eyes filled with the question Towerhill has seen in the eyes of so many dying men. Some of the sloop sailors are up in the rigging with muskets. Another volley rakes the deck.

Suddenly the sloop heels violently and snaps straight back to the horizontal, the motion shaking shooters out of the rigging like falling fruit. They fall onto the deck and into the river. Another explosion and the main mast cracks and falls, the sail dropping over the fallen sailors and the others on the deck like a shroud. A third cannonball cracks into the sloop's stern and the cannon flies overboard, the gunner embracing it, an unthinking reaction that drops him into the river. The sloop lists to the side and Towerhill sees a British frigate, the name *Phaeton* clear on its bow, broadside to its victim and to the scow. The frigate's cannons roar again and the sloop's foremast falls, the whole ship shuddering under the impact, more sailors jumping overboard. Another volley and the slaves watch agape as the sloop sinks, the red-haired sailor still in its bow, still shaking his fist at them as the water closes over him.

The *Phaeton* looms over the scow, smoke tendriling up from the mouths of its port-side cannons. Chapman, Towerhill thinks; he had put the boy out of his mind, sees him now, grinning down over the ship rail, waving at him. Two sailors throw down two ropes, bow and stern, Ulysses and Mingo catching and securing them. The British sailors pull the scow snug against the hull of the larger ship, the two vessels bobbing up and down in tandem. More ropes are lowered; these are to be the way up. Neb grabs one, loops it around his right wrist and forearm, grasping it with his right fist above, his left below. Towerhill looks up at the row of white faces along the gunwale, sees Lieutenant Scott, who waves and then salutes languidly. There is something reluctant about the gesture, and his face seems grim, lips set in a straight line. MacDougal steps up next to him, eyes widening as he takes everything in. He grins broadly at Towerhill, leans over to whisper something into Scott's ear. Scott shakes his head. Towerhill grabs Neb's shoulder.

"Wait. Let them take the women and children aboard first."

At Towerhill's grip Neb turned with a snarl, but it fades quickly, comprehension blooming on his face. He lets go of the rope, turns and snatches Duncan, a five-year-old, bare-arsed under his flax shirt, and ties the rope around his waist.

Towerhill closes his eyes for a second. Rebekkah's blinding of Bertram had forced them to abandon their original plans, but he had known from the beginning that Scott was expecting him to bring only male slaves, men of fighting age. If the British do not pull Duncan up now, he will have the ropes thrown off and they will be on their own. There is a second's lull, but then he hears Scott shout, "What in God's blood are you waiting for? Get that pickaninny on board!" and the people on the barge watch in silence as Duncan, his bare legs and little arse swaying like the clapper of a bell under his flax shirt, is yanked quickly up to the deck.

So it is that they board. Step out of their lives. The women and older children are able to grab the ropes as Neb had, looping it around one wrist, and using their feet to help brace themselves against the curve if the hull. It is not an easy climb. The ropes fastening the two vessels together have been tied as tautly as possible, but there is enough separation for their hulls to crash into each other and several times Towerhill thinks they will lose someone into the river, to be crushed. He can still hear the crackle of musket fire, but they are on the side of the ship—starboard—facing away from shore and will be protected, even if they are in range. They are not. He smiles, thinking about the frustration and fury that the militiamen must be feeling. The British could cannonade from the port side, but that would rock the ship too much, further endanger the boarding.

He goes up last. As soon as his feet are on the deck, Scott and MacDougal come over.

"Welcome, Mr. Towerhill," Scott says, and extends his hand. Towerhill shakes it, then lurches, somewhat off balance, annoyed that Scott helps to steady him. He plants his feet apart.

Chapman comes up next to him, still grinning, a tall, skinny ten-year-old who has worked the dock and the crabbing boats, his mother on Thomas Hallam's portion of the plantation, his father dead. "Heard the shooting and shouting, Towerhill," he says. Towerhill kisses the top of his head.

"Good lad," Scott says.

"Brought the whole clan, did ye, Digit?" MacDougal asks, his eyes glinting.

Towerhill ignores him, hoping that in their pleasure at rescuing his people the presence of women and children will be accepted as a fait accompli.

A tall, middle-aged officer, bewigged and striking in a black uniform with gold epaulets, is striding up to them. The men crowding the deck step aside for him, their bodies stiffening as he brushes by them, as if from an invisible wake. They have not come to attention, but may as well have. Towerhill is suddenly heavy with fatigue: the rescue the pinnacle of a day in which each second had required a wrenching intensity of attention—a normal state for a slave, but a thousand times more fiercely concentrated today—and now something in him has started to relax. He shakes off the stupor. Recognizes that the day has come to its point in this man. The words *striding* and *striking* immediately form in his mind—an old and now involuntary habit of trying to assess and cage the whites he meets within a few descriptive words. Now, looking at the officer, he understands that his impression has little to do with the uniqueness of a black uniform in a crowd of redcoats. There is a sense of coiled energy in the man's movements, a *bristle*. His eyes, light blue against a grooved, sunburned face, are bright and fixed upon Towerhill as if the two of them are alone on the deck.

"Mr. Towerhill, it is my pleasure to introduce you to our host from the Royal Navy, Rear Admiral George Cockburn," Scott says dramatically.

Cockburn nods slightly, still staring at Towerhill, as if he is waiting to gauge the effect of his name on him. Towerhill doesn't disappoint, lets his eyes widen slightly, part of it an act, another part stunned at the fleshed reality of this man, whose name he has overheard Jacob and the other plantation owners speak with disgust and fear, changing its British pronunciation—*Coburn*—to their own American usage The first syllable a sneer. But their emphasis always on the second: Cock *Burn*.

Burner. Raider. Looter.

"On behalf of his majesty's navy, I welcome you and yours," Cockburn says formally, glancing over at the wet, bedraggled, bloodied crowd of Negroes standing uneasily on the deck, looking about, blinking, as if trying to fathom the great shift their lives have suddenly taken. "I congratulate you on your liberation and have no doubt that you will serve his majesty proudly, not as slaves, but as free men."

The words sound planed and smooth, as if spoken to an invisible chronicler hovering at his shoulder. Nevertheless, Towerhill is reassured. The British need them. He does not trust any white man. He does not trust these white men. But he trusts their need of him and his people. He salutes Cockburn and extends his hand. Cockburn hesitates as he sees Towerhill's fingers, the odd sixth appendage, eyes him as he might some fantastical creature emerging from this American river.

All of the Negroes and much of the crew are looking at them. Towerhill's hand is still extended. A faint smile plays on Cockburn's lips, as if to indicate he understands the challenge. He seizes the hand firmly, and Towerhill hears his people stir and murmur. There is a note of pleasure in the sound, but no cheers, and he is proud of them for that, pleased that like himself they have not been seduced by gratitude into trust or adulation.

As he looks at Cockburn, trying to read their future in this man's face, he hears the crackle of musketry from the shore. He salutes again and then turns and walks to starboard. The militiamen are on the dock and along the shoreline, a thin cloud of smoke curling above them. He raises his eyes up the hill, to the manor house straddling its crest. It is intact; the fire in the kitchen has either died out by itself or been doused. Perhaps by Jacob and Sarai. The memory of them, naked, moving next to each other, stabs him.

The British officers and MacDougal are looking at him. He points to the hill. "Would that house be in range of your cannons?"

Cockburn laughs. Like a portrait come to life. It is the first genuine human noise Towerhill has heard emerge from his mouth.

"We shall see, my dear sir, we shall surely see." He waves at the shoreline, at the militia. "But let us work our way to it. Metcalf!" he shouts, and a tall, thin sailor snaps to attention. "Have those scum fired upon us, gunner?"

"That they did, sir."

"And what is my command in such situations?"

"Why, not to fire unless the scum offer resistance, sir."

"I could not have said it better." He puts a hand on Towerhill's shoulder. "D'ye hear my sable friend's question?"

"That I did also, sir."

"Then make it so."

Metcalf yells a series of commands. The starboard guns open up. Towerhill's people cheer as the militiamen scatter. His people. About ten militiamen have gathered at the dock and are firing their muskets at the ship. Metcalf barks another order, and within seconds the dock splinters, lists, collapses, dumping the shooters, dead and alive, into the river. Marines at the railing and in the rigging open fire on them as they struggle in the water. Next to Towerhill, Neb clutches his arm, hard, his eyes shining.

Many of the slaves—Towerhill needs to stop thinking of them with that word—are stuffing their fingers into their ears. The cannonade works up the slope of the hill, churning the soil, sowing iron into the earth. A cannonball skips over the ground, once, twice, smashes the stone sundial.

Metcalf is screaming elevation figures, and the helmsman, at Cockburn's command, tacks the ship closer to shore. A single militiaman stands and points his musket at them and a puff of smoke erupts, seemingly silent, from his barrel, the act useless at this range.

Towerhill turns away from the others and leans over the rail, between two of the cannons, and watches as the corncrib catches fire under the barrage. Now the side of the tobacco barn staves in, the roof sagging impossibly. The barrage moves up the hill, and finally the cannonballs start crashing into the manor house. One smashes into the skewed front door, flinging it aside. He pictures the delicate latticework of the curved

Chippendale staircase splintering, collapsing, the intricately carved shell alcove dissolving to dust, the detailed woodwork over the mantel cut to pieces, all the work of his hands smashed back into its atoms. Obliterated. Flames—not in his mind's eye now, but in the living world—billow from the upstairs windows, Yael's smolder fanned to new life. MacDougal comes up next to him, stares into his face with great curiosity, his smile an echo of Towerhill's own as he stands, feet braced on the heaving deck—Towerhill watching Towerhill burn to ashes.

JACOB

___

A LOUCHE SMILE

They are near the Quarters when the manor house goes up behind them. Jacob's back is to it, but he feels the heat on his skin, and he stops and turns to see the end of the world, a sight his eyes decline to miss. Sarai stops also, but she refuses to look, or perhaps she is staring down towards the river where Towerhill waits. Jacob is holding her hand tightly, but with that thought he loosens his grip. He will not hold her if she wants to join the others. He understands that a part of him wants her to make that choice, to leave him as stripped and emptied and free as he feels watching the flames, the weight of that house and her servitude lifting from him in the rise and billow of smoke; and he laughs.

"We need clothing," Sarai says. She is standing in the classic pose, her hands affecting modesty, and in that gesture he is made aware again of their nudity, and he thinks, Is there a stronger sign than this of how a man can lose the world and gain it in a single moment? The flames behind them have changed the quality of light, bathing the air with a wavering, charged luminosity. From where they stand, he can see the open fields and the five thickets of forest that grow down the slope to the river, like the fingers of a hand. The British frigate flashes fire and the rippling shock of the explosions jars his bones. Red earth spouts up from the fields as if the gunners are attempting to murder the land itself. He turns from the sight, his mind running from it, a hare searching frantically for a hiding place, and lets his eyes rest on the river. Its surface crinkles and sparkles in the sunlight, as it does on any other day.

Sarai puts both hands on his shoulders and shakes him, her eyes desperate. He can read her thoughts in them: has she chosen a mad man to shepherd? He shakes the lethargy out of his head like a wet dog juddering off water. The first slave cabin is just down the hill; he takes her hand again and they run over to it. What if its inhabitants remain there, deciding whether to run or to stay or to murder? But the place is empty—through the empty doorframe he can see inside to the packed clay floor and the hearth, an iron pot still hanging above it. He ducks into the doorway, the ceiling low, the joists hitting his head when he tries to stand straight. He has not been in a slave cabin since he was a child. The smell of the inhabitants still lingers thickly, an acrid pall of sweat that over the years has permeated and intertwined with the cold clamminess of the clay, the dust of the ground oyster shell used in the whitewash on the inner walls, ceiling, and joists. It stings his nostrils. Sarai is overturning the corncob-stuffed grain sacks used as mattresses. In a corner he sees a heap of cloth next to a fiddle made from a turtle shell. He recognizes the fiddle; it belonged to Samuel, who played it for their amusement on Christmas and other holidays. Jacob remembers Samuel's broad smile, which now, like the rest of the world, he must question as false.

Sarai flings open the door to a root cellar near the hearth; he had not seen the outline of its trap entrance in the dirt. It is perhaps five feet deep, no more than the girth of a large man in its width. Another part of the world hidden from him; another louche smile. Have the inhabitants of this house gone with the British, or are they hiding somewhere, waiting to come back here, to the only home they have known, to the familiar smells they have left embedded in the walls? As Sarai rummages in the hole, he walks over to look at the pile of cloth: some shirts and trousers, the arms and legs tangled, but the shape calling to mind those who wore them so that the heap takes on the aspect of a pile of corpses. Sarai comes up next to him, holding a bag of something heavy—food, he presumes, from the root cellar, but also a Piscataway war club, which should not have been there. How long had insurrection been planned? Why did the person who hid that club leave it? Sarai puts it down, plucks up a large shirt and pulls it over her head. He finds some trousers, too small, and a shirt, too big, and pulls them on also, the smell heavy, the coarse flax rough and itchy on his skin. There is nothing for their feet, which are scraped and bleeding, a fact he is suddenly aware of as he covers the rest of himself. Sarai rummages into the pile, throwing the clothing aside to reveal a hoe. She hands it to him. For an instant he wants to smile. Has a just God truly turned the world upside down, so that now he will go to the fields, take on the role of slave? It is just his mind at play; she means it, he knows, as a weapon.

There is another volley from the British cannon, shaking oyster-shell dust from the walls. Sarai nods to him and for the second time this day they leave a home behind. To their right is the thickly treed gulley, one of the fingers of the forest that point down to the river. The route Towerhill must have followed. He points the other way. He does not know how many slaves Towerhill took with him to the English, how many have stayed, whether any of them would shelter them or do them harm.

He sees Sarai has no doubts as to the choice. She clutches the war club.

TWENTY-TWO

SARAI

WHAT MAKES THEM POSSIBLE

She thinks back to the way he laughed when he saw the manor house go up in flames. His house. If not for that laugh, she would have left him. The thread between them is that thin. Yet it winds and binds her heart. A part of that same heart still urges her to break away, rush to the river, to the ship that will carry off Towerhill, just as another ship called *Jesus* had carried both of them to this place. A boy and a baby pressed together as she had been pressed to this man in the darkness of the priest hole. She remembers the hatred in Towerhill's eyes, the way it had flared into the eyes of the others in that room. Would they take her with them, or would they kill her? She is not sure which choice she wants.

She sees a line of militiamen downhill from them, crouched in a sunken depression in the earth, trying to shelter from the bombardment. Their path to that shallow haven is marked by uprooted tobacco plants and the corpses of their fellow militiamen, not all of them intact. As she looks at the men, living and dead, she recognizes Thomas Hallam, his face and figure forming sharply before her eyes, reminding her of how she felt when Jacob had let her look through a spyglass and she saw a tree and a stone and then a ship grow large and clear in the circle of its lens. She has no spyglass now;

it is the familiarity of Thomas Hallam's form, the arrogance and surety in the set of his shoulders and neck, in spite of the way he crouches, that clarifies him for her. *Here is your choice, Jacob.*

"Here is your brother," she says aloud, during a pause in the bombardment.

He follows her gaze and his eyes widen in surprise and she wonders why she must always reveal to this man what is in front of his face. But the thought, rather than driving her from him, draws her closer. He has been brother and friend, master and servant, father and child and lover to her, all at once. And her heart leaps as he shakes his head without an instant of hesitation and tells her they must hide in the trees, must avoid Thomas. Choosing to sever what binds him. Her heart leaps and her heart falls. At knowing what she has been given and what she has lost. The tug she has been feeling all this day. No, longer than this day. It threatens to pull her apart. She suddenly hears Auntie Rebekkah's voice in her head. *You is truly fucked, girl,* it says.

"We must get to the creek," she tells him.

He hefts the hoe, looks at it as if it has appeared by magic in his hands. "And then what?"

She thinks, He does not know what the land he thought was his conceals in its folds and waterways, of the secret roads of the night world.

We must find Joseph, she thinks; he should be nearby, preparing for Towerhill's now usurped plan.

"Come," she says.

They run for a ways down the gulley, then cut across a meadow, to a scrim of trees that zig-zags to the northern border of the plantation. Of Towerhill Separation. They had joked, she and Towerhill, about the prophetic irony contained in those words. Now it has happened. Towerhill has separated from Towerhill. He has left his own name. What will he be now? What will she be now, and what will Jacob be? We were naked and newborn; surely we need new names as well.

They are no longer naked, but an imp in her cannot help but see and be amused at how bothersome Jacob finds his new clothing, his new skin, as he pulls the rough cloth away from his chest and crotch, reaches down to scratch.

She needs to keep that imp. She has chosen this man today, and she understands that there will always be a corner of her heart that hates him for that choice. That only such small rebellions, such tiny internal subversions, will make them possible.

They plunge down a kind of sunken path, depressed by nature—an old creek bed—but deepened further by design and by nocturnal traffic. There are sections that those who use this path have deliberately let grow wild, and she uses the war club to push aside clinging wild grapevines and the scratching thorns of wild roses. The trees close around them and though she still hears the cannons firing—less frequently now, the volleys more ragged—their noise seems distant, like the memory of noise.

Then a noise very much in the present: the crack of a stick broken by a sudden weight, a rustle of leaves, a curse, and then more voices. She should have known they would not be the only ones to use this route. She slows, listening, then stops, causing Jacob to almost run into her. "What . . . ?" he starts to ask, speaking as loud as a free man who has never had to run and hide. She presses her fingers to his lips. But it is too late. The voices stop. A moment later, she sees the small group of slaves that has been just ahead of them. She hears a mutter and then a rustle of movement coming towards them.

Two men and two women: Toby, Neal, Milly, and Daisy, all of them field slaves. They carry bulging burlap sacks slung over their shoulders, but Toby also has a scythe and Neal an iron bar, held loose at his side.

"Massa," he says.

"Good morning, Neal," Jacob says. "Fine day for a stroll in the woods, wouldn't you say?" Cool as that.

There is another volley from the ship, cannonballs screaming though the air overhead, no longer at such a distance.

Neal nods swiftly. "Massa say it's a good day. What y'all think? Think is a good day, we come see massa and his nigger, this place?"

"I think it a fi-ine day," Toby says, drawing out the word, flicking something off the blade of the scythe. The group spreads out a little, forming a U around Jacob and Sarai.

"Toby, let's just git," Daisy says. "Man always treat us good."

"That's right," Toby says. "He treat Lucius and Sally real good, y'all think?"

Sarai says, "That was Bertram."

Toby smiles broadly. She thinks: It was a mistake to talk.

"'That was Bertram,'" he mocks, imitating her diction but pitching his voice high. "But Bertram gone now, girl, that right? You see old Bertram? How Auntie Rebekkah finish him?"

"Old Bertram not be seeing anything," Milly says.

"Old Bertram be seeing hell," Daisy says.

Neal laughs. "Now y'all can go visit him, that man."

"You and this white man's whore," Milly says, staring first at Jacob, then at Sarai.

She and Toby are working their way behind them, though the narrowness of the trail makes this difficult. Sarai hefts the war club, sees Jacob gripping the hoe with both hands. Toby laughs.

"Y'all know how to hoe, massa?" He spits. "You want, I show you."

Another volley of cannon fire splits the air.

Neal giggles. "Hear that?"

Daisy bends down, drops her sack, picks up a large stick, grunts with satisfaction.

"Sarai is not with me willingly, Neal," Jacob says. "I forced her to accompany me."

They all stop. A broad grin splits Neal's face. "Hear that? Missy Sarai force to 'company. You think she force to 'company all her days living in the big house?"

"Massa's house," Milly says. "Force her to fuck, that what you saying, Massa Jacob Hallam?"

"Massa Jacob Hallam," Daisy repeats. "And his nigger don't know she his nigger."

"Don't know she a nigger a-tall," Milly says.

Toby lunges forward, lifts the scythe over his head. As he starts to strike, Jacob thrusts the hoe, handle first, into the man's nose. He cries out; his face spurts red. At the same moment, Sarai smashes the war club onto Neal's skull, but the wood—old and rotten—breaks and falls apart. Toby is clutching his nose, out of the fight for an instant, but Daisy swings her stick, slams it into the back of Jacob's knees and, as he falls, beats at his head, his shoulders.

"Massa Jacob Hallam," she says again, a kind of wonder in her voice, and raises the stick over her head. Sarai screams and jumps on her, clawing at her eyes. The cannons boom, a string of explosions, and this time the balls come crashing into the trees nearby, splintering trunks. Daisy hesitates, but Neal doesn't. He brings the iron bar down in a hissing arc onto Jacob's legs. Sarai hears the meat-thud, feels a second of relief it isn't the crack of a bone. Another British volley splits the air, the cannonballs crashing even closer now, one seeming to fall in a plumb line from the sky, stripping the branches from a loblolly as if someone has run a giant hand down its trunk. Neal hits Jacob again, and now Daisy is striking a flurry of blows at clawing Sarai.

Toby is up now, his nose streaming blood, the scythe still gripped in his right hand. He steps forward, and Sarai sees the feathers of an arrow protruding from his mouth, its head pierced through the back of his neck. She has not seen its flight. It is as if the arrow has formed suddenly from his mouth. She hears a whir and this time see another arrow in the air, just for an instant, before it punches though Daisy's wrist. Daisy screams. The cannonade has stopped. For a long, suspended moment they all stand frozen, in a tableau. A strangled gargling spills from Toby's mouth; he seems to be trying to chew the shaft of the arrow. He falls. Silence. There are no more arrows.

A low growl is coming from the trees. Rage stamps Neal's face and an echoing growl spills from his lips. He leaps towards the noise, his fingers taloned. Sarai hears a flurry of leaves and then Neal's body seems to fly backwards from the trees, and she sees that his throat has been torn out, flaps of skin hanging like wings from his neck. Milly screams, staring at the wound. She looks at Sarai, her eyes wild, then turns and grabs at the shaft of the arrow sticking through Daisy's arm, pulls her away, back down the trail, Daisy stumbling and moaning.

Sarai stands still for a second. The silence feels heavy, unnatural. Then she hears Jacob groan. She runs over to him. He is unconscious, breathing raggedly. She sits down next to him, more because her legs have given out than by choice. She looks at the wall of trees.

"Come out, Joseph," she says.

TWENTY-THREE

JACOB

─

LIGHT AS AIR

They stand on the hill, outside the ruin that gave the plantation its name, and watch new ruins emerge below, as if whatever past destruction had been visited on this place is rippling out, calling the remainder to it, structure compelled to slide into chaos. Jacob feels . . . nothing. No, that is not true. He feels a weight lifting from him in the billows of black smoke, its rushing absence making him aware of its presence, a black, cancerous mass he has lived with so long he has not till now known it was there. He is light as air. But his leg hurts like hell. He laughs. Sarai looks at him with worry, no doubt fearing that the beating he has endured has affected his senses. It has, but not as she thinks. Like the fire, it has liberated him. From illusion. From the slavery of slavery. He laughs again. At the cleverness of the phrase. At his pathetic pride in his own cleverness. At the truth of the phrase, anyway. Now Joseph looks at him and nods, eyes glinting.

Joseph. The mystery of Joseph. The mystery of what he is. Of what they want him to be.

"Would you go to Towerhill?" Joseph asks, and for a moment Jacob is taken aback. Can Joseph bring time itself to a halt, grip its heft, reverse it? But no, of course, he speaks of Thomas's portion of their inheritance, still extant, not of Towerhill Separation. From which Jacob has been separated. From which he has been spared. He giggles again.

"You must stop that," Sarai says.

"Yes. Quite. You are correct, Sarai. As always."

She grimaces. "Stop it."

"Yes. I shall. In a moment."

"Not to Towerhill," she says to Joseph. And adds, as if necessary, "Plantation."

No, Jacob thinks, not to Towerhill. Not to Towerhill the place nor to Towerhill the man. Not to the slavery of one or the embrace of the other. They are coffled together, he and she, skin and soul. They have been made aware of their nakedness and thrust out, east of Eden. There is only one place they can now go.

They wait in the ruined tower until nightfall. Below, stripes of glowing embers outline the ruins of the plantation, like a sketch in lines of fire. Now and again shadows disrupt those lines, figures moving among them. Are there still slaves on the place, salvaging what they can? Most of the Quarters remain intact, though apparently some of the people burned their own cabins before leaving, an action he now understands in the marrow of his bones. Yet he also understands those who did not leave with Towerhill, fearful of leaving what was familiar, what gave them a framework in which to live. What would happen to them? Surely the militia and the patrollers would come, if they were not there already, come to gather loose property. Save it from the terror of freedom.

The militia. A tremor ran through his veins. Since Sarai had pointed Thomas out to him, he had not wanted to think of his brother. Did he still live, or had he perished in the British bombardment or by the hands of vengeful slaves?

"I should go down there," he says, almost to himself.

"No," Sarai says. "No, you should not. There is nothing there for us."

He sways, as if in a strong wind. The last word from her mouth is as dense with meaning as a poem; he can unwrap it into a universe. He understands. But he must go.

"Not to go with him. Only to see if he lives or is hurt. He is still my brother."

She puts a hand on Joseph's shoulder. "This is the only brother you need."

"He is gone," Joseph says.

Something sharp presses into Jacob's heart. "What are you saying?"

"I do not mean killed. I saw him among the militia. They have gathered their wounded and dead; they have left."

Can he believe Joseph? His desire to do so is so strong that he can't trust it.

"Wait here," Jacob says. "I will return soon."

He limps painfully down the hill. In places the earth is cratered, faint tendrils of smoke leaking from the pocked ground. An emptiness that comes from more than the pall of silence that hangs over everything; it is oceanic after the thunder of the bombardment, but also an internal barren-ness: what held him here has unraveled in his heart. As he reaches the ditch, he sees a pair of hands clutching the edge, as if their owner were about to pull himself up, peer over the slight berm. When he draws closer he sees that the rest of the body is gone, the wrists, somehow, neatly severed; the corpse probably taken by the man's comrades. There are other body parts scattered about. He nearly steps into a steaming pile of intestines. Meat. Is any of this meat Thomas? Brother meat.

He looks back at the ruined tower. He can see the forms of Joseph and Sarai. He is too far away to make out their features, but he can tell they are looking at him. Waiting for him. Us, he thinks. We sort. He turns and starts back to them.

They take a circuitous route through the forest, avoiding the St. Andrews Road and other byways. Joseph leads them to paths that are invisible until they are on them, but then run as clear as lines on a map among the trees—hickory and pin oak and loblolly. Jacob has hunted in these woods, walked through them seeking shade and broody solitude; as a boy he had played in them with this man and with Sarai and Towerhill, but now Joseph reveals what his eyes had apparently not yet been ready to see.

They finally come to a narrow creek, where Joseph draws aside thick brush tangled with wild rose to reveal a shallow drift skiff. Jacob knows where they are now, where they will go.

PART TWO

WOLVES

MARCH – JUNE
— 1814 —

ONE

TOWERHILL

———

NEW AND WONDROUS PATTERNS

He stands on the deck, finding his balance, looking out at the river and the shoreline. Scott and Cockburn stand next to him. A moment in near silence after the screams of this day, as if whatever future they have entered now has taken in a breath as it settles into its new form. A few sounds drift to him—the soughing of the sails, the creak of the ropes, sailors calling to each other. His own people are still on deck, gathered in the stern; they form a nebulous, dark mass, its edges blurred by the hard sunlight reflecting off the water, but every face turned towards him, their stares as heavy as chains. MacDougal stands nearby in the shadow of the main mast; is he there to guard the admiral? He catches Towerhill's eye, nods and grins his crooked grin, one corner of his Iroquois-carved mouth higher than the other, tugging at his nubbed ear as if signaling something, its meaning as enigmatic as the man.

They are far downriver from the plantation now, though Towerhill can still see smoke staining the sky when he looks north.

"Lieutenant Scott," Cockburn says suddenly, "you promised me a number of fighting men, men who know the territory. You promised among them a rather remarkable individual, a servant who spoke like a master, an oppressed African who spoke like a gentleman and who comprehended like a soldier, who might become a leader for our Colonial Marines."

Scott shuffles uneasily. "Yes, sir. And I . . ."

"And I, and I, and I . . . and I what, Scott? I will tell you what 'and I' brought to me. A bloody tribe, that's what. A bloody exodus. D'ye know what makes a tribe, lieutenant? Men and women and squalling brats and suckling infants. A bloody tribe." He shifts to Towerhill. "That I am now expected to shelter and feed; is that correct, Mr. Towerhill?"

"We can be of use to you, sir. All of us."

Cockburn looks again at the people clustered near the stern and then slowly turns and stares into Towerhill's eyes. "That is why you are here, *sir.* To be of use to me, and, through me, to his majesty. But Lieutenant Scott promised me fighting men. I understood that was also your promise to him. I did not hear any referent in that oath to the presence of your women and children, nor any reason we should tolerate their presence and cost."

Towerhill feels cold fingers squeezing his heart. "Then what is it we would be fighting for? We will all go then, and damn you."

Scott turns on him. "God's teeth, watch your tongue when you speak to the admiral, Towerhill."

Cockburn waves his hand, as if brushing away Scott's words. "You would be fighting for your own freedom, Mr. Towerhill. For kit and keep and for his majesty the king, as do we all."

"That means nothing to me."

Scott flushes. "Sir, may I speak freely?"

"When have you not, lieutenant?"

Scott looks directly at Towerhill. "As you say, sir, Towerhill has broken his promise. We do not need to tolerate this insolence."

"And yet, Scott, it is through your good offices that they are here at all."

"As you wished, my lord. I followed your orders."

"As you always have, my dear Scott. Please speak freely."

"As I always will, sir. But you knew my reservations about using these people."

Towerhill stares at the two of them, speaking as if reciting lines on a stage. What is he witnessing? He fights an urge to wrap his hands around Scott's throat. In the corner of his eye, he catches a movement, sees Mac-Dougal shuffle, tug again at his ear.

"I think it a low and unworthy tactic for us," Scott continues. "'Tis a beautiful river, this. Wider and bluer than the Thames. All of this," he makes a motion as if scooping the country towards himself, "could be our own pleasant countryside. These Yankees could be our own good yeoman peasantry. Yet we play the robber, plundering and ruining them, dancing about the wreckage."

Towerhill follows Scott's gaze to the lush green countryside, pastures jeweled with wildflowers, richly soiled fields corrugated in orderly rows, orchards heavy with fruit. Scott seeing England in these American land-scapes, a gush he has heard before from English guests visiting the plantation before the war. What Towerhill sees are dark forms bending over and over as if in prayer between the rows of tobacco plants, their faces lifting whenever the ship draws near, their glittering eyes seeing a promise in the ensign flapping from its mast. He draws in a breath, tamps down his temper. There is a throb in his sixth finger; it thrums up behind his eyes.

"It seems insidious to bludgeon these people with the very property we steal from them," Scott says. Looking pointedly at Towerhill. Property who has stolen himself.

This is a different Scott from the man he had met clandestinely before the uprising. Though Towerhill had never doubted, even then, that the lieutenant had donned a mask he thought necessary to wear during the act of seduction. His own mask talking to Scott's mask. He looks over again at MacDougal, the maddening grin twisted on the man's face, as if he can hear them and is amused at the reversal of his role and Scott's. *Why do we need these savages, sir?* Towerhill remembering now the conversation on the hummock where he had met the two men. He glances aft again, towards his people, observing how MacDougal, feet planted wide, has placed him-self between him and them. He can see Neb, who has moved out from the rest, and is staring at him, a grin weirdly mirroring MacDougal's at play on his lips. *Gone to the big house again, have you, Book?*

"We are at war," the admiral says to Scott. "As we were in France and Spain, lieutenant. I do not recall you being so delicate with those populations."

"They did not so much resemble our own."

Cockburn turns. Stares into Towerhill's eyes for a few seconds, before speaking to his aide.

"Enough, Mr. Scott. I have heard you. Now the debate is over. Our task here is to drub Jonathan. To bludgeon by the most painful means possible. That is all. The men will stay. As for the females and pickaninnies . . ."

If he seizes Cockburn, tips him over the side, Neb will see, will come to them, bringing the others with him. Could they take the ship? As Cockburn's sentence trails off, both British officers turn to stare at him, as if gauging him, something assessing in their look that stops him. Before he can speak, Cockburn holds up his right hand, palm out.

"Mr. Towerhill," he says, "let us go into my cabin to settle this matter. I can feel the air here slapping against my skin from all the flapping ears and wagging tongues on this deck."

Better there, Towerhill thinks. The close, private quarters would shield the two whites from the view of MacDougal and the others.

The air in the cabin is thick with heat and sticky with dust. A map of the Tidewater region is spread on a table in the center. Cockburn stands over it, one hand hovering, a finger darting down to touch the parchment here and there, as a bird of prey might. There is no design or pattern Towerhill can see in this tapping, only some custom of his body. He watches the admiral's finger go up the Chesapeake, up the Patuxent, writing Towerhill's past and future. Cockburn lifts it, points it at him. Like a pistol.

Towerhill moves closer. The admiral does not step back, again meets Towerhill's stare with his own, his gaze frank, eyes crinkling in what seems to be some private amusement at the small test he understands that Towerhill has put to him in that move.

"We are all well schooled at whatever tasks may be needed," Towerhill says finally. "We will fight for you and we will bring others to fight for you. We know this country as no white man can. Our women, and even our children, can hunt, fish, cook, clean, repair your sails, your wooden hulls, wash and sew your clothing, make your sailors' shoes. They can bind your wounds and they can wash and comfort your broken, and they can bury your dead. They can clean your weapons, and they can fashion them. And use them as well, for that matter. Our fight today began with a blow struck by a woman."

Once again, Towerhill putting his people up on the block. Display and utility.

"Then I'm curious, Towerhill. Except for the first and the last, what you describe are the same tasks your people did as slaves, are they not?"

Cockburn drawing the thought from Towerhill's mind. The admiral hooks a finger and gestures at him, as if to pull out a response.

"We would do these tasks as free people. In our own interest. And in the interest of your cause. You are here to fight for your nation, admiral. I bring my nation with me today, to this ship."

Cockburn laughs. And in that sudden bark, in the lock of their eyes that follows, the quick flutter of a grin between Cockburn and Scott, Towerhill comes to understand that all has been decided already, all his intercourse with the admiral a reconnaissance into the heart of his intentions, designed to force him to defend his people's presence here, to feel that their fragile acceptance depends on a British largesse that can be summarily withdrawn. To reveal perhaps as well the savage's ability to control himself, to think while under attack, to find and utter the words, as if reciting a vow, that encompasses what will be required of him and his people. It is indeed the mirrored performance of the little drama Scott and MacDougal had played out for him on the hummock, with Scott taking on MacDougal's role now. *Why do we need these savages, sir?* A role. Precisely the right word. Though a part of him, kernelled in the years of his life that had required him to know what white men were thinking, also knows that whatever play-acting Scott has just danced through at the admiral's command are couched by the lieutenant's own true beliefs. Towerhill does not give a tinker's damn, feels instead a small swell of admiration for Cockburn. It has been a long time since he has learned anything from a white man. Too many times, he knows, the British have underestimated their enemy out of arrogance and contempt; it has cost them dearly. He prefers to be with this man and his careful scouting.

"A nation, is it?" A look of amusement creases Cockburn's face. "Not a tribe, then? And these others of which Mr. Scott tells me . . . ?"

"Wesorts, sir," Scott says, rolling the word in his mouth, suddenly looking relaxed, the performance finished. "Half-breeds. Runaway slaves, Indians, whites. Swamp dwellers. They . . ."

"And are they a nation, Towerhill?" Cockburn interrupts.

"So people say," Towerhill replies. Thinking, so Joseph would have them.

Cockburn turns to him, hearing the hedge in his words. "What about you, Towerhill? Would you use that word?"

"Yes, sir, I would."

"And why would that be?"

"They share a history of murders."

Cockburn laughs, snorting. "I see, I see. And is that what makes a nation?"

"'Tis the glue, sir."

The admiral brings his palm down hard on the map. "Well, Wesort, they-sort, to blazes with what sort they are, or have, or have not. Do they know the land?"

"They are the land."

"How poetic. You know what I am asking."

"Lieutenant Scott asked me the same question. They will not fight for you."

"But will for the Americans?"

Towerhill hesitates. Joseph deserted him. He still feels the sting of that betrayal. But none of that is the concern of this white man and his tests.

"Nor for them," he says.

He looks away from Cockburn and Scott, lets his eyes fall on the mottled beams of sunlight streaming through the porthole. Dust motes rise and fall in some gentle current of air trapped inside this cabin, tiny planets visible, then invisible, then visible again as they turn to the sun or leave it, their swirl reflecting the turmoil in his brain and breast on this terrible and miraculous day. He stares at the sunlight and the dust, straining to see what new and wondrous pattern will form from the now scattered atoms of his existence.

"I see." The admiral nods. "Quite. One finds it all in the name."

TWO

SARAI

‒

A WITHY CAGE

That night they sleep on a low hummock at the edge of the swamp. Joseph goes ahead, to ready people for their arrival, he says. To be sure they are not immediately killed—or sold—is what he does not say. Nor needs to.

They have nothing to cover themselves, a fact the mosquitoes soon discover. She watches Jacob staring at a coven of them, clustered, feeding, on his forearm, and she reaches over and crushes them. The spurt of his blood stains her fingers. "Meat," he mutters. She wants to shake him. She wants to fuck him. She needs him inside her. It is not love, she tells herself, but a hunger in her bones, a hollowness that needs to be filled, so different from what she felt during their lovemaking on the plantation, when she could never lie with him without some corner of her mind sensing the invisible, judging presence of Towerhill, without questioning if—no, how much—of what she was doing was whoring for gain and privilege, a soiling that repulsed yet excited her. It is all gone, that. In the leveling circumstances of this day, a door to love has opened. But in the newness of themselves, now, here, she wants only the skin. Yes, meat. The warm human flesh of him. She wants it after the death today. She wants it in the giddy freedom of this night. She pushes him to the earth and lies with him,

130

face to face, but when she reaches into his trousers, the rough garment of a slave, he is soft in her hand. For some minutes, it is enough to feel him, warm and smooth and still, and cradling him in her palm, his helplessness, the power that has drained from him, touches her. But only for a few seconds: then she growls, deep in her throat, a noise that startles her, and she pulls his trousers down, takes him in her mouth. She runs her tongue into his slit, tasting the saltiness there, but he remains soft and finally puts his hands on her head and pushes her away, his face stricken. He is unmanned, she thinks, and for a moment feels a surge of frustration and contempt: is he only the creature of what he had thought to own? But only for a moment. Though she knows the seed of that thought will remain and then she feels a gush of tenderness towards him, as forceful as her lust had been and somehow a twin to it. She feels tenderness; she feels contempt. "Never mind," she says, thinking, as those words come to her lips, how they must be the very words so many other women have uttered to the stricken men they love—a shift in the power of their congress, piteous yet somehow sweet. So many thoughts run wild through her trenchant mind now. There is a kind of doubleness in everything, a part of her lying with this man, another part hovering above the two of them, studying, weighing each idea and sensation. It is something she has never experienced before, a complexity that is an unexpected gift of freedom.

She sleeps.

Awakens to Jacob, pressing down on her, her trousers pulled down, his face intent with a need to erase the failure of his body. Something in her clenches hard against that need; it is a reassertion of his power that has nothing to do with her. She twists her hips to the side, pulls her garment back up, and pushes him from her. He closes his eyes and lies back, accepting it, and she puts her fingers on his lips, smoothes their tight grimace away, until he is gentled and comes back to her. She kisses his forehead, the closed lids of his eyes.

They sleep.

She dreams she is running through a swamp with Jacob, though sometimes it is with Joseph, sometimes Towerhill. They flow more than run; she can still feel the warm mud under the pads of her feet, the water splashing from their legs, the white tail of the doe they chase bobbing up and down, growing closer. They speed through the reeds brushing against their flanks; excitement rising in their throats, they speed past the burning house, past the bed in the burning house, the island hovering like a cloud on the horizon, receding even as they run towards it.

Joseph awakens them. He does not touch them; she opens her eyes and he is there, his eyes glistening, but she had felt his presence slide into her sleep. Looking up at him, a nimbus of sunrise around his head and the dream still lingering behind her eyes, she remembers Jacob's words: *What the hell are you?* There has always been that mystery about Joseph, whispers among the slaves, and among the overseers as well. *Ilimu*, shape-shifter, he was called by those slaves who still remembered Africa, the word drawn from their own memories and from the werewolf legends the Wesorts encouraged to keep outsiders away from the swamps. From the stories Joseph, she suspects, cultivated about himself. His usual silence. His occasional tendency to howl. It was all nonsense, of course. With the three of them, Joseph was playful, happy, sad; he bled when scratched, he cried when beaten, he raged when mad, he stood shoulder to shoulder with Towerhill and Jacob and pissed into the river and did not, Towerhill said, lift a leg to do so.

And yet, when he was not with them, they would pass on to each other with a delicious thrill, the stories they'd heard about him. They remembered how he had first come to them, following them, his unseen presence scraping like fingernails along their nerves as they paddled further and further into the swamp. It was this memory that had come into her dream last night, as it has on other nights, this memory and the quickness with which he had killed yesterday, that takes her now to these dire and foolish contemplations.

"Good morning," Joseph says.

She and Jacob untwine, her body stiff and sore. Jacob stands and looks at the water, then crosses himself, kneels, and prays. She goes behind some blueberry bushes, relieves herself, and, while she still squats there, picks as many berries as she can hold and brings them back in her cupped hands. She offers them first, from politeness, to Joseph, who to her relief refuses: she tries to discard the nonsense she has been thinking about him, but cannot help imagining the quick dart of his rough tongue again her skin. Jacob licks the berries from her palm, his tongue, also to her relief, awakening a sweet frisson that sings through her nerves. And then they get into the boat and paddle into the morning, to whatever it will bring.

Which is the withy cage in which she and Jacob now hang, separated from the world by a lattice of willow branches crisscrossed in front of their eyes.

THREE

JACOB

—

EMPTIED OF HIMSELF

How can this be him?

Jacob recognizes the whiny foolishness of this thought even as he pushes his face against the cage's crisscross of willow branches. Yet the depth of transformation in his life seems absurd and somehow unfair. Two days before he had lain on clean linen and watched sunlight dance rainbows on the walls through a cut-glass goblet still half-filled with the deep ruby of the Madeira wine he had shared with the woman in his bed.

The woman is still here, though the press of Sarai's weight against him, and his against her, their faces so close that their breaths are plaited, is now an intimacy born of discomfort and humiliation. Her eyes are closed, her cheeks and forehead smeared with sweat-streaked dirt. As are his. There is something, he tells himself, he should be learning about the ease with which all that cushions one from the brutal world can be stripped away; some pious wisdom in the humiliation of his situation, some joy, even, that he and the woman he loves have been brought finally to the same level. But all he feels is hunger, and heat, and a maddening itch on his neck and shoulders. At least the cage is narrow enough so that he can scrape his back against its slats, and his gratitude at this fact strikes him as so disproportionate that he laughs.

Sarai opens her eyes, looks at him and blinks, as if the sight, his presence here, surprises her as much as it does him.

"I'd be grateful if you would share that with me, Jacob," she says.

"Share what?"

"The source of your laughter."

He strokes her cheek, flaps his hand weakly, trying with this gesture to indicate their condition, the events of the last days, the fact that they are hanging in the air like caged parrots. "It seems that I am extremely happy to discover I am able to scratch my back."

She stares at him, then laughs, then laughs louder, until Jacob can't help but join her. Their laughter spills uncontrollably; their bodies, filthy, itchy, covered with rags, shake; the cage sways madly. The sun has started to come up, and he can make out the spiked logs of the palisade. Zekiah Fort. The palisade enclosing his memory of this place from his childhood. He begins to imagine they have never left it, never gone back to Towerhill; what if this is the true continuation of their lives, and their lives on the plantation have been a dream? They seemed imprisoned now in Joseph's dream, and whatever intrigues that dream has spawned. Joseph had brought them to one of the log houses, then had left; they were seized and hustled to this cage moments afterwards, as if the grim group of men who burst into the dwelling had been waiting for Joseph's absence to act. As they surely were.

Several women are squatting near a small fire, cooking a pot of crabs. At the sound of laughter, they turn to stare at Jacob and Sarai, and then the laughter catches them, too, and they begin to chuckle, shaking their heads. One, an older woman, says something sharply, and a girl with matted, kinky hair, its tufts tied with blue ribbons, rises from the group and comes over to them with a gourd filled with water, balancing it carefully, graceful as a dancer. As she offers the gourd through the slats, he hesitates, wondering if the gesture is a form of torture, the water saline. But Sarai seizes the gourd in both hands and drinks deeply before he can stop her. She closes her eyes as she swallows and then hands the gourd to him. As he gulps the water down, feels it soothe his parched mouth and cracked lips, he tries to read their fate in the girl's eyes. But her face is a mask, not only expressionless but literally a mask: a parenthesis of blue lines engraved from her forehead down across her cheeks.

"Where is Joseph?" he manages to croak to her as she retrieves the gourd. The girl says nothing, only turns and walks back to the fire.

Where is Joseph? Jacob feels as if he is suddenly emptied of himself, has been poured onto the dirt shadowed by their cage. All the foundations of the world are sand. He recalls the way they've laughed, just seconds before, as if it has happened years ago, as if he is hovering outside the cage, viewing two mad people, their violent sway a gauge of their insanity.

"He will come," Sarai whispers, as if she has read his thoughts.

But he does not come that night. Or the next. Time becomes something fluid in that enclosure. They stop asking each other about him, try to stop asking themselves. As they broil in the sun the women bring water thrice more. Each time the women glance furtively around themselves, and he knows by the gesture that their mercy is a forbidden act. Sleep is another mercy; their bodies, weakened, easily release them into dreams, until the border between waking and that hazy realm dissolve and he is back in their hidey-hole in his bedroom, he and Sarai pressed close in the blackness even as they are wood-bound in this cage. The walls of the hidey-hole are beaded with acrid sweat and the sharp stink of dung stings their nostrils, as if they are in the gut of a beast. He is in the withy cage; he is in the hidey-hole and then he is above it, seeing Towerhill Separation from the height of some spiraling osprey or hawk, the house, its walls swelling and receding, the acres of tobacco plants swaying, the earth heaving in rhythm with their breathing, with his own ragged breathing and with Sarai's, the skein of creeks pulsing from their veins. It all moves, in and then out, in and then out, and on each exhale he strains towards release, hangs on the edge of freedom, only to be sucked down again. In the dream, he feels a need to empty his bladder, a pressure that brings him back to the reality of the cage, the stink as he voids, fouling himself, mourning the loss of fluid as it leaves him. Sarai, her eyes closed, touches his cheek and then kisses it; he can sense her trying to retreat back into the saving grace of sleep. As he does. The sway of the cage bringing them back, and waking them again, and allowing them to slip away, and each time they wake together, heated skin adhering to heated skin, and he thinks: this is our true wedding.

"This is our true wedding," he whispers. Sarai stares at him.

"Yes," she mutters. "Just as my girlish dreams would have it."

They both begin to laugh again, and again the laughter seizes them, and this time he fears they will not be able to stop; they will end as two bird-plucked piles of dancing bones, a picture that makes him laugh even harder, painfully, through the swollen tissues of his throat.

When he opens his eyes, Lombroso is standing in front of the cage.

FOUR

SARAI

—

GAUNTLET

She recognizes him at once. The square, broad jaw, his nose, the almost lipless slit of his mouth crowded in the center of his face. The face of the man who had once tried to sell her. His cheeks sag more than they once did, wing further down over his jaw line, and two grooves are carved deeply around his mouth, but his eyes bore into hers with the same coldness she remembers now, as if that memory has been waiting to hatch in her brain. She feels dread swell in her throat. Jacob reaches out and squeezes her hand. Lombroso. She had once asked Joseph about the origin of that strange name, but all he knew—or would say, for perhaps it was to be kept secret from outsiders—was that it had belonged to one of the Wesort founders: white, black, or Indian, he did not know, but a man (or a woman?) who had created the law of the Wesorts. The law of separateness and unity, Joseph had said, for the Wesorts are to live apart from the world, bonded by their mix of blood.

That mix is written in the faces of the men who stand, in two lines, outside the cage. Some are black, one as white as Jacob, or more so—the man seems bleached almost to transparency, his hair as pale as his skin, his eyes pinkish. A few seem pure Piscataway. Most, though, including Lombroso, carry the swirl of bloodlines she sees in Joseph. Separateness and unity. But the main factor that seems to unify them is their age. None is young. Each man holds a club, some with one hand, swinging it against an empty palm, others gripping it with both hands. Their clothing is ragged: some wear coarse, long-sleeved shirts, homespun trousers and tunics; some wear headbands; others are shirtless, with withered, sagging dugs. A gauntlet of old men. She can hope for the infirmities of age. Their faces, unlike Lombroso's, are expressionless.

He opens the cage door. Sarai and Jacob twist out of the narrow entrance, scraping skin. No one speaks. The only sound is the thud of clubs into palms, like perverse applause at their appearance. For a second she and Jacob stand motionless. Then she breaks away, turns, starts to run. Tries to run. Not to escape; she knows that is hopeless, but out of her body's need to move, to find itself, after her long restriction. But her legs, cramped for so long, fail her. She feels the muscles twist and flutter under her skin and it is as if the earth has been yanked away from under her. She falls to her knees and then on to her face. She breathes in sand, snorts it out, as she is wrenched to her feet. One of the old men smashes her shoulders with his club; a second blow lands on her elbow and sends a shock through her body. Jacob is on his knees, a trickle of blood coursing down the side of his face.

"You should not be here," Lombroso says.

"Clearly," Jacob mutters, and she feels a surge of love for him. They look at each other and laugh again, as if laughter is their anthem. Lombroso waves them forward and they begin to walk, and then, as best they can, run the gauntlet. As the blows rain down on them, she has the presence of mind to note that the Wesorts are avoiding their heads. They are not, apparently, meant to die. She reels from the blows. Waves of pain. A black spot forms in front of her eyes. A circle that fills itself in. She is dimly aware of Jacob again reaching over to steady her. A short, fat man, his creased belly bulging like a reverse set of buttocks over a pair of canvas sailor's trousers, smashes his hand, and Jacob grunts, stops, draws himself upright. She feels a wave of pride. In him. In herself. She spits at the fat man, generating a windmill of blows. She staggers forward, weathering them. And then they are finished. The blows stop. Her ears ring and the world lurches in front of her eyes. She sees one of the old men, black as Africa, catch her gaze, and nod, as if, she would like to think, in respect.

They cling to each other, their flesh bruised and bloody. In front of them, cabins, little more than shacks, are strung on both sides of the path, among the loblolly pines. People, mostly women and children, are lined along the path; they look gaunt, half-starved, the children naked, with bulging bellies and protruding navels. She looks more closely at the dwellings, mainly to take her eyes away from the people. There are many more cabins now than there were when she had been here as a child, though the structures are a jumbled mixture, as if they reflect the black, white, ochre faces staring at her: post-and-beams, simple lean-tos, shacks of scrap wood and deer hide. Their commonality is shoddiness: mold, rot; sagging roofs, where there are roofs; walls leaning. She sees two, no—she's sees another in a copse of trees—three Piscataway longhouses; had those been there when she was here before? Their tops sag, and there are gaps in the reeds: they look like structures built from a dim memory or notion of what they should be, and she immediately thinks, *Joseph.* Where are the fierce and feared Wesorts, the shape-shifters and swamp shadows who people the stories told to frighten children?

A crude pine-board table stands in the center of the path, just before it bends in front of one of the longhouses. An old man, dressed in buckskins, sits behind the table on a wooden stool. His face is striped with black and ochre lines. A wolf's head, skull gone but its form preserved—ears, eyes, muzzle, frozen snarl, yellow fangs—sits atop the old man's head. Sarai is transfixed by the stare of those four eyes, two below, two above. At one moment, all seem equally dead; at another, all are bright and alive and return her gaze. On the table is a line of oyster shells. A pit of dread opens in her stomach. She and Jacob are being prodded along the path. A wail rises from the women, as if they are mourning at a burial. She feels herself, and now Jacob beside her, suddenly stagger, as if they've been physically struck by the noise. Whipped. A gauntlet of sound. She conjures up their room at Towerhill Separation, walls aglow with some inner whiteness, spinning around them as if it were weaving sanctuary. Two men seize Jacob's arms and try to drag him to the table. He spins, manages to slam the crown of his head into one man's nose; it bursts into blood and she feels a flicker of satisfaction. And fear for him. Two other men grab him. The eyes in the wolf's head bore into hers. Lombroso moves to stand next to the man.

"Listen," he says, and slaps Jacob's right ear and then his left. "Listen. Tell Joseph."

"Where is he?" Jacob asks, staring into Lombroso's eyes. Sarai feels a brief stir of hope at the sound of Joseph's name; Lombroso's command to deliver a message reassures her that they are not going to be killed. She waits for his next words. But he only smiles.

Two women have come up on either side of her; they hold her firmly and bear her away from the table, whispering soothingly in her ear. The men push Jacob to the table. The wolf-head man picks up a shell, leans over casually, and slashes Jacob's face, two red lines appearing on his right cheek as if they have burst forth internally. Another man, squat, with broad shoulders, veined muscles bunching his arms, seizes Jacob's wrist and forces his left hand down flat onto the table. She hears the bang as his hand hits the table and then a smaller thump, drowned by his scream, as the edge of the oyster shell cuts through his two smallest fingers. The man holds them up in triumph, two pink cylinders of flesh.

—

They are back in the cage. The women who had held her have packed the two stumps of Jacob's fingers with mud and wrapped his hand with a poultice of leaves bound with rawhide strips. They have smeared mud on the cuts on his face as well. Better than their touch were the quick words one whispered to her. *It is not us. The old man forces us.* Sarai wraps her arms tightly around him; for a moment he tries to break away, as if shamed by his weakness. His skin is hot and spongy with sweat. As the two of them had been carried away, the wolf-head man had grinned at them, drawing back his thin lips to reveal scarlet gums, three blackened teeth set in his lower jaw like tombstones, one in his upper jaw filed to a fang. He held up his left hand, pointed to the middle and forefinger. "Tomorrow," he said. Then he fingered his nipples and pointed at her. "Tell Joseph," Lombroso had said. Would the letters of his message be formed from bits and pieces cut from the two of them? She recognizes that thinking of that notion as absurd will not prevent it from happening. She holds Jacob tightly, feeling again, she cannot help it, the change in their relationship that these upheavals have created, the subtle shift of power from him to her. Another kind of absurdity, the ironic kind, for she is dangling and caged and about to be diced. In her embrace, his trembling stops and he falls asleep, or at least pretends to. She falls asleep herself, truly, drifts in and out of a dream of being buried alive, feeling a plug of mud being packed into her nostrils, more mud filling her throat, her womb, she can smell the cold clay of it as it encases her, the weight filling her lungs from the inside even as it collapses her chest.

When she awakens, Jacob is still in her arms. She closes her eyes, but the fierce sun burns orange through her lids, its heat pressing like thumbs against them. She hears the sound of the cage door being opened, and she shudders and holds him more tightly and opens her eyes.

To see Joseph, staring at them, his pressed lips trembling with anger.

FIVE

TOWERHILL

—

A HISTORY OF MURDER

The Blackies, MacDougal inevitably called them, when he was being polite, but the name bestowed upon them by the British was *Colonial Marines*. What they call themselves is *free*, though saying it is more a prayer than a self-description they yet fully believe. Within the Negroes' battalion, those liberated from Towerhill Separation and the neighboring plantations are but one company, though their ranks have swelled daily, reinforced by runaways as slaves all along the Tidewater Chesapeake rally to the British, many inspired by the example of their revolt. They keep *Towerhill Separation* for a company name, for a rallying cry, and they remain tightly knit. Cockburn is wise enough to let them stay together and to do what they know how to do best. Which is to ravage the ground they once watered with their own sweat and blood.

They were trained, armed, and outfitted at Tangier Island in the Chesapeake, where MacDougal was happy to take on the role of overseer, and Towerhill strained to keep his people, and himself, from killing the Scot. He told them that the control they all needed to learn was no different from the clench of heart and soul and hand they had to live with as slaves. But several—Neb, in particular—chafed under the close order drilling. "We

143

gonna Indian for them, Towerhill, why we need this dancing?" But Towerhill understood why, came to value MacDougal's skill at it. They were honing to a purpose. Honing into a nation, readying for their own history of murders, though in truth the forming roots of that nation had already been soaked in blood. And no one complained about the weaponry drills. They had been forbidden to hold firearms all their lives; now the weight of these weapons rifles in their hands was like a physical manifestation of their changed and charged condition.

Before the company's first action, Towerhill had accompanied a column of white marines on a raid led by the admiral himself. They had burned their way across the St. Mary's peninsula, from Sotterly Plantation to Coles' Landing. There was only token resistance from the Maryland militia, and Towerhill learned nothing from the marines about fighting. But much about how to be Cockburn.

The raiders' main enemy was the heat. It was Maryland-summer hot, a wet, woolen blanket pressing into their flesh. The former slaves had long learned to ignore it, but it threatened to fell the English soldiers in their cumbersome garb, lugging their packs, their loads of ammunition and weapons. Men swayed in their tracks, fainted; others simply lay down, exclaiming they could march no further. But after the plantations had been put to fire, the American militias were rallying; there was only one way back to the ships, and any men left behind would certainly be slaughtered. Cockburn, tall, sunburnt, his battered, gold-laced hat askew on his head, walked over to one of the fallen men and picked up his Brown Bess musket. "What is this—Englishmen tired after a little stroll in the countryside? I'll carry it for you, then, if 'tis too much a burden." He walked down the line of men, peering into their faces as most turned away in embarrassment. A musket slipped from the nerveless finger of another soldier; the man, panting, his face fish-belly white, collapsed to the ground. Cockburn strode over to him, snatched up the weapon as if it were weightless. He picked up another musket, then another, cradling them effortlessly in his arms, marching crisply, shoulders thrown back, staring straight ahead. The soldiers began to sit up, get to their feet, their faces flushed now with shame more than heat. "No, sir, please, we'll walk," said the man who had collapsed, a Private Musgrave, and he rose unsteadily to his feet. One by one, the rest also stood, reached out, and gently extracted the weapons from Cockburn's hands.

Towerhill watched the admiral carefully throughout this incident, wanting to learn why and how he continued to earn the love and loyalty of his men. There was no secret. He drew his energy and strength from his need to possess energy and strength. If Towerhill would be Cockburn, he needed to ignore the fatigue and the heat that had sapped men's will and live up to his own legend. Live up to and add to it. By the time they were back on the ships, without having lost a man, the story had already spread. It was not the first or the last of such tales to ripple among the sailors and marines; and as Towerhill discovered, the telling was not as spontaneous as one might imagine. That night he observed Scott describing the admiral's actions to a group of men knotted on the deck; after they dispersed Towerhill saw Cockburn, standing in the shadows near the helm, catch Scott's eye and nod slightly to him, Towerhill, black in black shadows, catching it also, learning something else about leading soldiers, about the kind of legends that might be created to help turn slaves into soldiers.

His company's first action had been to seize an island, Blackistone, as a land base. From it and from the *Phaeton* they have since raided along the Potomac and the Patuxent, hitting Graham's Landing, Broome's Island, Cremona Plantation, Mulberry Hill, and others, burning where there was any resistance, carting food, furniture, clothing, and especially livestock back to the ships. Freeing those slaves who would be free, swelling the ranks of the Colonial Marines with more fighters as well as with carpenters and smiths and wainwrights and cooks and laundresses. Cockburn prefers the first, but the white sailors and marines take more pleasure from the skills of the latter. At first many of the black women grumbled at finding themselves performing the same tasks they had done for their masters. But as Towerhill predicted, they have come to enjoy, if not the tedium of their labor, the idea of doing it as free women who are paid for their work. And several among them—Sally one such, fighting side by side with Lucius, and more ferociously than him—have insisted on participating in the raids. The women are too fierce for Towerhill to deny.

But something has diminished in Lucius. Towerhill hears members of the company say that Sally has taken the place of his missing eye, hears others say, No, 'tis not that particular dangling orb she has replaced.

SIX

JACOB

—

WE ARE A COUNTRY

To be in this place, Jacob thinks, is to return to childhood, that time before the complications and divisions of the world had driven them into the unnatural state of their relationship on the plantation. They no longer need to engage in a façade that had existed only for form's sake, every slave and overseer on the plantation knowing that Sarai came to his bed. No longer the continual tug, the nag of doubt in his heart, that it was only his power over her that had brought her to him. The sense, always, of a third presence between them, a vision of Towerhill, a dark form with mockery and hatred shimmering in his eyes.

All that is gone, he thinks. They are both free, back on the island they had claimed as their own when they were there as children. They can shed the past in this Edenic place, though, when he makes that comparison, Sarai snorts, runs her fingers over the bumps on her skin, and wonders aloud if Eden had had so many mosquitoes and chiggers waiting, as the story went, to be named.

—

He doesn't remember how many days it has been since their liberation from Lombroso at Zekiah Fort. After Joseph rescued them, they were taken to another old longhouse concealed among pines and thick blue-berry bushes. Joseph had ten other Wesorts with him, nine men and a woman, dressed alike in fringed deerskin garments. In the past, Jacob had seen most Wesorts dressed in the same homespun clothing that all of the small-holder white and freed black farmers and tradesmen wore. The dress some of them wear now, he understands, is part of Joseph's design to bring them back to their Piscataway roots, an idea Sarai treats with the same cyn-icism she had expressed about the bucolic nature of their island. Designed, she said, to separate them from blacks, in white eyes. And perhaps in their own. Perhaps, he admitted. But their cage, the gauntlet, the cutting oyster shells, the painted faces on Lombroso's people harked back to tales sifted through memory and need. Lombroso was creating his own rival legend. But the ten Wesorts who had come with Joseph were younger than the people with Lombroso. They had helped Jacob and Sarai out of the cage, and then they stood in a loose, dangerous, utterly silent semicircle as Lombroso and a few of the men who had been in the gauntlet came to confront them. Joseph walked up to Lombroso, bringing his face so close their breaths mingled. After a moment, more Wesorts than Jacob had seen before emerged from houses and came to stand silently behind Joseph. Lombroso had turned, walked away, the other old men scrambling after him, muttering, their shoulders slumped as if in imitation of their lead-er's posture. As soon as Jacob and Sarai were out of the cage, Joseph had grasped his wrist, raising the hand gently as Jacob gasped in pain. Joseph had caressed the wrapping, as if his touch would heal Jacob.

He had been told, he explained, that the British had burned the cabins of several Wesort farming families living on the edge of the swamp, but when he and his warriors arrived they had found the places intact. A ruse, he said. To get him away so that Lombroso could undermine him by abusing the guests under his protection. It was not a challenge he could let stand.

As he spoke, Jacob's hand throbbed and waves of dizziness, fever and fatigue rocked him, the ground shifting, threatening to rock him off his feet. "He mentioned something about sending you a message," he said.

"A message?"

Jacob held up his mutilated hand, touched the cuts on his face.

Joseph nodded. "The old ways," he said.

After Joseph left, he had slept. When he awoke, he was sitting naked under moonlight on a low stool, Sarai perched on another stool next to him. He had no memory of how he had been placed there, no idea of how long he had slept. Time itself had seemed to thin and drift off, as if to erase his history before depositing him here. He and Sarai were surrounded by women. He recognized some as those who had given them water while they were caged. The women brought water again, pouring it over them, scrubbing and scraping their skins with cedar branches. Jacob's hand still throbbed, but he felt the pressing enclosure of the cage being stripped from him with each rough stroke. When the women finished, they brought clothing, simple homespun garments: a shirt and trousers for Jacob, a dress and a shirt for Sarai, soft deerskin moccasins for both.

—

The island is used as a hunting camp, and Joseph has constructed another of the old-style Piscataway longhouses there. It is much smaller than the dwellings that Billy Tayac, a full-blood Yeocomico who served occasionally as a hunting guide for Jacob's father, once described to Jacob. He spoke of oblong structures large enough to hold a number of families. Joseph wanted to go back to that usage, but he failed to get people to live in the ones he had constructed or repaired at Zekiah Fort. "Ain't gonna live like ants, all crowded in the same hill," said Jimmy Savoy, one of his supporters. "Y'all put Savoys, Proctors, Swanns in one place, we gonna kill each other." Joseph had given up.

Now the smaller structure he built on their island has become Sarai's and Jacob's house, though often they sleep outside, preferring the evening breezes on their skin. Joseph taught them to use a mixture of thyme and deer grease to keep the mosquitoes away; the smell was not unpleasant and the paste worked some of the time, though it clung unpleasantly in the growing heat of the summer. The quality of that heat, now strong enough to bead sweat on their foreheads, is their only sense of time, and if Jacob could erase even that temporal marking, he would do so gladly. They are, he wants to believe, outside the current of time. There are days when not a word passes their lips. The two of them are an island. As if they have taken on the isolate essence of the place in which they dwell. His hand heals, but the finger stumps itch, and sometimes his invisible ghost fingers and the scars on his face ache enough to wake him. Yet in the mornings, when he opens his eyes, the first thing he sees is a fine line of sweat on Sarai's upper lip, the way it pools in the delicate indentation under her nose. The way it tastes when he leans forward to lick it, tang of salt and skin. The shape of her lips, their corners turning up into a smile as he traces them with his tongue, the taste of her, moving her out of dream and into presence in a way she had never been to him when she had been his slave, never could have been. Each time they make love in this place he feels as new and whole as the smooth skin that knits over a wound. "As if we are being born as our own child," Sarai says.

"We are a country," he says.

SEVEN

SARAI

———

HER COUNTRY

Next to what Jacob insists on calling the short longhouse, Joseph had built a sweat lodge, smaller, and circular, not oblong like the dwelling. Long ago, he tells them, when the Wesorts were closer to the Piscataways, sweat lodges were a tribal center, and the Wesorts treated the shedding and scraping of dirt and skin that occurred there as a religious ceremony: a rebirth. And so that is how Sarai tries to feel as she wraps a softened deerskin around herself and pushes through the labial slit of the opening and into the air.

Only to wish to move back inside again, into the dark, warm, moisture-beaded curve of the lodge. For Joseph has come to visit. And standing next to him, with a smile on his lips that does not reach his eyes, is Jacob's brother.

She is not born anew, only back into the harsh, intruding light of a world she already knows.

Thomas moves stiffly; he has a broken nose, still plastered, and had been wounded in both legs and in his right shoulder. There are bumps under his skin where shrapnel still lodges, he says, displaying his injuries while ignoring the new scars on his brother's face. Though, clucking, he does touch the stumps on Jacob's hand, a strange grin broadening on his face.

Sarai goes into the longhouse and dresses. When she comes back out, the men are squatting around a fire near Thomas's beached canoe. She arrives in time to hear the purpose of this visit. Thomas has come to Joseph, he says, to try to get the Wesorts to join the fight against the British.

"Old Lombroso wants no part of it," Thomas tells them as they tear bites of meat from a rabbit Joseph has roasted on a stick. "He caged you, mutilated you, as I understand, so as to bedevil our friend here." He pats Joseph's back, and Sarai thinks she sees a stolen glance between the two men. It opens a door already set ajar in her mind. Was Joseph complicit with Lombroso in that little folkloric drama in which they had suffered? Was it a play to create both initiation and obligation? She tries to erase the thought from her mind. It does not reflect what she knows of Joseph's nature. And if she says it aloud to her man, the words might taste enough like the bitter fruit of knowledge to drive them from this garden.

"Our friend understands," Thomas continues, his hand still on Joseph's back. "He holds the vision for his people to . . ."

"Return runaway slaves to their masters," she says.

He turns slowly to her. "Be still. Only my regard for my brother lets you sit at this fire to hear our conversation."

Jacob stands. "This is her place. Hers and mine. Accept that or leave now."

Her heart sings.

Thomas grins, nods slightly. She can see the calculations spinning in his eyes, understands he will not allow his anger, his disgust at her presence with his brother, to undermine whatever he is planning with the Wesorts. He has always been that transparent to her; and she still possesses the slave's skill of being able to read the slightest signal, the tick foreshadowing anger, petulance, acceptance, retaliation, in a white man's face. A skill she will keep.

Jacob sits again. Joseph looks at her. "There will be no more slave catching," he says.

"So then we have agreed . . . ," Thomas begins, but Joseph raises his hand, palm out, and Thomas falls silent.

"Why would you join the Americans?" she asks Joseph, and both Thomas and Jacob turn to look at her. At the way she has spoken that word.

Joseph replies, "Sister, we live here."

"And you think they will let you do that, after they have used you?"

"Let us do what?"

"Live."

"They will have no choice."

She laughs.

"'Tis true," Jacob says to her.

She stares at him, feeling the earth shift under her. Shift her away from him, as if those two words he has uttered so wistfully have the power of an incantation.

She says nothing. She picks up a stick and began drawing circles in the dirt.

"I am leaving," Joseph says. "Speak to each other, and think of your words. The two of you will join me later."

"The two of you?" Thomas asks.

"After you have left," Joseph says evenly. He rises, claps the dust from his trousers, and walks away.

Thomas stares after him for a moment, then shrugs. He passes Jacob a flask of Madeira. "So be it," he says. But Sarai can see his anger.

"What would you have of me, brother?" Jacob asks.

"For the British it's a matter of *éclat*," Thomas says, stroking his plastered nose. "*Éclat*," he repeats.

"I heard you, Thomas. Should we have this conversation in French? Sarai understands it, if you mean to keep anything from her. Whatever we speak about, I will relay to her later in any event."

"I care not what your whore hears or understands, brother."

Jacob slaps him across the mouth.

Sarai looks away from them. A school of dancing minnows ripples under the sheened surface of the water. She concentrates on it for a few moments, taking the vision into herself, feeling the dance in her blood.

"This is the second time you have insulted Sarai," Jacob says. "If you call her that again, I will break your teeth. Brother."

Sarai turns to look at the men again. Thomas sits very still. His only movement is the tremble of his hand on the hilt of his sword. She watches that grip, the knuckles whitening. The men stare at each other, eyes locked. Then Thomas sighs. "She is not important. Amuse yourself as you like. I've dallied myself in that manner." He stills his trembling hand, lifts it from the sword hilt, and opens his palm to Jacob. "I am a guest, you say. In this place. What are you doing, in this *place,* brother? What are you doing when your country needs you?"

"This island is my country."

"How marvelous for you."

"I ask you again: what do you want here?"

"You. You are still on the rolls of the 36th."

"Don't be ridiculous."

"Listen, brother. Your country—your true country, Jacob. I know your heart—is in mortal danger."

"It will survive without me."

"Nothing stands between the British and Washington," Thomas says. "If they take it, Ross has promised to burn it to the ground."

"Don't be absurd."

"Listen to me. The British are sending thousands of troops, veteran battalions of the campaign against Napoleon. What regular army we have is still on the Canadian border. We depend as always on the state militias, and you know how bloody casual they are, all those young fops preening once or twice a year, when they can be bothered to muster, in uniforms their mothers and sisters design. And now the Maryland and Virginia militias, thanks to the British, are occupied with their darkies."

He steals a glance at Sarai, as if to gauge the effect of that last sentence. She looks away, gazes again at the water. How has she never noticed its myriad textures and movements? A silver vein of current courses through darker water; a breeze riffles the surface. Thomas's words run with it, as if from a distance, each flowing into the other, devoid of meaning. Ross. Armstrong, Madison, Monroe, Winder. *Éclat,* he says. Van Ness, he says.

"General Van Ness—the banker—now commands the Washington militia. A good man. He is also pressing the president, that miserable dwarf, to take action."

Thomas is speaking the language of another country. Out of place and disturbing in this air, next to this water.

"Towerhill," she hears him say. The name like a slap on her own face.

"Repeat that," Jacob says.

She straightens up, her stick suddenly still, the circles stopped.

"He and his niggers have been formed into a special battalion. They know the land, guide British raiding parties and ambushes, reveal—and destroy—our side's ambushes and counter-offensives. As guides and scouts for us, the Wesorts would be an effective counter-force."

"What do you want from me, Thomas?"

Thomas strokes his nose.

"Lombroso insists his people keep to their tradition of neutrality. It's a policy many of the younger Wesorts, under Joseph, are inclined to oppose, and I am sure they will prevail."

"Then why do you need me?"

"I don't. Not for that."

"Then what?"

He closes his eyes, as if tired of looking at his brother. But then suddenly he seizes his brother by the shoulders. "Don't be a fool. Join with Joseph, as our liaison. I am authorized to grant you a captaincy. It is a way, brother, for you to come back to us. Redemption, Jacob. I'm sure many would be willing to overlook the . . . mistakes you have made." He nods at Sarai.

Jacob flings Thomas's hands from his shoulders.

"Leave now," he says.

"Brother . . ."

"Leave before I forget the meaning of that word."

Thomas reaches out to gingerly touch the nubs of Jacob's two fingers. "Whatever our differences, brother, I know we still share a sense of patriotism, a belief in the hope of this country. I know you will not stand by while that hope may be erased from the earth."

—

"Is that what you want?" she asks Joseph later that day, sitting next to this same fire, next to him and to Jacob. "To have your people join them?"

"My people," he replies bitterly. "Sister, we need to fight on their side to *become* a people. We are nothing now. I pretend we're still Piscataway. But it's only play-acting. All of this." With a swipe of his hands, he sweeps away his dreams. Sarai looks at him, surprised at his admission, surprised at her own sadness. "The Piscataway, those who are left, will not have us," he says. "Nor the whites. Nor the blacks. No, we will not, as you say, *join* the Americans. We will *be* Americans. And once we are that, we can become Wesorts again. We have started building, rebuilding at Zekiah Fort. The clans are coming: the Swanns, the Thompsons, the Harleys, the Proctors, the Queens, the Newmans, the Savoys. Thomas has promised to obtain the deeds, now, if we fight the British. It will be as it was."

He wipes sweat from his eyes and looks earnestly at Jacob, at her. Pleadingly. It is not the kind of look she associates with him.

"There is a tremor in the land around us," he whispers. "I feel it. A surge into some unnamed future that one must be part of, or be left behind."

This is the first time he has put words to this secret nested deep in his heart. She knows this. And she knows he needs them to agree with him. But that is not her task. Not her future. She rises and walks away from the men, walks to the edge of the water. She needs to be away from them. From their certainties. A breeze ripples through the cordgrass. Each stalk is crusted with small snails, passengers swaying in the moving air, little receptacles for the words that come unbidden to her ears from the conversation that continues without her.

"Is this what you want?" she hears Jacob ask Joseph. His question echoes her own, his voice a disembodied whisper.

Joseph says, "The Americans see us as traitors, no matter how often we claim to take no side. And in the end, the British will be gone, and we will still be here."

"And other Wesorts feel as you do?"

"Enough of them do. As I said, your brother has promised us the deeds to Zekiah Fort, to the land around it."

"And you trust him?"

"As you've seen, there are already enough families there, families and young men, over a hundred people. We will be a town. Will you join us?"

"I am with Sarai."

Said as if it were a question.

"She is my sister, Jacob. As you are my brother."

"Yes. But where we see freedom, she sees servitude. I know. I see through her eyes. This is what has occurred within me. A gift, perhaps, of the cage that held us."

"You think it's that easy? Did each day in the cage include enough years to shift your sight?"

Joseph speaking the words that have come into her mind.

"No. I merely see more clearly what I have always seen."

"Then what tempts you to join your brother?"

Speaking the words that she has dreaded to think.

But Jacob does not deny them. He is silent for a moment. Then says: "The nation was created by an imperfect opposition to servitude. We must continue to exist, if that promise is to be made perfect."

We? Sarai thinks.

"You will join me, then. As liaison."

It is not a question.

"Only if she will."

It is a question. To her.

But the look she glimpsed in Jacob's eyes when his brother spoke of fighting the British has driven a spike into her heart. Why does he find the idea of burning Washington absurd? How can he find that idea fantastical yet imagine the life the two of them have chosen and are leading? She knows this man, as the women in the Quarters would say, arsehole to crown. To see the burning of Washington as unthinkable reveals how much he abhors the thought, how his mind flees from it. Tells her, in spite of his protestations, his angry dismissal of his brother, how deeply bound he still is to that world they have left. *We are a country,* he had said. This man who thinks, as Joseph said, that his brief time in a cage and the sharp pain of brutally separated flesh are enough coin to allow him to see through her eyes.

But other things are true also. They have touched each other as if to shape themselves out of the lap of the water around them and the weave of shadow in the trees. They have shared what a country shares. A language that fits only their mouths, is shaped only to their tongues, that reaches past shadow and skin to a center that is elusive and delicate, as smooth and liquid and difficult to grasp as yolk in a wooden bowl. A history built on death and pain. She thinks, we are a country in that way also, aren't we, my love? After Thomas left, before Joseph returned, they had fallen on each other frantically, as if to rebuild and reclaim what Thomas had violated. Ignoring her monthly flow, against the customs of the Wesorts and of their own peoples, the customs of the countries in which they once had lived. But the yearning in his eyes when Thomas had spoken of joining the militia stayed with her as they came together, and at the end she felt a blossom of flame at the place where their bodies locked, their center. And when their bodies had spasmed together, as they always did in this place, she felt he was spewing ashes into her.

Jacob has been exiled from his world, and now his brother and Joseph have shown him a way he can return. For him there will always be a way to return; for her that idea will always be shrouded in dread. He says he understands. But he doesn't, not as she does. Now he looks away from her, at the rippling corrugations of the water, the flower-jeweled marsh, the picketing border of trees on the far horizon. She watches as Joseph follows his gaze, feeling them both, found brother and chosen lover, recede from her, as if to that distance, and she wonders, not for the first time, at the choice she made to go with this man in that close hidden room behind the wall of his bedroom. A dark hole, a withy cage, a sweat lodge. It's as if she needs to emerge from three births in order to see the world with new eyes. But the landscape Jacob saw when the door of the cage opened was different, would forever be different, from the landscape that she saw. For him, there was limitless horizon, a promise that can still be kept; for her the sapling bars are still crisscrossed in front of her eyes, are still standing between her and the shimmering possibilities of that distance.

So she tries now to let herself see the vision he holds sacred in his secret heart: the city she has never seen, only heard described by him and, in a carpenter's detail, by Towerhill. The New Jerusalem for which both of her men yearned: one to build; one to burn. She constructs Jerusalem in her mind's eye from their words: the great capitol with its two wings and its library of thousands of books; the white-washed Georgian mansion that is the president's house; these palatial buildings rising from muddy, rutted lanes and heaps of refuse and dung and pestilent swamps. And then she lets herself envision what her lover has refused to see. Imagines it on the parchment that unrolled in her mind as she held him. Her white lover. Her white-washed lover. She takes the flaming candle from that vision and touches it to the parchment and it bursts into flames—porticoes and columns burning upward; roofs collapsing into dust; thousands of books, none of them holding the names of her people, curling into ash; a fiery mansion, built by their bleeding hands. And her heart rejoices. What does it mean when what horrifies him delights her?

And she thinks of Towerhill, who would light that candle if he could. And allows herself to wonder again if she has come to the right country.

EIGHT

TOWERHILL

A WRAPPED PROMISE

By mid-June they are at anchor on the Potomac side, just inside the mouth of Breton Bay across from Newtowne Neck. Towerhill stands at the railing of the *Phaeton,* trying to peer through the morning mist to the land. He has not slept; last night, whenever he began to drift off, his mind plagued him with strange, fragmented visions, his sixth finger burning and swelling until its nail burst forth into the prong of a claw, curved and black and sharp. Visions of Joseph, his lips drawn back revealing a black tongue, sharpened rows of teeth, blood running from the side of his mouth. Visions of running through the forest, a howl filling his chest as if someone were painfully pumping air into his lungs, then bursting from his lips. Snapping awake, Towerhill cursed Joseph, his wolfish friend. The transformations, Joseph had said, were of spirit, not of physical form, but many believed he was a shape-shifter. A belief Joseph nurtured. Towerhill understood. He had been a shape-shifter all his life.

The strangeness of these visions lay not in their subject but in the horror with which they filled him: this morning should bring him a feeling of accomplishment. In a week, after a feint to burn some plantations to the north, they will raid the county seat, Leonardtown. It is the point where he first met the continent beyond this mist—five years old, but born that day, born and borne over the same water that shifts and swells now under his feet.

The forecastle hatch opens and MacDougal emerges. Towerhill thinks that perhaps this is the morning he will smash the twisted smile off that devilish Scottish face.

But MacDougal, as if sensing his mood, only nods and advances over the deck with a slight, repeated dip of his right shoulder, a slight drag of his right leg, infirmities that, like his cropped ears, are a legacy of his torture at the hands of the Iroquois. Is it in spite of—or because of—those wounds that Towerhill always senses a coiled power about the man, some pent energy that hovers at the border of violence?

"Good morning to you, Digit," MacDougal says.

Towerhill doesn't reply. They stand in silence, both looking towards the shore. As the light, at first only a muted, diffused glow behind the morning haze, strengthens, the weave of the mist starts to pull apart in places, giving them glimpses of the land through those rents.

"'Tis a bonny country," MacDougal says.

MacDougal's gaze, his posture, his words bring the memory of Lieutenant Scott back to Towerhill, that same cast of hungry eyes over the land. He is so tired of these people. "Does it remind you of Scotland?" he says. "Or of the Thames? Or whatever other pissy stream flows through your memory?"

For a moment MacDougal does not answer, only continues to look at the country. Then says softly: "'Tis a wrapped promise, Digit."

Towerhill turns to look at him. The light dimly sketches MacDougal's form and face in the same manner it roughly drafts the land stretched before their vision: the brief radiance of this dawn light allows men to reveal what they hold tight to themselves in harsher illumination.

"You're more intelligent than you want people to think you are, aren't you, MacDougal?" he asks, though it is not really a question.

"Ah, you would know, Digit," MacDougal grins. He reaches up, caresses the stub of his right ear with his nubbed finger. "The one who owned you,

Jacob Hallam, was it? He would have freed all you niggers? So Lieutenant Scott tells me."

For the second time this morning, MacDougal surprises him. "Not in his lifetime," he answers.

MacDougal laughs. "You trust English promises of freedom, do you, Blacky?" His lips are twisted into the strange smile he always presents to Towerhill, triumphant because the world has once again proven he understands its grim ways.

Towerhill does not reply. No, MacDougal, he thinks, I trust in nothing. I view them in the same light they view us. By their value to us.

MacDougal screws his eyes shut, his face still turned to the shore, as if in doing so he can capture what he has seen more clearly in his mind. "My father was a carpenter, like you, Digit. He could lay the foundation of a house, see the whole finished structure in his mind. See the future, as it were. As if he had him a sixth finger." He opens his eyes, waves at the country. "You're right, you know. Place reminds a man of whatever he would be reminded of."

Who is this man Towerhill has known only as a scraping against his nerves, an irritant to his eyes? He says aloud, "What is that for you, Mac-Dougal? A scrap of trees, a meadow, a stream in some cold valley? Or a mother, a father? Do you have a woman some curve of the river calls to your mind? A child? What are you, MacDougal?"

The Scot turns to him, opens his eyes. They are pale, pale blue in this light and glow fierce and incandescent. "I had me all of that, Digit. Just as you ken." He waves at the shoreline. "No mountains here; I've lost them; they're as gone as my woman, my bairns. But I had them. High as God's beard. Round as my woman's breast. Put an ache in you, to look at them. And we Scots had the green, the green of this place, all aglow, soft at the edges at this hour, just as it is here now. We had that. Had British too, Digit. Sassenachs. And vultures circling over the dead meat. And wolves. And niggers. Aye, that's right, Digit. Had us white niggers as well, ye ken?"

"Why did you leave it?" Towerhill asks, though he understands that MacDougal has already answered the question.

MacDougal laughs harshly. "Why, I took the king's shilling. So now I'm the king's nigger, as long as his majesty will have me. Just like you, Digit."

He spins on his toe and heel, soldier-sharp, though there is something self-mocking in the movement, and in the salute he gives Towerhill as he leaves. His words stay, though; not only his last, parting volley, the hints of his lost, lingering past, but the yearning Towerhill heard in his dawn words, the ache of loss, the ache for what the dawn promises, over and over, in spite of the harsh truths of the coming day. The country that reminds them of what they wish to be reminded of. The country that reminds them of what they wish to forget. The wished-for country. Once he, too, had allowed himself to be seduced by it, by the ache in the way men tried to catch the land in their words. Once he had wanted to fight for those words, believing, like a child; certain that the world would form to his own wishes; that the mere act of releasing them into the ether would allow them to worm into and alter the minds of men. A wrapped promise unwrapping. Once he had succeeded in ignoring what he knew to be true by the truth of his own enslaved life. That he now takes the shilling of those who believe a God-given hierarchy is the natural order that governs heaven and earth, that it is from these men that he and his may obtain their freedom, is a source of sour irony. At times like these—rarer and rarer for him—when he contemplates such contradictions, he misses Jacob. He misses their debates. He misses the opportunity to push Jacob's face into the results of his hypocrisy. Into the rotting stink of it, as it emanates from the corpses he now leaves in his wake. And he misses Sarai in the same way. The little girl who hung on his words. The sister who shared the pages of the books in the Hallam study, an unveiling of a world they otherwise could not comprehend, no more than a field slave could, enmeshed in the chains of an enforced ignorance. The lover he had imagined to be flesh of his flesh, heart of his heart. The wrapped promise of her. Again believing what he needed to believe. Again ignoring out of convenience what he knew of human greed and desire. He wishes she could be with him. To watch as he burns to ashes all she believes can be hers.

NINE

JACOB

———

SHAPE-SHIFTING

He was taking them to be born, Joseph had said. Jacob remembers how Towerhill had scoffed at the stories about the Wesorts' ability to transform themselves into wolves, seeing it as a clever ploy to protect themselves from the encroachments of the outside world. "Children's tales to terrify grown men; a stratagem," he'd said to Joseph, who of course merely smiled mysteriously, causing Towerhill to laugh and clap him on the back. Jacob had always thought Towerhill was correct. But in spite of their shared cynicism, he feels a frisson of dread now—or perhaps hope. Hope in the possibility of transformation. Of shedding his skin and stepping out of his history. So, yes, he will name it hope, whatever else it is that drives him to be here as they glide through the dark water, among the trees, in a small cedar dugout.

It is near sunset. He paddles from the bow as Joseph steers from the stern, Sarai between them. None of them speaking. He feels his missing fingers, pain shooting through them as he grips the paddle. Breaths of mist rise from the surface of the silty brown water and cling like webs to the reeds, which stand so motionless they could be brushstrokes on a grey canvas, their colors leaching in the half light. The air is thick and wet and clings to their skins, as if vampirishly drawing out their sweat to replenish itself. They have not been traveling very long, but he does not know where they are. Or perhaps he has been here before, but its features have been transformed into strangeness by the hour, by the purpose of this journey. They weave through a thicket of dead loblolly pines, white as bones, buzzards squatting on their spiked tops in silent audience, the boat moving sluggishly through the miasmic mist of the swamp, heat wavering around them like the dreams of water. In minutes, or hours, or days—his sense of time has fled, and the dying light trembles in his vision—a dark hummock rises in front of them. He looks back at Joseph, who nods, and cleaves the water with his paddle, one, two strokes, and then the feel of the bow scraping along the sand.

A small natural berm ridges up just past the pebbled apron of the beach. They climb over it. The interior of the isle is much like their own; indeed, a twin of it, like one's doubled self in a dream, a quality created perhaps by the opaque light. They walk silently through the same thickets of locust, poplar, and chestnut, the ground scattered with chinquapins, to the same center circle of pin oaks that anchors their own island, the country of Jacob and Sarai.

Where their longhouse would have been, though, is only a sweat lodge. It looks ancient. The one on their island had been hastily constructed: bent saplings and woven reeds covered with blankets, reeds, and sailcloth. The understructure here is the same, but the frame is shelled with tightly woven sheets of reeds and bark, blackened with age and use, and scrawled with red letters, some of them in obscure shapes: broken circles and spirals; the suggestions of animals; some, to his surprise, Hebrew letters and seals of Solomon. He starts to question Joseph, but Joseph puts a finger to his lips. Another dugout, raised on two supports made of lashed, crossed branches, stands near the arched entrance. In it is a line of gourds, their tops cut off, each filled with a different dye: ochre, blue, green.

The three of them remain silent. The overlapping squares of birchbark flap slightly in the breeze; the whole structure creaks and groans, the noise reinforcing an illusion of motion, of expansion and contraction, as if the lodge is breathing. Looking at the dark arch of its opening, Jacob feels a sudden knife of fear. To enter that, to be devoured by that darkness. Does he truly want that wished-for transformation, now that the wish is about to be granted? Does he want to leave the certainty of known pain for the unknown? Joseph nods at them and strips off his deerskin shirt and trousers. Jacob starts to undress, but then, looking at Joseph, hesitates. His two finger stumps begin to ache again, as if in warning. Sarai has already shed her clothing and is looking at him questioningly.

"Why do you hesitate?" Joseph asks. "You enter the sweat lodge in your skin."

"Joseph, what will we be . . . ?"

"That is the question we are here to answer."

"Is there to be any more . . . bloodletting? Any use of oyster shells . . . ?"

Joseph notices where he is staring, and laughs. "Ah. No, don't worry. I would not sacrifice more of what is already scarce enough."

Sarai stares, at first not understanding. And then she does, and smiles. "Not to worry, my love. Nor would I permit it."

"Thank you. Though I would have desired you to raise some objection to Joseph's premise."

"On that you must stand on your own."

As Jacob undresses, Joseph walks over to the dugout. Next to the gourds are three branches, their ends fluttered into fiber. He dips one branch into the green paint and, without hesitation, draws three perfectly straight lines across the top of his chest, then three more on each thigh. With the blue, he paints two circles around his nipples, two more on the sides of his hips. With the ocher paint, still solely by feel, he draws across his forehead a single horizontal line, and then three vertical lines, growing from it, one on each end of the base line and one in the center. He closes his eyes now and chants words Jacob cannot understand but that seem to hover just at the edge of meaning, as if reminding him of something once important to him, something he should remember but can't, something that would explain everything, the way illumination in a dream does, only to flee at the instant of waking. He opens his eyes, and realizes he doesn't remember closing them; sees Sarai opening her eyes as well, her face reflecting the same bafflement he knows marks his own face.

"Sarai next," Joseph says, and repeats the painting process on her. He calls Jacob's name. Jacob stands still, eyes closed, as Joseph applies the paint to his skin. He feels two of the lines covering the scars on his cheek.

They enter the close darkness. Jacob expects Joseph to immediately light a brazier, as is usual. But instead he sits, and when Jacob and Sarai move to take their seats at the compass points of the lodge, as is also the custom, he shakes his head and bids them to sit on either side of him so that their flanks are touching. Jacob now sees that there is no brazier. In its place is a pewter box, the metal tarnished and blackened. Next to it is another gourd, this one filled with water. Joseph dips his fingers into the water, leaves them to rest there. He begins to chant: *"And I will take you from among the nations, and gather you out of all the countries, and will bring you into your own land."* He raises his fingers, wet and dripping, and touches their foreheads.

Jacob sits, waiting. Feeling nothing. The words are familiar, from the Bible, he is certain, though he cannot pin down the verses. Joseph's eyes are closed; he rocks back and forth between them. Sarai's eyes are closed also. Only Jacob's are open, the prosaic poles and inner walls of the lodge looming solidly around him, the shadows growing, reaching towards them. Were those chanted words from the Wesorts' history, or were they invented by Joseph to create their history? How much of what they are doing is playacting?

Joseph says, "Now you may question me."

Jacob spreads his hands helplessly, looks at the stubs of his fingers.

"What are we doing here, Joseph?" Sarai asks.

"You already know the answer to that question."

She flushes. Jacob is suddenly impatient with mysteries and ceremonies and unanswered questions, with this man he has known since they were children, cloaking himself in this enigmatic, aboriginal mystery.

"In Christ's name, Joseph. Do you truly become a wolf?"

His words sound absurd in his own ears.

Joseph laughs. "You said once, or perhaps it was our absent friend Towerhill"—Jacob sees Sarai start, feels his own heart thud in his chest— "that it was a legend we encouraged to instill fear in our enemies and, for that matter, in our friends, so that we would be left alone. You were correct, as far as that goes."

"As far as that goes?"

"We give men what they want to see in us."

"Then it is not real," Sarai says.

We are like children, Jacob thinks, needing to believe in fantastical tales.

"In another way, we give them what they want to see in themselves."

"Joseph, please."

"To be a wolf is to see as a wolf."

Jacob closes his eyes, exasperated.

Joseph begins again to chant. "*And the eyes of them both were opened and they knew they were naked,*" he sings, and the words are tuggingly familiar, evoking hours spent memorizing and reciting Bible verses, but with a slight twist, a difference, in context and in form. "*And the man said, 'I heard Thy voice in the garden and I was afraid because I was naked and I hid myself.'*" Joseph opens the lid of the pewter box and extracts three fibrous green bulbs. "*And in the beginning there was no knowledge of separation, all was the dream and there was no separation between the dream and the garden. So Tawsin who was the father of the Wesort and Nanjemoy who was the mother of the Wesort taught us.*" He turns to Sarai, gently pushes open her lips, and places a bulb in her mouth. "*And in the beginning there was no separation between man and tree, between man and animal, between man and man, between man and woman, and each grew within the other's skin and all were Wesort.*" He sinks his hand, palm up, into the water gourd, cups the water to her mouth, and she drinks. "*This was the dream and this is the dream and we live in the dream and we live for the dream, Wesort.*"

And then he does the same for Jacob. And chants. "*In the beginning was the word. The beast is in the word. All its fierceness. All its love. All its vision. The fierce heart of the wolf. The tender heart of the wolf. Until the word is spoken there is no wolf. When it is spoken, the wolf births into its form. It grows out of the word. It spins itself free from the word. It cannot be caged. It is a wolf.*" He pauses.

"To be a wolf is to see as a wolf," he says again.

Moonlight comes through the smoke hole.

TEN

JOSEPH

⸺

THE MOON COMES INTO US

We light no fire. On this night there is no heat and no smoke and we stare up at the smoke hole in the roof as the moon slowly fills it, at first merely the edge of a silver coin, cutting the blackness, pushing away the darkness, its milky light flowing into and illuminating all the corners and crannies of the lodge. The shadows from the lodge posts and framing poles elongate and crawl along the packed dirt floor, shifting the shapes of objects and transforming them, as if their true *orenda,* their inner spirit, has been released to our vision, its purpose so luminous with clarity it makes my eyes ache. The moon enters us as it enters the lodge. Enters me. Enters us. We each feel it differently. On this night, I feel it in the stirred heaviness of my sex but not only there. A tumescence of the whole body. Flesh and spirit are one.

Pain. The pain of birth, if that act were felt by the child as well as the mother. Multiplied in his flesh. As if the conception and the tumble into flesh all happened at once. But this pain is fleeting, gone almost immediately from memory, as the child must forget his rending passage into the world once he emerges from his mother's body.

Now I feel unutterable delight as I open to the world, my skin bristling, each follicle an appendage touching the world, as if the air itself has become part of my skin and I can feel all the quickening of lives moving in it. It is not distracting, this expansion of myself. No more than the rhythm of my breathing or the involuntary beating of my heart. A deer, a mile away inside the swamp, thrums softly on the edge of my perception as it chews tender stalks of marsh grass; I feel its breath, its heartbeat; the smell of its warm musk tendrils into my nostrils. I look at my companions and feel how they share the sensation. Holding the plants, remembering now when they were first put into my hands. No, not remembering. The ancestors are here. In the smoke. From the smoke. They are as I dreamed they would be. Heads shaven except for warriors' locks on one side, faces painted half-black, with ochre lines and circles on their chests and legs. They tower over me. They look at me with scorn.

I feel unutterable grief. At the loss that will come. It is always there, a pulling weight on the heart, the knowledge that what I have become is finite. As finite as the movement of the moon across the sky to die at the door to morning.

The grief that the man remains.

The moon comes into us. If you could see it enter, I imagine it would look like a flow of phosphorescence in the blood, the way those streaks of luminescent silver we see in the black water of the river thread and pulse, as if the reflection of the full moon is diffusing into the water.

What do you think you are the old ones ask.

You.

They laugh.

Get out of here. This is not your place. Do you think these plants will change your blood? Red nigger. Fish-belly white Indian.

You.

No. They laugh again, stomp their feet, shake a feathered gourd rattle in my face.

Wesort, they say. You sort, they say. Not us. You can't have us.

ELEVEN
TOWERHILL

—

AMERICA FELIX SECUNDUS

He is waiting for Neb, who has become his second-in-command; they are to meet here before the reconnaissance patrol to Leonardtown leaves. The plan now is to meet some of the leaders of the local slaves, garner what information they can from them, encourage an uprising. Neb will not be a part of it. Towerhill considers what he must say to him. Neb is his best fighter, but his savagery has gone too far. There were a number of times when he killed men who had already surrendered and who may have had useful information, other times when he killed noncombatants who simply fell to his attention, when he was long past battle rage. At Coles' Landing, Towerhill had gone into a cabin after he saw Neb emerge, wild-eyed, covered with blood, and found the inhabitants, a husband, wife, and two small girls, with their throats cut. These were not rich slaveowners; the man was a former indentured servant who'd been granted a few acres, a hoe, seeds, and a musket after five years spent laboring in the tobacco fields of the America Felix Secundus plantation. His wife had been a tavern serving wench; the girls looked to be only two and three years old. They were laid out in a neat row inside the cabin, like a statuary group representing Family. Their threadbare shifts were soaked with blood; blood was pooling on the clay floor, soaking into it, so that he could not help but step in it. The three-year-old's eyes were still open, wide with a puzzlement which pierced Towerhill. He knew that Neb had had two small children, a boy and a girl, they and his wife sold separately and sold south by Thomas Hallam, after which Neb had been relocated to Towerhill Separation. He understood what the sight of that intact family circle must have evoked in Neb when he burst through the door of the cabin. But his comprehension didn't serve to answer the question in that child's eyes.

It isn't until the seven members of his shore party are on deck, clad in coarse Osnaburg slave garments and fully armed, that Neb makes an appearance. Towerhill gestures for him to come to the gunwale.

"You'll not be coming."

Neb spits over the side of the ship. "And why's that, Book?"

"Because I order it."

"You overseein', Book? That it?"

Towerhill says nothing, only holds his gaze. MacDougal comes up behind Neb, who senses a presence, glances over his shoulder. He takes in MacDougal, clad in slave clothing, face blackened with charcoal, and grins humorlessly.

"That how it is, Book?"

"You will call me sergeant."

"Yes, *sir*, Sergeant Book. Yes, *sir*."

Towerhill understands there will come a reckoning between the two of them; if it must be now, then so be it. But Neb turns suddenly and walks away.

"You spurn him, Digit," MacDougal says. "But what he has done is exactly what Cockburn wants from you people."

"Let's be going,"

It is early evening but the moon is bright, too bright. The seven in the recon party climb down into a skiff, and Achilles, at the oars, maneuvers them among the dozens of barges being prepared for next week's raid. Towerhill wonders at the accuracy of the word *raid*: the action being planned is longer in preparation and larger than any in which they have so far

engaged. Cockburn will be landing about fifteen hundred troops, including the Colonial Marines, to take the town. Gossip among the marines and
sailors has it that the excursion is a rehearsal for a larger invasion, though it
is uncertain whether the target will be Annapolis, Baltimore, or Washington City itself; whether the goal of the war will be a quick dose of humiliation and punishment to the Americans in retaliation for their atrocities in
Canada, or actual occupation and the return of the country to the British
Empire. Around and behind the barges float the ships of the British fleet,
extending out to the Potomac past Newtowne Neck. Ships of the line with
seventy-four guns, frigates, schooners, bomb ships riding low in the water,
laden with deck-sized mortars, their firepower many times greater than that
he had seen churn Towerhill Separation into flame and dust. More boats
and troops are arriving every day, commanded by Cockburn's superior,
Rear Admiral Sir Alexander Cochrane, sitting in regal splendor aboard the
Tonnant, an eighty-gun warship captured from the French. Cochrane and
Cockburn. *Cock One and Cock Two,* the British sailors and marines have
begun calling them. Picking up the way the Colonial Marines spoke the
admiral's name. Pronounced as the Americans wished, never mind how
the Brits said it, and spoken with a pause and a grin between syllables, the
second sometimes drawn out into a menacing hiss.

Cock *Burrrrn.*

Towerhill takes a deep breath. Most days, he resists any feeling of being
wrapped to the British and their purpose; what he burns, he burns from
his own heart: he will be no white man's match. No white man's cock. But
now, surrounded by the fleet, he allows himself to feel that he is a part of its
massive power: he, Towerhill, sergeant of Colonial Marines, once the slave
of those against whom they are now so greatly arrayed, once as owned and
powerless as any dung-arsed cow mooing in the field.

Cock *Burrrn.*

The shallow-draught troop barges bob gently up and down, their hulls
looming darkly over the skiff as Achilles rows past. Only about three
hundred people live in Leonardtown and the only resistance expected is
from the 36th American Regiment, reportedly mustered there. The 36th.

Thomas Hallam's regiment. Has Jacob survived and joined them, as he almost did at the beginning of the war? Where has Sarai gone? Milly and Daisy told him of their encounter on the day of the uprising, the murder of their men. The image of Jacob and Sarai flits through his head, though mostly he has tried to keep these two people he'd once called brother and sister out of his mind.

The dark water is streaked with phosphorescence. It rises with each dip of the party's muffled oars, glows in their wake. They have left behind any equipment that might rattle or clank; they have bound scabbards and water gourds tightly to their bodies to prevent noise. All of them are Towerhill's best scouts: Achilles, Craney, Mingo, Ned, and Sally. This last choice does not make MacDougal happy. But, again, Towerhill can't say no to her, or think why he should. She is a skilled scout and a better fighter than Lucius—whom he leaves behind. Neither objects. It is true, he thinks: of the two of them, she has taken the man's part.

From Breton Bay, they slip down the channels among reedy hummocks and into Macintosh Run, a narrow creek that snakes through thick marsh and into thicker forest where the dark branches of trees, heavy-leaved in the July heat, overhang and tunnel it. Towerhill has timed their entry with the high tide; otherwise, the run would be too shallow. As it is, their boat scrapes bottom in places, and twice they must portage through the woods when fallen trees bar their way. He is grateful for the obstacles; they are what keep others from using this waterway. Twice he is startled by heavy splashes as beavers roll into the water to avoid the skiff.

He begins to see moonlight filtering through the branches, a sign the woods are thinning out into the farmland around the town. A minute later, he spots a twist of white cloth speared by an overhanging sycamore branch. It has been cut or torn so that six strips dangle down. Six fingers. The sign slaves have been using to mean Towerhill. He taps Achilles, who nods—he has already seen the signal—and digs in with his left oar until the boat bumps against a steep mudbank. Craney stands up in the bow and grabs an overhanging sycamore branch, pulls the skiff closer to shore, hoists himself silently over the lip of the bank, peering into the darkness, listening. When he is satisfied, Towerhill hands him the tie rope and he loops it around the sycamore's trunk so that the bow holds tight to the bank, though the stern continues to drift on the upstream current. When the party members are all ashore, they pull the boat up behind them and conceal it among the foliage as best they can.

They lie belly-down in a circle and wait. Mosquitoes whine in Towerhill's ears, and soon he feels the itch of their bites on his face and hands. He stays perfectly still, and not one of the others stirs. He is proud of their self-control. During training on Blackistone Island, he and MacDougal had made their fighters stand rigidly to attention for hours, ignoring pains and itches and other torments. It was not a hard discipline for former slaves; the only difficulty was training themselves to do it from a condition of freedom. Now they lie perfectly still, their breathing controlled, their Baker rifles trained on the curtain of tree trunks splashed with moonlight.

They do not have to wait long. Towerhill hears a branch snap, a rustle of leaves. He tightens his finger on the trigger. The leaves part directly in front of him. To his relief, it is the person he expected, Jebediah Barnes, a slave from America Felix Secundus plantation, who emerges from the trees. Towerhill peers beyond him into the darkness. He had expected to meet more slaves from that ponderously named place. *America Happy and Blessed.* The main house is located, conveniently for their intelligence, just above the bay, in the town itself, and the Negroes there have been steadily feeding information to the British. Before liberation, Towerhill had once been hired out to work on the restoration of the manor, a handsome, two-storied Georgian dwelling he looks forward now to burning. *America Infelix Maneo.*

Jebediah is a tall, skinny man of about thirty. Towerhill dealt with him before the war, in some of his night trades between plantations, and knows he is intelligent. The man is peering around uncertainly; he cannot see them. Towerhill calls his name softly and rises; the others follow suit. Jebediah smiles, his teeth flashing in the moonlight, and steps forward to grasp Towerhill's shoulders, staring into his face as if he is searching for something, or for someone. Towerhill nods, but again looks past him, into the woods.

"Where are the others?"

"Just me," Jebediah says. "Figure I be enough. Do what we need, say what we say. Too many patrollers out tonight."

Towerhill nods. "Any trouble getting here?"

The other five members of the patrol form a circle around them, weapons pointed out. He, Jebediah, and MacDougal squat down in the center.

"No. But they're twitchy-like. Skittish and delicate round us. Looking sideways. But looking hard."

"They?" MacDougal asks.

"White folk." He grins, touches the black paint on MacDougal's face. "They been hearing about you. The risings, the other plantations. Afraid to get used to cleaning their own arses."

"Let's not waste time here, Digit," MacDougal says.

Jebediah ignores him. "Hearing what they been nightmaring about, all their lives." He grins again.

In the darkness someone—Achilles, Towerhill thinks—sighs loudly. A sound full of satisfaction at what he's just heard.

"That's my king's shilling, MacDougal," Towerhill can't help saying.

"Aye. So let's earn it and be gone. What can you tell us, Blacky?"

"We got weapons hidden, here and there. Enough. Got all the men you need. Soon as you come, we rise." Jebediah closes his eyes. "We rise," he whispers.

"Where are the Yankees?" MacDougal asks. "Where, how many? Come on, lad, speak. Be useful."

"Old Carberry's regiment were here, across Newtowne," Jebediah says. "36th American. But gone now. Saw you all's ships so they gone."

"Say that again, boy." MacDougal is staring at Jebediah.

"Say it all you need. 36th gone. Only militia here. Here and there. Left cartloads of stuff, Carberry did. You come on, take it."

Towerhill feels a stab of disappointment. His dream of coming back to this place was apocalyptic, an advance through thunder and a rain of fire. And if the 36th was here, a long-sought meeting with Thomas Hallam. But Hallam is gone, and, without resistance, Cockburn will not burn the town.

"Well, then," MacDougal says. "We'd best be going now, Digit. Return and share the joyous tidings."

"Go on back, then," Towerhill tells Jebediah. "Get your people ready. We attack in one week."

"We ready, Towerhill. As soon as we hear your name." He holds up both hands: five fingers extended on the left, only the forefinger on the right. Six fingers.

"The legendary Digit," MacDougal snorts, as Jebediah rises and vanishes into the woodland.

Now Towerhill whistles and the others gather to him.

"You heard?"

They nod.

"Then we'll head back. Quiet as shadows, right?"

Sally asks, "Why not stay a little while?" She touches the hilt of the dagger she wears in her belt.

"No," he says, and starts to say more, but hears a shout from the woods, from the direction in which Jebediah vanished. And then another shout. And then laughter.

Sally laughs, too, a strange echo. "Patrollers," she says. "They got that boy."

"Digit," MacDougal whispers, looking at him. "Don't. We must go."

Towerhill ignores the Scot, waves his hand back and forth swiftly, as if he is slapping the air. The others spread into a line, a few feet between each, and move towards the noise, silently and in synchronicity, as if they are the same body. Except for MacDougal, who stands firm, feet planted.

But as they advance, he comes from behind, scurrying to keep up. It is that haste which trips him, and he falls heavily, crashing through the brush, his Baker rifle discharging. Towerhill curses, runs forward, the line sweeping with him. The patrollers—five of them—react more slowly. They are just turning, their mouths gaping in surprise, as the patrol bursts upon them. Slowly but also too quickly, for three patrollers raise their weapons, two muskets and a sword, and Towerhill's people fire. He winces at the noise: silence has become a kind of religion on these reconnaissance missions. But silence is moot now. The three are down, all hit with head shots, but the fourth patroller, a boy in his teens, with long blond hair tied back and a crust of acne on his face, is mounted; without a sound or a glance at his companions he wheels his horse around and gallops off through the trees. The fifth white man is armed only with a whip. Before the shooting he had gathered Jebediah's collar in his fist and is now frozen in that position. Jebediah slowly turns and grips the man's—the boy's, Towerhill can see now—collar with his own hand. So linked, they stand.

The patroller cannot be more than thirteen or fourteen. His face is twitching with a fear that sickens Towerhill. That infuriates him. *What they been nightmaring about, all their lives.* He is that nightmare now, to this callow child. Towerhill drops his musket, snatches the whip from the boy's hands, begins to rain blows on his shoulders and back. All of his cold strength, his years of sawing and fixing and hammering, his life spent clenching back his rage: all of this surges into his hands. The boy tries to run, but can only get as far as the circle of black faces around him, cold-eyed and expressionless, except for Sally, who wears a slight smile on her lips as she fixes her eyes to his. The whip raises dust off his shirt and then cuts through it, slash after slash, red droplets checkering through the cloth until the shredded fabric falls away and reveals his white, white flesh, striped with red. He runs, stumbling, screaming, until finally he collapses at Towerhill's feet, grabbing at his ankles, as if in supplication. Towerhill kicks his head until he releases his grip. He does not stop whipping. He can see the cleaner white of bone glinting through the parted skin; it looks luminescent to him, a blurred glow in the moonlight. He does not stop. Out of the corner of his eye he sees MacDougal gather himself and knows what he thinks of doing. If the Scot steps forward to stop him, Towerhill will kill him.

It is Jebediah who finally reaches out and grabs his wrist. They both stand very still, staring into each other's eyes. The boy is in a heap at his feet. He is a child. Towerhill looks at his own hand, the six fingers gripping the whip handle. How good, he thinks bitterly, that he left Neb behind. He flings the whip into the weeds, turns, and walks away.

When he glances back to look at the others, he sees that MacDougal is gone.

TWELVE

SARAI

—

A VISITOR

"Are you disappointed?" Jacob asks her after they return to their cabin. On their island. In the world. But not back, she thinks. She is unable to look at the objects, at the things around her, and see them as she had seen them before. This is not a blessing or a curse, nor is it a choice, no more than a newborn chooses to enter the hard world beyond the womb. "Is it real," they had asked Joseph, half-mocking, meaning would they sprout fur, fall to all fours, and howl at the moon? She recognizes the absurdity of the question now. A part of her knew the wolf lived only in her mind; another part now knew that did not matter, even if the transformation she experienced last night came only from her hunger for alteration, coaxed out by the bitter excretions of whatever fibrous plant Joseph had placed on her tongue. It is another way she has changed since yesterday. "It was a property of the plants," she says. "I have read of such things. It was not real. But that does not make it untrue."

They are sitting on the deerhide they have spread on the ground. She feels its soft bristle as she runs her hand lightly over it, feels the quick of the life that it had wrapped.

"I know," he says.

"But let's not talk about it."

He nods. She touches his face, feels a surge of grief, a premonition of loss. It is as if a blind woman—not blinded, but a woman who has never seen—has suddenly been given sight and comes to understand what she has lacked in her perception of the world. How that lack had led her to choices that, fully visioned, she would never have made.

She goes to the fire pit. Several coals still glow faintly, though she doesn't remember starting a fire when they returned; it seems to her they had fallen immediately into a deep, dreamless sleep, as if whatever dreams nested in their minds had already been released through the ceremony, their transformation, whatever their experience in the smoke lodge might be called. She blows on the coals, places some dried twigs over them, and kindles a fire before she realizes there is nothing to eat. She glances around helplessly. Jacob is looking at her. "There's nothing to eat," she says.

"I'm ravenous," Jacob says, and they both laugh at that choice of words, their understanding of each other's humor, their mutual hearing of the unspoken *as a wolf* in his remark. The secret, private language that connects them. The wolf grows from the word. It cannot be changed. That is what remains of last night. The connection. We sort of people. She is bound to them now, bound to the yearning of a dream she cannot name, but that Joseph has touched into her mind, as if he has struck her forehead with his palm as she once saw a traveling preacher, a free black, do. Remembering the three of them now, sitting in their expectant, reverent solemnity, bare-arsed and painted, chanting bits and pieces, strings of words that for all she knows grew from Joseph's own needful mind, she suddenly thinks of the Quarters, a warming fire, a Christmas Eve, men and women mumbling drunk on stolen grog, singing nonsensical words to someone's dissonant pluckings on a tortoise-shell banjo, seeing revelation in the leaping flames, seeing it dissipate like thinning smoke in the cold, clear, merciless light of the next slaving day. She is bound to them now and yet a part of her, some other mangy wolf that dwells within, still runs off helter-skelter, furtive, belly touching the earth, through the marsh and forest. Runs towards Towerhill, as she remembers him at the church, eyes blazing with rage and expectation. Towerhill towering. In the fever dream that was last night, she had padded through an endless, sere plain, flat but punctuated with thorn bushes, towards a hillock where Towerhill stood waiting. What did it say to her, that bitter plant sending such a dream to her, when surely her dreams should have gathered towards this man sitting here with her, a smile on his lips at the sight of her, his skin dappled in coins of light? She feels a tightening knot of lust in her loins, as strong as the hunger for food, chooses to ignore it, as if compelled to prove some mastery over herself. As if unsure which image, the dream-memory or the solid, available, loved man across from her, has generated it.

"When you first took me," she says, using that word deliberately, looking around at the reed dwelling that encompasses them now, "when I was fifteen? I remember looking over your head at the books in the study, trying to feel I was inside one, inside a story."

She rakes the coals with a stick. Why had she said that out loud, brought that memory into this space?

"I think we have some dried venison," Jacob says.

—

Later in the morning, as Joseph had requested the day before, they paddle to Zekiah Fort, coming hard upon it before it reveals itself, like another dream emerging from Joseph's mind. More work has been done since last they were here—shacks repaired, children playing in the dusty paths; neat rows of corn patches in clearings at the base of the hill. Joseph is, she sees, taking the *fort* part of the name literally, starting to repair the palisade of sharpened logs around the inner circle of cabins and the longhouses, one of which Joseph has taken as his home and a kind of meeting place. She realizes now how much the place has started to resemble the prints of the old Piscataway villages she saw in the Hallam study.

They look inside the longhouse, but it is empty. She and Jacob sit outside. After a few moments, she sees a strange white man striding purposefully towards them, Joseph a few steps behind him. The white man is clad in coarse slave garb, the tunic torn and ragged and his face streaked with black, as if he has been caught in some stage of racial metamorphosis.

The black, she sees, is from some sweat-streaked paste. Both of his ears are cropped, and his nose is scarred, broken, crooked. A British Baker rifle is slung over his shoulder. Beside her, Jacob stands up, gripping a piece of firewood. The man grins, holds out his hands, palms forward. Several of his fingers are crooked, as if they have been broken, and the small finger on each hand is missing.

"Nay, dinna poke me with your stick, Master Hallam. Most times I meet with our friend here, I dress in mufti, so to speak. 'Twas haste and opportunity brings me to you in these clothes."

"Sergeant MacDougal is a friend," Joseph says.

"Sergeant?"

"Late of his majesty's Colonial Marines," the man says. He flaps one hand to his forehead in a casual salute, then extends it to Jacob, still grinning. "Pleased to make your acquaintance, Master Hallam."

Jacob stares at the hand, keeping his own at his side, refusing the connection the man is trying to make. The brotherhood of the mutilated, Sarai thinks. MacDougal sighs, turns to her. "Ah, the lovely Sarai." Her name rolls off his tongue in a soft burr. "I have heard Towerhill speak of you, me darlin'."

She is speechless. It comes to her that she may still be in the fever dreams of the night before, that this apparition, rank with sweat, may be an envoy from those visions.

"Speak with some deep bitterness, I'm sorry to tell you, lass. Though seeing you here, in glory, to be sure, gives me an understanding of the depth of that well. What a loss to him you must be."

He reaches up as if to stroke her face. Jacob strikes his hand aside before she can move back.

"What the hell is this, Joseph?"

Joseph squats, remains silent, as if waiting. Finally Jacob sits down, and Sarai follows suit. MacDougal stares at them, still grinning, shaking his head as if in wonderment. Finally, he sits also, painfully, his knee joints popping audibly.

"Sergeant MacDougal has been in liaison with your brother, providing information about the British."

"A turncoat," Jacob says.

An envoy, Sarai thinks.

MacDougal looks at him, the grin frozen on his face, a glint of anger in his eyes. "Well, laddy, that's a bit of a two-headed coin coming from a Yankee, in't?"

"Is that what you are, MacDougal—a two-headed coin?"

"Could say. What I do say is you should know a man's history before you open your gab. But tell me something else, laddy. What do you name yourself, hiding here in your little Eden with your dusky Eve, while your countrymen bleed?"

She sees Jacob flush, and her heart sinks. An envoy, she thinks again. Thomas's face floats into her memory. Words birth wolves, Joseph had said last night.

"That's enough," Joseph says. "Jacob has already agreed to join us. He is my brother."

Agreed when? she thinks. She looks to Jacob. He doesn't meet her eyes.

"Aye, and Lombroso is your father. Dinna seem your family loyalties strike too deep."

"I didn't know that," Sarai says.

"Not by blood," Joseph replies. "We all called him that, at one time. Father."

She wonders if she can believe him. Seeing again Lombroso's face through the bars of the cage, behind the table, oyster shells laid neatly along its rough plank. Searching for Joseph in those features.

"His inaction will destroy us," Joseph says.

And what if it is the opposite, my dear brother wolf, she thinks. What if it is your action that will destroy us?

"Listen, laddy," MacDougal says. "We dinna need your chief, your Lombroso, nor the rest of your clan to strike a great blow against the English. All I need are you, Master Wesort, and a few dozen of your men and a swift and secret passage." He makes a whooshing noise, puffing his scarred cheeks. To indicate the swiftness of that passage, she supposes.

"A swift and secret passage where?" Jacob asks, his eyes lit with an interest that stabs her heart. "To do what?"

"*Where* is Leonardtown, from which I just came. *What,* Master Jacob Hallam, is cut off the head of the serpent: Beast Cockburn himself."

THIRTEEN

JACOB

―

WELCOME TO THE MADHOUSE

Sarai stares at MacDougal. And then at him. "You are all insane," she says.

MacDougal laughs. "Welcome to the madhouse."

He wants the Wesorts to get him close enough to shoot Cockburn. He knows the way the British will come, knows Cockburn's custom of staying with the lead elements. Needs only a raiding party of people who know the land to get him into place.

Jacob's eyes stay on Sarai. She sits with her shoulders stiff and hunched, her head down, as if protecting herself from a strong wind. He wants to lay his hand on her bunched muscles, feel the warmth of her skin, feel her relax under his touch. But he knows if he touches her, she will shake him off. He knows what she hasn't said. She is against the plan not because, or not only because, it is insane. She is against what the plan will accomplish—their plunge back into the world. She would have them stay where they are, in their fools' paradise. That phrase opens in his mind in a kind of angry hatching, surprising him; just yesterday, just hours ago, he would have never have described their sojourn here with those words. That noun, yes, but never that adjective. He understands Sarai, knows that since his brother's visit she has been dreading the choice that Thomas and now

MacDougal have brought them. To fight for his people is to fight for those who enslave her and her people; it risks, as well, returning them to the unbalanced life they shared before coming to this place. But he believes, he reassures himself again, that the country for which he will fight offers them a truer chance to become the island of their hearts.

MacDougal picks up a slender stick, smacks it against his palm. For a moment the group remains silent, no sound but the slap of wood against flesh, the constant insect thrum in the marsh—whirr of katydids, buzz of mosquitoes—and an osprey's cry like an exclamation point. The Scot squints at Sarai, the sun in his eyes, and finally speaks.

"They'll come up from Breton Bay, march straight up Washington Street, here." In the sand he draws squares—houses, representing the town—and two parallel lines for the street. "Make a strutting parade out of it. Show their power. They know there won't be resistance; I doubt Cockburn will even put out flankers. Though that man of yours, Towerhill, he's got sense in his wooly pate. He might deploy his blacks, if the English pricks have the sense to listen to him."

"Why do you think you know what Towerhill would do?" Sarai asks angrily. As if, Jacob thinks, only she should own the key to that secret black heart.

"I fought with him, my dear. Trained him some. Learned from him more. He's my brother-in-arms. I don't say those words comically or lightly. My brother-in-arms. And he feels the same about me, I know. What that means? That he will hate me strong. Means he's too damn dangerous. But that's the chance we take. They have flankers, I avoid them." He taps the sand drawing. "Come up through the houses, they're nice and thick here"—he taps again—"and into this one. Hide until the admiral arrives."

"Why that one?"

"It belongs to James Links, one of our agents. More important, 'tis behind the Haslip store. I think I can get Cockburn to make a wee visit to that place."

Sarai shakes her head. "And then we are caught and hung. Why don't we just shoot ourselves here, save ourselves a walk and a choke?"

"We? Who is *we*, lassie?"

"Answer her," Joseph says.

"Ah, the British will be in confusion, losing Cockburn. Confusion and disarray." He rolls the last word out again, as if tasting it. "Dis-a-rraayy."

Sarai turns to look at Jacob. "Towerhill will be there," she says, hurling the name like a spear. "How disarrayed do you think he will be?

"Aye," MacDougal says. "Quite right, milady. He is not likely to become discombobulated; we will not depend on that. Ah, I will miss Digit. I truly will."

"Digit?"

MacDougal holds up his left hand, spreads his fingers, brings the stick up next to it, and for an instant, with his new Wesort eyes, Jacob sees his old friend wiggling those six fingers at him as if laying a curse. Feels his own missing digits.

"Aye, Digit," MacDougal repeats. "If he sees me—sees us—he'll want to chase. But the British will not dedicate too large a force for that."

"After the murder of their commander?" Sarai asks incredulously.

"Even then. They have great plans in motion, lass. They can't let too many men chase ghosts in the marsh."

"What plans?" Jacob asks.

MacDougal shrugs. "The invasion, of course, as your brother must've told you. Though whether 'twill be Baltimore or Washington City, I cannot tell. But listen. And think on it. Think on how we may bleed them a bit." He draws a large rhombus in the sand with the point of the stick, cuts an oval bite out of its bottom. "Leonardtown." He pokes the oval. "Breton Bay. Come down Macintosh Run, to the east." He draws a line to the bay. "Infiltrate, up through the town. After doing the dirty deed, come out this way." He draws a line out from the town. "Thick forest here. We have you and your Wesorts and Thomas's militia here, an ambush force to slow them down." He continues the line. "Here, more militia, with your brother. They keep coming, we'll bleed them fair." He prods the stick once, twice, three times into the earth. "We'll keep striking them, right until we disappear into the forest."

"Towerhill," Sarai says, hurling the name for the second time against Jacob.

"Aye, Towerhill. I know. It's risky. A matter of surprise, of finding and taking opportunity. It may not work. But I think it's worth the gamble, given the stakes."

"Insanity."

He turns to Joseph. "You get me close enough, is all I ask."

"We need more details, MacDougal. How do we get out from the town afterwards?" Jacob asks. He is picturing Leonardtown, the narrow mud-heaped streets, the square at the end of Washington Street, where two black children had been sold into his life.

"We again, is it? Got a mouse in your pocket, laddy?"

"Call me laddy again and I'll knock you on your Scottish arse."

MacDougal laughs. "Ah, *there's* Master Hallam. Good. But here it is: there is no we. I get in close on my own. Get out on my own. 'Tis safer and easier. They will be in shock, for a moment at least. I'll go back the same way, not to Links's, of course, but down this alley, through the woods here. Like I said. You and a squad or two of the others will be here"—he pokes the stick—"and here, shooting a bit, delaying them."

"No," Joseph says. "I'll go with you, into town. In case you miss him."

MacDougal grins, Jacob seeing in it a flash of triump: Joseph's participation will fold the Wesorts fully into the war.

"And I'm going," Jacob says.

MacDougal shrugs.

"And I," Sarai says.

MacDougal's grin widened. "Welcome to the madhouse," he says again.

FOURTEEN

TOWERHILL

A RETURN

The fleet crowds Newtowne Neck, disgorging landing boats laden with marines into Breton Bay. The marines are packed in so tightly they must hold their Baker rifles vertically against their chests. Each boat is a small forest of bayonets. Towerhill stands in the bow of one of them, feeling a light mist of spray against his face, staring ahead. He does not let his eyes go to the woods where he left that flayed child.

"Sit down, man, damn your eyes," Cockburn yells at him. "Jonathan's a fine shooter; I should have no need to tell you that, sergeant."

Their boat is less crowded than most of the others, for the admiral has chosen to come ashore with Towerhill, chosen, in fact, to give the Colonial Marines the honor of leading the attack—Towerhill still cannot bring himself to call this landing of fifteen hundred troops a raid. Some of the white marine officers had grumbled at the order, given as they assembled on the flagship deck just before dawn; he saw Scott, predictably, purse his mouth as if he had eaten something foul.

He will return to Leonardtown with a weapon in his hands and power at his back, wearing the red coat of his country's enemies. Back to the town square where, as a small boy, hastily washed of the effluvia of his dead mother, he was displayed and sold on the auction block. Pried from her dead arms in the hold of the slave ship *Jesus,* pried from the memory of her face and name, from everything of her except the feel of those arms, death-grip tight around him, and the death stink emanating from the body of the woman who had given him life. His own arms wrapped around baby Sarai, pried as well from her own mother as she died in childbirth. Since the uprising, every torch he lit and touched to a house or a field has been a liberation of his heart, and in Leonardtown he will burn the portal of his birth into this country.

Cock *Burn.*

He sits down in the boat, still facing forward. There are no sounds beyond the creak-splash-creak of the oars, the hiss of parting water, the faint squeak and rattle of their equipment. Acting on the intelligence his patrol gathered, as well as the lack of any resisting fire from the shore, Cockburn has spared the town from a cannonade and mortar barrage. As they land, Towerhill tries to capture and hold the image of his armed self ascending onto the point of land, the Leonardtown Wharf, where he first set his bleeding feet on this continent. But the attempt is futile; his consciousness about what he is doing makes his need to enshrine it in his memory seem false, an artifice. There is only the purity of the moment. It is enough. The wind and spray in his face, the water they move over, the wharf, and the white clapboard houses on the hill swelling up behind it.

The rowers ram the bow of the boat up into the fringe of cordgrass along the shore, and the landing party leaps out over the gunwales, Lieutenant Scott first, waving his sword dramatically, although the effect is lost when his feet sink into the mud and he has to sheath his weapon to pull them out, nearly losing a boot along the way. The last members of the party to disembark push the boat out of the cordgrass so the rowers can get it back into the bay and out of the way of the boats coming in behind them. Ten boats with ten marines in each have now come ashore; theirs is first, but only barely. Cockburn, once clear of the mud, draws his sword and poses like a statue in the grass, though his black hat tilts over his eyes and he pushes it straight with the hilt, an un-martial gesture. Neb spits. Each blade of grass under Towerhill's boots looks sharp and distinct from its fellows. Everything around him seems magnified and slowed.

As soon as they clear the shore, they fall into formation. It is not the way they fight, not the way he and MacDougal have trained the black marines, but they have drilled enough to be able to form and move in ranks sharply, and to fight in that insane way if so ordered. As it is, what they are doing now, given the lack of resistance, seems like a parade. A demonstration of power. Though Towerhill still designates two squads, Neb leading one, as flankers, to parallel their march up the street, spot and flush out any ambuscade.

As he and Scott yell commands, he feels the absence of MacDougal from his side. When he reported his desertion to Scott, the lieutenant's face had reddened and he cursed, but otherwise did not seem surprised. Neither was Towerhill. But he missed the man. The black in that white man.

He scans the windows in the nearby houses, hoping someone will take a shot at them. The windows remain shuttered. Closed eyes. Walls like stupid faces. He looks up the street and peers into the alleys between the clapboard houses, many of the spaces occupied by the corn and vegetable gardens the townspeople have been growing because of the scarcity or unreliability of food supplies from the raided plantations and small farms. Their presence, evidence of his marines' effectiveness, raises a small spark of pride in his breast. He hopes to see some of the slaves who have been waiting for the arrival of the British. But the town seems empty, the cornstalks between the buildings swaying like mocking representations of the missing inhabitants.

The troop's first objective is the brick courthouse at the crest of the hill, near the America Felix Secundus manor house. He knows the main street up from the wharf is called Washington, but it is now unmarked save for a scrawled slogan, *Butcher Cockburn!,* painted on the side of a house. Cockburn comes up next to him, looks at the defacement, grins. "Adjective or verb, what do you think, sergeant?"

"Undoubtedly both, sir."

"Undoubtedly." Cockburn looks at the boats behind them, disgorging more marines. "We had best move these men forward."

"Aye, sir." Towerhill spins around to face the front rank. For a second he pauses, taken by the sight of them, standing straight in their red tunics, their smartly plumed leather top hats slightly cocked, narrow side brims worn left side up, right side down, a style the black marines have adopted as their own. Their Baker rifles, bristling with two-foot-long bayonets, are held at identical ninety-degree angles, so from the side they might seem like a single weapon. The company looks as sharp and dangerous as those bayonets. Something swells in him. A short time ago, these fighters had been stooped, shuffling wraiths, shadows of men, their rebellious, free natures expressed only in furtive mutters, the subtle camouflage of song and the equally subtle ways in which they would sabotage their labor, a sharp clandestine mockery of their masters. Now they are wolves. His people.

FIFTEEN

JACOB

___

THE FALSE WORLD

They are dyed and stained black from moccasins to skins, Sarai, smiling in not-so-secret amusement at Jacob's transformation. She wears a man's trousers and shirt. "Wouldn't it be better," he asks, "to wear the customary garments of the townspeople?"

"Aye, if we were mixing with them instead a' sneaking about like the wee, scurryin' shadows a' mice," MacDougal says. He waves at them, brings his nubbed hand back to his own chest, and then flings it out again, encompassing Joseph, Jacob, and Sarai—two scarred and nipped white men, a black woman, and a half-breed Indian, all draped with gunpowder horns, knives, cartridge pouches. MacDougal carries a pistol and his Baker rifle, Joseph the same; Sarai and Jacob have Brown Bess muskets: all British weapons that MacDougal had been stealing for the Wesorts. "Best we keep in mind how odd we be. It'll give us the *aspiration* to stay out of sight." Jacob agrees, thinks of his phrase *customary garments*, the first word describing nothing they had experienced since fleeing the plantation. Since fleeing Towerhill. The double meaning of that name, a joke since their shared childhood, had shifted now into a single looming countenance.

By now, twenty Wesorts are in position near the group's route of retreat, in the thick woods east of town. If MacDougal had expected more, he didn't say so. Nor did he comment on the ragged array of their patched-up garments, and the ancient or makeshift weapons most of them carried: old muskets, bows, tomahawks, spears, crude war clubs.

Thomas Hallam's militia company was to join them there.

Before leaving, Joseph had taken Jacob and Sarai into the sweat lodge, had pressed the bulbous plants on their tongues. *This is my madness, eat of me.* The plants, or the words Joseph chanted, or their own eagerness to be altered, heightened their senses; that was the plan. Jacob can still feel the stir and skim of life in the atmosphere around him, as if the air is an extension of his skin. *Sneaking about like the wee scurrying shadows a' mice.* The sensations are not as powerful as they were the first time; the *orenda* in these plants was not, Joseph said, as strong. But as the mission grew closer, he had been taking more and more of the plant, discarding sweat lodge ceremonials, focusing only on the need to be altered. His eyes, pupils dilated, loomed large in a face that seemed to grow as thin as a blade, as narrow as a stab. He worried Jacob, worries him more now. Looking at Joseph's face, he sees nothing to contradict that impression. For the first time he questions his friend's judgment. Tonight, he thinks, they need to remain anchored in what Joseph calls the false world. False or not, it can kill them. Yet when he had been offered the plant, he took it.

Macintosh Run is narrow and serpentine and shallow, snaking through the thick forest to the north and east of Leonardtown. Too shallow, in places, for the canoe; they must drag it over rocks and fallen trees and branches. Even afloat the canoe claws and scrapes along the branchy bottom. In two places large trees block the run completely, and they must portage through thorny underbrush. Jacob thinks it's good that they will try not retreat this way. Their plan, which seemed so clear and probable to him when they discussed it, now seems slipshod, full of holes, too dependent on luck. And to what end, if they succeed? Cockburn will be dead. Yes, that. If that. There will be that. And it will force the Wesorts to the fight on the American side, and he knows Joseph sees this weave into the bosom of the greater nation as a kind of salvation and legitimization. But Jacob is not as certain. Sarai's doubts nest in his own heart. It is as if, after the sweat lodge, all the myths of their childhood have come into question. Was there truly such a nation as the Wesorts, or did such an entity exist only in Joseph's desire for it? Was there truly an America? He knows two of the men in the ambush party waiting outside Leonardtown, George Swann and Hunter Reed; both are small-hold farmers who would sometimes hire slaves from Towerhill Separation. Did they share Joseph's conception of themselves? Would they want to move their families to the village Joseph dreamt of at Zekiah Fort? The thought of dying, of risking Sarai's life, in a flawed plan for two causes he has come at times to doubt—the Wesorts and his country—leaves him feeling hollow and sick. Yet here he is. Here we are, he thinks. We sort of people. Welcome to the madhouse.

Their route into town is part of the madness, so insane, Jacob tries to believe, that it might work. They knew the British will land from Breton Bay; if their timing is fortunate and if MacDougal's information still holds true a week after his desertion, they will arrive just before the troops fully occupy the town. They will take the run almost to its spillage into the bay, conceal the canoe in the reeds there, and move up the hill parallel to Washington Street to Links's house. Relying on British arrogance to dull British caution.

"But dinna count on any of that," MacDougal had warned. "Well, count on the arrogance. But don't take them for unbloodied fools. Every man a' them and all their officers have spent the past decade fighting old Nappy. They know their trade. As do the Colonials."

As they near Breton Bay, a reed-strained breeze from the land touches Jacob's skin; the scents of silt and salt prickle in his nostrils. He feels skinned, his senses so open he wants to scream, to tuck himself into a ball. Again, he silently curses the plant, Joseph for giving it to them, himself for taking it. They paddle the canoe into the reeds, sink it, and wade through the shallow water. The mud sucks at his moccasins with each step, sawgrass whips into his face, a million mosquitoes whine in his ears. The reeds are sliver blades swaying around him, flashing bursts of light into his eyes, needling his brain. A sudden throbbing pain stabs behind his eyes. He kneads his scalp, sees Sarai stop also, and Joseph, the same stunned look on their faces. Joseph clutches his head, his eyes tightly closed, and begins to rock back and forth in the water, a groan spilling from his lips. Mac-Dougal stares at Jacob, mouth agape, then slaps him hard, turns, wades a few steps ahead. Freezes. Waves at them to get down. They squat, holding their weapons and powder above their heads to keep them out of the water, and then move forward in a crouch, awkwardly frogging through the silty water. A water moccasin flows away from them, and Jacob thinks that would be the shape he would shift into now if he truly had such power and not some alchemical puppetry from a vegetable.

But when he parts the reeds, and can see the bay, he gasps. Suddenly he understands, *knows,* the origin of the pressure inside his skull. The narrow is filled with the dark shapes of ships—lanterns splashing light on decks and hulls, bobbing on top of masts, the breathing of hundreds of men filling his ears, panic gathering in his breast. *"We are in the false world,"* Joseph had preached. *"The world of dreams is the true world and we are the dreams of ourselves."* If that were so, Jacob wishes he could awake and be somewhere else.

He hears a rustle that is not wind off to his right, and then the sound of metal striking against metal, the squeak of leather. MacDougal holds up one hand, but they have already stopped. The Scot slides off into the reeds. After a minute, Jacob hears a sharp cry, a harsh, rasping sound, and his nostrils are suddenly thick with the smell of blood. The three crawl forward until they see MacDougal straddling a log, his eyes glittering, his dirk in his hands. A red-coated corpse floats near him, face up, a second, gaping mouth on the neck under the first mouth. The log he sits on bucks a little and MacDougal plunges his knife into it and withdraws it quickly, plunges and withdraws, three, four, five times, and Jacob can see now it is not a log. The sentries' bayoneted muskets float nearby.

There is a light spatter of rain.

"We best move quickly now, darlings," MacDougal says.

SIXTEEN

TOWERHILL

―――

HEAVY ON THEIR BONES

The strike of their boot heels against the cobblestones echoes from the walls of the houses that line Washington Street. The echo increases the sense of emptiness that emanates from them; Towerhill sees them as if their frameworks were termite-softened and collapsing inward, their paint and whitewash thinned and faded so that the grey-brown of the boards beneath shows through—as if, in his mind, the town were collapsing of its own rot, becoming a memory of itself. Though when he looks again the buildings are sturdy as ever. He sees a shadow flit across an upstairs window, raises his rifle to it, and calls a halt. The suddenness of his command causes the troops behind his company to bump up against his people, a kind of shudder moving through the whole column as its inertia is blocked. Scott, red-faced, runs up to him.

"Why the hell are you halting, sergeant?"

Towerhill waves the barrel of his musket at the windows. "I saw movement up there, sir. I want to send men through the houses as we advance."

Scott stares where Towerhill is pointing, and snorts. "Bloody phantoms, sergeant." He scratches his chin. "But I suppose you are correct. Send out more flankers."

"Aye, sir."

Towerhill tells Achilles and Craney to join Neb and take their squads through the houses, and he keeps his troops in position until they are past the halfway mark towards the town square atop the hill. Now, as they advance up the street, small piles of loot—silverware, china, clothing, an occasional sword, pike, or musket—build up outside the front doors of houses, and the faces he glimpses in the windows now are not fleeting and featureless, but twisted in anger or weeping.

The wharf and now the town square. As if he is marching into his own past. The slave auction platform also stands empty, haunted by the ghost of himself, a naked and shivering child who had just made that same march up from the river, shuffling and coffled; as they move through that place, he can feel again the weight of those cold chains on his neck and ankles, the weight of Sarai in his arms. A tremble goes through the ranks, and he knows he is not the only one feeling that icy press on his skin. He tries again to brand this moment on his mind: what it is to march armed and with armed brethren through this place.

As if called up by the feeling, drops of rain spatter against his neck. He looks into the sky. Clouds have rolled in. He curses silently, sees Neb look up, grimace also. A summer downpour will make any burning they will do difficult, perhaps impossible. The rain falls harder, becomes greasy on his skin, but then, miraculously, sputters out. Still, the sky threatens, pushes an urgency into his steps.

By the time they reach the courthouse, some of the marines have lit torches. Although Cockburn will not let them ignite the town, the brick courthouse and the jail next to it are known to be militia headquarters and will be burned.

They break into the jail; Achilles smashes the iron lock with the axe he had once wielded on Towerhill Separation to chop wood under Caleb Hewitt, and then to chop the overseer himself on the day of the uprising. There have been reports that British prisoners or American traitors are being held here, but the cells are empty. Recently empty: a plate with hardtack is still on the floor of one cell, along with a reeking puddle of piss.

More of the marines have lit torches by now.

As they move in on the courthouse, three women—two white, one black—stand in front of the door, the two whites with their arms folded defiantly. One is middle-aged, the other younger; she glances over at her companion every few seconds as if searching for an example of what attitude to assume. Which is, Towerhill supposes, a posture of brave defiance. It is a good choice, certain to impress Cockburn, and especially Scott, who has come up beside the admiral now. They both like to play the chivalrous enemy, and Towerhill fears that these two white women will give them the chance. They are of a height—the younger one blond, the older perhaps also fair-haired, though gone now to gray. Both wear the crinoline and lace of planters' wives. The black woman, tall and thin, stands behind them; she glares at Towerhill, her eyes filled with hatred.

"Greetings, my ladies," Cockburn says, taking off his plumed hat and waving it across his knees as he bows. "And whom do I have the pleasure of addressing?"

The older woman steps forward. Her lower lip is trembling slightly. She narrows her eyes; their lids are thick and, to Towerhill, appear hooded, reptilian. Apparently he is not the only person who sees the woman in this manner; behind him, in the first rank, he hears Sally gasp. He turns to see her making a sign against the evil eye; she moves protectively in front of Lucius.

"Mrs. Janet Thomson," she says stiffly. "And Mrs. Eliza Key."

"Rear Admiral George Cockburn, at your service." He bows. If they hear the slight twist of mockery in his words, they do not acknowledge it. At the sound of his name, the younger woman, Mrs. Key, looks at him in horror or fear, and backs away, until she is pressed against the wall. Mrs. Thomson turns her serpent's eye on him.

"Permit me to introduce my aide-de-camp, Lieutenant James Scott," Cockburn says.

"Delighted," Scott mutters, removing his hat and bowing also.

Mrs. Thomson turns her eye on Towerhill, sweeps it along the ranks of black soldiers. Her lips curls. "Is it your intention to burn this place?" She has drawn herself up, eyes blazing. The Negro woman lays a hand on her arm.

"Sister," Towerhill says to her, "you may come with us."

Scott glares at him. But before he can speak, the black woman spits at Towerhill. "Be gone, devil," she hisses. Her mistress smiles at her.

"Hush yourself now, Mattie," she says.

He feels a wave of heat behind his eyes. It must show, for the white woman takes a step back, while both Scott and the slave woman take a protective step forward. A strange dance.

"Towerhill," someone calls from the ranks.

As he turns, he sees several Negro men, and one woman, emerge from the shadows to the left of the courthouse. Jebediah. One man is armed with a scythe, and another, a squat, broad-shouldered man, holds an axe.

"We here, Towerhill," Jebediah says unnecessarily.

"Join the others." Towerhill points towards the ranks.

"Yes," Mrs. Thomson says. "Join the other scoundrels." She waves a finger at Jebediah. "I know you, boy."

He smiles broadly at her. "Think so? That right?"

Scott turns on him. "You will shut your damned hole and get in formation. Now." He glares at Towerhill. "Control your men, damn you, sergeant."

Jebediah is staring at him, still grinning, but his mouth twitching. "Something I got to tell you, Towerhill. Something y'all need to know."

Cockburn raises his eyebrows. "Let him speak, sergeant."

Jebediah grins, throws an awkward salute at his forehead.

"Stop playing the fool," Towerhill snaps.

"Yes, sir. Stopping now, sir. Thing is, sir, Haslip's Sundries? Back down to Washington Street? I hear tell the soldiers left it full. Had to clear off too soon, I'm saying."

"Full of what, man?" Cockburn says.

"Why, admiral, sir, full of soldier things. Muskets, balls, all that."

Cockburn smiles. "Hah, Scott, do you see? Do you see the value of what we have cultivated among these people? Where is this store—is that what you said?—where is this Haslip's located?"

"I know the place," Towerhill says.

"Excellent."

Towerhill looks at the courthouse, suddenly afraid Cockburn will order him away, back to Haslip's.

"Sir, should we . . . ?"

"Let us finish here first, sergeant."

"Very good, sir. Fall in now," Towerhill tells Jebediah.

"Into what?" he asks, still staring at Scott. But he moves off, stands next to Sally.

"A fine company," Mrs. Key says, looking at them, her mouth working as if she needs to spit.

"And you condone this vandalism," Mrs. Thomson says to Scott, ignoring Cockburn completely.

But Scott just shrugs. "We are at war, madam. Please cooperate. I will help you any way I can. But please cooperate."

Cockburn snorts. "Burn it now, sergeant," he says.

"Sir . . . ," Scott starts.

"A moment, sir," Mrs. Thomson calls.

He spins around impatiently. "Mrs. Thompson . . ."

"Thomson."

"Mrs. Thomson," he corrects. "And Mrs. Key. Please return to your homes."

"Would you burn a place of God, admiral?"

"I beg your pardon."

Towerhill steps forward. He feels the ranks behind him stir, waiting for his signal. Cockburn raises his hand, and he stops.

Mrs. Thomson steps in front of him, training her cold, hooded eye on him.

"Not only men judge in this place. We use it also for worship. It is our church."

Cockburn laughs. "To the god of George Washington."

"To the almighty God of both British and Americans," Mrs. Key says, her voice high and shrill.

The admiral looks amused. "Please, ladies. Step aside."

"Sir," Scott says again. Cockburn stares at him impatiently. Towerhill stares at the courthouse. It calls for fire. He feels like a flame himself, hungry to pull brick and mortar and board into his essence. "Perhaps, sir, we might act graciously here." Scott turns and looks at Towerhill, and the ranks behind him, starting to surge forward. "Sergeant, you will hold your marines back."

Cockburn closes his eyes, blinks them open, as if just coming awake. Towerhill feels something fall in his heart.

"Ladies," the admiral says, "I pledge you this. We will search the building. If we find nothing subversive inside, I will let it stand."

"You are the subversion here, sir. What you will find inside is the necessary minutiae of our lives. Births and marriages and deaths and deeds."

Towerhill's hand grips the staff of the torch, tightly, more tightly, then opening and closing his fist as if he is strangling his own rage.

It comes to him that the necessary minutiae regarding his own enslaved life must be recorded in this place; the courthouse is the repository for records of all slave sales in this southern part of Maryland.

"If that is all the building contains, it will be preserved," Cockburn says. "You have my word."

The two pull out the sides of their dresses and curtsey. Towerhill sees a bloom of malevolent flowers.

"That is all we ask, admiral. You are more gracious than . . ."

He looks at Mrs. Thomson, a slight smile playing on his lips. "Yes? Than what?"

"Why, than the monster whom I had expected to meet when I heard your name," she says evenly.

He laughs loudly. She and Mrs. Key and the slave woman turn and leave.

"Sir," Towerhill says to Cockburn, "permission to begin the search."

Scott looks at Cockburn sharply. "Sir, may I have permission to use my own men?"

Meaning white marines.

Cockburn's face reddens. "Sergeant Towerhill will conduct the search. How many men do you need, sergeant?"

Scott starts to speak again, but when he looks at the admiral's face, he holds his tongue.

"One squad should do, sir," Towerhill says. He turns to his troops, certain his expression will betray him if he continues to look at these white men. He has forgotten how to wear the mask of the slave. "Sally," he barks, "bring your squad up."

It is dark inside the courthouse. The light from their torches licks up the walls, like a vision of the consummation he wishes for the place. There is a dampness in the plaster covering the brick, a smell of rot and mold that lies thick in his nostrils. As he steps forward, he senses the darkness closing behind him. Their shadows, his shadow, dance on the walls, and for an instant of panic, he feels as if he is being absorbed.

The courtroom takes up most of the bottom floor, rows of benches facing a table, three large throne-like chairs behind it. The squad shuffles among them, looking subdued. Then Josephus, a former slave from Cremona, sits in the center chair, bangs the butt of his musket on the table.

"I the judge," he yells out. "Judgment coming down."

Sally, catching the anger in Towerhill's eyes, turns and barks at him, "Shut your mouth, fool. Get to looking."

There are three anterooms off the courtroom, a desk and books of records in each. He sits at one desk as the others pull books from the shelves, pry open boxes, search in alcoves for places arms might be stashed. Using their skills as people who had once had to hide things in order to keep them. Sally and the others stack books and single documents, not yet bound, before Towerhill. Mrs. Thomson was right. Minutiae. Sales of acreage, pigs, cows, all chattel but slaves. Land-dispute judgments. The record of a trial of two men who had murdered another for his wagon and tools. A fisherman who had killed his nephew by drowning him in his nets.

Marriages and births. He throws them on the floor, grinds his heel against pages, feels them rip like flesh.

"They more downstairs," Sally says. He nods, rises.

"Towerhill, we go with you."

"No. Keep searching here. Find something."

"Find what, Towerhill?"

"Something that will let us burn this place."

The stairs to the basement are narrow. The walls seem to press in on the sides of his head as he descends; the further he goes, the more the pressure. A part of him is drifting, with the tall flicker of his torch flame, the shadows, and for second time this day he thinks of his mother, a woman he remembers not at all, except as the flesh he pressed against in the hold of the ship that bore him here. As the damp walls press on him, he holds the strange sensation of being hulled again in that ship. A cry escapes his lips and he tries to shake the madness out of his head. In a moment he will put the torch to whatever he can burn in this place, burn himself up in its conflagration.

A heavy wooden door stands before him, a sign on it. Records. He flings it open.

The ledgers and records of slave sales are on shelves against the back wall. Each leather-bound ledger is marked by a year. He pulls them down, one year after another, piling them on the floor. He opens each one. Lists of names, ages, dates of sale, prices. He is piling corpses on the floor; they lie jumbled around his feet; he feels them clutch at his ankles, moan. The moan fills the room, echoes back at him. My sisters, my brothers, my fathers, my mothers. He realizes he is muttering those words out loud. The names, the strange African names that open some echo of recognition in him, rise in a cloud from the pages and scrape like nails across the skin of his face. He takes up another book. The leather covers are green, mildewed; they threaten to crumble in his hands. He opens it. The year inscribed on the front page is 1785.

He finds himself and Sarai on the thirty-sixth page.

Boy, five years of age, with mother (dec'd). Accompanied by infant girl, mother also dec'd.

He rips out the page. The boy has no name. Whatever name he was given, was given to him here. He holds the page to his torch. This, at least, he can burn. As it catches, and is quickly consumed, he feels something leave his body. His heart, perhaps. His soul.

Someone calls his name. *Towerhill.* He starts, looks around, his neck suddenly cold and clammy. The sound echoes against the walls, trapped. He looks at the ashes swirling in the air. They form into a trace of letters, come together, call him.

"Towerhill, come on up!"

He shakes his head. The sound has come from above.

As he walks out of the building's large oaken front doors, he thinks of lying to Cockburn, fashioning some tale that will allow then to burn the building. But it is of no use. Cockburn would demand to see the proof. This edifice will stand like a tombstone, heavy on their bones.

When he steps out into the air, he seems to enter a different day: the sky has darkened with clouds. Lightning licks the sky. He sees Jebediah speaking to Cockburn, who is nodding gravely. He walks over to them, stands to attention, salutes.

"Anything, sergeant?"

"I'm afraid not, sir."

"Pity." For a few seconds, the admiral seems at a loss. "Well, let's see if Jonathan has left behind anything of interest elsewhere; give you the chance to burn something, cheer you up, sergeant. Your glum countenance sours my damned appetite." He looks around. "Where the devil is that boy? No matter. You mentioned you knew the location of that store he mentioned?"

"Haslip's, admiral."

"Absurd," Cockburn laughs. "Well, let's take a look.

SEVENTEEN

JACOB

SHADOWS

They work their way up into the town through the alleys behind the houses. Jacob tries to think of the four of them as shadows. The houses are dark, except where the bottom edge of a curtain doesn't quite meet the sill and candlelight flickers between, like the fluttering gleam of a blinking eye. The British are mustering at the bay end of Washington Street, the synchronized tramp of their feet sending tremors through the ground, the shrill cries of their commands broken by the shielding houses in between. Still, at times it seems as if someone is shouting next to his ear, and he winces involuntarily, feels his testicles contract. He strains to pick out Towerhill's voice. The sense of clarity and connection he gained from Joseph's plant has become a curse, a nightmare from which he is unable to wake. But Sarai, next to him, seems calm, peering ahead and then, feeling his eyes on her, turning, reaching to squeeze his arm.

They can't stay parallel to Washington Street all the way to Links's house; in places they have to go around or between houses, at times through small gardens and corn patches or through the thick blueberry bushes that grow wild in uncleared alleyways, right up to the street. Once they have to wade through the mud and shit of a sty. A few buildings—stores, an inn—are close, too close, to the street. Jacob can hear the British vanguard starting to tramp up the hill. He catches a glimpse of the wide cobblestoned street, grass growing in the seams among the stones, and suddenly sees a small group of blacks armed with scythes, axes, and hoes moving in their direction, shouting and singing, waving their tools in the air. He freezes, grabs Sarai's shirt sleeve to hold her back; Joseph and MacDougal also freeze. MacDougal looks at Jacob, nods, points up the street.

As they start forward, they again hear the clomp of boots against cobblestones. Many boots. Too close. Jacob looks off into the darkness to the left, thinking to flee in that direction, when MacDougal grabs his elbow, points to a small patch of corn growing in the garden plot next to the house. The Scot gets down onto his belly and crawls into the corn, the other three following, each heading to a separate row, trying as much as possible not to disturb the stalks. The ground is nubbed and hard-ribbed under Jacob's belly, and his belt buckle and ammunition pouch press into him painfully. When he is almost midway through the patch, he grasps the base of the two stalks nearest to his head to keep them from swaying. The stalks and his own dripping sweat create a wavery green veil before his eyes, though he can still see the street through the row's narrow gap. A few drops of rain fall on his neck; the air is heavy and damp, a boil about to burst. The house fronts on a parallel alleyway behind Washington Street; he can hear the soldiers, the rattle of equipment, their shouts and laughter. He can see their red coats, their black faces against the white of their shirts and wigs: Colonial Marines. The plumed leather top hats on their heads seem identically cocked to an angle, the left side of their brims up and the right side down. The style speaks to a cohesiveness and unity of purpose that sends a chill through him. They carry the same Baker rifles as MacDougal and Joseph do, but with two-foot-long bayonets attached to the barrels. One of the marines turns towards him, and Jacob feels his eyes penetrating through the stalks. His heart jolts. Not from fear but from recognition. Nebuchadnezzar. Neb. He's long been aware that Towerhill has taken his, Jacob's, people—yes, he will still think of them that way—taken them over to the British, but this physical confirmation strikes him like a blow. He remembers, after Thomas had sold Neb's family and sent him over to Towerhill Separation, how the man had tipped his hat, smiling and nodding with the usual obsequiousness, but then, with a seeming deliberateness, staring straight into Jacob's eyes, allowing his slave mask to slip, to reveal his rage and his intelligence, like secrets he felt he could expose with impunity. The act suggested an intimacy, a knowledge of Jacob's ambivalence, that had both touched and troubled him.

Now Neb turns away, is no longer staring in his direction. Jacob sees him grin bleakly and speak to another black—Craney!—and point to the door of the house in front of which they stand. Craney wears the same corporal's stripes on his sleeves as Neb does. The other marines stand in a semicircle, waiting, some with their muskets trained on the curtained upstairs windows. Craney nods, smashes the butt of his musket against the door, and then kicks it repeatedly until it falls off its hinges, the movement so practiced it speaks to experience, repetition. The marines pour into the house, their howls mixing with high-pitched screams from the inhabitants. He hears a shot, and then another. Laughter. A window upstairs is smashed, shards of glass flying out, glittering, into the street. In a few minutes Neb and Craney come out, followed by another corporal—Jacob recognizes Mingo now, another face emerging from mists of memory into a transformation more deadly than the lycanthrope metamorphosis he had dreamed for himself. Mingo grips the elbows of two terrified teenage girls dressed in their night shifts, hustles them out into the street. One falls to her knees, weeping. Another black marine—Jacob does not recognize him—drags out a portly, red-faced man, his mouth working as if he is chewing something frantically, a trickle of blood dripping from the corner of his lips. Other marines follow, some carrying candlesticks, a chest, pewter mugs; they pile them neatly in the street. The portly white man says something, raises his hands, and without a word Neb slams his musket butt into his jaw; Jacob can hear the crack of the bone from where he is lying. The man drops like a sack of rocks. The girls are silent for a shocked second and then begin to scream hysterically. Mingo, shaking his head, says something sharply to Neb, who just grins at him.

The marines move up the street, leaving the girls kneeling over the man Jacob assumes is their father.

MacDougal has crawled up next to him, whispers in his ear. "Come on, laddy, need to move now."

Jacob works his way backwards out of the corn patch, waits until Sarai is out also. She turns to him, but he looks away, unable to meet her eyes. He is unsure why. When he looks again, he catches the twitch of pain moving across her face, and then it is she who refuses to meet his gaze.

They continue up the street parallel to Washington, and then loop around the court house, turn into an alley, and out again. The rear door of a house opens a crack and then wider; a tall, bald, saturnine man in a vest—Links, Jacob presumes—staring out. He frantically motions them inside. The house is dark, illuminated only by the daylight leaking around and between a curtained window. Jacob stumbles over an item of furniture, its sharp edge hitting his thigh. Links lights a candle. The effect is conspiratorial, theatrical. He feels a sharp need in himself to fold everything that is happening into the safety of the ridiculous. It is not working. He thinks of Neb's face, contorted with hate and glee. But the name that comes to him is Towerhill. He feels his presence everywhere. Sarai is staring at him. He meets her eyes this time, tries to smile. Her face flickers in and out of his vision in the candlelight. He is unable to tell if she smiles back.

"What are we doing?" Joseph asks MacDougal.

But it is Links who answers. "You need to leave here. Quickly. You saw what happened to the Jacksons."

"Dinna fret yourself, man," MacDougal says. His brogue, Jacob notices, has seemed to grow thicker, MacDougal playing at being MacDougal. "Blow out that flame, and we'll wait. 'Twill all be well, Master Links. You'll be here to bore your bairns with legends of your heroism."

Links doesn't move. MacDougal sighs, leans over, blows out the flame.

In the murky grey light, Jacob tries to move closer to Sarai. His leg, the other thigh this time, runs into the sharp edge of the table, and he stumbles on something else—a stool?—as he moves. In his mind he hears the name *Towerhill* again, in Sarai's voice, as if she is whispering into his ear, as if she is flinging it at him like a weapon. He is too far from her for the whisper to be real. But he freezes in place.

They wait like that, connected only by the sound of their own breathing. The silence around them like a wall. At times he can hear shouts from outside breaking it, the occasional report of a musket. Once a woman screaming. After what might have been five minutes or five hours, time fluid as water for him, there is a soft knock on the door. A very polite British soldier or the person they have been waiting for. Links opens the door. The man comes in.

Links lights the candle again. A glimpse of a black face. MacDougal quickly pinches the flame out.

"No need," he says. Then: "Good to see you again, Jebediah."

"You got it?"

"You tell them?"

"All done. They coming and they coming quick and mad. Best get to doing whatever you want to be doing. I'm gone, hear? Give me what you promise."

Jacob hears clinking as MacDougal hands something to the black man.

"How I know it's all here?"

"Shove it up your black arse, coin by coin."

"I gone."

"One minute."

"No minute."

"Nay," MacDougal says, "just one," and Jacob hears a soft thud, a gasp, something bang against the table. Sees the short struggle as a dance of shadows. The word "you" in a whisper, a whimper. A thump. The sharp, acrid smell of shit.

"They fuck," Links says. "In my house, MacDougal?"

"Help get the purse out his hand. Fucker gripped it like a proper Scotsman."

"I'm going to scream," Sarai says, the strange calmness of her voice contesting her words.

"Then you kill us all, lass. Man who can be bought and paid for can't be trusted not to sell us as well."

"You've killed me too, you son of a bitch," Links says. "They'll find the body here . . ."

"Nay, we'll lug the bugger out with us; they'll figure we done it. Figure right, too. You'll be gone, Links. Or stay and die, if you want. Only stop pissing my time away, you whiny sod."

"Come on, then," Links says. "And damn you to hell."

He leads them—with MacDougal dragging Jebediah's body—to a door in the back of the room, opens it to a gap between the rear of his house and the rear of the two-story clapboard building facing Washington Street. The store. Jacob can't remember the name of the owner. Knows it isn't Links. Remembers MacDougal replying "bait" when they had asked him what was inside. What they all are now. The situation, what they will do, still doesn't feel quite real to him. It is as if he is watching himself from some-where outside his own mind, a bemused spectator of a play whose premises are too melodramatic to draw him inside its world.

"That will be just fine," MacDougal whispers to Links. He is breath-ing heavily. There is another patch of corn between the store and the next building. MacDougal releases Jebediah's collar, lets the body fall. "On your bellies, children. And goodbye to you, Master Links, unless you would like to join our little party."

But Links is gone already.

EIGHTEEN

TOWERHILL

—

ALI BABA'S CAVE

Haslip's Sundries is on the bottom floor of a two-story building a short distance past the courthouse, next to another alleyway thick with corn. Its one window and door are boarded up. The marines rip the boards off, and Towerhill sees Cockburn grin, his face suddenly alight. "Open sesame, James; it seems we have found Ali Baba's cave." The walls are lined with barrels, dozens of them. They pry the lids off. Balls, gunpowder, rifles, bayonets, all left intact and all left quickly, as Carrington withdrew the 36th American from the town. There are two bedrolls, inscribed with names: Captain Forrest, Captain Millard. Perhaps they had been billeted in this room.

Scott comes up next to Towerhill, suddenly friendly, claps him on the back. Towerhill stands near the door with a logbook, tallying as the working party goes through the tedious process of emptying the building of supplies—he counts a hundred barrels. After they are loaded onto wagons confiscated from the nearby livery, he strikes a spark onto his torch and, as soon as it flames, tosses into the front door, before Scott has a chance to be chivalrous again. Cockburn stands next to him, looking pleased with himself. Soon his face is lit in the flickering light of the fire. Towerhill's own face stays stiff and dark. He tries to see these flames as tindered by the paper he burned in the courthouse. But this tiny conflagration is not enough; it is too small to join with and feed the flame in his heart. Cockburn laughs, the sound drawing Towerhill's eye to him. At the same instant, he sees one of the cornstalks move slightly. Move in this windless day. There is a flash of lightning and the crash of thunder. Cockburn's laugh ends in a sharp, loud bark. Without thinking, Towerhill shoves him to the side, bringing his body in front of the admiral's. At the same instant, he sees the flash, sees a quick tongue of fire lick out from the corn patch between the buildings. Something slaps his leg, at the thigh, and spins him around: Cockburn's indignant face, the building, the shadows beyond from where the flash came, a figure in those shadows. He fights against falling, trying to ignore the pain, which grows from that first blow against his leg to a red-hot sear he feels to his marrow, as if the fire he desired has come into him. There is another loud bang, and from the corner of his eye he sees the top of someone's head explode. He can't see who. He runs towards the shadows behind the building, raising his rifle. He hears another shot, feels the air disturbed as a ball zips over his head. A disembodied head forms out of the darkness, the mouth grinning at him, the head shaking, as if disappointed in him. A body forms under the head, the whole apparition rising from the corn like an alien plant. The shooter's rifle—a Baker like his own—is on the ground, but his hand holds a pistol, the barrel trained on Towerhill.

"MacDougal," he screams, raising his weapon, his leg buckling.

He sees the mouth form the word "Digit" as the Scot fires, feels the ball sear his side, the blow knocking him sideways as he drops his rifle. Feels himself draining away, as if he were water falling from a broken vessel.

As he falls he hears his men rushing up behind him, hears Cockburn screaming at them, sees again his face, and then as the darkness begins to claim him, glimpses three other faces form and then fade from the stalks of corn next to MacDougal, all three half-lit by flames from the burning building. Joseph. Jacob. And Sarai.

The rain begins falling, hard now.

NINETEEN

JACOB

A REUNION

They crawl forward through the corn until they have a clear line of sight onto Washington Street, and then lie parallel to one another, one in each row. Jacob hears shouts again, from up the street. He is lying in a patch of corn planning to kill an ogre, as if he has been enveloped in a game from his childhood. It is all comically, cosmically ridiculous. He feels a giggle bubbling behind his lips, clamps it in. A part of him understands that he is attempting to retreat into the comfort of absurdity. With that thought something clicks in his head, and everything becomes very real. He is here, the musket he aims at the street heavy and cold and solid. A leaf from the stalk caresses his face, raises an itch. The prosaic touch of it is real. The smell of blood and shit is still in his nostrils. What had the man's name been? Jebediah. The sound of boots hitting cobblestones in unison from up the street. Louder. Louder. Sarai, lying in the next row. The row of cornstalks between them, the silence between them plaited into those plants. Towerhill is coming. Jacob places his left hand, palm down, on the earth and rests the front of the Brown Bess's barrel on it, its weight pushing his hand down into the dirt. To his left, he sees that MacDougal has pushed up a little parapet of soil to help support his weapon. He follows suit. Towerhill, he thinks again. He thinks of their island, the miles between that place and Sarai and himself seeming more the measure of years than of distance. He wishes to be there. He wills them to be there. Towerhill stands between it and them. The sharp retort of the boots are loud, and he can hear their voices now, see the first redcoats approach the building, muskets and bayonets pointed at it. He can't see the entrance. Hears the crash of musket butts against the door, the words "Ali Baba" in an excited, high-pitched voice.

The street blurs. He wipes sweat from his eyes. And there is Cockburn, the living man emerging as if from the satirical broadside that MacDougal had shown them: the wanted posters the militia had posted on buildings and trees throughout the county. Only staring at him for a second, the second it takes until Towerhill appears next to him. A wave of hatred so strong it seems to shift him out of his own skull flashes through him. He trains the barrel of his musket on Towerhill, the weapon brushing against the cornstalk next to it. Towerhill glances up, seems to be staring directly at him. The admiral throws back his head and laughs. A flash of lightning. The crack of thunder. Towerhill shoves Cockburn to the side. MacDougal fires. The sequence is jumbled. A swath of red opens on Towerhill's thigh as if splashed on by a paintbrush. The blow spins him around. Everything slows. Another British officer is shoving Cockburn back. Joseph fires. The officer's head explodes. Jacob sees Towerhill flinch, as if slapped. He is aware of his finger on the trigger. He has not moved. Towerhill is rushing towards them. He rises, as does MacDougal, and now Sarai and Joseph also, growing from the corn. Everything in him is focused on Towerhill. On killing Towerhill. Towerhill screams MacDougal's name. No, Jacob thinks. Me, Towerhill, look at me. He pulls the trigger. At the same instant, Sarai reaches across and slaps up the barrel of his musket. He hears MacDougal's pistol fire.

The rain comes down, hard.

PART THREE

THE NEED FOR FIRE

JUNE–JULY
— 1814 —

ONE

SARAI

―

CULLODEN RUN

They lay under that rain in the bushes and between the trees along the banks of Bledsoe's Run. "Culloden Run," MacDougal says, chuckling at whatever meaning to himself the joke has. She does not care to know. She hates his madness, hates that she allowed herself to be seduced by it. Hates herself, as if she'd shot into her own heart the shock and disgust she saw in Jacob's eyes when she diverted his weapon. Though she would do it again. To lose both him and Towerhill would be unbearable. She had not thought so clearly of her action at the time. She had not thought at all. She had simply known that if Jacob's musket ball had penetrated Towerhill's heart it would have slain both him and her love for the man who had fired it. How could she tell him that? That she had been certain they would die in the corn patch, could not abide that murder as the last act of their lives together She had seen Towerhill, for the first time since they had left the plantation, standing fierce and free, and she could not bear to see him, what he had become, what they had once both dreamed of being, slain by the man she had chosen to take the place of that dream. It would have been the murder of a hope that had once driven her, that still pulled at her heart. She had abandoned it, had replaced it with Jacob. With a different kind of hope. "We are a country," he had said. Well, that was lovely. But to enter the blurry border of that unformed land had meant leaving too much of herself behind.

She would leave. She had left already, the instant her hand had shot out, as if by its own volition, to strike aside the musket barrel. She understood that now. Not to Towerhill. Not to anyone, but away from the mistake she had made. She would leave this man she loved, this man who had fought for what could never be hers. Who wanted so fiercely to believe they shared what a country shared, language and memory and death and love that the world could be shaped to such vision. But no, they were not a country.

In the corn patch, she had lain near Jacob, as close to him as she could, knit to him by the certainty that they would die. She is next to him now, here, still held by the same certainty. But he has not said a word to her since their mad scramble out of Leonardtown. Out of the madness of Leonardtown. MacDougal had been correct about that at least. "Nay," he'd said while they were planning the assassination, "they'll not all come running at us, all arse over teakettle. Too damned disciplined, that'll be their weakness. They'll get themselves into formation first, officers shouting orders, yelling 'damn your eyes' and some such, before they come marching after us." All true. In the sudden driving rain and confusion they had been able to slip into the maze of back streets and then the surrounding forest as the British and the Colonial Marines shot up the houses and shredded the corn patch. Links, still eyeing MacDougal balefully, had led them to a finger of forest before disappearing himself. They had come perhaps another five miles at the run, led by Joseph. The twenty Wesorts, joined by Thomas's militia company, another forty men, were waiting at the rendezvous point. Thomas solemnly shook hands with Joseph, but then wagged his head in disgust and disappointment when they reported that as far as they knew Cockburn had survived. Now they lay, the four of them and the Wesorts, along the run, its water rising, the militia lined perpendicular to them, hidden among the trees on the other side. They wait to die, she thinks. Wait for Towerhill. Playing soldiers in the woods as they had as children. She, the youngest, the only girl, always made to be the redcoat. Or an

Indian. Until now Thomas Hallam had never joined those games. And today Towerhill would play the redcoat.

Sodden gnats circle in front of her eyes and a drop of rain runs down her nose, rivulets flowing under her collar, soaking her back. The branches and leaves of the oak tree that canopies the run have grown heavy with the rain, and droop dangerously over them. The bank here is thick with dripping ferns and the run flows clear between mossy rocks and over white pebbles, its surface frothed by the rain. It is a beautiful place to die, she thinks. The rain creates a kind of intimacy; the harder it falls, the more she can live in the illusion of being cut off from the flow of time. The Colonial Marines, what her former brethren call themselves, will have picked up their trail by now. We should keep running, Joseph had said. But MacDougal insists that they wait here. Perfect position for an ambuscade, he says. And they obey. It is something else she has learned. A new raindrop of wisdom. Men will obey the maddest among them. Towerhill will come, MacDougal assures them, but they and the Wesorts, their woodcraft as good or better than those chasing them, will kill some marines, move back into the forest, keep picking them off as they come. Keep killing her brethren. Until their brethren kill them. She is certain that MacDougal plans to die. Their failure to kill Cockburn has sucked something out of him. Has affected the rest of them. They, she, feel like the shadows they had striven to become. Like segments of MacDougal's mad dreams, even madder now, the Scot muttering to himself, giggling at some dialogue playing out in his brain. And Jacob, hollowed by failure and fatigue and disappointment and her betrayal, seems content to follow the direction of his madness. To drift dreamily into the peace of death. No. It is not the way she wishes to leave him.

She leans over and grabs him by the shoulder. Shakes him.

"We should go."

He stares at her as if she is the one who is mad. Joseph has turned and is staring also. MacDougal has laid his face against the barrel of his Baker rifle. He turns it towards her now and then back to the rifle. "'We must go,' says her ladyship," he croons to the barrel. "We must go, o'er the mountain and through the bonny glens."

Jacob still hasn't said anything, but Joseph nods to her.

"Yes. You and Jacob should go. Disappear." He smiles. "You may know a place. It may be waiting for you."

"Aye," MacDougal says. "There 'tis. He's right, our Wesort friend. We sort, you see, don't need you. You should go. You should disappear into the sweet, soft mists of sweet soft love. Be gone. All gone. Run along now, my little sere lassie. Get to your sweet swiving in the glen." He giggles again, sings. "Oh, the sweet swiving in the glen, the sweet, sweet swiving in the glen."

Jacob is staring at him. "Shut your foul mouth, MacDougal," he says.

"Ah, MacDougal's foul mouth," MacDougal says.

He reaches over and pulls the bayonet from its scabbard on his belt, fixes it quickly to the rifle, kisses it. Places the tip of the blade against Sarai's throat.

"Desertion 'tis a terrible crime, you ken? A terrible, terrible crime for a soldier who's taken the king's shilling." He giggles again. The sound is so incongruous coming from this bloody man that it chills her blood. He brings his face close to hers, the gnats circling madly between them, the rain beating on her head.

Both Jacob and Joseph have risen, their weapons trained on MacDougal. "Bit of a dilemma, in't?" MacDougal says, and presses the point a little harder. "Perhaps m' ladyship may wish to slap up my barrel? Real quick-like." She is afraid to breath. She can see Jacob's finger tighten on the trigger, his knuckles white.

MacDougal grins madly at him, withdraws the bayonet. "Not to worry, laddy. I'm just playing with you a tad. You and the lady wish to run, please do. I'd dinna want anyone here who dinna wish to be here. I like to choose my company, times like these. That's the lovely thing about hell, lassie. You get to choose your company there."

"We're not going anywhere," Jacob says. She looks at him. At her lover who did not know she had already left.

"We're not going anywhere," she repeats.

MacDougal laughs. Madly.

They wait in the rain until first light, Bledsoe's Run swelling and slowly rising towards them. She raises her face to the rain, catching the drops that roll off the leaves on her tongue. After a time, she goes off to piss behind some blueberry bushes, ready to ignore MacDougal if he tries to stop her. But he only turns his head as she rises, a grin still pasted on his face. The rain spatters on the leaves around her, echoing the spatter from her body. Her bladder always feels full these days. Inspired by the rain. She returns to her position, her indent in the earth already puddled. The effects of the plant have worn off. In spite of the wetness and the danger, the day and night have been too long and too full and she feels waves of fatigue roll through her, pressing on her brain, as if it, too, is growing heavy and sodden, gauging itself by the rise of the creek. She fights her weariness, fights to keep her wavering musket trained on a thinning of the trees that marks the faint trail they followed and along which the British might come. Or Towerhill, his face staring at her from the shadows between the trees. They have held here too long. She knows it; she knows the others must know it; but the waiting has become a kind of faith in which they no longer believe but are afraid to leave behind. She feels a wave of nausea, her stomach clenching as if a fist is gripping her from the inside. The rain whispers through the canopy of leaves over her head. Drips coldly on the back of her neck. She imagines the droplets gathering in the cups of oak leaves until their heaviness pushes the edges of the leaves down and lets them overflow, drip onto her. Her mind floating to that picture. Brushing over the veins of those leaves, their wet shine, as if she can trace their delicate net with her fingers. She stops fighting sleep; there is too much relief in the thought of letting go of the clenching tension she has felt in her heart since they began their insane mission. She sees Towerhill's face, his skin wet with the same rain that touches her skin now, his eyes boring into hers. Knows if this man next to her raises his musket to shoot Towerhill down she will again push the barrel of that weapon aside, stand in front of its fire, and let the ball burst her heart. She tips into the edge of sleep, surrendering, letting it take her. Her eyes fall on a sodden clump of leaves, drifting down the run as if matching the drift of her mind. She sees herself and Jacob and Towerhill floating down the Wicomico on the cusp of everything. She needs suddenly, fiercely, to piss again. The leaves catch on an outcrop of rocks, hold for an instant, feathering out, and her mind catches and holds also, something nagging at her, and then she is wide awake with knowing. Knowing as surely as if she can feel Auntie Rebekkah's hard hand pressing on her belly—*you is truly fucked, girl*—what weight has been pushing so insistently against her bladder. Knowing where Towerhill will go. Two things impossibly in the world together.

TWO

TOWERHILL

—

BOATS

He leans against Craney as they enter the house behind Haslip's. Candles have been lit on the shelves and in the sconces and Dr. Sandman, the battalion surgeon, is already there, as is Cockburn, staring at Towerhill with a strange kind of puzzlement, as if the wounded man is a battle for which he needs to calculate a strategy. Sandman sweeps dishes and pewter pots from a table in the center of the room. "Get him on there, man. Quickly." Towerhill shrugs off Craney and lies down, feels Sandman cut through his powder-burned trousers and shirt, feels him bandage his leg and side, Craney helping him. The faces in the corn patch come to him, wavering in the air. He hears the rain beating incessantly against the roof. Cockburn paces back and forth nervously as the doctor works, occasionally jerking his face towards Towerhill, then looking quickly away, as if in shame.

"Damn your silence, Sandman," he finally explodes. "How is the man?"

Sandman looks up from his work. "Flesh wounds, sir. He'll be fine, so long as there's no corruption."

"Good, good," Cockburn mutters angrily. Towerhill understands his mood; the admiral is not so much annoyed by the attempt on his life as he is at being indebted to the man who saved it. Towerhill looks down at the floor. His soldiers had carried Jebediah's mud-crusted corpse inside; it lies close to the legs of the table. As Sandman finishes his bandaging, Towerhill gazes down at the corpse. It models the fate he would have met if MacDougal had shot an inch to his left. The corpse is open-mouthed, open-eyed, staring at Towerhill with an expression of astonishment that probably would have been his own death mask as well. He has seen it before, vows to configure his own face in anything but that mask of foolish surprise, if he has time before he goes. Though he has watched enough men die to realize he surely will not.

"I assure you, he'll be avenged," Cockburn says, pointing at Jebediah. "We'll catch the Yankee bastards."

"This house should be burned," Towerhill says. His first words since screaming MacDougal's name. Since seeing Joseph, Jacob, and Sarai, three strange stalks growing as well from that patch of corn.

Cockburn nods, his mouth set in a grim line. Towerhill sees the twin fires of candlelight reflected in the admiral's eyes, like some poetic mimic of his own wishes.

"It should be burned," he repeats. "The town should be burned."

"Yes," Cockburn says. "As you say, this house. As an example." The admiral gestures at the ceiling. "But as for the town, the rain . . ."

"It will burn," Towerhill insists.

"Of course, man, of course. But your orders now are to recover."

The door swings open and a white soldier Towerhill does not recognize enters, along with a gust of rain. A lieutenant. His uniform and boots are caked with mud and there is a smear of it on his cheek. The officer closes the door, salutes Cockburn, stands at uneasy attention.

"Report, damn you," Cockburn snarls.

"We didn't apprehend them, sir. They fell back too quickly."

"More than a thousand men in this shite-heap of a town, lieutenant, and they cannot *apprehend* the sneaking little cowards who tried to assassinate your commander?" He sweeps his arm angrily towards Towerhill. "And the good sergeant who saved me?"

"My apologies, sir. It appears they are no longer in this shite-heap."

"Are you mocking me, lieutenant?" Then, as if naming the rank reminds him of something: "Where in blazes is Scott?"

"Searching, sir. They moved very quickly. We traced them to the forest east of town; my men are following, with help from the sergeant's, ah, marines, who know the area. With your permission, I will rejoin them."

Towerhill sits up, swings himself off the table, his bare feet inadvertently kicking Jebediah's corpse. "Call them back," he says.

The lieutenant turns to stare at him. "I beg your pardon, sergeant. I am speaking to the admiral. And I am not accustomed to taking orders from . . ." His hand goes up to touch the mud smear on his cheek, as if it contains the word for which he is searching, but he catches Cockburn's furious gaze, and sputters into silence.

Towerhill ignores him. "Get me some damned clothes," he says to Craney.

"Orders from whom, Lieutenant Merriman?" Cockburn asks coldly. "From the man who saved my life? Perhaps I should change what you are accustomed to. Perhaps the wrong man here carries the king's commission."

Merriman is sweating, his skin pale under the smear. "Sir, I meant no . . ."

"Shut your damn hole."

"Let me take my company," Towerhill interrupts, indifferent to both Merriman's insults and Cockburn's outrage. Seeing only the four faces growing from the corn patch. He nods at the lieutenant. "If this fool goes after them, he will just be ambushed. I know where they will go."

And where they will not go, he thinks.

Merriman reddens. "Sir . . ."

Cockburn is shaking his head. "Towerhill, I'm grateful to you. But this is not the time. I need you and your men for . . . well, for what will face us now. You know that."

He knows that. The invasion. The arrival of General Ross and the army. It is the first time Cockburn has referred to it in any way. But Towerhill does not care. "It will not take me long, sir."

"You cannot be certain of that. I cannot be certain of that."

"I can," Towerhill says.

Cockburn closes his eyes as if clamping down a fury he is struggling not to let loose on Towerhill. Opens them. "Sergeant, I said you have my gratitude. But do not call too much on that debt, do you understand?"

Towerhill does not bother to reply. He can barely hear this white man, yet another would-be father. *Cock Burn.* He sees the faces among the cornstalks, sees them burn, seared by the flames consuming his own heart.

The admiral is looking at him, one eyebrow raised.

"I understand," Towerhill says.

"Then what do you . . . ?"

"Boats. That is all I need."

THREE

JACOB

—

THE DISTANCE BETWEEN THEM

Jacob sees her face alight with fear, her hands trembling on the musket barrel. The thought that she is breaking brings a parallel tremble into his heart. A realization of how much his own strength is drawn from a need to match hers.

"What do you mean?" he asks. She repeats the three words she has just whispered, then adds, "They should have been here by now," and he sees Joseph's face, alight also, not with fear, but with a terrible understanding. Joseph stands abruptly, emits a long, shrill whistle, and some of the Wesorts strung along the ambush site rise and begin moving towards the run, hefting their weapons. "Come if you are coming," Joseph says to him, his voice tight. "Or stay and be fucked." The words disturb Jacob more than the sudden movement does: he has never heard Joseph curse before. He looks at Sarai. She stares into his eyes.

"They have boats," she says again.

MacDougal suddenly laughs. "Ah, my Digit," he says, nodding. "My good, good Digit."

"How can you be so certain he will try for Zekiah Fort, girl?" Thomas Hallam asks indignantly.

She doesn't bother to answer. Because she does not need to, Jacob thinks. Because it's Towerhill. The boy his father had taught to play chess and then could never beat. He turns to Joseph. "They will hold him off. Until we get there." Kill him, he thinks, looking at Sarai. Kill the black bastard. Kill the nigger. The word emerging in his mind surprises him as much as Joseph's curse did, bobbing to the surface like a rotten branch he has been trying to push under water for years.

—

It is, Jacob calculates, about twenty miles overland to Zekiah Fort. Where and when they can, they follow the net of old Piscataway and Wesort paths and even the main road, gambling that the bulk of the British are behind them in Leonardtown. Having no choice. Joseph is sure that, traveling by water, Towerhill will loop out of Breton Bay from Leonardtown, head north along the Potomac, then swing into and up the Wicomico, landing south of the thick swamp and then sweeping up on foot through the more navigable fields and woodlands at its eastern edge. Jacob supposes he is certain as well, though his sense of connection to the world around him, the effect of Joseph's plant, is long gone, leaving only a pit of dread in his stomach. That dread and his own hatred are in truth all he has to sustain himself, for thirst trumps even his hunger; his throat is too dry and swollen for him to pay attention to his empty, rumbling belly. He says nothing, even when they pass by freshwater streams and a farmer's well. While the rain lasts, he can tilt his head back, let the drops fill his mouth. When it stops, the air remains heavy with moisture, but heat presses like two hands on his forehead. They run silently and without cease, all with the same intent expressions on their faces, eyes hard, gleaming with hate and desperation. Running alongside a tobacco field, they pass a farmer and his wife repairing a worm fence; the couple, in the act of lifting a rail, freeze and gape at them. Thomas doffs his hat. Surely anyone seeing them lope by silently, panting, their tongues hanging, would be reminded of the Wesort wolf stories. He wishes they were true. But that belief is gone as well. Vegetable magic. He craves the plant, but only for the energy he knows it will give him; he sees that same hunger in Joseph's dark-circled, haunted eyes. His blood is sludged with exhaustion, his limbs heavy. He keeps running. Sarai stays in front of him, silent, just out of his reach. The distance between them remains the same, yet with each step he feels she is pulling further and further away.

FOUR

TOWERHILL

—

THE WISHED-FOR FUTURE

Towerhill loses two people even before the company arrives at the palisade. Nestor and Yael were among the original thirty-six from Towerhill Separation, and their loss tears another strip from his heart. He blames himself. The route from their mooring point on the Wicomico to Zekiah Fort had skirted the swamp and was an easy march through meadows and light forest. But the Wesorts had scattered spring traps and dug bear pits along the easiest access routes. The local white farmers did not venture into the area. This he had known; he'd been warned by slaves who'd escaped the traps, by others who had been caught by the Wesorts and returned for rewards. He had known, but in his haste and hatred he'd ignored his knowledge.

He makes the company, makes himself, stare down into the bear pit filled with sharpened stakes. In falling Nestor was stabbed through the neck, and he died instantly. But Yael is gut-pierced, and she looks into Towerhill's eyes as she writhes on the stake, her mouth gaping, her body voiding, before her light goes out. He doesn't look away. Neither do the others. Neb stands by his side, nodding, his eyes gleaming, a new brother in this new world, fleshed emissary from his bitter heart.

More cautiously now, he sends scouts ahead, and the company moves through the woods toward the Wesort settlement. At last light on this long day he catches sight of the palisade atop the small hillock. It seems to assemble itself as he watches, as if the stripped trees of the forest are congregating to press against each other, stand between him and his first memory of this place, a huddle of huts hard against the swamp, a mix of mixed people. *The feared future* had been the words that gathered into his mind then, a phrase he remembered Cedric Hallam uttering when he had told of seeing a platoon of black soldiers charging at him in a South Carolina swamp. *No, the wished-for future*, he had thought. He had been a child thinking childish things. Until he'd been whipped into adulthood.

The palisade is strong and sturdy but the gate is open, no one on guard. Why should there be? The wolf is away, hunting or being hunted, only the cubs and the toothless left in the hidden den. They enter silently, gathering in the space just beyond the gate. Bristling with bayonets. His people. The feared future. Under a smoky haze, a profound hush lies on the village, a murmuration of sighs and creaks and breaths. He is uncertain whether those whispers are really here; he cannot be in this place without sensing a pentimento, his memories whispering beneath the imposition of the present. As he thinks this, a musket fires. He sees the muzzle flash from between two houses, feels the brush of the ball pass by his head; it tears the jaw off Hiram Forrest, just come to the company, just seventeen years old. From the corner of his eye, Towerhill glimpses a dark form running between two sagging shacks. As he raises his musket and fires, Neb howls, the same sound that had burst from his own throat at the bear pit, that had poured from him when he saw the four faces in the corn patch, that weaves now with the volleys they are firing into the houses. The howl carries him forward into this red evening, so that even after it no longer bursts from his mouth it fills his skull and shifts his vision. He runs forward, Neb cavorting in a mad dance at his side, and he thinks: Joseph does not know what a wolf truly is.

FIVE

SARAI

—

FILINGS TO A LODESTONE

At first the palisade looks intact, and for an instant Sarai allows herself to hope that they have arrived in time, or that they have been wrong, that Towerhill has never come here. But then she sees the smoke. Joseph rushes forward, only to be yanked back by MacDougal. "Not so hasty, lad; they may be waiting for us." Joseph turns to stare at him, and at this look Mac-Dougal drops his hand and shrugs. The Scot, she thinks, seems to have come back to himself. It is the rest of them who are seized by madness. MacDougal peers around, bright-eyed, nodding at what he sees, as if it is calling up memories of other ruins he holds in his mind. Her only other ruins have been Towerhill, the plantation and the man. She understands she will have more now. Joseph and the other Wesorts ignore MacDougal, run inside the palisade, screaming until the screams become a keening wail, the sound stabbing her, growing louder as they pass from house to house, or what were houses. There is nothing left but ashes, patterned along the lines of what once were walls. Those walls and everything they had held have become heaps and smoldering outlines. Some of the heaps are small, oblong, and when she sees Nick Swann step from the ruin of his house holding two such in his arms, tears streaking his ash-smeared cheeks, she turns away. In the center of what must have been the town square, where Jacob had been mutilated, there is a burnt corpse tied to two large planks fastened into an X. The nails that hold the arms and feet to the crossbeams are still intact. Lombroso. The features are unrecognizable, but she is certain it is him, and she wonders what Towerhill would think if he knew he had avenged not only their childhood betrayal by this man but also Jacob's more recent agonies. She tries to see what had been here before, to see this place as if through the eyes of the child she had been. She thinks, He had to burn it. She knows him as she knows her own heart. He had to burn it and them from his memory and from the world. Whatever flames were lit here, she knows she has helped to light.

When they leave, they are as husked and broken as the place itself. Ashes blow from the gate of the still sturdy palisade, but Joseph's carefully repaired wall of spaced, pointed logs has become pathetic, as useless as the skin of a corpse.

Sarai looks away from it. The meadow that rolls down the slope from the gate is jeweled with wildflowers, pink Maryland meadowbeauty and milkwort, bright purple hyssop skullcaps, white Queen Anne's lace. After the rain, the air is heavy and languid, the stink from the compound contesting the perfume of flowers. They walk aimlessly and individually down into the field, no longer a cohesive group, but mourners leaving a cemetery, each wrapped around his or her own stunned grief. A thicket of loblolly pines and cedars marks the border of the meadow. Nick Swann is in front. His friend, James Hewitt, hurries to catch up to him. Struggles to take one of the small, cindered corpses cradled in Swann's arms. As Swann turns to snarl at him, flashes erupt from the tree line. For an instant she ties them to the bright riot of the meadow flowers, but then she hears the solid, meaty thunk of lead balls passing through the corpses of Swann's children and into his chest. A scream fills her ears, louder than the sudden gunfire all around her, and it takes a willed catch of her mind before she realizes it has burst from her own lips. Out of the corner of her eye she sees MacDougal yelling at her, waving at her to get down, but now Jacob is next to her, with Joseph on her other side, and she feels a mad elation as the three of them run towards Towerhill, inevitably, pulled like filings to a lodestone. Nothing can touch her, she is coming home, the trees drawing closer, dark faces and bright red tunics scattered among them, tongues of flame licking towards her. Jacob's brother has reached the tree line; as he does, a small group of blacks surrounds him, raining blows with their rifles, and then Neb, laughing, yanks him back by his hair and she sees him draw a scalping knife along Thomas Hallam's hair line. Can't hear his scream. Sees Joseph's chest erupt in a red blossom. Sees a black marine—she doesn't recognize him—step from behind a tree and drive his bayonet into Jacob. Sees Towerhill's face now, in the shadows of the trees, his eyes fixed to hers in hatred, as they had fixed on her when she was in the corn patch, as they had fixed on her when she was wrenched naked from the blackness of the priest hole.

PART FOUR

PASSING THE FIRE

AUGUST–SEPTEMBER
— 1814 —

ONE

TOWERHILL

—

A CONFLUENCE

He stands next to Cockburn and Scott on the rocks at Point Lookout. Looking out. The fleet of fifty-one ships crowds the confluence of the Potomac and the Chesapeake Bay. Frigates, seventy-four-gun warships, troop barges, schooners, sloops, bomb ships bristling with long-range mortars. In spite of himself, Towerhill feels a thrill race through his veins. This power into which he is subsumed. As if he has shared the emotion, found it too large to express in words, Cockburn flings his arm out, draws it back to his chest, encompassing the fleet.

They are awaiting a skiff to take them out to the flagship for a meeting with Vice Admiral Cochrane, as well as Rear Admiral Codrington and another rear admiral, Pulteney Malcolm, who had led the troop convoy bringing reinforcements from France. The commander of those troops, Major General Robert Ross, would also be there. Except for Malcolm, they all outranked Cockburn. Ross was to lead the ground expedition, a task that until now had been the admiral's. Ross had not wanted to come, Towerhill has heard the troops whisper, reluctant to leave his wife's skirts and still suffering from a bad neck wound he'd received this year in Spain.

"How does all this strike you, Mr. Towerhill?" Cockburn asks, waving again at the fleet. Out of the corner of his eye, Towerhill sees Scott stiffen, no doubt annoyed that the question has been addressed to Towerhill. To the nigger on this particular cluster of rocks.

"Impressive, sir," he says.

Cockburn snorts. "It's a pretty picture at least. And Codrington is a good man; his idea, y' know, to recruit your people for the Colonial Marines—he began the corps down in the Caribbean and Florida. But now the admiralty's promised us twenty thousand men and sends barely five thousand."

"General Ross still seems . . . uncertain about attacking Washington," Scott says.

"General Ross needs to extract his finger from his arse."

"A feat of which I hope he's capable, sir."

"Well, that's what determines our purpose today, lieutenant. We must encourage the good general to ex-digitate."

"It will not be easy, sir."

"Quite. All will depend on how far up said digit is inserted."

Digit, MacDougal whispers to him, grinning madly, his face shifting in the current and sparkling with sunlight, looking up at Towerhill from just beneath the shifting sheen of the water.

Scott spins to face Towerhill. "You find this amusing, sergeant?"

"I find the image comical, sir."

Cockburn laughs. Scott hesitates for an instant, still glaring at Towerhill, but then allows himself a smile.

"'I would enjoy seeing such a depiction, sergeant," Cockburn says. "Something in the heroic mode. One foot forward, perched on the prow of the *Tonnant.* One hand brandishing a sword. The other occupied as has been suggested." He raises his hand and then presses his palm against his right eyebrow, not—Towerhill realizes—mocking that imagined heroic stance but staring out, impatiently, at the water.

"Where is that damnable gig?" he growls.

"The signal, sir," Scott says. "It will be . . ."

"The admirals await. My *superiors.*" Cockburn curls his lip. "What is it the marines call us, Scott? Myself, Cochrane, and Codrington?"

"I'd rather not say, sir."

"Do you think I haven't heard it before, man?"

"Two cocks and a codpiece, sir," Towerhill says.

"Hah!" Cockburn says. "Hah! Do you hear that, Lieutenant Scott? Do you know what I can do with men like that? God's teeth, of course you do. We're the bloody bastards who whipped Boney. Do you remember France, lieutenant? Do you remember Spain?"

"Quite, sir," Scott says quietly.

"Of course you do." Cockburn grins fiercely. "Towerhill, what about Malcolm? 'Two cocks and a codpiece.' What do the marines do about Malcolm's unfortunate name?"

"Why, they lament he lacks the spelling to join the other pricks, sir."

"Hah! Do you know what Jonathan calls me, Mr. Scott?"

"I do, sir."

"Rather not say that too?"

"Cock Burn, sir."

"Yes," the admiral says, and there is no hint of laughter in his voice this time. "Yes," he says again. "Bloody Jonathan can't get his republican tongue around the King's English." He squints at the water. "Where's that boat? We need to be there, Scott. I don't want that cock and that codpiece listening to our reluctant general without the opportunity to bring some bollocks to this damnable meeting."

Towerhill follows the admiral's gaze, as if he is searching also for their transport to the *Tonnant.* He isn't. He looks for the rocket ship *Erebus,* where he has been told Sarai and Jacob are being held, isolated from the other American prisoners, defined as spies and assassins, not soldiers. But it is impossible to discern that one dark silhouette among all the others off the point. He is not certain that she is—that they are—on that ship. He could have made inquiries and pinned it down. But he has not. He will not think about them. He will not think of Zekiah Fort. Let it waft from his memory like the ashes it has become.

There is a flash at the stern of the *Tonnant,* followed by a red streak arcing into the air and the burst of a signal rocket. "Our masters call us," Cockburn says dryly.

A breeze touches and cools the sweat on Towerhill's forehead, stirs the fringe of sawgrass past the rocks along the shore. He can see the shadow of a large ray just under the surface, the creature darting back and forth swiftly, as if confused by the suddenly populated water. He is dimly aware that Cockburn and Scott are still talking, but he lets their voices become part of the sough and heave of the waves, the breeze whispering in his ear. To the west, he can see the shoreline of Virginia, past the picket of masts; to the east, the Chesapeake Bay. He thinks of another ship with captives in its hold, come up this gateway into America, this sword-thrust of land into the confluence of waters. Thinks of a woman chained to the deck and clutching two children to her breasts, one a child born between continents, the weight and darkness of the new land waiting for her outside the thin wooden walls of the ship, its waters lapping insistently against the dank, dark boards of the hull. Perhaps some of it leaking through, forming a rivulet that flows over the deck like a tongue of the new world, licking at her and the infant she holds at one breast and the child he had been at the other, that water tasting them even as they fed. Even as she curses it and kisses it back, trying still to taste Africa, to keep it as long as she is able on her own tongue.

TWO

SARAI

—

EREBUS

The priest hole. The withy cage. Now this. It occurs to her that the only time she and Jacob are truly together, even more than during the conjunction of their bodies, is when they are so wombed. A joining that never survives its birth into the world.

The river or the bay—she is uncertain of their location—swells under their supine bodies, rises and falls as gently and regularly as breath. Some of it, of whatever body of water rocks them now, leaks in between the boards; they are lying in a brackish pool, the air around them dank and clammy. Their prison this time is a small, walled-off space, a brig created by the curve of the bow, its roof so low they can only lie or sit. The ship— she saw its name and its rockets, before they were first cast down into the dark—is the *Erebus*. At first the darkness here had seemed complete, like the silence—except for Jacob's raspy breathing; he is still unconscious—but gradually she has come to see small cracks of light and hear other sounds: the creak of wood, muffled laughter, a sharp curse, footsteps overhead, the lap of water against the hull. She rolls onto her side, the movement painful, the manacle cutting into her ankle, and runs her hand over Jacob, from face to legs. There is a trickle of blood at the corner of his mouth,

243

but the main wound, the bayonet tear, is at his side. The British surgeon had wrapped a bandage over the cut, around Jacob's waist, but when she touches it, she feels wetness, though the light in the brig is too faint for her to see if it is water or blood or both.

Jacob groans, mutters something; she thinks she hears the word *Culloden,* as if MacDougal is speaking through his mouth. She touches her lips to his forehead. His skin is burning. She kisses both of his closed eyes, feels them move under his lids, under her lips. What is he dreaming? For an instant she feels a stab of envy at his escape from the consciousness which keeps her chained next to him. But here they are. She rolls against him, gets her arms around him, holding him to give him her warmth, to take warmth from him.

His weight in her arms, the chafing weight of the chains on her ankle, brings her back to the first time they had embraced. Not the casual hugs and skin brushes of their childhood, but the moment the press of his skin on her own had opened an inchoate ache of need for him, a throb of desire in her groin along with a nagging bitterness at the presumptive sense of ownership in his touch, at her own need, at her traitorous body. That moment which had marked her womanhood had also presaged her future, the contradictions that even here, lying with this man in their own filth, continues to tear at her. She closes her eyes, sees the three of them sitting at the edge of what might be the same water which rocks her and Jacob now. Sees the flash of rage in Towerhill's eyes as Jacob puts his arm around her, draws her to him, Towerhill tightening his lips, saying nothing to this brother. Who, after the Zekiah—after what the Zekiah had first meant to them—they both had come to understand was a white man, a master.

The boards creak in the darkness of this jail. Face to face, his breath on her skin, she can see Jacob in the greenish half-light. His features look unformed, vague; she rearranges them in her vision, sculpts him as she moves her fingers over his face. She feels the bristle of his beard, rubs her face against its roughness. He stirs, groans. Shouted commands, a snatch of song, the clank of the anchor chain being raised. The ship seems to leap forward, freed; she can feel it in her bones.

They are moving; she knows that, but time has become as liquid as water, a day and a night and another day all running together, marked only by faint increase or dimming of light, sailors opening and closing the trapdoor overhead, throwing down scraps of dried meat or dry tack, raising or lowering a bucket of water, the bucket that contains their waste. She hopes they keep each bucket separate for its purpose, but she cannot be certain. She eats and drinks very little, has tried to limit the voiding of her bowels. Perhaps for this reason, because of the uncertainty of the bucket. The phrase sounds vaguely philosophical to her. The Uncertainty of the Bucket. Its purpose anchors them to tyranny of the physical world, the prison of their bodies' needs. Jacob wakes from time to time, but his flesh feels like fire, and the words that spill from his mouth are babble; he speaks whatever story is running through his dreams. She feeds him by chewing, softening, the hard scraps of foul meat and then pressing them into his mouth; takes mouthfuls of water and kisses them into his mouth, though a few times now she has been able to raise his head, bring the bucket to his lips. When he pisses, or she senses or guesses he needs to, she holds his penis over the other bucket. Sometimes she guesses wrongly and he wets himself. He has not shat himself. She is grateful for that, but not overly concerned. If he does, she will clean him. She wonders at her lack of disgust, if it is a creature born of the necessity of their situation, or if Jacob has become her child. The thought makes her laugh, madly. After all of this, has she become his handmaiden again? His mammy? No. She feels no difference between her body and his, this man she was going to leave, an intimacy that is beautiful in its manifestation, terrible in its cause.

More shouted orders. The anchor is dropped. She feels the ship strain against its pull. No difference between her body and the ship also; she imagines its wooden struts curving up from her ribs, the cold water heaving against her back. Why not? She is a ghost in the dark, formless, liberated; she can be anything she wants. She can be a wolf. She hears a heavy, scraping sound, the clang of metal against metal, as the rockets she glimpsed are moved into position. The ship is preparing for battle.

THREE

TOWERHILL

HOT AS AFRICA

From the top of a high bluff, his God's-eye perch, Towerhill watches the fleet struggling up the Patuxent. The sense of overwhelming, monolithic force he had felt at Point Lookout has been scattered and broken by the twists of the river: sloops, brigs, schooners, and frigates water-bug ahead of the long lines of warships that tack ponderously from one point to the other. Laden troop barges, water almost reaching their gunwales, wallow upstream in a slow, straight line, Congreve rocket barges flanking them like protective sheepdogs. He recognizes the *Iphigenia,* Cock One's ensign flying from it—wonders who in hell's name would name a ship so: did the admiral leave a sacrificed daughter in England as an offering for victory in America? The *Tonnant,* too large for this passage, has been left anchored in the bay. Eventually, Scott has told him, even the frigates will have to be left behind as the banks of the river squeeze to narrows. Towerhill knows why, but would prefer otherwise. When he came to know that their objective was the capital, his memory had unnested the bombardment that had plowed and churned Towerhill Separation, the flames curling and spiraling from the windows of the manor house, the taste of dust and ash and freedom in his mouth, and then shifted that vision, as if it were a barrage itself, to Washington. There would be, he understands, an attack up the Potomac with the heavy bomb and Congreve rocket ships (including, he thinks, his mind going flat, the *Erebus*), but this thrust up the Patuxent keeps the Americans from knowing if the ultimate target is Washington, or Annapolis, or Baltimore; it leaves them uncertain about where to concentrate their defenses. The tactic is working; the slave grapevine has, to his, and Cockburn's, astonishment, reported no significant American forces between themselves and the capital.

Towerhill can see faces of white soldiers, like a row of shields, in one of the troop barges that has drifted close, too close, to shore, and too far from the protection of the other boats. The bulk of the army, under General Ross, is on the larger ships, but Cockburn keeps his accompanying marines, black and white, as a force ready to land if the Americans have situated gun positions along the river. There have not been any, also to Towerhill's uneasy surprise; a couple of guns in a spot such this bluff where he and Neb perch could have deadly effect. Some of the soldiers bobbing below look hangdog sick, while others stare gap-mouthed at the countryside. He imagines the lush greenness of it in their eyes after ten weeks spent tossing on the Atlantic; he remembers standing on the deck with MacDougal, how the Scot had painted his own idealized memories over the land. *A wrapped promise.* Remembers MacDougal's face, the way he had seen it at Zekiah Fort: blood-striped and mud-blackened, the pupils of his blue eyes dilated with madness. He had not been among the prisoners or the corpses, a fact that Towerhill admits he does not regret. He will kill MacDougal if he ever gets the chance. He hopes he will not. Something about the man still tugs his heart. He will not let himself think about it. No more than he will let himself think about the other two. He'll fish-pack them into the darkness of forgetfulness, just as he'd seen them packed into their cell on the *Erebus,* suspended between life and death. A marine had raised the trapdoor to give him a glimpse of them, embraced by their chains and each other, but shut the trap quickly, startled by the strained anger in Towerhill's shouted command.

He turns his attention back to the river. He and Neb are flanking the fleet on foot as it moves up the Patuxent, a scouting mission he had convinced

Scott to approve. *Yankees catch you, sergeant, and you'll be back under the whip in a tobacco field, if they don't hang you.* Cockburn is tense and testy, afraid of the way command control is slipping away to Ross and the army, increasingly annoyed with Ross's reluctance to see the expedition as anything more than a punitive raid: the general, it is said, does not want to take Washington. Towerhill understands, sympathizes, agrees with Cockburn, but can't bear how the admiral transforms his frustration into pettiness. He will no longer delicately thread his way through the rise and fall of a white man's moods.

The troop barge has come closer now, caught in the current. The men's faces seem stunned and haggard. They have been transported directly from the fighting in France and the peninsular campaign and are not happy to be here. Their grumbling pleases Cockburn. "Thought they'd be back in England, sporting heroes' garlands," he said. "Instead, here they are, charged to drub Jonathan, all mad primed, and cocked liked muskets."

"Cap'n Book," Neb says, tugging at the long hank of hair—Thomas Hallam's scalp—dangling from his buttonhole. The tug opens Towerhill's memory: Neb after the fight at Zekiah Fort, brandishing the scalp, whooping, saying the man wanted to play Indian.

"Where you eyeballing?" Neb asks. "Look there."

He points to the mouth of a small creek, just to their north. For a moment, Towerhill can't see what Neb has spotted, but then he makes out a woven mat of branches and reeds covering a boat, the lines of its hull clarifying in his vision. One of Joshua Barney's raiders: the American commander has been harassing the British with his shallow-draft fleet of about twenty galleys. They had bottled him up in St. Leonard Creek for a while, but Barney had managed to shoot his way out. As Towerhill watches, the American crewmen throw off the camouflage and row out swiftly from the inlet, the vessel's light sail furled but twenty pairs of oars sculling fast, the twelve-pounder at the bow manned, Towerhill sees to his disgust, by a black man. The galley moves between the slower British barge and the nearest ships in the fleet, which are too far away to come to its aid. The redcoat soldiers are cursing, bringing their muskets around to bear, but the Americans are already firing, their musket balls chopping at the men on the port side; Towerhill sees one soldier rise, clutch his face, blood flowing between his fingers, and then fall into the water just as a swell hits the boat. Gone in an instant, the long, twisty sentence of his life written from London alley, to yellow-dusted Spanish road, over a heaving sea, to be finally punctuated here in Towerhill's river. Neb is shaking him: "The fuck the matter with you, Cap'n Book?" When did Neb promote him? A shot from the raider's bow cannon hits the barge mast, and the canvas crashes down on the soldiers. He and Neb fire down at the Americans, Towerhill aiming for the black gunner. His round splinters the wood near the man, who glances up at the cliff face; Towerhill can see him grin, drawing his lips back, his teeth white against his black skin. He wants to put a shot into that mouth, splinter those teeth. He becomes aware that he is steadily cursing, a low murmur spilling from his lips. Some of the British are rising and managing to fire back now, the face of one boy appearing under a fold of the sail like a child peeking out from a blanket. One of the Congreve rocket boats swerves towards the troop barge; it's too out of range, but its crewmen load a rocket into the steeply angled rail launcher anyway. The sparks from the rocket's fuse are visible, even at this distance, the missile arcing up, trailing more red sparks, then bursting harmlessly, with a sound like clanging metal, against the white cliff face below Towerhill and Neb. Shards of rock fly up and splash into the river. The bow of the American raider heaves up on a wave; at its peak the black gunner sends a cannonball into the hull line of the troop barge. Wood splinters; Towerhill sees the boat stagger back like a man receiving a blow to the face. It lists, begins to sink, the Americans still pouring musket fire into it. The black gunner waves up at him, still smiling, as the raider pivots sharply, the port oarsmen dipping hard, those on the starboard raising their oars out of the water, the movement drilled and skilled. For an instant, Towerhill sees six fingers in that wave, blurred by distance. He dismisses it; impossible to see such details from here. A rush of hate swells in his chest and he trains his rifle on the bobbing figure of the man, fires again. Useless. The boat glides into the mouth of the narrow creek, Towerhill watching helplessly. By the time he looks back, the troop barge is already up to its gunwales in the water, some of the soldiers trying to slough off their gear, others sinking into the river.

"That nigger good," Neb mutters.

They rejoin the fleet at Benedict, arriving near dawn to watch the drowned men be resurrected, more than four thousand of them ferried ashore through the shoals and narrows, and not an American soldier in sight, nor, for that matter, any American at all among this scatter of rundown clapboard houses that styles itself a town. Towerhill is not sure where Cockburn is, and waits with Neb as troops disembark all around them. The drownings he had seen brings his eyes to the heavy load each man carries: muskets, powder, at least sixty lead balls, haversacks with extra clothing and rations—he imagines the cold clutch of that weight as it dragged men to the bottom of the river. A city of tents seems to spring up around them as they walk, as if his mind builds it with each step. Its neat rows mock the ramshackle town, empire displaying itself to colony. Pickets deploy, campfires spark like matches, kettles boil, soldiers work with a quick, practiced surety that puts his mind at ease: more, makes him feel again a measure of pride at being part of this force, not just his own people, but these hard, irreverent men cradling weapons that are like appendages of their bodies, men molded into a species for which he has no name but recognizes nonetheless. Men licked, as he has been, by the same fire. The encampment seems to grow even larger as he and Neb walk towards the town, the canvas of the tents bellowing out and sucking in, some huge creature fastening itself on the land. "'Ot as bleedin' Africa," a tall, whipcord-lean soldier says, wiping sweat from his eyes as he looks at Towerhill and Neb. "And here's the Dark Continent itself, come a calling." His grin takes the insult from the words. "Come 'ere, come sit with us, Africa, tell us the air 'ere ain't always made a' steam. Give us the lay a' the land." He presses his hand against his chest, the fabric of his woolen tunic as soaked with sweat as his red forehead, and waves at the small fire that he and the other men sit or lie around, flopped like dead fish on the ground. A kettle of boiling water is suspended over it, the fire reflecting like tiny red jewels in the beads of sweat on the man's forehead. "Come on, then, ha' a bit a tea with us," he says.

They do. The others sit up, squint at Towerhill and Neb as they palm their hot metal mugs. The thin man holds out his hand to him. "21st North British Fusiliers," he says, as if speaking his own name, as if it should mean something to Towerhill. And then it does, MacDougal again coming to his mind, the Scot spitting over the side of the ship, telling him that unit was coming across the Atlantic *Butchers of Culloden,* he'd said. *My new comrades-in-arms.*

They are here now, and MacDougal is somewhere in America or in hell, and now Neb acts the nigger for them, paying for his tea and hard biscuit. Brandishing a spoon as if it were a knife. "Cut massa throat, me. Cut Jonathan throat. Me free now." Rolling his eyes.

"Me cut 'em too, Blacky," says a tall soldier with a scar splitting his face in two. His lips up-curve and smile on one half, down-curve and frown on the other. He claps Neb on the shoulder. "But we'd rather cut some fine Yankee split-tail, truth be told. You know where we can find any of that, me fine burnt fellow?"

Neb laughs, too loud and too long, bangs his spoon against the kettle rapidly, one bang for each word, "Yes, yes, me like too, split-tail good." The men laugh, repeating the half-wit phrase. Towerhill rises, needing to get away from this man, his comrade-in-arms. The whipcord-thin soldier catches his eye as he leaves, and he nods to show his understanding of Towerhill's embarrassed disgust, the two of them forging a momentary fragile alliance against fools.

He finds General Ross's headquarters where he suspected it would be, in the largest of the sagging and ill-built houses. His carpenter's eye hasn't noted a tight join or true right angle in any of the hovels along the rutted mud road running through Benedict. At headquarters a sentry stops him, touches a bayonet point to his chest. He wraps his hand lightly around the blade, he and the sentry joined by steel and by stare, until Scott comes out and tells the man to lower his weapon.

Scott takes Towerhill's report, what there is of it, grimacing at his account of the destruction of the troop barge. "We saw that. Bloody helpless. Bloody Barney." He waves in the general direction of the river. "Our reports are that his famed flotilla is in the narrows north of here. Waiting to receive us. I look forward to that meeting. So does the admiral. Keenly. Do you know what Barney calls his flagship? The *Scorpion.* Pretentious scut. Seen scorpions before. Looking forward to stepping on that bloody insect."

Through the wall Towerhill hears Cockburn's voice, suddenly loud and angry, and he looks at Scott. Who grins thinly. "The admiral and the general are conferring on matters of strategy. Orders have arrived to Ross from Lord Bathurst." He sees the question in Towerhill's eyes. "The Secretary for War." Scott deepens his voice: "'You will consider yourself authorized to decline engaging in any operation which you have reason to apprehend would lead to failure or undue losses. You are not to engage in any extended operations at a distance from the coast.' So says the good Secretary for War." Scott barks a short laugh, Towerhill hearing an echo of Cockburn in it. The lieutenant nods at the door. "Our masters, Sergeant Towerhill, are parsing matters of proportion and distance and geography."

The two wait together, Scott uneasy, pacing, eavesdropping shamelessly. The walls of the room are stained with blotches of green and yellow mold, the smell thick in Towerhill's nostrils. A framed embroidered cloth, memorial of some dead wife or daughter, hangs crookedly on the wall separating them from the room in which the two commanders are meeting. "*As a flower plucked too soon / Sweet Adele has left her mortal form.*" He can hear Cockburn's raised voice as clearly if there were no wall, but Ross's is a mumbled whisper.

Ross: "————.—————.————."

Cockburn: "You are, by God, authorized to bloody well *not* decline to engage, general."

"————.—————.————."

"Winder has melted away; no one fired as much as a cannonball as we came upriver," Cockburn says. Towerhill thinks of a few shots that belie that statement. "What there is we can sweep aside."

"————.————.———."

"Bathurst is simply distancing himself from disaster. A disaster that will not occur."

"————.————.———."

Ross's aides, George de Lacy Evans and Harry Smith, come into the room. The three white men look at each other. Scott shakes his head. De Lacy Evans shrugs delicately, walks over to the wall, and straightens the framed poem. He runs his finger over the embroidered words, mouths "*thy mortal form*," and rolls his eyes at Towerhill.

Cockburn's voice is rising. "Give Emperor Madison the chance to gird on his armor and fight it out. Bloody Lord Bathurst isn't here. We are. The 85th. The 44th. The 21st. Veterans of the fighting at Fuentes de Oñoro, and San Sebastian, of the peninsula, of bloody fucking Egypt, Ross. You fought with them, you know what we have. We're here with some of the finest fighting regiments of the British army, arrayed against an ill-organized, rag-tag collection of militias. The only one of them with any steel is Joshua Barney and his bloody nuisance of a flotilla."

"_____._____._____."

"And what will you do with that army? I have a thousand marines as well, Ross. I have the Colonial Marines, my fighting niggers. I am not going to sit on the bleeding river and bob like a bloody cork."

The door flings open and Ross comes out, his eyes blazing; the gouged scar on the side of his neck seeming to glow red as well. He caresses it rapidly with his forefinger; whatever is pent up in him subsumed into that gesture, sweeps out of the room, carrying Evans and Smith in his wake.

But the next day, back with the company, Towerhill watches what seems to be a transformed and martial Ross, pretty as a picture, mounted on a prancing, snorting horse, its sweat-flecked black hide matching his black uniform and the hat he raises over his head. He bows to the soldiers of the 85th as they cheer and yell, "Huzzah!" Some of Towerhill's Colonial Marines cheer with them; others stare, shuffle uncertainly, before joining in. Neb throws back his head and howls, long and hard, until some in their company look at him uneasily, and fall silent. At Cockburn's insistence, they have been attached to the 85th's twelve hundred men, marching in the army's vanguard.

After the cheers die away, there is a brief silence, like a held breath, and then the commands of the officers and sergeants ring out and the army lurches into its march.

As he walks, Towerhill brings Sarai up next to him, liberates her form from the charged, fetid air, transforms her from the chained wraith he had last seen imprisoned in the blackness of the ship hold. Wills her to step forward, spin to him, as if she has been by his side on all of the dazzling, bright transforming days that have led to this road. To the place he will take all of them now. He glances to his left, as if to truly see her there, extant and proud of him. She disperses like the seeds of a dandelion, disintegrates with a breath into the iron-hot air.

Dust rises from their boots, coating their uniforms, sticking to the sweat running down their faces and forming a yellow paste on their skins. Small clouds of vapor hover like a miasma from the soaked wool of their tunics, mingle with the shimmer of heat in the air. His marines march smartly, keeping a fast past—they must reach Nottingham by this evening. The heat is familiar to them; they had years in which they shrugged it away from dawn to dark in the tobacco fields. He fears, though, for the white soldiers, these marchers through Egypt and Spain, who have no experience of a Maryland August, and is not surprised, after an hour or so, to hear the clatter of equipment, the shouts of sergeants, as men begin to fall out. Surprised a little, though, at the twinge of satisfaction he feels. Pride. He smiles wryly, chides himself for taking pride in a simple-minded ability to walk encumbered and in step with his fellows, singing the same cadence they once sang as they stooped to cut or pluck or weed the plantation fields through other inflamed summers. Such pride, he admonishes himself, replaces the whip but achieves its function. He has married his—their—interests to the interests of these white men, who will tolerate them only as long as their aims coincide. He cautions himself now to hold to a rigid inner vision of who these white men are, to remember that they will never come to know the world like his people have, will inherit it in different ways. *Come 'ere, come sit with us, Africa.* Yes. For a time.

Afternoon. The road narrows as they pass through a copse of poplars and oaks, thick with underbrush. A good place for an ambush, Towerhill thinks, just a second before he hears the crackle of musket fire and sees the flashes from the darkness between the trees. His men and the British pivot sharply and face outwards; the brigade's flank becomes its first rank, the men in that row dropping to one knee and training their weapons outward as the second rank instantly returns fire over their heads. Their reaction is flawless as a drill, though Towerhill berates himself for letting himself relax and be subsumed into the mindless march of the column. Why hadn't he put out flankers? Ross or Colonel Thornton, the brigade commander should have done so, but since when had he subordinated his responsibility to them, let their arrogance creep into his perception?

There is no further firing. Two stretcher bearers run past him; they load up one man and carry him off. There is another volley, and he stiffens, as do the others around him, but it comes from inside the woods and he recognizes the distinctive sound of the British army's Brown Bess muskets. So there had been flankers. Moments later, he glimpses red uniforms through the screen of trees, and then six men break through the underbrush, two carrying a corpse wearing a red and blue uniform crisscrossed by white straps and an odd leather helmet crested by a large black feather. The uniform looks new, has the aspect of a tailor's display, a vision reinforced by the unlined smoothness of the man's, the boy's, face—a puffy, well-fed visage. Towerhill lets himself see a planter's privileged brat playing soldier. The boy's throat has been torn away; the shot that killed him was close; he can see powder burns on the collar. One of the soldiers holding the corpse twists that collar, hauls up the body, and dumps it in front of Thornton's horse. The animal rears slightly, then prances sideways. Another soldier drops a Harper's Ferry rifle next to the body, and the party salutes the colonel. He returns it sharply. The brigade cheers, Towerhill's marines joining them. The man who had raised and dropped the corpse catches Towerhill's eye, nods easily, grins: it is the tall, thin soldier who had invited him and Neb for tea. Towerhill nods back, tosses an easy salute.

FOUR

SARAI

———

ENTWINED

There is a kind of freedom in being imprisoned, she thinks. To be held rocking in this dark womb entwined with her silent fetal twin, *entwined* with her *twin*. Here there are no more choices to be made, no more paths to enter. She lies face down, growing into the damp wood, *rooted,* if you will, sir. Tendrils pushing out from her pores into the fiber of the wood until there is no difference between flesh and wood and then the wet of the river, seeing its mud-clouded water now under the ship, brushed as she descends into it by crabs, rockfish, rays, and now the blue face of a drowned man, mouth open in astonishment, weighed with musket and kit and sinking into the sediment. Her sight skittering like a crab. Towerhill told her how his six-finger visions seized him, but she had dismissed it as a kind of brag. Towerhill mantling lies as prophecy, himself as prophet. She had not understood until now. From outside the walls of her world, she hears the boom of cannon fire, muffled, from a distance, and she is sucked back into her mind, hears shouts from the sailors, their running footsteps thudding above her head. Drills. The foolish excitements of the world all going on without her. She lacks Towerhill's sixth finger, but if she wills it, her trenchant mind may float away again, pass through these walls, briefly feel the rasp of the wood inside her skin, agitating the atoms of her body, and then falling away so that now she soars upwards, away from the depths, now she is an osprey, screaming osprey screams, circling above the masts, the ships spread out beneath her.

She tries to remember the other ship, her first ship, knows memory and story are so entwined themselves it is impossible to separate them, knows it doesn't matter. It is the past, not the future, where all things are possible. The future is a wall and a chain. The past is a stage. Joseph's voice. *And in the beginning there was no knowledge of separation, all was the dream and there was no separation between the dream and the garden. And in the beginning there was no separation between man and tree, between man and animal, between man and man, between man and woman, and each grew within and without each other's skin and all were Wesort. This was the dream and this is the dream and we live in the dream and we live for the dream, Wesort.* Stir this, use a sassafras stick, or it don't take, Rebekkah says. You know that? You see what I be doing here, these two days? Put ashes in the barrel, boil down the grease, just so. Know when it be ready. Cool it, shape the cakes. Who else know how? Massa? You? Some other nigger? Who know how to pull a baby, he get all twisty up? Just me, Auntie Rebekkah. Auntie Rebekkah ain't going nowhere. I here, and I know here. She spits in the pot. Grips Sarai's wrist, hard and unrelenting as a manacle, her fingernails puncturing her skin, a bracelet of blood springing to the surface, falling into the water, dispersing outwards, webbing among the hummocks and reed islands and wooded copses of the Zekiah, her brothers, her lovers, tall on either side of her, their shadows cooling her. She watches Jacob staring at a coven of mosquitoes clustered, feeding, on his forearm, and she reaches over and crushes them. The spurt of his blood stains her fingers. "Meat," he mutters. The boat rocks. She grows smaller. The image of Rebekkah pushes her back into the womb of another ship. Her tiny body pressed not just to this man's flesh, but among rows and rows of Sarais packed into *Jesus,* sweat and piss and blood gluing them to the deck. She turns her head, and all her mirrored others turn their heads, this way, that way, their eyes glowing, a sailor opening the hatch and screaming, seeing only the symmetrical lines of eyes, all blinking in unison. Turns this way. That way. All of her bodies, spread through the dark hollows and veins of *Jesus,* chain-fastened and immobile, except for her heads. She turns to the left and sees now that instead of her endless, wearily repeated self, next to her is Jacob, and as far as she can see down the dark, peripherally narrowing corridor, it is she and Jacob and she and Jacob and she and Jacob. She knows who she will see if she turns her head to the right. She does not. She rolls over, sees the man next to her, chained with her: Jacob, always Jacob, a scrim of spittle on his lips, runnels of sweat on his face, pushes her face close, the acrid smell of him in her nostrils achieving what the chain on her ankles cannot do. Fastening her back to time.

FIVE

TOWERHILL

—

PIG POINT

The company, which has stayed on shore and is ahead of the rest of the army, flanks Cockburn's little fleet of shallow-draught barges, keeping it in sight as the river narrows, expecting to find enemy gun emplacements at every rise of the shoreline. At points the foliage is too thick near the banks; the water diffused into broken sparkles through the net of leaves or curtained completely by tangles of honeysuckle and wild rose, so they have to swing further out and lose sight of the river and the boats. Towerhill feels a sense of relief each time he sees them again, intact. Un-attacked. They are far upriver now—perhaps, he estimates, twenty miles from Washington—the sense of closing on the city singing in his blood. No American force, neither militia nor regular army, has appeared to stop them, neither on land nor on water. There have been a few attempts at ambushes, a few sharpshooters hidden in the woods. "Nuisances," he heard Scott call them, and although more men have dropped from the heat than from enemy fire, he doubts the three men killed would use the same word.

Near Pig Point, the river tapers so much that even from shore he can see the buttons on Cockburn's uniform, the curled plume rising over his hat, the admiral standing dramatically at the bow of his gig, spyglass to eye,

259

posing for a statue of himself. As the gig and the other boats round the point, he sees Cockburn's head jerk back, as if something has struck the lens of the telescope. He follows the instrument's line of sight, his heart lurching as he sees what has struck Cockburn's eyes. All seventeen boats in Barney's flotilla lie in the river just past its bend, directly in the admiral's path. Barney's own sloop, the *Scorpion,* flying an American flag, is at the head of the line. Cockburn's triumphant shout rings across the water, and Towerhill motions his marines to get down; they string out smoothly along the bluff, their rifles trained on the flotilla. As he glances over them, Sally catches his eye, smiles broadly, and raises her rifle to him. That gesture snagged hard against the memory of her body dangling helplessly as Bertram violated her, a vision seared alongside all the other visions that have since burned behind his eyes, but always connected to the night he met Scott and MacDougal. The latter is gone but Sally is still here, strong. Growing stronger as Lucius seems to grow weaker, though she cares for him ferociously, as if he is her child more than her husband. He lies next to her on the bluff now, one-eyed, unmanned, his shoulders trembling slightly. She reaches over and lays a hand between the wings of his shoulder blades. As he notes the gesture, Towerhill feels something like hope shiver through him, the thought that many versions of a true self may lie laced and tangled in a person, ready to be pulled free if the end of the right cord is tugged. Don't you see, he thinks, returning to the silent discourse he carries on all the time with Sarai and Jacob, chained in their dark carapace in his brain, his eternal and vigilant audience. Don't you see how it all lies dormant and snugged down by the past in each of them, his people? That it is for him, with his sixth, measuring finger, with his carpenter's eye that can see the final shape that might be built, to leverage that weight off their shoulders, let their true form uncoil, let them shape themselves to measurements they had not known they contained?

He groans aloud, feeling a surge of disgust at his need for their witness, at the hollowing, inchoate sense of loss he feels from Sarai and Jacob's absence from his life. The book-buttressed shrine of their childhood now only a taste of ash in his mouth.

Enough. He turns his focus back to the flotilla. Something about it makes him uneasy. Why are the barges so close to each other? He sees anchor ropes stretched taut from their sterns, the boats straining forward in the current, then snapping back. His gut clenches. He can't see any sailors on board. He swings his eyes back to the river. Cockburn has drawn his sword, is waving his barges on; does he expect to duel with Barney? Towerhill looks back at the flotilla.

"Open fucking fire, Cap'n Book!" Neb yells at him, and when he doesn't respond, Neb shoots anyway, with three, then four, then five of the others joining it, their rounds splashing among the barges, one thunking into the sloop's mast. Towerhill leaps up, shouting at them to stop. He can see a web of thick, black lines fanned out over each empty deck, their pattern growing clearer as he stares, their meaning edging at his brain. A small ball of fire erupts from a clump of holly bushes on the other side of the river, floats and darts through the air, closing on the stern of the last galley; there is a lag in his brain before Towerhill recognizes it as a bobbing torch, clutched by a black man in a green uniform. The cannoneer who had sunk the troop barge: Towerhill is certain of it. He rises, shouting, points his Baker, shoots, the whole line of marines now leaping to their feet also and opening fire, the ground just behind the man's feet erupting in geysers of dirt. Out of the corner of his eye, he sees Cockburn turn his face towards him, Scott seizing the admiral's arm, jerking him down, waving at the sailors to lie on their oars, just as the running black man tosses the torch onto the deck of the last galley, turns his face up as if to once again grin at Towerhill. Some other, uncoiled possibility of himself, moored to an old, abandoned dream.

The fire races from boat to boat, a glowing incandescent spider web threading before his eyes, leaping finally onto the *Scorpion*. Towerhill can see, as if his sixth finger has snagged and slowed time, the fire outlining each board in the hull of the sloop and then the wood bulging outwards and flying apart, dissolving into its elements, showering the river with debris that splashes across the surface and re-creates a transient form of the boat. He swings his eyes back. Scott is dragging a cursing Cockburn down from the bow, as some of the British soldiers, confused, set up a cheer that is drowned out as more of the barges explode. Something whizzes past Towerhill's ear; he feels its heat brush against the skin of his face, turns to see an oarlock embedded in the tree trunk behind him.

The flames from the boats billow up into a single pillar, rising hundreds of feet into the air, and then spilling down in tendrils of black smoke. Towerhill sees the white faces of the sailors, the black faces of his people, all tilted upwards like rows of shields. Cockburn is standing again, beating on the back of his tiller man, pointing to the riverbank. The gig quickly makes landfall, the admiral cursing all the way. He jumps ashore below Tower-hill's position, near the burning sloop, as Scott scrambles to keep up with him. Cockburn jabs his sword at the flaming boats his face red and furious. Barney was the one American commander Towerhill had heard him speak of with respect; Cockburn badly wants the fight. Ross, Towerhill knows, will squeeze Cockburn out if he can; the column of smoke rising before them may be the final punctuation mark on the admiral's plan to take Washington. His only mission had been to parallel the march of the land expeditionary force with his fleet of small boats, to protect the land army and find and destroy Barney. That has been done, fight or no fight, and Towerhill feels his throat thicken with dread. Too many of his own hopes depend on the admiral's gamecock ambitions. He does not, will not, see the fire he craves in this solitary column of black smoke.

The admiral is jabbing his sword at something, shouting, and Scott joins in. Towerhill grasps the issue immediately. One of the last of the galleys has not caught completely on fire. There is a line of flame on the deck, licking at the small sail, but it has not spread. Hearing Cockburn and Scott, several British sailors race to it, and Towerhill shouts for his people to help. He scrambles down the slope without waiting for them, thinking to jump on board, but two of the white sailors have already pulled the boat close to shore with its hawser; another leaps onto the deck and slashes the sail lines with a cutlass, bringing the sail down on the sputtering fire. Towerhill hears Cockburn yelling, "Good man!" The admiral is standing next to a clump of blueberry bushes, feet planted; behind him there is a stir in the leaves. Alarm skitters through Towerhill's mind. He cries out, pointing his rifle at the bushes. Cockburn looks up at him, his face darkening. Scott sees the frown and swivels towards Towerhill, raising his musket just as Towerhill fires into the bushes. Leaves fly up. He hears a kind of groan, *uhnn,* not a wail but a note of acceptance, or the fulfillment of an expectation. Another shot. A round flies past his face; he can feel its breath on his cheek. Towerhill raises his rifle, sees Cockburn pushing down Scott's arm, yelling a name, pointing.

Four sailors and one of his own people, Sally, have scrambled into the blueberry patch and are hauling out the sniper, his legs slack, his features clarifying in Towerhill's vision like something floating up out of a dark pool as Sally grabs the man's hair and tilts his face towards him. The cropped ears, the crooked teeth fencing a mocking grin. "Ah, Digit," MacDougal says, and is about to say something memorable, Towerhill is certain, as Scott smashes the hilt of his sword into his mouth.

—

Towerhill goes to MacDougal that night. The man has been bound with heavy chains to the mast of the remaining barge. His head is tilted back, almost in the same position it had been when Sally yanked his hair, and his eyes are wide open. Towerhill follows their gaze. The sky is cloudless and jeweled, but MacDougal is not looking at it; his eyes are fixed on the rope tied to the cross spar. Towerhill squats down next to him and holds up a jug of whiskey. The sentry, Achilles, scowls, but doesn't say anything, just turns his back and continues on his post, along the burnt-out hulls of Barney's flotilla.

"You'll have to help me a bit," MacDougal says.

In the moonlight he can see MacDougal's lips are bruised and swollen, a thread of blood runnelling his chin from the right side of his mouth. Towerhill brushes the blood away, brings the jug up to MacDougal's mouth. The Scot closes his eyes, drinks deeply.

"Ah, Digit," he says, as if continuing the sentence he had begun before Scott smashed him, "a stubborn nature was always my downfall."

"And bad aim."

MacDougal laughs. "There is that as well."

Towerhill drinks deeply from the jug, tasting blood with the whiskey. MacDougal nods at the rope swinging above his head. "At least your mates will be spared that," he says. It takes Towerhill a second to understand that MacDougal believes Sarai and Jacob are being held as prisoners of war and as such will not hang. He thinks of correcting the Scot's perception, but doesn't see the point.

"You're a deserter."

"Nae, Digit. I was a deserter from my cause the minute I put on the red coat and took the king's shilling. But it didn't take, as you noticed."

Towerhill tilts the jug up to MacDougal's lips, watches his Adam's apple move as he swallows. He is aware of the swinging shadow of the rope. Achilles comes back, hawks loudly into the river. Moves off again.

MacDougal is looking straight ahead now. He nods at the night, at the shore, at some vision in the vast darkness past the campfires of the soldiers. "It's always just across some strip of water for us, me and you. Wider for you, I know. Once, when I was with the savages, after they'd carved me into a shape more to their liking, they took me up to the top of the mount they called Elseetoss. Lovely name, that. El-see-toss. Like singing. It's the highlands, Digit. Not this flat, foul, watery place. From that place, from Elseetoss, you look west and the mountains go on forever, all nuzzled up with clouds. Like you can see them dreaming."

Towerhill waits for him to say more. But MacDougal just turns to stare at him, his eyes holding stars. The river laps against the side of the boat, moonlight silvering it in flat sheets that here and there shiver with quickenings of life. It's enough for Towerhill, this flat, watery place.

"Give me some more of that pisswater pretending to be whiskey."

Towerhill raises and tilts the jug again. Watches MacDougal swallow.

"Digit."

He waits for MacDougal to say it.

"Ever see a hanging? They say it can be quick, your stem snaps. But they never make it quick, the Sassenachs. Stretch it out, so to speak."

Towerhill doesn't say anything.

"You know what the worst horror of it is, Digit? Not the shitting and pissing; I dinna mind giving all that shite to the English. No, the worst is, when it's done, I'll be as black as you."

SIX

SARAI

—

THE CHILDREN OF JESUS

Time is not an anchor. Or it is the chain to which the anchor is secured, sometimes taut, sometimes slack. In the slack she drifts back, floats in a cold darkness laced with shivering tendrils of light until the anchor chain snaps taut again and now she is back in the belly of *Jesus*. As the child stirring in her belly is in the ship of her own body. Waiting to be born from chains into chains. To be born nailed to the cross of itself. She is back in *Jesus*, a tiny scrap of a person, pressed to the steaming flesh of her chained people, with them, of them. The memory of it as real as the skin on the hand she looks at now in the gloom of the hold, fluttering her fingers before her eyes. The memory of it a lie. Her past a construct gathered to her mind from Tower-hill's stories, the foundation that carpenter had built for both of them. Their true history torn from them as they had been torn from it. A cold, hard corner of her mind knowing the vision of the past that had just encompassed her had come to her from the heated skin of her lover, his body wrapped to hers. Had come to her from the darkness and groans and creaks of this prison that held her now, rocking her on the same water that had brought her here in that first ship. She hears the curses of the sailors penetrating down through the deck. Pulling her back to this place. *Erebus. Jesus.* Both.

Jacob stirs against her, moans. His body only heat and bones. Skin thin as paper. His mind as adrift as hers. More. He has not said a word; his eyes, when they flutter open, see nothing. His hand on her abdomen, mindlessly drawn to the new life he must feel under his palm. His lips around her nipple. As the child Towerhill's lips had once pressed against her mother's breast, or his mother's breast, or their mother's breast. Jacob's mouth slips away. She has no milk. But something flows from her, thin and transparent. She cradles his head against her again, feels the draw of him. She floats away. *Erebus. Jesus.* Her mouth searching for sustenance at his mother's breast, the five-year-old boy who would be Towerhill next to her, both of them sucking greedily, in unison, their mother stroking their backs, saying yes, yes in an English a corner of her mind knows can't be hers. A third child, still and cold, laid at their feet. His skin white in this sea of black people.

Their mother. Her mother. Their mothers. Their stolen past a rocket burst of possibilities. How true were the stories? Towerhill had been certain that the dead child was a boy. Is he reborn in her belly now, that child, or is he in this man next to her whose soul is also wrapped so strangely to hers? The baby girl and the five-year-old boy, too old for the breast but starving, both of them pressed between the two women, one living, one dead. Pressed between the rows of chained people. The living and the dead. The terrible embrace of her people. Had they been sisters, her mother and Towerhill's? Had Towerhill truly been five? Six? Older? Younger? And the darkest question of all, always there but never spoken by either them: what if there was only one mother, Towerhill truly her brother. It doesn't matter. They were the children of that dead womb. As are she and Jacob now. Wesorts. The children of *Jesus.* The children of *Erebus.* The anteroom of death.

She feels the strong suck of Jacob's mouth at her useless dug. The child inside her kicking sharply against the wall of her belly, starving inside her. A memory built of taste and smell and sound coming to her: her mother's skin going from hot to cold, the nipple swollen in her mouth dry and abrasive, the stink in her nostrils like something alive and writhing. The void when her mother is torn away. Her wail and Towerhill's rising to heaven: the birth cry of their rage.

Jesus. Erebus. The ship then and the ship now rock together, disembodied voices, curses filter down to her ears, the wood creaks and groans. A merging of what she cannot possibly remember but does. The closing of a circle.

Had she been born on that ship? It had to be. It had to be, Towerhill had said. She and their nameless dead brother or sister. It had to be what? The rush of water and blood from her mother onto the deck stained and foul with the effluvia of all those who had been and would be affixed to that place. Trickling down through the hair-thin cracks, to flow into the sea where both their, no, both her mothers had finally been thrown, drifting to the bottom, their hands raised back to the ship. Their lives the gift from both those mothers. Or of one. She does not know. She sits up, pulling her nipple from Jacob's mouth, the transparent liquid that had begun flowing from her trickling from the side of his mouth. She kisses him, tastes it. Bitter on her tongue. The child inside her kicking frantically. She bends to feed herself from herself. Knowing only that she must live. Knowing only that this child inside her must be born and must know its story.

SEVEN

TOWERHILL

⸻

BLADENSBURG

He first sees the cloud of dust out of the corner of his eye, a reddish stain
spreading against the hard cerulean of the sky, perhaps a mile to the north-
west, and for an instant, his eyes stinging with sweat, his head throbbing
from the heat that presses like wet palms against the sides of his forehead,
he has hope of a summer thunderstorm, the cooling relief of rain. But as
the column turns a bend in the road and Bladensburg comes into sight like
a painting creating itself along the river below them, he hears a murmur
ripple through the ranks ahead of the company—they had been plodding
silently, mindlessly, letting nothing more than their own bovine momentum push them forward through the heat and their own exhaustion—sees
shoulders stiffening, a kind of tremble passing through the mass of men,
marked by a metronomic bob of their muskets, and he knows the rising
cloud he sees does not mark rain.

At the beginning of the march that morning, when Ross had finally
agreed to advance on Washington, the men had cheered, surged forward
eagerly, grinning at each other. The white soldiers had been three years
fighting in the Penisular War, and upon their victory had been yanked to
this shore instead of home; they had been spit upon and cursed by people

who looked like their own countrymen, ambushed and whittled down by sharpshooters, denied the chance for outright, decisive battle when Barney had blown up his own fleet. Both they and the Colonial Marines knew of Ross's reluctant caution, Cockburn's urgent encouragement: the admiral understood what they needed. An hour into the August heat, though, soldiers, the hard veterans of France and Spain and Egypt, had started staggering, a few, and then more, and then dozens, falling to the side of the road, often in mid-step. The thick dust that had risen from the feet of those still marching stuck to their sweat, coating everyone, caking their faces, turning whites and blacks into an army of yellow men. Ross had ridden up and down the ranks, urging men on, pointing to Towerhill's people, none of whom had fallen, as examples. To shame them, Towerhill supposed. *The niggers are still marching.* He marched to his own cadence chant in his mind: *sell or be sold, sell or be sold.* He closed his eyes for a moment, seeing as he always did these days the grinning face of MacDougal, the tightened rope gouged into the flesh of his neck, the whites of his eyes bright red from burst capillaries, his skin as black as he had predicted. Perhaps, as he'd told MacDougal, perhaps a whip-wielding Bertram in each company and a few years of first-to-last light in the tobacco fields baking under this same sun would have helped to keep the white soldiers on their feet. Or perhaps a vision in their heads of the shimmering city that awaits further down this road, built on their backs in the name of a dream of freedom forbidden in their waking lives; perhaps the fire they would bring to that place would have kept them marching. Perhaps if they were those white niggers you told me about.

At about ten, Cockburn riding up next to Ross, whispering urgently in his ear, the general had finally called a halt. The army had collapsed in place. An army of puppets with their strings suddenly cut. Ross, resplendent in his black uniform ("Bloody sod dresses in mourning garb," Towerhill had heard one of the white marines whisper. "What's he telling us?"), his saber held aloft as if he were seeking an enemy to charge, rode back and forth along the flank of the column, shaking his head and muttering to himself. "Cast his die," James Scott said, sotto voce, to Cockburn, and

Towerhill saw the two officers, mounted on their horses above him, hold each the other's stare for an instant. As if feeling Towerhill's own stare, Cockburn suddenly looked down at him, shrugged, and waxed eloquent. "We are the dice, and we have all been cast, lieutenant," he'd said, still looking at Towerhill. The roles of the two men—Ross reluctant, Cockburn pressing to advance—had once again been reversed. Until yesterday, Ross's unwillingness to continue to Washington had been reinforced (Scott had confided to Towerhill) by another message from Admiral Cochrane ordering the army to stop and withdraw back to the Chesapeake, Cochrane certain the Americans would mount a daunting force to defend their capital city, one much larger than Ross's fewer than five thousand men. Towerhill's scouts and the slave grapevine had confirmed the numbers; a few thousand militia from Washington, Georgetown, Maryland, and Virginia camped at Long Old Fields within marching distance, twice their number near Bladensburg, northeast of the capital. The British forces had only a few cannon; the Americans surely would outgun them. Barney's flotilla had been destroyed (though Barney and his flotillamen had been spotted with the forces at Long Old Fields), the Americans had been humiliated, and the army's purpose honorably achieved. Why risk a disaster? Cockburn had urged Ross to ignore the order. He commanded the army, didn't he? Cochrane was only a sailor, like himself. Did the army come this far simply to turn around? The troops were eager. Their soldiers, the veterans who had defeated Napoleon, would not be defeated by the foppish militias they had seen arrayed against them. If they turned back now, Jonathan would crow that the British had retreated. Had run. In Canada, Cockburn reminded Ross, the Americans had burned the town of York to the ground. Where was the justice, where was the bloody honor, in simply marching up nearly in sight of Washington just to turn around and march back?

In the end, Ross had agreed. And now seemed carried away by his decision, driven with a purposefulness Towerhill has never seen in him before, that in part, he supposes, must have been spurred by the whispers he had heard among the general's aides that it would be General of the Army Ross, not Rear Admiral of the Navy Cockburn, court-martialed if the Americans defeated them after he'd ignored Cochrane's orders to return to the fleet.

The dust that had arisen from the American forces is settling now. On the other side of the Eastern Branch, the ground in front of them, its fields and meadows broken by copses of wood, rises about a mile to a low ridge. The opposing lines of infantry and artillery are strung out along it, bayonets or sabers catching the light and flashing here and there. The hill he is on lets him see everything as if a map had been spread before them.

Cockburn throws his reins down to him, and Towerhill steadies the white horse as the admiral dismounts. The animal's nostrils flare, tremors running through his sweating flank. A sudden knot of anger tightens in Towerhill's chest. He has not come here to be a house slave. Since the last attempt on his life, Cockburn has insisted that Towerhill accompany him. He is not flattered, fears he has become some kind of token for the admiral, a nappy-headed talisman to rub for luck. He looks over his shoulder, searching out the ensign of the 85th Light Infantry: his company had remained attached to them. He spots them towards the rear of the brigade. He needs to be with them.

Ross rides up next to them and dismounts, nodding to Towerhill but not handing him his reins. His horse, its coat as black as the general's uniform, snorts nervously, its hooves dancing. Cockburn's white stallion nudges its head into its neck, as if to calm the other horse; Ross's horse whinnies, turns to bite. As if mirroring the animals, Cockburn places a hand on Ross's shoulder. Ross throws it off. He paces, still wielding his saber, pointing it at the town, the river, the land, as if he could stab them all. Towerhill following its direction, trying to see it as Ross and Cockburn do. Bladensburg, lying along a bend in the Eastern Branch, looks empty, deserted, though he supposes the inhabitants could be inside their homes. As he watches, more British soldiers flow into the town, their red coats brightly delineating the pattern of streets. When they near the river, gunfire crackles and Towerhill sees flashes from the woods across the water. One of the British soldiers falls violently backwards, as if yanked from behind, the splash of red from the top of his head visible from where Towerhill stands. The first dead. Ross either doesn't see or ignores the casualty. He rises on his toes, laughing aloud, pointing the saber at the river. At, Towerhill sees, the narrow bridge across it.

"Intact," Ross says to Cockburn. "Why in Christ's name would the fools leave it intact?"

Cockburn shrugs. He puts his spyglass to his eye, scans the opposite side of the river. "They astonish me at times. Brave enough, but they're not soldiers. But look beyond the bridge, Robert." He sweeps his hand, encompassing the countryside, turns to Towerhill. "How many men have your scouts counted?"

He repeats the number.

"Six thousand fools," Ross says. "Look at their lines. They have the least number of men nearest the river; the other lines too far apart to help each other. There must be a mile between them. Winder is a bloody dilettante. How did he think he would come to their aid? And look at them." He sheaves his sword, puts out his hand impatiently. Cockburn hands him the spyglass. "Look at them. They are *motley*, Cockburn, motley. Bloody militia. It's as you said. Bloody militia against the soldiers that defeated Boney."

He is rising and settling back and forth on his toes and heels, but Towerhill hears something strained in his voice, as if he is trying to convince himself. The scar on his neck somehow seems more pronounced, almost inflamed. George Evans and Harry Smith ride up, their faces alight with excitement. They dismount, cluster around Ross.

"Militia that can shoot quite well," Cockburn says. "Did you hear that firing? They have rifles—I have seen them shoot accurately over a hundred, a hundred and fifty yards. Sergeant Towerhill."

"Sir?"

"Please pass me your weapon."

He hands his new rifle to Cockburn, who makes a show of putting it to his eye, aiming across the river. "Name it, sergeant."

".54 caliber Harper's Ferry rifle, sir."

"Towerhill took this," Cockburn says to Ross, who is fidgeting impatiently now, "from the deserter we hung, the man who tried to assassinate me."

"I know the story, sir," Ross says shortly.

"Our Brown Bess muskets are good for perhaps thirty yards, our Baker rifles better. But how many of our men have rifles? Bloody Cochrane laughs when I suggest it, but it will be the future." He claps Towerhill's back. "Made sure as many of my marines as I could got them, isn't that right, sergeant? Bakers."

"Yes, sir." Seeing MacDougal grinning at him from a corn patch, but his tongue protruding, black and turd-like, as it was on the day of his hanging.

"Exactly. Shoot the eye out of a squirrel, our Jonathan. And the ones in blue? Those are not militia. Regulars."

"Your point, sir," Ross snapped.

"My point is just past that bridge." Cockburn waved at the trees. "There. Do you see the glints and gleams from those woods? If they have sharp-shooters there, and we can be certain they do, they can sweep the bridge. And there, to the right. Cannon. Do you see them? Six pounders, I would say."

"I have seen them. I have seen how exposed they are. They have no idea how to use embrasures effectively."

"Still," Cockburn says. "I suggest we ignore the bridge, hit their flanks. The river may be shallow enough to cross on foot, up and down stream. We have no idea how many cannon they have."

"I agree, sir," Harry Smith said.

Ross snorts. "Do you, Harry? Admiral, if I may remind you, the Navy's presence on this battlefield is only a courtesy I extended to you."

He is quivering, not, Towerhill sees, with nervousness but with eagerness, the man having, it seems, but two extremes: too much caution or too much ardor.

Cockburn stiffens. "Sir, I offer you council. You may . . ."

He stops suddenly, distracted by something that catches his eye. Towerhill follows his gaze towards the river. He can see the 85th mustering at the edge of town, the rows of black faces in his company at the brigade's rear. A drum starts beating; they are moving forward, without orders, to the bridge.

"What in the bloody hell is Thornton doing?" Cockburn looks aghast.

"Ha," Ross says. "Ha! Just as he should."

"Sir . . ." Harry Smith starts. But Ross swings into his saddle, draws his saber.

"Initiative, Cockburn! Initiative!"

He wheels his horse around and charges towards the bridge. Evans and Smith glance quickly at each other, wheel their horses around, and gallop after him.

Towerhill begins to run towards the river.

He hears Cockburn yelling at him to stop. Below him, some of the British soldiers are sheltering behind houses. But the 85th has already started across the bridge. Excited shouts rise from the other side of the river, under the steadily mounting cracking of the rifle fire. The bridge is narrow, the British forced to march three abreast as they go onto it. Rifle and musket balls smash into the ranks, shredding flesh and bone as if someone were chopping at the soldiers and marines with an axe. He runs towards the river as if in a dream, everything too slow, his body too heavy. He needs to be with his people. Rounds buzz over his head, near his face, close enough that he can feel the hot brush of them on his cheek. Someone slapping meat. A sound he can never remember when the fighting is over but that floods back instantly to him now. Then he is on the bridge, a wall of red-coated backs in front of him, between him and the company. The British still marching in step, unhurried, silent, insane, the front ranks falling as they step off the bridge, funneled into the American fire. Not only there, though. A cannonball splashes into the river, raising a water spout. Another hits a man next to him, carries off a leg. The soldier, white, young, looks at the instantly cauterized stump, thin tendrils of smoke rising from the shredded flesh, and turns to Towerhill with a question in his eyes, as if mildly puzzled. Towerhill glimpses the leg, floating in the river. He pushes the unbalanced boy aside, shoulders through two other white men, and he is with his people, Neb turning to grin at him, his face still caked with yellow dust, furrowed with rivulets of sweat and blood. "Cap'n Book joining us from the big house. Must be desperate, children, house nigger's here." Other faces turn towards him, smiling: Sally, Lucius, Achilles. Triumphant screams rise from the other side of the river. The British soldiers are preternaturally silent, grim; his own people taking the cue from them. The two cannon he had seen open up from the other bank take out the three men in the front rank, reload, their balls falling into the middle of the column of red coats. They are funneled into the fire. And then are off the bridge, fanning out in the open field. Flashes of gunfire from the trees, the deeper boom of the cannon. He nearly trips over a corpse; Sally grabs his arm, steadying him. He does not see Lucius. Sally nods to him and her jaw flies off. Something strikes his forehead. She is still clutching his arm. He has to pry apart her grip to move forward. She drops behind him, the sight of her desperate eyes, her tongue wiggling obscene and serpentine, melding into the memory of her hanging from a tree in a dark forest, at the beginning of the long march that has taken them here. He knows the two pictures will now and forever be braided together, knows all in an instant that is a scream in his mind and is gone and his mind is cold and rigid as it needs to be.

He sees Colonel Thornton, still mounted, just off the front of the bridge, waving his troops on. A ball thuds into the side of his horse, sending it over as if shoved by a pair of hands. Thornton leaps off as it falls, still waving his sword, charging at the American line, which has now moved out of the trees; his men leaping after him, over the clumps of their own fallen. There is a roar from the British now; the weeks of heat, death, and frustration they have felt finally given a target.

Towerhill reaches up, brushes his forehead, fingers finding something hard clinging to his skin. He pulls it away. Them. Two of Sally's teeth. He flings them from him. He is somehow in the field past the bridge, but has gotten separated again from the company. A horse whinnies loud behind him and fearing to be trampled he turns to see Ross and Cockburn, along with Scott and the other aides, charging off the bridge, Cockburn's gold epaulettes glinting. The admiral throws his head back and laughs, committed now, Towerhill sees; they are all cast die. Soldiers from the other brigades are finally fording the river above and below the bridge. Why hadn't they done so before? He can identify the 44th East Essex, and the 4th King's Own. The Americans, no more than a hundred yards away, begin shifting their fire onto the soldiers in the river. Cockburn sees him, raises his sword, still laughing. Scott's horse goes down. Towerhill loses sight of him. The cannonade and the rifle fire from the American line shifts again, smashes into his people. To his right is a small ring of piled stones; two of the British sailors have set up a Congreve rocket tripod in the small, sheltered area, eighteen-pound rockets piled next to them. Not too sheltered, he sees: the bodies of two other sailors, both head-shot, lie near the rocks. One of the live sailors, a thick, bearded man in a striped tunic, pulls a lanyard and a rocket flies off and arcs towards the enemy line. The angle of the launch is set too high: the rocket trails a dramatic shower of red sparks, but falls harmlessly into the tree line. Towerhill leaps over to the rock formation. "Down," he screams, "Bring it down." The sailor stares at him blankly, and Towerhill kicks the tripod legs out further, bringing the angle of the trough down, pointing the rocket directly towards the American ranks. Rifle balls ping and whine off the stones, send a needle-sharp spray of broken rocks into the face of one of the other sailors, a small, broad shouldered man Towerhill had seen before on the *Tonnant*. He screams, clutching his eyes, blood welling between his fingers. The bearded sailor—Towerhill recognizes him also now, the *Tonnant's* gunner's mate—grasps what he is doing, adjusts the angle of the rocket further down, pulls the lanyard, pushes Towerhill away from the back blast. The noise deafens him. The rocket flies straight into the American ranks, the warhead exploding, shrapnel slicing ribbons through flesh.

They load another rocket. The gunner's mate's face is black with powder. Before Towerhill can adjust the angle, a great blow knocks him to the side. When he looks up, he sees it is the flank of Cockburn's horse, not an American shot, which has hit him. The admiral towers over him, grinning madly. Scott, horseless, leaps over the small parapet of rocks to his commander, his forehead furrowed with worry, screaming at Cockburn, gesturing at him to get down, Towerhill seeing it all in pantomime, unable to hear a word. But Cockburn doesn't dismount. He leans over and pats the gunner's mate on the back, praising him. As he bends further, the stirrup leather of his saddle suddenly, magically, parts; it takes an instant for Towerhill to realize a shot must have passed just under Cockburn's leg and hit below his saddle flap. The admiral looks down, annoyed, and dismounts quickly just as the saddle starts to shift. The gunner's mate suddenly grabs his throat and falls backwards, blood bubbling from the wound as he falls and his hands flap apart. Cockburn kicks the body to the side and tries to wrestle the next rocket onto the launch trough, waving impatiently to Towerhill to come help. They swing the rocket around and Cockburn raises the angle slightly, aiming it to arc over the embrasure holding the three American six pounders. Cockburn's face is alight with glee. The admiral playing gunner's mate. Scott catches Towerhill's eye, shrugs, wordlessly sharing an understanding: after the destruction of Barney's flotilla, there is no place for Cockburn in this land campaign, his sailors and marines now under Ross's command. But no chance he would stay out of it either.

He pulls the lanyard, letting the rocket fly. It explodes harmlessly against the raised embrasure in front of the cannon. Cockburn curses, turns to muscle up another rocket. Scott grabs his arm, points. The British are pouring off the bridge now, most of the army on this side of the river, and have forded further up as well, their formations moving forward inexorably towards the American line, which has started to fall back. Towerhill searches over the ground for his company, cannot see them. What he can see are the other American brigades on the low hill to the southwest. Ross had been right: they are too far away to aid their fellow militia here.

His hearing comes back with a rush now, waves of sound crashing into his ears. The British are cheering, the sound almost as loud as the gun and cannon fire. "Keep firing, man," Cockburn yells in his ear, the admiral and Scott muscling another rocket onto the launcher, sending it spiraling at the retreating troops, smashing a hole in the ranks. "Kill the buggers!" Some of the buggers are still shooting, a platoon or a company stopping to fire back at the advancing British, Scott still trying to push Cockburn down.

Towerhill can see more rocket positions have been set up, the gunners imitating what their position has done, using the Congreves as cannon. Chunks of lead mow whole ranks of men down, Cockburn nearly jumping up and down in excitement. The American line has broken, the Americans running back towards the heights, some of them dropping their weapons. The air is laced thick with smoke.

Towerhill cannot grasp that the short meeting of the headquarters group on the other side of the river had taken place less than an hour ago. It had happened in a different life time. He glances up at the sky, trying to orient himself back into some ordinary sequence of hours, but the sun is a dulled silver coin, it edges blurred, hazy behind the pall of smoke all around them. It must be about two in the afternoon. He peers around, his eyes burning from gunpowder, spots the company moving up on the right flank, Neb still in front of them, still unwounded. If he grins, calls him Cap'n Book, Towerhill will kill him. But when he joins them, Neb says nothing, doesn't even look at him. Towerhill keeps himself from scanning the ranks, seeing who he can no longer see. When he touches his forehead, he can still feel the imprint of Sally's teeth. He pushes down the sudden gush of grief. All of them are caked with blood and dust. The remnants of the first American line are still scampering, panic-stricken, abandoning weapons and wounded, towards the rise where the rest of the army is entrenched, waiting on a slope about a thousand yards in front of them. Straddling the road to Washington.

That is what comes to him. The knowing of it tightening all of his people to him, as if by invisible cords, their veins threaded by death and purpose, even their breaths panting in syncopation as they trot forward. Everything from Sally's rape, from the sound of a scream and Mingo's first blow, swinging an iron bar to the head of a boy named George Adams, has been honed to this point. These men in front of them who would affect to be their masters, blocking the road to their capital.

His eyes pick along the slope, trying to read the terrain, spot the enemy positions along the low crest even as they draw closer. He knows, from his scouts and informants among the slave population, who must be on that ridge: Winder, Walter Smith's Washington militia, the federal regulars commanded by William Scott, a battalion of Beall's Maryland militia. Jacob and Sarai coalesce out of the smoke; he sees them not as accusatory eyes glittering in the darkness of their prison but as they had been. As the children they all had been. Watching what was unfolding here as if in a book-lined room by a fireplace, listening to the stories of the Revolution Cedric Hallam would tell them. The wrapped promise of those stories that he would unwrap here, now, this day. He wants them here to see this. To witness this. To be with him. His Revolution.

The ground begins to angle up now. The company trots faster. The yellow cloud begins to thin and disperse, or the distance has closed enough now to where he can see the American artillery. Three, no four, no five guns, eighteen and twelve pounders. The black man who had set off the explosives at Pig Point is next to one of the eighteen pounders. A surge of rage goes through Towerhill, so strong he almost stumbles. He squints, hoping the man is only an apparition conjured by his hatred; he would prefer madness to the reality of this presence, which means that Joshua Barney's flotillamen have arrived at the battlefield. He had thought them too far away to get here in time. But there is no mistaking them, canvas sailors' trousers rolled up to their knees, open white shirts. What must be at least a company of American marines stands in front of the guns, they and the sailors standing rock-steady, maintaining fire discipline, waiting for the British to come into range. He can see Barney himself in their center, feet planted apart. He is ignoring the panicked soldiers scurrying weaponless through the marines and flotillamen. Barney's men, their faces stamped with contempt, step to the side to let them through, taking the cue from their leader, though several of the marines spit on men that come close enough to them.

"Shit," Neb says.

Towerhill's eyes are drawn again to the man next to the eighteen pounder. He is certain now it is the same man he who set off the explosives at Pig Point. But he is not the only black among the flotillamen. A third of the force must be black. Fighting for their chains.

"Fighting for their chains," he mutters aloud, though he may as well have repeated "shit." Neb is looking at him curiously. He realizes a low growl has been spilling from his lips. He doesn't try to stop it. It catches, the people next to him and then the whole company emitting that rumbling snarl, the rage he feels vibrating through the ranks.

The cannons open up.

"Up the 85th," someone shouts from his right, and he sees Colonel Thornton, horsed again, saber drawn, one instant as idealized an image of a soldier as a statue, the next his new horse falling, its forelegs sheared off, spraying blood. Not only his horse. The cannon, pointed directly at them, are firing grapeshot and canister, blasting clusters of musket balls that cut swathes through the soldiers. Thornton has managed to leap off his horse as it falls, but something slashes open a swath on his trousers near his thigh, blood bursting from it, and he falls over. The white soldiers of the 85th, enraged, continue to charge, but Towerhill feels frozen in place, the company's momentum halted, as if his people are suddenly confused by the sight of the black soldiers in front of them, a man swinging a fist against an opponent he suddenly realizes is his own image in a mirror. As he gathers himself, out of the corner of his eye he sees one of his men leap forward, screaming, charging ahead of the company towards the cannon. Lucius. His one eye blazing, his mouth open, so that the roar of the cannon fire seems to be pouring from it. The sight stuns Towerhill, stuns all of them for an instant, and then the grapeshot shreds Lucius and they are all screaming, running towards the cannons, the American marines rising from their positions, charging forward to meet them, absurdly yelling "Board them, board them," as if swinging onto the deck of a ship. He screams the two words that come unbidden into his own mouth, *Sally and Lucius,* as if he is calling them back from the dead, not certain he is doing it aloud until he hears the others take up the cry as the Americans crash first into the men of the 85th, and then are among his people. All around him men are grappling, stabbing, clubbing at each other, grunting as if scything a field. He fires his rifle into one man's face, stabs another in the gut, feeling the bayonet strike the bones of the spine; a fetid stink of shit assailing his nostrils along with the gush of blood as he draws the bayonet out, strong and stinging enough to momentarily replace the sharp, prickling stench of the cordite. Further up, the cannon crews are reloading, though everyone is too mixed together now for them to be able to fire. He clubs another man in the jaw with his rifle butt, looks up, trying to see the black cannoneer, fighting his way through to get to him. If he can kill him it will be over. He somehow knows this. Then they are among the cannon, overrunning them. He cannot spot the black gunner anywhere, bayonets a burly, bearded white gunner instead, the fuse still sputtering in the man's hand.

"Ross, Ross!" someone yells, and, insanely, there he is, his blood and sweat-streaked horse rearing as he lays about him with his saber, the scar on his face inflamed and blazing. He hears the names the Colonial Marines are yelling and screams them himself, "Sally and Lucius," the cry picked up by all the white British now, no idea of whose names they call but laughing madly as they yell the two words. Towerhill looks to the general's right and left, and then, unsurprised, sees Cockburn, the grin still pasted on his now blood-webbed face, giving it the aspect of a grotesque mask. The American marines start to fall back, somehow getting themselves into line, firing into the mass of British. As they retreat, the two forces un-entangle, redefine into their own formations again, the gap of ground between them littered with the dead and wounded and lines of knapsacks, thrown off during the charge, the packs and the corpses somehow equivalent in his eyes.

It is as if neither side can move now. They stand and pant, tongues hanging out like dogs, the strength drained out of their limbs. Towerhill yells at his people to reload. Unnecessarily; they are already doing it. They face the rank of the remaining marines and flotillamen and as if on a signal both sides begin pouring volleys into each other. As if all of it has boiled down to this essence. Two groups of humans standing and murdering each other while one group screams the names of two lovers, words drained of meaning. Firing, ramrodding down packets of shot and powder, raising weapons, firing again. Or falling. It goes on for years and centuries. The people he freed are dying on this ground. It goes on until a hand grasps his shoulder. He spins, nearly bayonets Scott. The lieutenant's mouth moves but Towerhill can hear nothing. He shakes his head, feeling his logy brain swell against the insides of his skull. Scott leans closer. Ross wants him to move over to the Americans' right flank, hit the Maryland militia on the hill there. Brooke's regiment will strike the other flank. "The general has decided," Scott yells into his ear, pointing at the flotillamen and marines, "to stop trying to entertain these particularly gallant gentlemen."

"Tell the general," Towerhill yells back, "that I approve."

The 85th keeps firing at the center positions as the company about-faces, and then wheels to the left, moving along a small stream. He spots Ross's and Cockburn's horses, rearing in front of the troops, Cockburn still determined to stay in the fight. They are facing the hill held by the Maryland militia now, Beall's unit. Musket fire flashes from the yellow cloud of dust and gun smoke blanketing the low summit in front of them, at first a few shots, but then a fierce volley blasts from the American position. A low, grim chuckle runs through the ranks of his company: they must still be about two hundred yards away and these troops are armed with muskets, not rifles: they are too far out of range. Neb steps out, cavorts in front of their line to remind them of their shortcomings, laughing at the little geysers of dirt erupting in front of him. Towerhill yells at him to get back into the formation, yells at all of them to form their lines, still refusing to look at the gaps in his ranks as they do.

Ross, scar blazing, the black plume on his hat bobbing as his horse prances, raises his saber and screams something. "Charge," Towerhill supposes. Or "Shit." It doesn't matter. The line is already moving forward. A volley of musket fire rolls down the slope, some of the balls slapping solidly into flesh, taking out men in the front rank. Another volley. The British lower their bayonets and continue trudging up the hill, their heads bowed, like men walking into a storm.

And the American line dissolves. One instant they are on the top of the hill, reloading frantically, and the next they are running piecemeal and panicked down the other side. For an instant the British stand uncertainly, and then a roar goes through the ranks and they surge forward, still in

formation. Moments later they are on the top, watching Beall's Maryland-
ers scatter and run into the woods on the other side.

From where they stand now, they overlook the center of the American
line to their right, where Barney's flotillamen and the marines still are
standing firm, exchanging volleys with the British on the slope below them.
Towerhill sees that in this position they can fire down at Barney's men,
without much danger to themselves. That same realization moves like a
current through all of them; without a word of command they begin pouring fire down onto Barney's position. Towerhill can see individual faces, see
men he hits fall. But the black gunner is nowhere in sight. Barney himself
stands with his feet planted firmly apart, hatless, his gold epaulets still
strangely clean, next to a twelve pounder, one instant yelling commands,
the next crumpling to the ground, clutching his right leg. He struggles to
his feet, bracing against the cannon, his men still firing down the slope and
now, futilely, up at the redcoats on Bealle's hill. One of the flotillamen,
a different black man, takes Barney's arm, helping him to stand. More
men fall under the withering fire. Towerhill can see Barney bark an order.
Almost instantaneously the remaining flotillamen and marines form into
lines, and—carrying their wounded and dead—begin retreating down the
other side of the rise, the rear line peeling off and marching down the slope
while the remaining squads, facing front, keep firing at the British still
coming up the hill, the flotillamen's and marines' withdrawal as orderly
and different from the other American forces as their fight had been.

Suddenly Cockburn, still mounted, is next to him, reining in his horse.
He points his sword at the lower hill, at Barney, then brings the hilt up
to his forehead, saluting his foe, mouthing, Towerhill is sure, some fine
phrase. He can hear nothing, only the ringing in his ears. But he can read
Cockburn's thoughts: without one fine, brave enemy, the victory would
be too cheaply won. For an instant he is unable to summon the cynicism
with which a part of him—the part that had not gone through this day—
knows he would usually regard such sentimentality. He feels suddenly tied
to Cockburn and to Barney, to all of them, white and black, to his own

and his enemies, as if they had all been convulsed out bloody but corded together as brothers from the womb of this day.

Dinna be a poetic fool, Digit, MacDougal whispers in his ear. *You'll still be a six-fingered nigger to them, enemy and ally, when all this is finished.*

On the lower hill, the British line has nearly overrun the flotillamen's position. Barney, still yelling commands, suddenly collapses. Others join the man holding him up, trying to pull him away, musket balls from above and below spattering the rocks around them now. Barney gestures angrily, staggers away, fighting off their hands; he must be telling them, Towerhill understands, to abandon him, save themselves. The worthy foe. He is suddenly filled with a white hot rage at the man. While they are still arguing, the small cluster of flotillamen is swarmed by redcoats, Barney standing at bay, surrounded by a ring of bayonets. He shrugs, raises his hands. "Don't touch him!" Cockburn, still next to Towerhill yells, futilely; he cannot be heard. It doesn't matter; the soldiers have seized Barney unharmed and Ross is already galloping over to continue playing the chivalrous gentlemen. MacDougal whispers, *You know the thing I don't like about it most, the most horrible thing, Digit? Not the shitting and pissing oneself; I dinna mind gifting all that shite to the English. No, the worst is, when it's done, I'll be as black as you.* He watches Cockburn and Ross and Barney and is filled with disgust, his little brotherhood-in-arms reverie dissipated into smoke. He understands once again, no ghostly urging from MacDougal necessary, the difference between him and his people and these officers to whom war was a game, death or defeat only making the stakes higher, a good enemy necessary to underscore their own bravery and generosity of heart in the stories they would one day tell in manor halls, while for him—and for his—the courage, the proficiency, the victory of men such as Barney would mean only lives clamped back into bondage. Neb is right, he thinks; MacDougal, that white nigger, was right. Kill him. Kill them all.

Washington lies before him. Him and his. That is all he will take from this day. All the gift he can give Sally and Lucius and the others who have fallen with them.

He glimpses something out of the corner of his eye. Further up the slope, the black cannoneer, his man, darts over to one of the eighteen pounders, stuffs something into the barrel. There is an outcrop of rocks shielding the gun, and Towerhill realizes he can't be seen by the men who have taken Barney. The other soldiers around Towerhill, including Cockburn, have seen the gunner also and are yelling to their compatriots below, firing down at him, Towerhill knowing what the man means to do as if he is in his skin, the task he will not leave unfinished. Musket balls ricochet off the rocks around the man, splinter shards of stone, raise puffs of dirt near his feet. He ignores them, lights a sputtering fuse, steps back, and—Towerhill is certain—looks directly at him. Grins. White teeth flashing in that black face. The cannon explodes.

As the smoke clears, Towerhill sees him zig-zagging away, scampering over the crest of the hill to the rear, one hand over his head, waving farewell.

EIGHT

JACOB

‒

WE ARE AMERICAN SOLDIERS

Consciousness returns in increments, not to his mind, but in a slow inventory of his body, piece by piece calling attention to itself, as if he has flown apart, needs to reassemble. Piecemeal. He becomes aware of his toes because he cannot feel them. Something cold and hard clenches his ankles. His knees burn; his ribs are hot metal bars under his skin. His heart beats painfully, as if it's being squeezed and released in a punishing grip. Air rasps in his lungs, a pair of bellows lifting and lowering his chest. A tick of blood in his veins. A distant whisper trickling into his ears, are if they are rediscovering their function. An acrid sting in his nostrils. Something stinks. His eyes ache. His eyes. There is something, his mind tells him, that eyes can do. What? He searches for an answer. It comes to him. He opens them.

Sarai's face, smudged with dirt, fills his vision.

His mouth. His tongue. His lips. "Hello," he says.

Tears fill her eyes.

"You've come back," she says, and he wants to tell her that her face, sensed just beyond the grey pall that has settled on his mind, is the agency that has drawn him to return.

"Don't speak," she says.

He doesn't. He tries to sit up.

"Nor rise. You're weak."

He becomes aware again of the cold, hard grip around his ankles. Looks down and sees the manacles. The floor beneath him is moving up and down. A ship. A flood of memories. The Zekiah. Joseph falling. He feels himself leaving again.

Cold water splashes into his face.

"Is that necessary?" Sarai asks someone, sharply.

"Nay," another voice says, nasal, unpleasant. "But 'tis certainly amusing."

He squeezes his eyes open and shut, tries to remain awake. There are two dark figures standing next to Sarai, who, he now sees, is chained as he is to the deck. The torn shift she wears is streaked with filth. One of the figures resolves into a red-coated soldier, his face and body seemingly constructed of a series of blocks, though Jacob does not yet trust his vision. The soldier is holding a bucket. It takes Jacob a few seconds to connect it with the water that has just been dashed into his face.

"You will desist, corporal," the other figure says. He leans forward, places a hand on Jacob's forehead. Jacob makes out a sharp nose, bushy eyebrows, a look of concern. "This man is a prisoner."

"Begging your pardon, Dr. Grieves, sir. He's a fucking spy."

"I told you," Sarai started, "we are not . . ."

"What you are is a nigger whore," says the corporal. "And lucky to be one; that pickaninny you're whelping may save you from the hangman's rope, lass. So shut your gab."

"His fever is broken, my dear," the other man says to her. Is he a doctor? Dr. Grieves, Jacob thinks. Dr. Grief. He is still half in a dream, tries to cling to it, retreat into it. Shakes his head rapidly against that urge. The doctor says, "Do not allow the corporal to disturb you. The disposition of this case is still undecided."

"We are American soldiers," she says.

The corporal laughs. "Thank the Lord for that. Means I get to go home again. The kind of shite soldiers your lot has—nigger whores and white men gone to the savages." He swings the empty bucket toward Jacob. "You should've joined us. Our blackies are *fighters*, lass; I seen them. You want your belly swelled, they'd have done it for you, smooth as goose grease."

Jacob is trying to sit up again. The corporal puts a boot against his chest, pushes him over.

"That is quite enough, corporal," the doctor says, his voice rising. "You're dismissed."

The corporal scratches his crotch. "Begging your pardon, sir, I have orders . . ."

"You now have other orders, corporal. From me."

"Mr. Grieves, sir, these two are dangerous."

"They are chained, weak, and helpless. And under the protection of Admiral Cockburn. Who will hear of their treatment."

"Have it your way, sir." The corporal rises, vanishes.

"Are you well?" Jacob asks Sarai, recognizing the absurdity of these drawing-room words as soon as they leave his mouth, released into the dark, fetid air, the pressing curvature of their new prison. He is giddy, the fever throbbing behind his eyes a diaphanous, shifting veil between himself and the world. As if she reads his thoughts, Sarai raises her hands, gestures around them. Answers his question. They look at each other, filthy, manacled, chained, and a brief laugh spills from their cracked lips, inundating him with relief and a strange gratitude. They are a country. Dr. Grieves stares at them quizzically, shakes his head.

"You're still feverish," he says to Jacob. "But you'll survive."

"Apparently to be hung as a spy."

"As I said, the disposition of your case is still uncertain."

"We're prisoners of war," Sarai says.

"These matters are not in my purview." The doctor purses his lips. "As I understand it, the force with which you were captured was . . . irregular. Not army or militia."

"We are American soldiers," Sarai says again. She places a hand on Jacob's arm, as if to link them, places her other hand on her belly.

The corporal's words suddenly come back to him. *That pickaninny you're whelping may save you, lass.* He stares into her eyes. She holds his gaze without blinking. Nods. Lifts her hand, picks up his, and moves it to her belly, pressing it down onto her skin.

NINE

TOWERHILL

PASSING THE FIRE

It is no more than six miles from Bladensburg to Washington City and the late summer twilight still lingers as they come in sight of the twin buildings of the Capitol, its sandstone blocks glowing red in this last light, rows of windows dark and ocular against it. They stop at a crossroads just before the complex. Mansions line the street, and their windows are dark as well, though in one Towerhill thinks he sees a candle flare up and go out, like a blink. Cockburn nods to him and he in turn nods to Neb, who walks forward into the road, holding a white flag of truce. They need to be certain, Scott told him, that the town has surrendered. Towerhill had wanted to carry the flag himself, but Cockburn had forbidden it, told him not to be absurd. For a few hours that afternoon, camped at Bladensburg, he had been afraid he would be robbed of whatever sense of culmination his entrance into the capital would provide, afraid, at first, they would bypass Washington altogether or that only the white troops would be allowed to enter the city. But General Ross had made it clear how he wanted to use the black marines. "It will be fitting," he said to Admiral Cockburn, "if Sergeant Towerhill and his Colonial Marines lead our *parade* into that— what do you call it, George?—that 'nest of buggering vipers.'"

Scraping their eyeballs with the sight of black men with guns, their nightmares unbound into their waking lives. Just say it, Ross, he had thought, tightening his lips to keep the words in. Seeing in his mind the plantation he had burnt to free himself, all the plantations and houses and towns after that, a pyre to commemorate and incinerate the years of his enslavement, a line of burnt offerings that would end here.

—

Now Neb walks into the street. At first he simply struts, but then, as some of the white soldiers laugh, he begins bobbing and dancing, waving the flag vigorously, acting—to Towerhill's anger—the fool for them. But the shot that cracks through the air does not come near Neb. It strikes Ross's horse. For an instant, there is complete silence, the British frozen in a tableaux. The horse whinnies once, not loudly, and a shudder travels through its flesh. It collapses slowly, as if allowing its master time to safely dismount. During the day's fight, it had been as untouched and unflinching as its rider, charging with him into the thick of combat. Towerhill knows, has been told repeatedly, that this horse carried the general through all the fighting in Spain and France. Now he sees Ross kneel by it, holding its great head in his hands and murmuring to it, tears running down his cheeks as his aides stand by uneasily. "There will be no punishment unless there is resistance," Ross had ordered. Towerhill feels a surge of gratitude towards the animal. Its death will burn a city.

All of them standing and watching Ross's farewell to his horse as if it is a stage play. Another shot rings out; he sees the flash from the window of one of the mansions lining the street. A soldier from the fusiliers falls, clutching his stomach. More shots. One rips a hole in Neb's white flag; he waves it with more energy, still dancing in circles in the street, jumping up and down and laughing. Another strikes near Cockburn's horse, the animal rearing, and then two more soldiers go down; his marines and the British are firing back now, squads running into the mansion. Towerhill yells at Craney to follow him; he runs to the other side of the Capitol in time to see a group of Americans, none in uniform but all armed with muskets, laughing and clapping each other on the back like schoolboys playing a prank as they run down the hill in the direction of the White House. He stops, shoots, his people opening fire also; one of the Americans clutches his head, spins, falls. His comrades, no longer laughing, scatter, abandoning him. For an instant Towerhill considers following them. But then he feels the heat of the flames behind him. When his squad comes back to the street, the shooters' mansion is on fire, and George Evans is battering at a padlock on the Capitol doors with the hilt of his sword. The lock swings back and forth, undamaged, until Evans curses, steps back, draws his pistol, and shoots it off.

Some of the marines rush forward into the south building, following Ross and his aides. The House of Representatives, Towerhill recalls. He had studied the plans for these buildings when he had been hired out to the architect William Boulton; he had been taken to Washington to see the start of the construction. Whose black hands had finished the task? Towerhill studies the tangible buildings themselves now, coldly, methodically, only his sixth finger twitching, as if it is the gauge of some inner turmoil. The two structures are made of enormous blocks of sandstone, and their roofs are iron. But between them—he knows the plans are to join them under a great dome—is only a connecting wooden passageway. It will burn. The rest must be put to fire from the inside out.

Cockburn and Scott enter with some of the fusiliers, who are carrying a tripod and several Congreve rockets; the admiral, apparently, has become fond of them. A mistake, Towerhill thinks. He hurries after them. Just inside the door, an old slave dressed in silk pantaloons and a white wig tries to block his way. "Where you going, nigger," the old man demands. Towerhill grabs him by the two sides of his vest, lifts him, and puts him aside. High firestone columns rise to support a vaulted ceiling and glass skylights, with red silk curtains hanging ceiling to floor, and creating what seems to his eyes a jarring opulence against the elegantly simple architecture of the room. A huge carved eagle, wings spread, and a marble statue of a woman holding a document stand above and behind the rostrum at the head of the chamber. The Constitution of the United States of America. He remembers Cedric Hallam, Jacob's father, standing as he read the document to

Jacob and himself. A believer in educating darkies, if not freeing them. His eyes shining, his lips trembling. Reading to his captive audience in the book-lined sanctuary that had been his study. The sanctuary of lies. The repository of lies.

Cockburn, laughing like a schoolboy, has set up the tripod and—before Towerhill can warn him—sets off a rocket aimed at the ceiling. It bursts in a flower of red, showering sparks and shrapnel that ricochet off floors and tables and, surprisingly, do not kill anyone. Cockburn, his face blackened by powder, looks uncharacteristically embarrassed for a moment, but then recovers himself, and stands on the speaker's chair at the head of the room. "What say you, gentlemen?" he yells, his voice echoing. "Shall this harbor of Yankee democracy be burned? All for it, say aye!" Most of the men laugh, and yell aye, a wave of giddiness running through the room.

A hand claps Towerhill on the back; he spins, bringing his rifle around, nearly shooting the white soldier smiling at him. "Here be even hotter than blooming Africa, ain't it, Blacky," the man says in MacDougal's voice, his face and form blurring for a moment, and then coming back into focus as the tall, lean soldier from the 21st, the man offering him and Neb tea before Bladensburg. Towerhill brings his rifle up to the vertical, in salute, and turns away. The soldiers are piling up furniture, lugging in desks and cabinets and chairs they've dragged from the offices along the corridors, slathering them with gunpowder paste, giggling and giddy. "Leave the bloody corridors clear," he hears Scott shout. Cockburn himself ignites the fire; it shoots up to the ceiling, a wave of heat fanning out. "More!" he yells. "More fuel for Mr. Monroe's bonfire!" He spots Towerhill. "What say you, my good sergeant? How shall we proceed? What more do we need to feed this republican blaze?" He lifts and lowers himself on his tiptoes, excited as a child, the flames reflected in his eyes.

What they need comes to him. "Words," Towerhill says.

He turns, searching the chamber, spots the old slave still near the entrance, and strides over to the man, calling for Craney, Mingo, and Neb to follow him. The old man looks at him defiantly.

"Where's the library?" Towerhill asks.

"Call the Library of Congress, here," the old man says. "And *the* library of *this* Congress ain't a place for no traitorous trash like you."

Neb has his knife at the man's throat before Towerhill can say a word.

"You take us, old man, or I carve you another smile."

"You do that, nigger."

"Leave him," Towerhill says, suddenly weary. "I remember where it should be."

He leads them down the connecting wooden corridor to the North Wing, passing the Senate on the first floor, then the Supreme Court Chamber, where other soldiers are already piling furniture into a huge pyramid, then upstairs, following his memory, where he flings open the heavy oak doors. Shelves, with thousands of books in them, stand above him on all sides. Hallam's study writ large. As his eyes brush the leather spines, he feels the words stir all around him, squirming on the pages, scurrying to slyly configure themselves to the prospects notched in his mind. Pretending to shape the world into beauty. Millions of words. A tower hill of lies. A little nigger boy, his brain crawling with insectoid words, spewing them from his lips as if they were his. As if he could own them. As if they could save him. The freak of nature. The educated nigger. The terror in their lives. He goes to the shelves, and begins gathering armfuls of the books, throwing them onto the floor. *This harbor of Yankee democracy.* Neb grinning at him. Cap'n Book. Laughing at him. Laughing with him. He laughs with Neb, two black men laughing together in the face of lies. *Debates of the British House of Commons, Journals of the Lords and Commons.* Law books. Glanvill, Hale, and Coke. Boswell's *Journal of a Tour of the Hebrides.* Bertram's *Travels. History of the Colony of Massachusetts Bay.* John Locke. *The end of law is not to abolish or restrain, but to preserve and enlarge freedom. For in all the states of created beings capable of law, where there is no law, there is no freedom.* Shakespeare. *Hath not a nigger organs,* he will proclaim to Neb, *dimensions, senses, affections, passions; fed with the same food, hurt with the same weapons, subject to the same diseases, heal'd by the same means, warm'd and cool'd by the same winter and summer, as a white man is? If you prick us, do we not bleed? If you tickle us, do we not laugh? If you poison us, do we not die? And if you wrong us, do we not revenge? If we are like you in the rest, we will resemble you in that.* Jefferson. Cedric Hallam standing like Moses descended from the mount, like God in his heaven, reading down to them. We hold these lies to be self-evident.

"You going read them all, Book?" Neb asks.

An analogy, Towerhill thinks. Neb is to Towerhill as Bertram was to Jacob.

Craney looks at them worriedly. "Admiral is waiting on this, Towerhill."

"Let him wait," Neb says. "Cap'n Book *reading*."

Towerhill points at the shelves. "Craney, you, Mingo; you remember the day the north barn burned?"

Craney looks at him, puzzled.

"You remember how we made a line, passed buckets?"

"Sure, Towerhill. Put out the fire."

"You get the others, get the British too, form a line, here back to Cockburn."

Neb laughs, seeing it. "Going to pass the fire."

Craney nods. "Sure, Towerhill. We can do that."

"Then go."

——

At first, they pass the books along the line of men stretching from the library back to the South Wing, but this is too slow, and soon soldiers are taking armloads, throwing some into the now-burning Senate Chamber, running more over to Cockburn in the other wing, throwing books onto the bonfire, the heat blasting back into their faces, woolen uniforms growing hotter, sweat soaking into the fiber, steaming, so that little clouds hover over their shoulders as they run. Other soldiers have found documents in the clerks' office downstairs and throw them into the flames as well. Towerhill tears down a damask curtain from an anteroom near the library, fills it time and again with load after load of books, running back and forth, panting, breathing in lungfuls of hot smoke from the burning pages, tasting their ash on his lips. Finally the room is empty, and he runs with the last load and flings it onto the fire. The books flare as they hit the flames, burst into flame themselves, pages swiftly blackening and curling. The heat has grown unbearable, and some men scream in pain as they inadvertently touch metal buckles or buttons. Fire runs up the silk curtains; the glass of the skylights melts and drips, molten glass falling on one man's back, threatening to torch him as his comrades roll him on the floor. Ross, sweat runnelling his blackened face, finally yells at them to evacuate the buildings.

Outside Towerhill stands with Cockburn, Ross, and the others watching from a safe distance, their features strangely animated and fluid in the light from the fire. It is full night now, but the flames shooting up from the two buildings and from the fires across town in the Navy Yard—set ablaze by the Americans themselves—illuminate the sky with false daylight.

Towerhill walks away from the laughing Englishmen over to the silent formation of his own people, standing in solemn witness, each of them, to a man and woman, understanding what the British will never understand about what they are seeing on this night. He walks back further, until he can take in all of the picture. But as the buildings burn, it is only the image of books flaring like moths drawn into a fire that he sees in front of his eyes, the books and a room where three children sit surrounded by other books, entranced by lies and promises. He wants to rejoice, to flicker and elongate and dance like a flame himself at this culmination for which he has been waiting and killing, his life a line of fire moving inexorably from the flames of the plantation's manor house to this blaze lighting the sky over Washington. Something loosens in him at this moment, a fist that has been squeezing his heart for so long he no longer knows it is there until it suddenly releases its grip. He has come to this place and has done what he has needed to do; he has liberated the words and now he can see them rise phoenix-like from the flames, their letters twisting and writhing, shaping into forms unforeseen by those who had fashioned them, released now into the world like unwrapped promises.

—

In the White House, the smell of roasted meat fills his nostrils. In the dining room, the table had been set, as if in anticipation of their arrival: a damask tablecloth, matching napkins, fine china plates, crystal goblets.

Now the light from their torches sparks gleams of fire from the silverware and crystal. For a few seconds, the small crowd of British officers, caked with ash, dust, and sweat, stand stunned. And then erupt into laughter. How good of Madison to prepare a feast to celebrate their victory. Will the famous Dolley attend them? One hears she offers quite a spread. Ah, Madeira wine; what aristocratic tastes these democrats have. The beef too rare, what? Not to worry, it will be Cockburned to a crisp soon enough.

And so on.

As the officers sit at the table, Cockburn waves a leg of lamb at Towerhill, motioning for him to join them. But he remains in the doorway. He is repulsed by their hilarity, though he cannot understand why. The faces— Cockburn, Ross, Smith, Evans, Scott, Glieg—all familiar to him, seem transformed, as if some devil beneath their skins has been unfettered. Scott spreads his hands, his gesture taking in the table, all the silver and crystal finery. "A feast worthy of the champions of republican freedom, what?" he says, directing his statement to the stray American they'd dragged in with them, coming across him as they walked to the White House. The plump young man is seated next to Cockburn, terrified and trembling, his white wig askew. He blanched when he'd been told the admiral's name. Now Cockburn throws an arm around his shoulder, pushes a wine-filled goblet under his nose with his other hand. "Come, good Yankee . . . what did you say your name was?" The man mumbles something. "What?" Cockburn shouts. "Speak up, lad! Display some of the boldness and courage your countrymen exhibited at Bladensburg!"

"Bold as rabbits," Evans laughs.

"It's Roger Weightman, sir."

"Of course it is not. It is Jonathan, yes? Roger Jonathan. Jonathan Jonathan."

The others at the table chant the name. "Jonathan, Jonathan, Jonathan."

"And what is your standing in life, Monsieur Jonathan?"

"Sir?"

"What work do you do, idiot?" Scott calls.

"I'm a bookseller, sir."

Cockburn laughs. "And I'm a book burner. Isn't that right, Sergeant Towerhill? Where are you going, sergeant? Stay. Stay while we make a toast."

He stands, dragging the bookseller up. Raises his goblet. "To peace! To
peace with America and to hell with Madison!" He drains the goblet, fills
it again, makes Weightman drink. "That's it, Jonathan. Quaff it like a man!
Quaff, quaff!"

"Quaff, quaff," the others call.

Cockburn releases the bookseller, lifts himself up, and pulls a cushion
out from underneath himself. "Know what this is, Jonathan?" He doesn't
wait for an answer. "Took it from your queen's dressing room upstairs, to
have me a small souvenir of our presidential feast." He raises, kisses the
cushion. "Belongs . . . no, *belonged* to your queen herself, Mistress Dolley,
wife of the rather swiftly vacating James. I will keep it to remind me of
her . . . seat."

The British roar. Except, Towerhill sees, for Ross. A faint look of disgust
passes over the general's face.

"And now let's have a dance. Show our American representative here
how John Bull spins!"

Smith and Scott get up from the table and dance, an exaggerated min-
uet, singing to each other, their voices pitched high:

> *A landlady of France,*
> *She loved an officer, 'tis said,*
> *And this officer he dearly loved her brandy, O!*
> *Sighed she, "I love this officer,*
> *Although his nose is red,*
> *And his legs are what his regiment call bandy, O!"*

"Come join us, my dear sable friend," Scott calls to Towerhill. "Show
us how Blacky can dance as well. No? Why not? Come back! Desertion is
punishable by hanging!" He wags a finger at Towerhill, and Harry Smith
sings to him, extending his arms:

> *Fifty I got for selling me coat,*
> *Fifty for selling me blanket.*
> *If ever I 'lists for a soldier again,*
> *The devil shall be me sergeant . . .*

Towerhill leaves the singers. Enters the kitchen. The place must have been abandoned moments before they arrived. Spits with joints of meat are still turning on the fire. A black man sits on a stool in front of the grate, singing softly to himself, drinking from a silver goblet. He turns to look at Towerhill, takes in the singed red uniform. His eyes are yellow and bloodshot.

"What are you doing here?" Towerhill asks.

"What's it look like I doing?"

Towerhill waves a hand at the kitchen. "All this. Who was it for?"

"Who you think lives here, nigger? It's for the president, when he come back."

"You're free, man. You can leave."

The man snorts. "Where *to,* Mr. Nigger Red Coat? I'm American. I'm here."

Towerhill stares at him, their eyes locked.

"Stay," he says to the man. "Stay and burn."

—

When he returns to the dining room, it is crowded with men from the 20th Fusiliers, Cockburn's sailors, and some of his own Colonial Marines. One of the white soldiers has piled all of the silver, plates, and goblets in the center of the damask tablecloth; he and another bring the two ends of the cloth together, creating a sack for the loot. Ross, his face still serious, tells the man to bring it all outside. He spots Towerhill.

"Come, help us, sergeant," says Ross. "There is still work to be done this night."

The general picks up a chair, puts it on the table. Swaying slightly, the other officers, including Cockburn, follow his example; along with the soldiers, they pile all of the furniture in the room on the tabletop. They tear down the curtains and add them to the heap; then the fusiliers spread on the gunpowder paste, as they had done in the Capitol.

"Towerhill," Cockburn calls. He is holding a torch. Towerhill walks over to the admiral. Cockburn hands him the torch, looking into his eyes, all drunkenness seemingly vanished. Towerhill raises it to him in salute, turns, and puts the torch to the edge of the tablecloth. It bursts into flame. A cheer arises, and the others begin throwing their torches onto the pile.

"Are your marines ready?" Cockburn asks, as they move towards the door.

Before Towerhill can answer, they are outside in the humid August air, which feels cool on his face after the blast of heat. He sees Neb, in front of the company, next to another company of white marines and sailors. The men in both groups hold long poles, topped with plate-sized balls of cloth smeared with gunpowder paste. They surround the White House.

"They're ready, sir."

Cockburn nods. "I owe a certain debt to you, sergeant. This evening's work is my first payment on it." He nods towards the building. The flames inside make the windows glow red. "You may proceed."

Towerhill walks over to one of the windows. He can see the flicker of flame inside, the shadow of fire playing on a corridor wall. He raises his rifle, smashes it butt first into the glass, a shard cutting his cheek as it falls, his tongue spontaneously licking out, tasting the blood on his lips. "Like that," he says to Neb.

"Break them up!" Neb yells, and the marines surge forward and smash the glass with their muskets. Mingo stands nearby holding one of the fire poles. Towerhill remembers him felling Adams with an iron bar, on the day of the revolt, the day of a beginning that has brought them here. Towerhill strikes a match and nods to the smith, who grins and lowers the pole. He touches the flame to the gunpowder-smeared ball. It flares. "Light them!" he shouts, and Mingo touches the flaming ball to the next pole, and the next. When all are aflame, the men throw them through the broken windows.

Fire finding fire.

TEN

TOWERHILL

―

DARKNESS

They burn structures all around the city the next day. Only government buildings, Ross orders, Towerhill bridling at the hypocrisy. Officers whip or shoot soldiers for looting or unauthorized burning, determined to show the uncouth Yankees how a civilized nation acts. But Towerhill is here to be the terror in their lives. Isn't that why he was recruited? He remembers MacDougal, speaking of Neb's atrocities: *What he has done is exactly what Cockburn wants from you people.*

His marines burn what they can. They burn until the white soldiers become black. Smoke lingers in his nostrils, clings to his uniform. He tries to capture and keep each moment in his brain, as if it's a box he can open and look into later. But the knowledge of what they are doing is too fantastical. He is living in something he's imagined for too long to trust its veracity; and when he lies down that night, sleepless, his throat raw from smoke, his hand still clutching and unclutching a torch he is no longer holding, he can recall only disjointed images of the day, a few places and incidents that for some reason stay in his mind. Near the War Office, a lone American horseman charging them, screaming, a pistol in each hand; Craney shooting him off his horse, offhand, casually, leaving the body lying in the street as the soldiers put the building to the torch. Shots fired at them from behind a house; a woman coming out to plead with them before they torch it but screaming when she sees their black faces. An officer accusing a soldier of looting, striking him in the face; the man's hat flying off, spewing silver gewgaws and balled-up silk scarves stolen from a house. The remnants of the Navy Yard, where, when they burn a shed filled with ships' ropes, cordage, hemp wraps, sheets, braces, noxious clouds of black smoke swirl up from barrels of tar, twisting hundreds of feet into the air. A sight echoed, strangely, later in the day when a patrol, ordered to blow up a gunpowder magazine, finds it empty and not knowing the Americans have thrown the gunpowder into a well, some of the soldiers toss a few lighted cigar butts into it. Their bodies, or parts of their bodies, scatter everywhere; perhaps thirty die—more than were killed in taking the city.

Four times during the day, Towerhill's company came across slaves; each time he invited them to come with the British. He is still furious about the looks of fear or disgust they cast upon him, as if he and they were not of the same flesh. *I'm an American. I'm here.* Hates that those words still echo something in his own heart. He thinks of Sarai, sees her and Jacob twisting around each other in the flames of Washington, their chained forms conjured in roiling, billowing, black smoke.

They burned until a storm rolled in late that afternoon, the sky turning pitch-black as if absorbing the smoke that had arisen from the city, great crashes of thunder and a violent wind tearing the roofs off houses and sending shingles whirling like shrapnel. A deluge that doused the flames, the work of his day, in minutes.

They left the city that night, exhausted, the marching soldiers stumbling and falling asleep on their feet. Retraced their steps to Bladensburg, where the battlefield was still scattered with the naked, bloated corpses of their own soldiers, stripped and looted; their wounded, those too hurt to load onto wagons and bring to the ships, left behind in American homes. Towerhill made sure that none of his people were among them. He saw that the throats of some of the black dead had been slit, their faces battered in: injuries that told him they'd still been alive at the end of the battle.

Four days later, he sits in Cockburn's cabin on the *Albion,* anchored off Benedict. Only the two of them are crammed into this small, close space, the porthole admitting shuddering rhomboids of greenish light that make Towerhill feel he is under the sea rather than on it. Cockburn is behind a pine-plank table spread with a map of Baltimore and its harbor; he is a different, quieter man, not the strutting braggart Towerhill had seen in Washington. Yet some of that man reappears when the admiral offers him a glass of Madeira, making sure Towerhill sees that its decanter bears the presidential seal of James Madison.

"Jemmy's wine," he says. "Towerhill, do you remember that horseman you shot out of the saddle? The man with a pistol in each hand?"

"I didn't shoot him. It was Corporal Craney."

Cockburn waves the name away. "A pity you can't be credited. The man's name was John Lewis, a sailor. He'd been impressed onto one of our ships, and escaped that day."

"Sir?"

A grin twitches on Cockburn's lips. Towerhill waits for whatever game is being played out.

"Lewis was George Washington's nephew. You can tell Corporal Craney he has spilled the blood of the great traitor."

"I will convey that to him."

Cockburn peers at Towerhill, waits for more reaction. When he says nothing else, the admiral sighs. "Lieutenant Scott feels our burnings in Washington were a mistake. That they will put anger into Jonathan's heart, steel into his spine. Do you agree, sergeant?"

"It is of no concern to me, sir."

"Meaning it is not in your purview?"

"Meaning I care not what they feel."

Cockburn grins. "Exactly the correct response." He taps the map with his forefinger. "Thus far, courage has prevailed over timidity in our general's heart. With the grace of God we will soon have good use for your marines. This war—if I may flatter the great Yankee skedaddle with that

title—will bring us a far fatter prize than Washington." He slams his fist on
the table. "We should have marched on Baltimore immediately. But our
superiors, with their good British sense of fair play, felt they needed to give
Jonathan more time to prepare his defenses."

Cockburn sharing strategy with a black sergeant of marines. Towerhill
wonders what he is doing here; he is too tired to play the grateful nigger, to
be this man's audience any more.

"Sergeant, when we were in the White House, you recall I mentioned a
first payment to you?"

"Sir?"

"You requested information about two of our prisoners. Information
and a visit. I ordered a hearing of their case."

Their case. As if their link is fated and inevitable. He says, "Sir, when will
that occur?"

Cockburn raises his eyebrows. "It has occurred already, during our little
excursion to Jemmy's house. I think you will be pleased with the outcome.
You may visit the *Erebus* tomorrow, if you still wish. As you requested, we
hold the woman guiltless, as she was a slave to the man, one of your people, and powerless. I will release her to your custody, if that is your desire,
or"—he glances at Towerhill's face—"if not, will simply have her released,
though not until we have taken Baltimore."

Towerhill says nothing.

"And as for the man—your former master, as I understand—you will be
pleased to know that he is charged with spying. The group he was with is
not part of the regular army or the militias. Irregulars are considered spies.
And spies are hung. At your request, you may attend that event, though it
may have to wait also until we have taken Baltimore." He taps the name of
the city on the map again. Towerhill focuses on his finger, watching it trail
up the Patapsco to the city harbor, press on the blue of the water.

"The boat where they are being held? Do you know the meaning of its
name?" Cockburn asks him.

"Yes."

ELEVEN

TOWERHILL

—

BREAD AND CHEESE CREEK

When he opens his eyes in the morning, he feels that finger pressing the center of his forehead, opening a starburst of pain behind his eyes. He tries to once again expel Sarai and Jacob from his mind. But the choice couched behind Cockburn's smile chains him to the floating prison that holds them in darkness, suspended between earth and hell. They are still together, Sarai refusing to be separated from Jacob, a desire respected because of Towerhill's perceived special interest in her. Or so Scott, dispatched to Cochrane with messages from Ross and Cockburn, returned to report to him. Making that statement into a question. Towerhill refused to answer it, let his silence pile up to the height of a gallows. Let them stay together, rotting in his memory as they were in that brig. Let Jacob hang.

In his dreams, he sees three shadows cast on white sand overlap and meld.

He is separated from them now in any event, the *Erebus* part of an eighteen-ship squadron that, as the bulk of the army lands and swings up the North Point peninsula to hit the city from the east, will branch off to follow the west dogleg of the Patapsco River into Baltimore Harbor, its rocket and bomb ships tasked to take out the forts defending the city. Baltimore is to be squeezed between two pincers, the army and the navy—though, at Cockburn's insistence, the admiral and his contingent of sailors, marines, and Colonial Marines will remain with the landing force. According to signals from their spies and sympathizers in and around the port, the land force would have to contend with a series of entrenchments, breastworks, and redoubts dug in or built up on a ridge east of the city and fortified with more than a hundred cannons, including thirty-two-pounders loaded with grape and canister. And a mobilized army of twelve thousand men, or fifteen thousand, or twenty thousand, depending on the proximity of the agents to that force or their perception of what Ross might want to hear. After listening to their reports Cockburn became apoplectic, cursing Cochrane's timidity, the two weeks he had spent hesitating after Washington, unable to decide whether or not to take Baltimore and thereby giving the Americans time to prepare for attack. "He's given Jonathan the time and the spine," the admiral snarled.

Their passage up this river has been very different from the thrust up the Patuxent. The banks here are thick with watchers so that Towerhill cannot scout the shore parallel to the fleet as he had done before. As the ships come into view, alerts flash through the countryside, panic flickering in the watch fires that are lit one after the other, drawing a flame-dotted line of the British progress. The ships sail by hastily built watchtowers and signal stations, each one spewing out horsemen who gallop out to forewarn of the fleet's position and movement. The banks of the Patapsco teem with refugees; standing on deck Towerhill sees hundreds of people, panicked by the burning of Washington and Cockburn's reputation, leaving their towns and villages and farms, their possessions piled into wagons. Cockburn's reputation and now, the admiral tells him delightedly, Towerhill's as well, their fears of a slave revolt given a face and an appellation. Wanted posters bearing his name and image, depicted as a snarling, apish creature holding up a clawed six-fingered hand and dripping with blood, are everywhere, tacked up on trees, houses, the sides of barns.

One such image stares back at him now from the front page of the *Baltimore Patriot and Evening Advertiser*. The newspaper is spread across

Cockburn's map table. To Towerhill's surprise, the admiral throws back his head and howls. "You're my wolf," he says gleefully, slapping the illustration.

No, Towerhill thinks, I'm your dog, Cock Burn.

—

They land just before dawn on September 12th, running the prows of the landing boats into a beach sheltered by a large sandbar. They leap off the boats and immediately drop to their bellies in the warm sand. It cups Towerhill's belly and loins with an almost sexual caress. For a few moments, they lie in silence, as if all of them—his company, the four thousand others that he and they are part of—are collectively holding their breaths, waiting for the flash of musket or rifle fire from the dark scrub of tree line before them. Nothing happens. Towerhill's people look at him for a signal, and he peers into the forest, watching for moving shadows under the branches. The black spars of the trees spike through milky moonlight. Seeing nothing, he rises, runs forward; behind him he hears the creaking, clanking, breathing noise of a body of soldiers moving en masse. He rushes forward in a crouch—moving in spurts of twenty, thirty, forty yards—then flings himself down again, and the skirmish line, the whole army, forms to the marker of his body. No one fires at them.

They lie in line until dawn. They are fifteen miles from Baltimore. At first light, Ross and Cockburn, both on horseback, join them from the ships, Ross on a new stallion, the scar on his neck flaring red. "I will sup in Baltimore tonight or in hell," the general proclaims as he dismounts. His aides repeat the phrase and it passes down the line to the ranks. Ross has a penchant for creating memorable locutions, designed, Towerhill supposes, to inspire the troops. This one, he judges, lacks originality.

The woods are thick here, and when the army rises and advances, it splits around the trees like a tide breaking around pilings. Already the day's heat is pouring down on them. After advancing for about two miles, Towerhill's lead scouts come across a large farm and report back. "Is it a prosperous enterprise?" Cockburn asks, and when Towerhill says yes, the admiral suggests to Ross they order a halt for breakfast, give the men a rest before battle.

The farmer, a dour man named Robert Gorsuch, is obsequious, feeding Cockburn, Ross, and their aides eggs and thick slabs of ham, but eyeing Towerhill nervously. Cockburn catches the look and cries out for Towerhill to join them at the table. But he declines to be Cockburn's feared hound. In fact, he'd rather sup in hell. The two commanders, giddy with anticipated success, sit and stuff themselves, undoubtedly coining more fine phrases.

Towerhill goes in search of slaves. But they have either already run away or have been hidden by Gorsuch. He finds a set of manacles in the darkness of a barn. The building smells of animal urine and moldy straw, a scent that stings his nostrils and brings him full-force to his visit to the *Erebus*— the space where Jacob and Sarai were held close and dark, stinking of sweat and shit and fear, and, still, under all of it, the smell of them, which is the smell of his own flesh and something rooted beneath it. Jacob had turned his face to the bulkhead, but Sarai, the skin on her face shrunken to her skull, a line of pimples under the sweat and dirt on her forehead, stared at him, her eyes luminous, and spoke his name. "Towerhill."

"You don't have to be here," Towerhill said. "They will free you."

"Free him," she said. "They will hang him."

"As he would have freed us?"

"Look at him," she said. "Is he still what he once was?" She reached down, touched the manacle on his ankle, Jacob stirring, looking at him now, eyes half-closed. Not pleading.

Towerhill laughed. He grabbed the chain, yanked it. "Do you think a few weeks of wearing chains makes you my brother? You'd need to wear them for a hundred years."

Jacob nodded. "You are my brother," he said. "You killed my brother." He turned his face away, pressing it into the wood, Towerhill's hand still gripping the chain, Sarai rising and lunging for it. As she tried to stand, stooping under the low ceiling, he saw what he had not seen before: Jacob's get swelling her abdomen, her final betrayal.

He leaves the barn now, shutting the door behind him, out of habit, out of a desire to close off that memory, keep it in the darkness.

Scott gallops over to him, looking impatient. Cockburn wants Tower-hill and a squad from the Colonial Marines with the advance party; the admiral and Ross will stay in the lead of the army.

Towerhill takes Mingo and five other men. As they go forward, the day grows hotter. Branches whip against their faces as the forest closes around them.

"Stay close, sergeant," Cockburn yells to him. Has he become amulet as well as dog for the man?

Gunshots suddenly punctuate Cockburn's order. The crack of Harper's Ferry rifles. Snipers. The admiral and the general rise in their saddles, peer into the thick woods, trying to spot the source of the fire. Two soldiers hurry toward them through the trees, carrying the corpse of a third. Ross curses, wheels his horse to the right, "We need more men," he yells to Cockburn. "I'll bring up the column." He slaps his reins, starts forward again. Towerhill hears another shot, sees a small eruption of red spurt from the black shoulder of Ross's tunic. He runs forward, as more rounds buzz past his head. Evans is already there. Towerhill sees Ross slump forward, the reins dropping from his hands. Before he can fall, Evans catches him by the unwounded shoulder, eases him to the ground, as the horse snorts and prances nervously. Towerhill turns to the direction from which the shots came and rushes forward, past the horror-stricken faces of the men already forming a tableau around the general. Two white soldiers, one emitting a steady stream of curses, run with him, zig-zagging among the trees. They spot the two snipers at the same time; the Americans are reloading. Tower-hill raises his rifle as he runs, opens fire; rounds from the other two soldiers burn past his ears. One of the snipers gasps, clutches his stomach; the other is head-shot, his forehead blasted away. The gut-shot man writhes on the ground. One of the British soldiers—a sergeant, Towerhill sees—has tears running down his cheeks; cursing, he sticks his bayonet through the snip-er's throat, puts his foot on the sniper's chest, pulls out the bayonet, pushes it in again. And again.

Towerhill goes back through the trees. Someone is yelling for a sur-geon. Evans is sitting down, Ross's head cradled in his lap, as another man—Towerhill does not know him—wraps a bandage around the general's shoulder and chest. Towerhill sees with a shock, just before the bandage covers it, that there is a second hole, this one in Ross's chest, blood pumping out. Cockburn kneels by him and Ross hands the admiral something—a locket?—says something Towerhill can't hear. Probably not he would sup in hell, a small cold part of Towerhill thinks. *We'll need more men; I'll bring up the column,* seems like a more fitting epitaph for the man, illuminating his nature better than whatever words he might be uttering into Cockburn's ear.

—

Mourning for Ross, or what Towerhill sees of it, is brief, and mostly an affair of the officers. He sees some of the enlisted soldiers with tears streaking their grimed faces, but more shrug, clean their weapons. Utter black jokes. Ross's command is taken by Colonel Arthur Brooke, a steady, blander presence. Towerhill's people seem more shaken by Ross's death than the white soldiers, a fact that bothers him until he is driven to understand it when Neb, stroking the hank of hair fastened to his shirt, berates them: "You niggers still think you need a massa telling your arses what to do? You be *soldiers.*"

—

Whatever mourning took place ends when the army arrives at North Point and finds three thousand American militiamen waiting for them, the left of their line hooking down from Bread and Cheese Creek, their backs against the forest, open fields of fire in front of them. Towerhill knows from the briefing he earlier attended with Cockburn and Ross that this is only a small delaying force: most of the American land defenses, the tens of thousands of men and hundreds of cannons the British expect to face, are entrenched perhaps five miles from here. The faces Towerhill can see in front of them now are grim and angry; he recalls Scott predicting that what happened at Bladensburg and Washington would steel the enemy's hearts. Cockburn rides out in front of the troops, galloping here and there on his white horse, waving his gold-plumed black hat with one hand and shaking his fist at the enemy, as if inviting them to a tavern brawl. As if reassuring his soldiers that nothing has changed with Ross's death. But Towerhill feels detached, feels none of the quiver of urgency he had felt at Bladensburg, the need to sweep these men from his path. Since Washington, something has burned out of him. *You are my brother. You killed my brother.* He knows Jacob was not speaking of Thomas; the knife point of those words—worse, the secret language he and Jacob still shared—thrusts to his heart. *As I had to, brother,* he had thought, but kept those words to himself.

—

The battle spools out in fragments of sound and image. He feels aloof, husked and indifferent. Perhaps the sensation is not unique to himself. How many years have these white soldiers been killing and dying? Egypt. Spain. France. Bladensburg. Washington. He sees soldiers from the 4th stop fighting to eat lunch, drawing rations from their packs as if at a picnic, waiting for their rockets, musketballs, and shrapnel to finish shredding the American line, then rising and advancing to be methodically shredded themselves as American cannons fire grapeshot and scrap metal—broken musket barrels, old locks, chains, hinges—into their ranks. The British quick-step forward, other soldiers filling gaps in the ranks as soon as men fall. Their bayonets are steady, and for the most part the men are silent, though a few cheer, a few scream Ross's name, a few spew curses in rhythm with their footfalls. Towerhill sees a heavy-set blond boy, his face blotched with pimples, shout, "Shit, shit, shit, shit," over and over, as if calling out a cadence.

Towerhill still feels nothing. The sense of hovering detachment makes him imagine he is already dead, his soul watching the curious, senseless strivings of the living, bayonets thrusting into meat, the heavy thud of bodies crashing into one another, grunts and screams, flashes, men sinking their teeth into each other's throats. The smoke is a thick curtain between himself and some overacted farce. Rents in it open here and there to reveal frozen pictures of soldiers locked together, their mouths open in screams he can no longer hear. Neb is leading Towerhill's company, pointing, yelling orders Towerhill should have been yelling. He lets him. MacDougal's bruised face, a black tongue formed of gunpowder smoke flickering from his mouth, swirls into view in front of his eyes, its features shifting into Jacob's mocking countenance. He thrusts his bayonet into that swirl, its point finding a throat, feels the slight, initial resistance of the flesh and then the ease of the slide. Slams the butt of his rifle into the face of a stocky, bald man with corded arms who comes at him with an axe raised over his head, the shock of the blow vibrating up his own arms. Beats in the man's head. When he looks up, drained as if from a hard job of work just accomplished, the Americans are retreating, the living shedding a trail of their dead as they back off the field.

Watching them fall back into the trees, Towerhill feels a heaviness moving through him, as if his mind and body is a sack slowly filling with water. As if his detached soul is reentering his body, learning anew the knowledge of weight. He knows the retreating militia should be pursued. But he is paralyzed with weariness. He struggles to keep his eyelids open. He is not alone. The army has become a single organism, overcome by a heavy, relentless fatigue that is both the opposite of battle rage and the price of it. It spreads through the ranks like contagion, immobilizing soldiers in spite of half-hearted commands from Cockburn and Brooke to pursue the enemy into the woods. Towerhill sits down in place, the others collapsing around him, and passes into sleep.

—

That night it rains heavily, washing away blood, soaking the soldiers lying heaped in the field, the living and the dead equally oblivious. MacDougal comes back to him all night, not as he had seen him during the hanging, the fifteen slow minutes it had taken him to choke to death, but with a face made of smoke and ash.

—

Towerhill awakens just after dawn to hear what he at first takes for thunder, bright flashes in the sky to the west, great booms, unearthly howls, and a continuous rumble that he feels in the earth when he puts his hand flat on the wet ground. The bombardment of the Baltimore harbor forts has begun. How much louder it must be for Sarai and Jacob in the *Erebus*. Though what they will be waiting for is the silence that will follow, the gallows standing in that silence. He remembers another boat, three children paddling towards an island painted along a horizon that continually receded from them. He is suddenly, fully awake, he, Towerhill formerly of Towerhill Separation, presently separated from his own heart.

He will not let Jacob hang.

TWELVE

TOWERHILL

———

BEGGING HIS PARDON

Cockburn's tent is lit from the inside by a lantern; his silhouette and Scott's play against the canvas. Towerhill starts toward the entry flap, and a second later feels the tip of a bayonet trembling at his throat. "Hold right there, Blackie." The sentry is a short white man, his hat dripping rain.

Scott sticks his head through the flap. "Towerhill." He gestures at the sentry to lower his musket. "It's quite all right, corporal. I know this man. Resume your post."

The sentry salutes, about-faces, and continues on his rounds.

"Are you a fool," Scott asks, "coming up on us this way?"

"I need to see the admiral."

"*Sir,* damn your eyes," Scott snaps.

"Yes, *sir.* I need to see the admiral, *sir.*" He will nigger all he needs.

He can see Scott's face, blurred by the rain, staring at him wide-eyed, visibly coming to a decision.

"Who is it, Scott?" Cockburn's voice.

"Sergeant Towerhill, sir."

"Towerhill? Let the man in."

The rumble of artillery continues; he knows the bombardment is occurring to the southwest, at the mouth of Baltimore Harbor, but it sounds as if it is all around them.

Inside, the tent is hot and dry. Cockburn is in shirtsleeves, his face haggard, his trousers and boots, like Scott's, mud-spattered and still wet, as if they have just been riding. He looks years older than he looked yesterday, though Towerhill can't tell if this impression is due to the lantern's flickering shadows.

"Your blacks fought well yesterday, sergeant. As always."

"Thank you, sir."

"You know, Towerhill, my opinion of your race was, at one time, very low. But you and your men and the other Colonial Marines have unsettled that notion." Cockburn's eyes suddenly brim with tears. He turns away quickly. "It was a hard day. For all of us. That man gave me fits: one day the timid lamb, the next the hungry wolf. But there was no doubting his courage."

"General Ross was brave when it came time to be brave, sir."

"Aye, there was that." Cockburn closes his eyes for a few seconds. When he opens them, his voice is firm. "Though he didn't always know when that time had arrived. What brings you here, Towerhill?"

"Sir, before the battle, you gave me information about my friend, and my former master."

"Ah, that. Well, be patient, Towerhill. He is not hanged yet. My understanding is that he has been transferred to Admiral Cochrane's flagship, in preparation—he and several other condemned men. Would you care to attend?"

"Sir, I would prefer to have no hanging to attend."

Cockburn raises his eyebrows. "Speak plainly, sergeant."

"I ask for parole for him, sir. You have sent other Yankee prisoners home, with pledges not to fight against us anymore."

Cockburn says nothing for a long moment. Then he looks into Towerhill's eyes, as if seeing something there he has not noticed before. "Offers of parole are for soldiers, not spies."

"He is no spy, sir."

"You will not tell me what he is or is not. He was captured with irregulars, armed but not in uniform, member of no militia or national army. Towerhill, do not strain my patience. Our loss yesterday, the loss to the army and to myself, does not incline me to mercy."

"Sir, you spoke of paying a debt."

Scott pushes forward, stepping in front of Cockburn as if to protect him. "You are going too far, sergeant. Get out of here before I have you arrested."

Cockburn holds up a hand. "That will do, lieutenant, and thank you. But Towerhill is correct. I always pay my debts."

"Thank you, sir."

Cockburn clenches the hand into a fist, raises a forefinger. "Once."

There is a long silence. The admiral raises another finger. "Twice."

"Yes, sir."

"I will not intervene in this matter directly," Cockburn says.

"Sir? If you will not do . . ."

"The hanging is set for tomorrow. I will request Admiral Cochrane look into the matter and decide."

"I beg your pardon, sir . . ."

Cockburn snorts. "Yes," he says, drawing the word out. "Precisely. You are precisely begging my pardon, Towerhill."

"But if the hanging is set for tomorrow, how . . ."

Cockburn raises his hand, stopping his question. He pauses and stares into Towerhill's eyes, as if his opinion of this black man has been unsettled also.

"There is a service you may render me, sergeant," Cockburn says finally. "I am sending Lieutenant Scott to Admiral Cochrane's flagship with a message from myself and Colonel Brooke. You will accompany him. While there, you may, if the admiral permits, beg him for this peculiar pardon. Perhaps you might even explain your strange reasons for this sudden change of heart."

"Thank you, sir."

Cockburn slaps the flat of his hand onto the map before him. "Damn you, I want you to understand the importance of his mission. I don't give a tinker's damn if the man's neck is stretched or not, and I don't give another damn about what has possessed you to risk my anger this morning. You dare to bring up what I owe you as if you're a merchant calling in a bill of services. I cannot decide if I admire your audacity or if you're simply a fool. Very well; this pays the bill. In finality. Your presence will be useful in making sure Lieutenant Scott arrives safely."

"Admiral, I do not need, . . ." Scott starts.

"I will determine what you need, Scott. Towerhill knows the country. If anything should happen to you, he may continue the mission. Towerhill, our survival and success depend on receiving heavy artillery support from the navy, delivered at exactly the correct time. We'll be attacking the American line, at Hampstead Hill. I'm sure you've already surmised that. The message Lieutenant Scott will be carrying to Admiral Cochrane informs him of the time of the attack—which will be tomorrow morning, at two o'clock—and emphasizes the need for bringing the naval bombardment onto the American line at that time."

Towerhill hears rain beating against the canvas, the continuous rumble of the distant barrage behind it.

"There will be a feint, to the Yankee right, a diversionary attack," Cockburn says, "and then we will hit their left with two columns. Your Colonials will be part of the feint."

"Yes, sir."

"Do you understand why I am telling you this?"

Towerhill nods in Scott's direction. "In the event that Lieutenant Scott is captured or killed. So I can inform Admiral Cochrane."

"Good. And you understand the importance of such a message and why I want men I can absolutely trust to deliver it?"

"I do, sir. But my request . . ."

"Are you mad, Towerhill?" Scott asks.

Cockburn holds up a hand. His face seems unnaturally white in the half-light of the tent; Towerhill sees for the first time the utter weariness in his eyes. "I will write a note for you to take to Cochrane, asking that he consider your request for this man's parole."

"Just consider, sir?"

Scott glares at him. But Cockburn ignores the question, looks him up and down. "Prepare yourself: inform whoever may take your place in the company about your possible absence. My hope is it will not be necessary to replace you. You will very likely be back in time to join the attack."

THIRTEEN

SARAI

A CURTAIN OF SMOKE

She had tried to fight them when they came to take him away, clawing at the face of one of the men—a boy actually, wide-eyed and nervous—drawing blood. The second soldier, older, with grizzled grey sideburns, slapped her, holding onto his musket with his other hand. When she fell back, he pressed the muzzle against the swell of her belly as her legs splayed awkwardly. "I'll shoot the both of you, missy," he said, and she knew he was not speaking of Jacob.

And now, with Jacob gone, she still feels as if something has been pulled out of her, an emptiness into which she is collapsing. She tries to believe that this other presence within her will fill the void, and perhaps in time it will, but she knows also there will always be a sigh of absence in the center of her soul. She will be freed, the soldiers told her, paroled when the fighting is finished and left in Baltimore. Freed from them, but still held by invisible chains to Jacob. And held by the visible chain of her skin to the servitude that will await her, a colored woman without papers of manumission or anyone to speak of her service. All dead or captured, we sort of people. Servitude awaits her and awaits the child inside her, born to one day be pulled away from her as she had been torn from the mother

319

she never knew. Wrenched from the womb of a mother and the womb of a ship. Her life, past and future, an endless chain of confinements and separations.

She moves her hands under her dress, flattens her palms on the warm mound of her belly. Feels the child quicken under them.

There is a roar all around her and she feels the ship juddering as it fires rockets at her country. Her country still. Those three words coming into her mind as if emerging from a depth. If she were allowed on the deck, allowed to see what is being torn asunder by the rockets of the *Erebus*, she knows that is what she would see: her country still, waiting for her across the dark water and dark itself—something huge and nebulous and unformed, its shape hazy behind a translucent curtain of smoke, only briefly delineated by flashes of fire.

FOURTEEN
TOWERHILL

——

MERCY

Neb sleeps with his hands clasped around his knees, his chin, on his chest, nested by the hank of Thomas Hallam's hair, one delicate strand drawing in and out of one of his nostrils. Towerhill remembers how Neb had pressed his face close to Thomas Hallam's at Zekiah Fort, the flash of fear in his eyes as Mingo wrapped his arms around him and Sally yanked his head back by the hair. Afterwards, Neb had brandished the scalp, shaking it in front of Towerhill. "Wanted to be an Indian, him," Neb had said.

Towerhill picks up a pebble and tosses it at Neb, hitting him in the forehead. Neb springs up instantly, the same skinning knife he'd used on Thomas Hallam in his hand. Which is why he has awakened the man from a safe distance. Neb squints up at him. There is no sleep in his eyes. Once Towerhill had wanted to kill him, if only to stop seeing the mirrored reflection of himself he glimpsed in Neb's eyes. Once. Now he gives over his command to the man, in case he does not return.

He and Scott, on horseback, cross the North Point peninsula to the shore of the Patapsco, staying well south of yesterday's fight to avoid American patrols. A gig, a sailor to row it, and a navy officer wait for them on the beach—a lieutenant, like Scott, who stares and raises his eyebrows

when he first sees Towerhill. On the bay, the bombardment is steady, deaf-
ening, the undersides of the rain clouds lit in red and white flashes. "Be a
bit rough, our little sea voyage," the lieutenant says. "Cochrane's moved
his flagship to the *Surprize*. Appropriate, in't?" He waves vaguely at the
bay, as if to indicate the direction of the ship. The sailor, his face grim,
says nothing, just rows, but the lieutenant is chatty with nervousness or
excitement. He points out ships and American fortifications: in spite of
the rain, the black square silhouettes of the forts in Baltimore Harbor are
sometimes visible, sometimes obscured by smoke, their walls reflecting
the flashes of the rockets and bombs. "McHenry, there," the lieutenant
yells, wiping rain from his eyes. "On the left, Covington and Babcock.
Damned Yankee names. Should all be called Jonathan, what?" They row
close to one of the bomb ships. "H.M.S. *Volcano,* rightly named, what?"
the lieutenant yells. Two gargantuan mortar guns fill the entire midship
deck between the two masts; when one of the 190-pound mortar shells is
fired, the hull shakes and the whole ship visibly sinks lower into the water.
Towerhill sees the beginning of its fiery curve into the air before the shell
disappears into the rain. And, apparently, into the water, as he never sees it
land and explode. Some of the shells are hitting the fort, exploding in red
and white bursts. Congreve rockets, sputtering and whistling, trailing red
sparks, arc up from other ships, or fly in straight horizontal lines towards
the American emplacements, their crisscrossing fire trails scribbling the
sky. Some hit; more seem to miss. He sees no return fire from any of the
forts; the British ships must be out of the range of their guns. The gig
is rocking back and forth violently, as if caught in a storm; the agitated
waves seem faceted, aglow in red and yellow. "*Devastation, Meteor, Terror,*"
the lieutenant screams over the noise, and it takes Towerhill a second to
understand he is naming bomb ships.

He grabs the man's forearm. "Where's the *Erebus*?"

The lieutenant looks down at Towerhill's hand, his face stamped with
disgust. Towerhill tightens his grip. The man doesn't speak but points with
his other hand. Towerhill can see nothing until a rocket is fired from a
point in the darkness somewhere in front of them and the flames from its

tail briefly reveal a low hull, a long dark form whose outlines blur and fade as the missile arcs until there is no delineation between boat and water and sky. "There," the lieutenant says. "Right there between heaven and hell. Doing its duty."

"Towerhill," Scott says. Nothing more. Towerhill thinks he hears a strange twilight-hour tenderness in his voice. He lets go of the lieutenant's arm, peers into the flash-illuminated, rainy gloom. He can no longer see the *Erebus*. Another mortar is fired from the *Volcano;* the gig has come closer to its hull, and the back-blast sink of the ship sends out a high-ridged wave that raises the smaller boat and then lets it down hard, slapping the water.

They meet Cochrane on the deck of the *Surprize;* the admiral is surrounded by a small flock of aides but stands apart from them, further down the rail, watching the bombardment through a spyglass. Rain drips from his wide-brimmed hat onto the lens; he curses and wipes it on his sleeve, then glances around to see Scott and Towerhill.

"Good morning, lieutenant. I've been expecting you."

Scott waves at the bomb and rocket bursts on the wall of the fortress. "It seems like a good morning indeed, sir."

Cochrane grunts. "Can't tell. Can't tell at all if all this damned lovely ordnance is actually hurting the buggers. They just sit there."

"They're bound to fall, sir. Jonathan doesn't have the guts to withstand a long bombardment. He's spineless."

"Yes, yes, of course, lieutenant," Cochrane mumbles, distracted. He slaps the copper-jacketed spyglass against his thigh. "What do you have for me?"

"Sir, might we go below?"

Cochrane raises the glass to his eye again, stands silently, his shoulders swaying slightly. More explosions blossom off the seawall of Fort McHenry. Towerhill sees two rockets fall within the walls, followed by a flash and a rising column of smoke. The British seamen cheer.

"Need more of that," Cochrane nods, and then looks up, blinking, at Scott. "Damn silly to be standing in the rain, don't you think, lieutenant? We should go below. Tell me what my firebrand Cockburn plans. *Toujours*

l'audace, Cockburn. Cockburn and Brooke, is it now? My condolences on
the loss of General Ross. Good man. Came through all that in Spain . . .
well, fortunes of war and all, what can I say? No doubt you grieve him
greatly, eh, lieutenant? As it should be, as it should be. Still, a lovely death,
I understand. Up in the saddle, boots on, so to speak, all that. Come."
Glancing at Towerhill. "Bring your man."

Towerhill follows the two officers below. The inevitable map is spread
out on a table in Cochrane's quarters, lit by two lanterns, their bases nailed
to the table top. He sees the harbor, the squares marking the American
forts, the city behind, their representation on the table, their twin actuality
through the glass of the cabin's port. Cochrane has unrolled and is reading
Cockburn's message. He chews his lower lip thoughtfully. The cannons
boom and the ship lists to one side, rocks back, the flame in the lanterns
elongating and contracting with the motion.

"Show me, lieutenant."

Scott indicates a crescent-shaped line, northeast of the city, with his
forefinger. "Hampstead Hill. The Americans . . ."

"General Smith," Cochrane interrupts.

"Whatever the blackguard's name, sir. They are dug well in, on a ridge-
line here, extending to here. Early this morning, we rode out and observed
their positions in person, the admiral, General Brooke, and I."

"Colonel Brooke, lieutenant."

"Yes, sir. I beg your pardon, sir."

You are precisely begging my pardon, Towerhill, Cockburn had said. Towerhill fingers the admiral's letter, held in a leather pouch against his chest.
He starts to speak, but then holds back, knowing how these men would
react to the interruption.

"By now, our troops have moved into position in front of the Jonathans."

"Of which there are how many, lieutenant?"

Scott hesitates. "We estimate from fifteen to twenty thousand men, sir."

"I see. And artillery?"

"We counted a hundred and twenty guns."

"Sizes?"

"All sizes, sir."

"The largest?"

Scott mumbles something.

"Speak up, lieutenant."

"Thirty-two-pounders, sir."

"I see. Loaded with grapeshot, no doubt. On the high ground. And your force is, what, less than five thousand? With how many cannons?"

"Why, as many as your ships carry, sir. Surely that is the point." Scott presses his finger down hard on the map, following the crescent of the American line. "These are militia. The people we have beaten again and again. By attacking at two in the morning, we can gain Jonathan's flank, hitting him here, at the left, where their guns stop, with two columns, and sending a diversionary column against their right. With your ships' artillery supporting our attack, at precisely the right moment, we will break them."

Cochrane remains silent, staring at the map.

"Sir," Towerhill starts.

"Shut your mouth, sergeant," Scott says.

Cochrane looks up, blinking, and speaks as if there has been no interruption. "We never meant to break them, Lieutenant Scott. Only to drub them. We have done more than that already with the burning of their capital, a foul barbarity I never ordered nor approved. Nor did the War Office."

"Sir, we . . ."

Cochrane puts up his hand. "I know your commander's desires, and I know his ambitions. Lieutenant, I will send a message back with you. You may read it, if you will. What I shall write is this. These forts will not fall. The one excursion I sent into their range of their guns was decimated. I will not waste more men on them. We will continue drubbing and then we shall withdraw. Without being able to advance beyond the forts, we will not be in range to support your proposed attack. I am not in command of the army. Neither is Cockburn. I will convey to Colonel Brooke that it is his decision in the end whether to attack or not. But I will not be able to support him and I will therefore recommend against it. My orders—our orders—are to move our force south, to New Orleans, and to therefore indeed have a force that can be so moved. To drub a while there, as it were."

"We can take them here, sir."

"We can sup in hell," Towerhill says.

Startled, Cochrane straightens up and stares at him, as if noticing him for the first time. The ape speaks. Scott glares. "Damn you, Towerhill . . ."

"No, quite right, sergeant. Well said. Colonial Marine, is it? You fellows have been quite fierce. And, it appears, quite sensible as well."

"Sir," Towerhill withdraws the message from his pouch. "This message is also from Admiral Cockburn."

Cochrane holds up a hand, palm out, against Scott's objections, and takes the paper with the other. "What's all this, then?" He reads, nodding, frowning. Towerhill waits. Cochrane hands the paper back to him.

"I see, sergeant. I commend your, eh, impulse towards mercy, especially since this is your former master. Quite commendable, your loyalty."

"Thank you, sir."

"But quite impossible also, I'm afraid. I have secured a pardon and man-umission for the woman, per Admiral Cockburn's request, but the man will hang, as soon as the bombardment is lifted. Our policy is quite clear. I can't let the example stand."

The lantern light flickers on the map of Baltimore, Cochrane's shad-owed face expressionless, Scott smiling slightly.

"You heard the admiral, Towerhill."

He has. The three men stand in silence, as if observing a moment of mourning. Cochrane sighs loudly, ready to turn his attention back to Scott. Towerhill feels everything slipping away.

"Sir," he blurts, "this blacky jus' want say goodbye to his old massa. He always good to me."

Scott looks at him in astonishment. He's never heard him putting on the nigger before. But Towerhill doesn't consider it much of a risk, present-ing a white man with the caricature he expects to see and hear. Cochrane turns to him, smiling, clearly touched and pleased by this utterance of servility that costs Towerhill only a few words and a piece of his soul. And that doesn't fool Scott for a second. The lieutenant starts to speak, but Cochrane interrupts.

"No, lieutenant, that's quite all right. As I said, he's shown commendable loyalty, both to his, as he says, 'old massa' and certainly, as I have heard tell, to us. You may see your good old massa." Cochrane seems to relish the words. He calls outside the door. "Sergeant Wilkins. Please escort this fellow to the brig. He has my permission to visit the prisoner in cell two." He glances at Scott. "Through the door only, Sergeant Wilkins."

As he follows Wilkins down the corridor and out onto the deck. Towerhill hears Scott still objecting. Outside, he feels rain on his face. The portside battery is firing, sailors shouting, cannons rolling back on their rails, bursts exploding on the sides of the fort, briefly illuminating its ensign. They enter a hatchway, descend into darkness. At the same time he is climbing, up into another fortress, the tower from which he took his name, the ruin that three children tried to imagine whole and complete. The fields spreading below them, verdant in the sun, the river sparkling, jewels of light dancing off its surface like silent laughter, schools of fish trembling the bright sheen of the water. The ship rocks back and forth with each volley, the noise growing muffled and dim as he and Wilkins descend. On the lowest deck, Wilkins lights another lantern. There is, Towerhill sees, not one brig, but a series of cells, tiny rooms, with padlocked doors and small slots at eye level. Something scrapes—fingernails?—in a crazed, private rhythm against the inside of one of the doors; a keening wail leaks from another.

"Do any of these cells hold a woman prisoner?"

Wilkins snorts. "No such luck, mate. All we got now are the condemned buggers. Got a pair of bollocks, every damned one. Here we are." He stops in front of a hatch with the number 2 painted on it, slides back the eyehole.

Towerhill peers inside. All he sees is blackness. He keeps staring until a part of the blackness delineates into an even darker form, hunched on the deck. He calls Jacob's name. Does he see the form stir? He feels a hollow in his chest.

"Let me inside, sergeant."

"Can't do that, Blacky. You heard the admiral. You wanted a visit, here you are."

"Look, he was my mate. No one is going to know."

"Very touching, that story. But I've got my orders."

"I understand," Towerhill says. Straightens up, turns, grins, slaps his hand hard against the back of Wilkins's neck, slams his face into the door-jamb, slams it again. The white man drops. Towerhill fumbles in Wilkins's pocket and finds a ring of keys. He begins fitting them one by one into the bottom of the large padlock. Wilkins groans, face down. A trickle of blood pools from what Towerhill assumes must be his forehead. He grips the sergeant's hair, yanks up his head, slams it down again. Someone is shouting Wilkins's name. A clatter of feet on the gangway. The fifth key clicks. He pulls the lantern from Wilkins's loose fingers and enters, closing the door behind him.

The stench is as heavy and fetid as it had been in Jacob and Sarai's cell on the *Erebus*, but somehow the strength has been hulled out of it; here it is more the dried memory of a smell. A chair, empty, stands in the center of the room. Jacob is sitting on the deck, his back to the wall. The shouts from outside are louder now, nearer. Towerhill turns the key in the keyhole and is relieved to feel the bolt slide home. He braces the chair against the door anyway, sets the lantern on the deck, and kneels next to Jacob, bring-ing his face close. Jacob's breath barely registers against his skin, but his eyes open. A slight smile plays on his lips.

"Towerhill," he says. "Towerhill." As if he is naming both the place and the man.

People are shouting and pounding against the door, a myriad of voices, muffled, coming from the other side. The angry voices of men and the laughing voices of children, all calling his name. He pulls Jacob to him and kisses his forehead, the skin hot under his lips. He releases him, draws his knife from its sheath, and slits Jacob's throat.

EPILOGUE

— 1833 —

SARAI

＿

THE MERIKAN

Sometimes she hears stories about the three of them, herself and her two men transformed into strangers who have stolen their names. *Kaiso* verses sung by women as they beat clothing against the rocks in the stream, as if that water had brought the words to them with its flow. Tales or fragments of tales recounted and made ribald in the drunken songs of black sailors in Port of Spain taverns, or told by the slaves still laboring on the sugar plantations. *Sing us a' the Six-Fingers, brother, sister.* Sarai gathers these to herself as, when she was a girl, she gathered small shells from the banks of the Patuxent, stringing them together to make a necklace for her invisible mother, furrowing the ground with her big toe, dropping the strung shells into that shallow scratch, and kicking the dirt, the soil on which her mother had never stepped, over it. Completing the voyage for her. Their lives a line strung from Africa. "In Africa," Auntie Rebekkah told her once, after Sarai had helped her with a birth, "what the old ones tell me, they cut the cord, bury it in the dirt there. Child always knows the home place, that way."

"This here Africa," declared some of the surviving elders from Towerhill Separation when the British deposited them on Trinidad. She did not doubt them then and does not doubt then now, as she stands next to her house. The corn in her garden is still low enough for her to see over the stalks to the green, jungled mountains, the rim of the verdant bowl where she now makes her free life.

She carries her mother to this place, and now Jacob and Towerhill as well, five shells taken from a water more azure than the Patuxent could ever be. Completing a different voyage. Her living tie to them stands next to her, barefoot and restless and smiling at her mother's foolishness: this tall, slender girl with coffee skin and eyes the color of the Caribbean.

She carries her two men with her, behind her own brown eyes, always thinking how they would see what she sees now, their eyes resting on trees heavy with plantains and sweet-flesh mangoes; how they would feel breathing air fragrant with bougainvillea and jasmine. Jacob at peace, finally freed of the chains that did not so much bind him as pull him apart. She still feels his lips tug at her nipple: her lover, her husband, her child, somehow all at once.

How would Towerhill have fared here? All of the Colonial Marines who were granted land by the British have given the names of their former companies to their villages, so once again and finally she lives in Towerhill, though her own mind still adds the word *Separation* to it. "Ah, woman, Book would be restless for the killing," an oddly gentled Neb, her neighbor now and the village head man, has told her. It had been like that for Neb, too, at first. But then he'd shed it, cut from it by a grief that surprised him as much as the British surprised him when they kept their word and brought them here. His years of murder suddenly committed by a stranger who'd left him with a debt he could never repay, even if he'd known how to count it and could name those whom he owed. Would it have been like that for Towerhill, his six fingers still scratching at his heart to find who he was? Sarai knows only that he was released by Cockburn before the British sailed to New Orleans; she does not know what happened to him afterwards. Neb had been a witness at his court-martial. "Was the killing of Jacob Hallam an act of vengeance or of mercy," the admiral had demanded. "Yes," Towerhill had said, and then remained silent, except to ask that Sarai be free to stay with the British fleet, if she wished. Some stories claimed that he was captured by American slavers in Baltimore and sold south. Others say he was free, seen in Virginia, in New York, even in Canada. Or that he disappeared into the Zekiah Swamp. But in many of the *Kaiso* verses, the ones sung by the women, the ones she wants to believe the most, he had headed west, into the unmapped, unnamed spaces of the country.

She kicks soil from her own field over the string of shells, sending it down to her mother in the earth, to the two men she loves. Hears a shout from a group of Trinidadian women passing by on the dirt road. "Come on, Mama," Anaya says impatiently. They are going to Port of Spain, where people are gathering in front of Government House to protest the apprentice law the British government has imposed: it declares that all slaves on the island will be freed, but will have to stay and work on the plantations for another six years as "apprentices." "*Pas de six ans, pas de six ans,*" the women are chanting. "Come join us, Towerhill," they yell at Sarai and her daughter. "Come join us, Merikans," they yell, that word they call her and her people here rising and echoing against the green hills.

— THE END —

AUTHOR'S NOTE

Historical fiction, by definition, tosses imagined lives and situations against and among actual people and events which are personalized and re-formed according to the demands of the narrative. Among the many real historical figures depicted in this novel are George Cockburn, Robert Ross, James Scott, Joshua Barney, and more. Actual events including Cockburn's raids on Leonardtown and other areas in southern Maryland, the battles of Bladensburg, North Point and Baltimore, the burning of the Capitol and the White House, and the participation of the Colonial Marines in those actions also inspired this narrative. The *Erebus* existed, as did the other named ships and their armaments. Zekiah Fort was a real place, and the Wesorts lived and still live in southern Maryland, though their early history, ceremonies, and connections to the War of 1812 as depicted in this book are fictitious, as are the characters of Lombroso and Joseph and their conflict. Most importantly, the institution of chattel slavery was real, and thousands of African Americans in the Tidewater regions of Virginia and Maryland did join the British during the War of 1812. They fought in the service of a hierarchical monarchy against a republic based on democratic ideals that were denied to them, but which they read as a promise they had to seize in order, as Martin Luther King, Jr., said, to bend the arc of history towards justice.

Many books, articles, essays, websites and people helped me construct the historical backdrop of this novel. The most important were Marc Leepson's *What So Proudly We Hailed: Francis Scott Key, A Life*; Peter Snow's *When Britain Burned the White House: The 1814 Invasion of Washington*;

Alan Taylor's *The Internal Enemy: Slavery and War in Virginia, 1772–1832*; Dr. Julia King's fine work at and about Zekiah Fort; Jeanne K. Pirtle's *Images of America: Sotterly Plantation;* Katherine Humphries and the rest of the staff and archives at Historic Sotterly, from which the listing and notices documents in Part One were adapted. I'm grateful to all of these fine scholars and sources.

I'm grateful as well to the University of Massachusetts Press for choosing *A Wolf by the Ears* for the 2019 Juniper Prize for fiction, and for the great work of their editorial staff. Many thanks to my wife, Ohnmar, for her patience and support; to my son Adam and daughter-in-law Rachel, for their love and for the precious gift of my grandchildren, Sanda and Isaac; to George Evans and Michael Glaser, for their steady support and friendship; to the College of Southern Maryland and my colleagues and students at that institution, who have given me more than I can ever name; and, finally, to the person who inspired this book: Lucille Clifton, for her friendship, for her words, and for her eternal wisdom.

JUNIPER
JUNIPER PRIZE FOR FICTION

This volume is the nineteenth recipient
of the Juniper Prize for Fiction,
established in 2004 by the
University of Massachusetts Press
in collaboration with the
UMass Amherst MFA Program
for Poets and Writers, to be
presented annually for an outstanding
work of literary fiction. Like its sister award,
the Juniper Prize for Poetry established
in 1976, the prize is named in honor
of Robert Francis (1901–1987),
who lived for many years at
Fort Juniper, Amherst, Massachusetts.

CPSIA information can be obtained
at www.ICGtesting.com
Printed in the USA
LVHW011554141220
674147LV00006B/1248